BONES *of the*
BARBARY COAST

BONES *of the* BARBARY COAST

A CREE BLACK NOVEL

DANIEL HECHT

BLOOMSBURY

Published by Bloomsbury Publishing, New York and London
Distributed to the trade by Holtzbrinck Publishers

All papers used by Bloomsbury Publishing are natural, recyclable products made from wood grown in well-managed forests. The manufacturing processes conform to the environmental regulations of the country of origin.

Library of Congress Cataloging-in-Publication Data

Hecht, Daniel.
   Bones of the Barbary Coast : a Cree Black novel / Daniel Hecht.—1st U.S. ed.
      p. cm.
   ISBN-13: 978-1-59691-086-7
   ISBN-10: 1-59691-086-0
   1. San Francisco (Calif.)—Fiction. 2. San Francisco Earthquake, Calif., 1906—Fiction.
I. Title.

   PS3558.E284B66 2006
   813'.54—dc22

                                                                2005037130

First U.S. Edition 2006

1 3 5 7 9 10 8 6 4 2

Typeset by Westchester Book Group
Printed in the United States of America by Quebecor World Fairfield

Is there a murderer here? No. Yes, I am.
Then fly. What, from myself?

—William Shakespeare, *Richard III*

FOREWORD

Introduction to
Stranger, Mirror: Crisis and Constructive Development
by Lucretia Black, Ph.D.

Fourth Annual Horizons in Psychology Conference
University of New Mexico, Albuquerque
December 8, 2005

I SHOULD STATE AT the outset that my experiences in San Francisco did not involve a supernatural entity or paranormal occurrence. My investigation into that unusual skeleton—the remains of a victim of the Great Earthquake of 1906, found in a lovely hilltop Victorian—ended as it began: an attempt to identify a particular human being and to learn more about his life, entirely through historical research and the study of his bones.

I was neither surprised nor disappointed. In fact, the majority of incidents I investigate do not involve actual paranormal phenomena. Most often, the reason is simply that there are none to be encountered: Reports of ghosts can derive from hoaxes, from mistaken interpretation of normal-world phenomena, or from psychological disturbances on the part of witnesses. Sometimes, too, my own sensitivities prove insufficient to determine whether a revenant is or is not present.

This should not be taken to mean that such efforts aren't instructive or don't carry risks for the investigator; my work on the San Francisco skeleton proved to be among the most meaningful and dangerous research projects I have ever undertaken.

1

I don't regard the absence of paranormal phenomena as "failure," because for me the real subject of any investigation is the human mind and the art of living. Most reports of hauntings, real or imagined, come from individuals in the process of some important life passage, some crucial psychological upheaval that derives from past experience and has profound implications for their lives henceforth. The paranormal crisis is nothing less than a paradigm collapse, which forces people to reassess their beliefs about the nature of the world and of human consciousness. These are often dangerous passages, but they are also full of positive potentials. The breakdown of habitual ways of viewing the self and coping with the world offers an unequaled opportunity for constructive personal development; properly managed, it can become a liberating and empowering turning point. For the observing psychologist, it constitutes a unique opportunity to understand what it is to be human, how our minds work, and what forces are operating below the horizon of our conscious thoughts and intentional actions.

Of course, paranormal phenomena are by no means the only catalysts for such a process. The discovery of the San Francisco skeleton proved a highly effective trigger, provoking both catastrophic and constructive development for all involved, myself included. In particular, my association with Cameron Raymond demanded a rigorous inspection of habitual assumptions and posed many questions that continue to challenge me. Likewise, the astonishing journal of Lydia Jackson Schweitzer provided a catalyst for what has proved to be an ongoing personal development process. I take comfort in knowing Lydia confronted similar issues, and came to similar conclusions, a century before me. As was common in her era, she was a skilled diarist; for me, to read about her joys and struggles was to discover a sister-spirit and was abundant recompense for the other frustrations of the case.

I am aware that my theory of psychology has been described variously by my peers as unusual, radical, renegade, or ridiculous. Though my graduate and postgraduate studies at Harvard were conventional, my experiences after the death of my husband proved to me that prevailing paradigms of human consciousness and behavior were insufficient to explain certain phenomena. I now believe that no theory of psychology can be complete unless it accommodates the reality that we are shaped to a considerable degree by relationships, in many forms, from the past and from beyond the grave. It must accept that fact that dying is a crucial developmental act for which we prepare, consciously or unconsciously, throughout our lives, and for which we are equipped by nature to "manage" as personalities. (Freud's latter year emphasis upon thanatos, the death wish, as a primary engine of human behavior demonstrates his emerging awareness of the important role of death in personality formation.)

Finally, just as psychology has had to adapt to the influence of the "harder" sciences of evolutionary biology and neuroscience, it will ultimately have to accommodate physics—including the bizarre domains of quantum mechanics and chaos theory.

From the start, I have relied on deep, empathic identification with others; in most cases I do not "see" ghosts or fragmentary personality residuals so much as "become" them. Similarly, I identify powerfully with my (living) clients and others met during an investigation; I absorb their characteristics, I feel for them and with them, I lose myself in them. I suddenly notice myself—or, worse, don't notice—speaking with another person's accent, feeling his or her arthritic joints, taking on a stranger's worldview, using gestures that are not mine. This is essential to understanding my clients' experiences, but it is a dangerous tendency. I have been able to maintain a clear sense of myself as a separate personality only through a great deal of discipline, assisted by the vigilance of my colleagues at Psi Research Associates, Joyce Wu and Edgar Mayfield.

Whatever its neurological mechanisms, this extreme counter-transference has been among the most difficult aspects of my process to explain or to defend as a therapeutic practice. In part, I blame this difficulty on the fact that we lack a vocabulary for such experiences, that our terminology is limited by the reductively mechanistic bias that currently dominates Western scientific thought.

Ultimately, however, I can't speak objectively of these experiences because objectivity is an inadequate tool. Human consciousness is not inherently objective. We experience our lives as vast, elusive, unending, and hugely variable subjectivities; life is knowable, explicable, or communicable only by the *sharing of subjectivity*.

We do have a word for such sharing or merging: *communion*. In Latin, the term means simply "mutual participation"; yet for us it also conveys, appropriately, profound spiritual and moral connotations. My communion with the subjective lives of others is therefore not readily susceptible to the scalpel of analysis; nor, arguably, ought it to be.

It is certainly true that my approach has led to unusual experiences, but I can honestly say it has never been my desire to seek out the bizarre or anomalous manifestations of the paranormal world for their own sake. The normal world is frightening, unpredictable, and dangerous enough to satisfy any such urge, if I had one, as the San Francisco investigation amply demonstrates. On either side of the dimensional mirror, my only goal has been to understand the truth; to better know what it means to be human—what we are, at bottom, what we are capable of, what moves us. What the mind really is, how it really works; what abides inside us in the places we cannot observe. What matters most about being, for our brief allotment of days, alive and aware.

And, yes, whether we are worthy beings or not; or, as Lydia Schweitzer so well distilled the question, how we choose to be worthy beings, or do not.

It is in this context that I present my case study of the psychosociodynamics surrounding the person known, officially, only as "UCSF Unknown Human Remains 3024." I proceed knowing that many of you will remain skeptical of my approach and conclusions; but I also know that others are willing to accompany me on this foray into distant and exotic territory. I take comfort that you, too, understand that the world is a far more mysterious place than we often assume, and that we live among what is, in many ways, a society of strangers.

Yes: Look to your left and to your right, right now, and you will see a stranger. Who is she? What motivates him? What past shaped her, what future awaits him? You cannot know.

If you find this an uncomfortable proposition, please remember—again, as Lydia pointed out—that stranger is also more familiar, more intimately understood by each of us, than we are typically willing to admit.

From this, I think, we can derive some measure of hope and solace.

I

AN UNINTENTIONAL AUTOBIOGRAPHY

1

T HE BONES HAD BEEN assembled in roughly their former working
order, a symmetrical array of odd, ivory-brown shapes that took up
virtually the whole length of an eight-foot stainless-steel table. Cree stood
at the foot of the pallet with Uncle Bert and Dr. Horace Skobold, head of
the University of California Forensic Anthropology lab, as Skobold introduced her to the skeleton.

"First, some generalities. From a cursory look at bone development, I'd
say our subject was male, about five-foot eight in stature, and between
twenty and forty years old. Race uncertain, given the, um, obvious developmental abnormalities."

Horace Skobold was a tall, apple-cheeked man in his midsixties, dressed
in khakis, a white shirt, and a bow tie. He paused to appraise Cree with
watery blue eyes that were owlish behind thick-lensed glasses. "Do you
have much background in anatomy, Ms. Black?"

"Unfortunately, no. More in psychology."

"Well, for an adult human male of his age and size, the phalanges—toe
bones—have very unusual proportions. The distal and medial sections are
extremely short and stubby. If I had seen them alone, I might have said
they indicated brachydactylia, type BHA1. The typical foreshortening is
readily apparent in the fingers as well."

Cree bent to look more closely as Dr. Skobold used a chopstick to
point out each feature. The bones of both feet had been arranged in two
fans at the end of the table: raying longer shafts ending in a series of
short, knuckly knobs. They had been dry-brushed but not yet washed,
Skobold explained, so as to preserve any instructive chemical traces or
DNA sources. He hadn't had time to do much with the skeleton since

Bert had brought it over from the San Francisco Medical Examiner's office.

The array on the table gave off a chalky, earthy scent that Cree was a little reluctant to inhale. Even to her inexperienced eyes, these bones didn't look right.

"But brachydactylia is contraindicated by other features," Skobold went on. "Such as the metatarsals, the bones of the foot, which are unusually *long* and rather delicate. Highly unusual. Factoring in aspects of the heel, I would guess that this man had a hard time walking on the soles of his feet. It's likely he would have felt more comfortable with his heel raised." The chopstick traced the various foot bones.

Skobold's style reminded Cree less of a distinguished scholar than of a small-town funeral home director—a sober air, blandly pious, resigned. Either he had faced some deep sorrow in his life, she thought, or it was something he affected because it seemed the appropriate tone around the dead. Whichever, it couldn't hide his enthusiasm for his work. He was clearly enjoying his presentation and like a good showman was saving the best for last. She dutifully studied the metatarsals as he talked about them, but she couldn't resist a quick glance at the skull. Though bones had never bothered her, she shivered at the thought of the living face those angles and protrusions had once supported.

As if feeling the same thing, Uncle Bert stood well back from the table. Or, more likely, he'd seen enough of the skeleton earlier, or enough bones and bodies in his lifetime, and was giving this show to Cree.

She and Bert hadn't had time to catch up at all, having come straight from the Oakland airport in separate cars. Given that they were already on the East Bay side, not that far from the University of California and the lab, Cree thought it made sense to begin by looking at the bones. Bert had called ahead to let Dr. Skobold know they were coming.

After so many years, she hadn't recognized Bert right away. She'd scanned the crowd around the baggage carrousel for several minutes before spotting something familiar in the tired, top-heavy-looking man in the rumpled gray suit. Their eyes met a couple of times before it clicked for both of them, and then Bert bulled through the crowd to give her a brief, clumsy embrace. Definitely a gentleman of his generation: He'd insisted on carrying her bags, even though it made opening doors for her awkward. He'd driven her to the rental lot where she'd picked up a little red Honda SUV, then she'd followed his Crown Victoria to Berkeley.

The lab was in the Life Sciences Building, a neo-Romanesque, gray monolith at the center of campus. Its big basement room and side offices were pleasant in a clinical way, well lit by overhead fluorescent tubes and a row of windows opening to a view of a narrow concrete light well and a slice of sky and treetops. The space was largely occupied by cranio-facial reconstruction projects and the tools the science required: Stainless-steel lab benches supported bones, computer terminals, microscopes, X-ray film viewers, equipment for making molds and casts, a variety of specialized measuring devices. The only disturbing element was a faint smell of rotting meat.

Most interesting were the clay busts, eight or ten reconstruction projects in various stages of completion. The finished ones were fully fleshed likenesses, but most were only partially covered by straps and pads of brown clay. A few were still naked plaster skulls, marked with index points and bristling with cylindrical spacers, indication of the painstaking effort required to build a recognizable face from anonymous bones. The completed busts were very lifelike; clearly, Skobold was a superb sculptor.

"Moving up," Skobold continued, "to the lower leg. Where we immediately spot a significant disproportion between tibia and fibula. This fellow has an extremely robust tibia—shinbone—with pronounced thickening at the proximal end, at the knee. By comparison, the fibula is unusually delicate. And the femur, the bone of the thigh . . . it's ordinarily about the same length as the lower leg bones, and is a reliable rough guide to the height of the individual. But as you can see, it's substantially shorter than the lower leg assembly. Remarkable, isn't it?"

"I'll have to take your word for it," Cree apologized.

The door at the far end of the lab opened and a middle-aged woman entered, wearing a lab smock and carrying several files. She nodded to them, then sat on a stool in front of one of the reconstructions and immersed herself in her work.

Skobold's watery eyes went back to his subject, and he tapped his chopstick on one of a pair of bones shaped like fragments of a ceramic bowl that had fallen and broken into two mirrorimage pieces. "The innominates—the pelvic bones—show many interesting characteristics which I'll need to study more closely . . . The spine, fairly normal except for the coccyx. Normally, the end of the tailbone consists of three fused vertebrae. But this fellow's aren't fused, and he has three extras at the end—supernumeraries, not common, but not unheard of . . . Moving up, multiple deformities in the scapulae, shoulder joint, and rib cage suggest that the arms would be better suited to projecting somewhat forward from the torso as opposed to depending downward from the shoulder in the normal way."

There wasn't really a rib "cage" at the moment; the individual ribs were laid out in a series of arcs, flat on the table. Several had been broken, their curves reassembled from two or three pieces.

Cree followed Skobold when he shuffled up toward the head of the table, but Uncle Bert's cell phone buzzed and he stepped away to talk. Something to do with trace evidence analysis, Bert apparently pulling a favor with the Crime Lab. As a veteran inspector with SFPD's Homicide Detail, thirty-five years in and retirement approaching, he was no doubt eager to clear his remaining cases.

Cree looked down at the splayed hand bones, stubby rows of knots and carbuncles. "Are you sure all these bones belong to the same person? Couldn't they be from several people of different ages, or have some . . . animal bones mixed in?"

"Actually, that was my first thought, too. We often receive remains of several commingled individuals, and it can be hard to sort them out. And you're right that there's a superficial resemblance to the features of certain animals. I am frequently asked to look at skeletal remains that prove to be of nonhuman origin. People bring in dog or deer bones, thinking they've found a murder victim or prehistoric remains in their backyard. But, no, this fellow is human and all these bones are his. Every bone accounted for, no redundancies. And the geometry of the aricular surfaces . . . the heads of the bones . . . shows they belong together."

Cree nodded.

Skobold glanced at Uncle Bert, still on his phone, then made a mournful face and rubbed his hands together with a gesture that conveyed both excitement and reluctance. "Well. On to the *pièce de resistance*. The skull."

Skobold took a position at the head of the table and picked up the cranium, a smooth orb intact but for an irregular, egg-size hole on its upper left side. Again he used his chopstick to point out each feature.

"The most obvious deviation is the unusual development of his maxillary bone and dentition—particularly the extraordinary length of the canine teeth. And, as you can see from the side view, the whole nasal and maxillary region is protruded by two inches or more."

He paused to pick up the jawbone, a long, narrow horseshoe with lower teeth that stuck up menacingly. With the expression of a parent regarding a troubled child, he fitted the jaw to the cranium and began levering it up and down in a biting motion.

"Striking, isn't it? Over the years, I've encountered a good number of deformed individuals. Hospitals and medical schools sometimes ask me to do morphometric analysis of fatal congenital deformities, mostly stillbirths or neonates, a few young children. I don't think I have ever seen this degree of elongation of the nasal, maxillary, and mandibular structures. Certainly never in an adult. Such extreme deformities are almost invariably accompanied by other problems that result in early mortality. The extent of his deviations from norms and the absence of a precedent will make analysis and reconstruction quite a challenge."

The chopstick hovered at the ragged nose hole and then went into it for most of its length.

"Note also the descended and enlarged sinus cavity. We'll be able to see it better when we get his X-rays, but even a cursory inspection shows that this fellow's nasal aperture has moved toward the end of the maxilar bone. He has a fully elaborated sinus cavity arrayed along a more horizontal axis than you would see in a normal human or one of the great apes, and suggests he had a superb sense of smell. Furthermore, the foramen magnum—the point at which the spinal cord enters the cranium—is located more posteriorly. The plane of the foramen magnum and the occipital plane converge in an acute angle, suggesting his head was carried somewhat forward from the neck and shoulders, rather than set atop the spine as we are used to. Among paleoanthropologists, such an angle typically implies a preference for quadrepedal locomotion."

Skobold rotated the skull and used his chopstick to demonstrate the likely angle. The head and neck would have been thrust aggressively forward.

Uncle Bert ceased pacing and put his phone away, but he still didn't join them. He stood, drumming his fingers on the counter and staring into the distance. He made a bulky silhouette, one big plug of a man, and looked to Cree like someone with a lot on his mind.

"Do you know what caused his death?" Cree asked.

"Well, the head injury is a presumptive candidate," Skobold said. "The sharp edges of the cranial hole and its crisp fracture lines tell me the injury occurred to living bone. But determining cause and manner of death isn't my job—the medical examiner's office does that, and they've already signed off on this as accidental death. No one's bothered with a post mortem."

"Why not?"

"Age of the remains. The general condition of the bones gives us some indication—their coloration and friability, the amount of rodent nibbling, and so on. Put that together with where the skeleton was found and the artifacts recovered from the site, we can safely presume this fellow died in the Great Earthquake of 1906."

"Yes, Bert told me. But to find bones that old . . . that's pretty amazing, isn't it?"

"Actually, in San Francisco, it's by no means unheard of. Bertie—how many Great Quake victims would you say you've handled?"

Bert looked up at the ceiling as he made an effort to recall. "Personally? This is my second. In the department, maybe six, seven in my time."

"You have to remember what a cataclysm that was," Skobold said. "A major city, turned to rubble and ash. Utter chaos, a quarter of a million people rendered homeless. Besides the known casualties, around eight hundred people were lost—presumed dead but unaccounted for. But bones are durable. So they turn up every few years during road or sewer-line work, or when some handyman is fixing up his basement, as with this fellow. Remains this old are deemed 'historical.' Which means establishing cause and manner of death isn't a pressing matter for Bert and his boys."

"So . . . will you be doing a facial reconstruction?"

"Oh, I wouldn't miss it for the world! But I really shouldn't begin until we're done with Norma Jean there." Skobold tipped his head toward the woman in the lab smock, who was applying a small white cylinder to the plaster skull in front of her.

Cree gave him a questioning look. The woman was Chinese, ebony haired, barrel shaped, hardly Norma Jean.

Skobold smiled with doleful amusement. "Not my assistant—that's Karen Chang. I'm speaking of her subject. We tend to give them names. You have to remember, they're almost all John and Jane Does when they come in here. We've tagged those remains as 3019. Our chap here is 3024. But the numbers are depersonalizing. Having a name helps you give your reconstruction more of a real . . . personality."

Cree smiled. "What's your name for this one?"

Skobold started to answer, then checked himself; the big eyes behind their lenses grew concerned. "Bertram did talk to you about our concerns? You're not going to . . . publicize this in any way, are you?"

Uncle Bert shifted, an unspoken signal of discomfort. He turned and came toward them, meeting Cree's eyes briefly. Clearly, he'd rather she didn't go into the details of her profession.

"I'm just here as a friend of Uncle Bert's," she said. That sounded stupid, so she clarified: "I call him Uncle Bert because I've known him since I was a kid. He was a good friend of my father's."

"I grew up in the same neighborhood as her pop," Bert explained. "Ben and I were in the Navy together, back in the old days. Cree was coming down to visit and it occurred to me that she'd be interested in our guy here. In fact, Horace, I thought she could help me look into him—she's a . . . private investigator, historical research is her specialty, so I thought I could kind of kill two birds with one stone. We'd get in a visit, she could do some legwork for me. I can't give him too much time, I could use the help. I figured she might find something that'd be useful to you, too, medical history or photos or something. If you're up for working with her."

Cree had assumed Bert would've worked this out with Skobold earlier, and she wondered how he liked having the arrangement sprung on him.

The proposition seemed to make Skobold uneasy, but he said somberly, "Of course, Bertie."

Skobold's expression stayed worried as he began to draw a dust cloth over the skeleton. He paused when only the savage-looking skull remained above the cover, and like a man putting his son to bed seemed to speak to it as he went on: "We consider confidentiality very important in this instance." He glanced at Bert and continued when Bert gave a nod of assent. "There are administrative, ah, sensitivities involved. This fellow is a most interesting specimen, but his remains have no medicolegal significance.

Historical, accidental death, you see. Neither Bert's bosses nor mine would be happy we're spending taxpayers' money to take the time to identify him."

Bert waved that concern away. "I'm three months to retirement—what're they going to do, fire me? And you've got tenure."

"In any case," Skobold continued, "I'm sure the owners of the house where the remains were found would prefer not to see their name in sensational news reports or have their home become the object of interest of curiosity seekers or . . . oddballs. Of which, I'm afraid, San Francisco has rather more than its share. And I can't spend my days fending off tabloid reporters or curious faculty members. Or students, God forbid! This isn't a circus sideshow. We have work to do. We take our work seriously."

"Of course."

Bert clapped Skobold's shoulder, but Skobold didn't look reassured as he drew the sheet up the rest of the way, over the long, jagged grin and fractured cranium.

"Wolfman, of course." Skobold looked embarrassed and unhappy at the admission. "How could we resist? We call him Wolfman."

2

Put us in a pot, Cree mused, *boil everything else away, and what do you get?*

Of the psyche or soul, the residuum could be enormously varied and was usually very subtle stuff; for most people, it could never be as convincing as the hard, stubborn stuff of bones. Bones were unique, biology intersecting geology, concretions of minerals made by living things. Of the physical person, bones alone remained to tell the story—provided someone could figure out what they were saying.

She was following Bert's car into San Francisco to look at the house, the bones' resting place for a hundred years. Bert had written the address on a scrap of envelope in case they got separated, but so far caravanning was no problem. The rush hour traffic, bottled up on the I-80 on-ramp, moved so slowly she never got far from his bumper. All she had to do was keep sight of the hump of the bubble light on Bert's dashboard.

A classic man of few words, Uncle Bert. In the airport, his conversation had been limited to *Hey, let me get that* and *You need something, cup of coffee, slice of pizza?* Like Pop, he'd grown up in lower-middle class neighborhoods in Brooklyn and still retained the accent after all these years on the West Coast. She got the sense he was a man who didn't spend much time in the company of women. Definitely a career cop, cop to the core.

Cree's investigations rarely involved contact with police. In six years, Psi Research Associates had been consulted on police business only three times. The main reason was that they were seldom asked; police tended to be skeptics, and even open-minded cops were reluctant to call in parapsychology types to help solve a murder case. One homicide detective had explained that it was a great way to get your balls busted by your brothers

17

in blue, and it invited sensationalistic press attention that didn't inspire citizens' confidence in their law enforcement agencies. Asking for help from somebody like Cree was functionally making a public admission that there were no other working lines of inquiry.

The other reason was that murder made for bad ghosts—the perseverating experiential echoes of a murder victim were often grotesque and tormented. After seeing what the first couple of cases did to Cree, Joyce and Edgar had insisted that she avoid investigations involving recent homicides.

Fortunately, Cree rationalized, that concern didn't apply here. These bones might be unusual, but they were old, and they didn't belong to a murder victim. And anyway, this wasn't actually a PRA job, this was just a personal favor for Uncle Bert, a pro bono investigation for an old friend on what struck Cree as an intriguing mystery. It had all come up quickly—the call from Bert that coincided with a gap in their work schedule. Edgar was off on vacation in Hawaii, which precluded his participation; Joyce had flown back to New York to be with her mother, who was recovering from a minor stroke.

Anyway, for all she knew, there were no ghosts involved, and this was simply a historical research job. Uncle Bert had bristled with skepticism when she'd asked him about supernatural elements.

Uncle Bert. One odd bird, Cree thought.

The Black family had mostly lost touch with Bert Marchetti after he'd moved out west. She remembered him only from early childhood: Ben Black's handsome Navy buddy, who used to greet her by kissing her on the lips as if she were a grown woman—his Italian showing, as Pop said. The men would sit at the kitchen table, smoking, drinking grappa, telling tales about Navy misadventures. Pop was naturally a more reserved person, but Bert's visits gave him a chance to let his hair down. They'd get too loud, laughing, and Mom would shush them, *You'll wake the kids!* and Bert would flatter her into submission and make her drink grappa, too, even though she said it tasted like garbage juice. In summertime, the men wore sleeveless undershirts. Cree and Deirdre liked Bert because he could always make Mom laugh—maybe because if Bert was a little unrefined, he was "romantic" in a way Pop usually was not.

Pop had admired him for moving to San Francisco, because not too many guys from the neighborhood ever managed to break loose. After a few years they had fallen out of touch, and Cree knew only the barest outline of Bert's life since he'd gone west: becoming a policeman, getting married, a long-ago divorce. He'd flown east for Pop's funeral, fifteen years ago, but since then they'd heard even less from him—just the rare late-night call to Mom, who would complain afterward that Bert was drinking too much.

Cree had been surprised to answer the phone and hear this voice from the past, the blunt consonants and grammatic ellipses so much like Pop's, the theme music of her early childhood. At this point, Bert was less a family friend than a semilegendary figure from the early years, the Brooklyn period of their lives.

The old man it had taken her so long to recognize at the airport had short silvering hair and a beefy chest and shoulders with a hard paunch to match. His gray suit bore the wrinkles of too much sitting, but his shirt was so white and crisp that Cree suspected he'd just put it on, straight from the package. As he'd bent to hoist her bags, his jacket had parted over the broad seat of his trousers and she'd glimpsed the gun he carried in a belt holster high on one side. He was about Mom's age, sixty-three, but he looked much older: weary, unsurprisable, pouched eyes, a downward tug at the corners of his mouth, doubling chins and jowling cheeks. His quick clumsy hug smelled of cigarettes and aftershave. His smile looked wary, as if it didn't know his face very well.

After the toll booth, the bridge rose and the view expanded: the bright water of the Bay, a tight cluster of tall downtown buildings with the pastel city spread on the hills around it. Emerging from the tunnel on Yerba Buena Island, she could see beyond the skyscrapers to the orange towers of the Golden Gate Bridge and the arcs of cable that swept to the hills of Marin. With the sun lowering over the Pacific, the crag of Alcatraz was stretched by its own shadow. An exhilarating vista.

The first time she'd come to San Francisco was during a vacation with Pop and Mom and Dee, when Cree was nine or ten. That was a decade after the golden era of the sixties, but forever afterward she'd thought of the city as a magical place, full of color and celebration and people who wore gypsy clothes and danced in the streets. She had found a part of herself then, a sense of who she would become. She felt it still, a thrill of expectation, an echo of a young girl's yearning for the dawning of the Age of Aquarius and the other world-birthing dreams of those Haight-Ashbury years of legend.

Wolfman—Skobold's nickname harkened to a very different legendary tradition. Cree had to admit her curiosity had been aroused: lots of questions surrounding those bones. Not the least of them was Bert. His aura was opaque, dark hued, but she sensed there were energies working beneath his impassive surface. She had to wonder why a weary cop three months from retirement would put in all this extra work on the hundred-year-old skeleton of a John Doe and call for assistance from a dead friend's daughter he hadn't even talked to in ten years.

They got off just below Market Street, then began working their way north toward Pacific Heights. Uncle Bert drove like a man who knew his town, leading her on a zigzag course through smaller streets. Cree loved seeing the neighborhoods again, whites and beiges and rainbow pastels, streets rising in a series of steps lined with San Francisco's famously tall, narrow Victorians. On the dizzyingly steep final slope of Divisadero, Bert's car disappeared and the gap between buildings showed only sky. Cree brought her car to a stop with its nose in the air, checked cross traffic, then bucked back hard as the Honda breasted the top of the hill. She crossed the flat and slowed when it seemed there was nothing but air beyond the hood; in another instant she pitched forward and the drop from Pacific Heights to the Marina opened beneath: houses clinging to the slope, streets stretching away into miniature far below and ending abruptly at the broad waters of the bay. The distant hills of Sausalito were bright with ocean sun, shadows in their folds. Directly below, Bert's car waited at the first intersection, turn signal flashing.

A minute later, Cree pulled behind him into a driveway on the uphill side of the house. They both got out and she followed him to the front sidewalk, where he lit a cigarette, inhaled deeply, and turned to look up at the tall façade.

"It's good we're coming in now," he said, "the contractors have gone home. Otherwise we'd never park within a couple blocks. Nice digs, huh?"

It was a big, mostly Italianate Victorian just a block down from the crest of the hill, with bay windows, bracketed cornices, elaborate pillars and or-namentation on the porches. The dusty, curtainless windows, one framing a stepladder, showed it was unoccupied and under repair. It was separated from its uphill neighbor by only a thin screen of green stuff that ran along the gangway where they'd parked, but the downhill side faced a garden terrace that took up a full additional lot and exposed the north wall of the house to the big vista. Given the slant, the far end of the terrace was a good sixteen feet above the street.

Cree made an appreciative murmur.

"Yeah, the new owners, they got to be millionaires," Bert said. "They'll have a real showpiece when they're done fixing it up."

"How do they like finding a skeleton in their basement?"

Bert flicked his ash with a tossing gesture. "Not too happy. They're moving from Boston, need the place ready by their move date, and it set the work back while we exhumed the bones. I still got the basement room closed off in case we want a second look, kind of a hassle for them. Plus they have a couple of kids, they don't want to put the kids off the new place, make it seem scary. I haven't told them about the unusual character-istics of the remains, why saddle them with that."

He looked up at the house, drawing deeply on his cigarette, apparently in no hurry to go inside. Cree shifted gears to match his tempo. If he was working himself up to confiding in her, she'd give him the time. Anyway, it was pleasant, here on the steep slope, with the long views, the late-afternoon sunshine. She tipped her face toward the sky and soaked it in.

"My social skills are a little rusty, Cree," Bert admitted. His pouched eyes slid over, reconnoitered her response. "I was in such a hurry to get to Skobold's shop I didn't even ask about the family."

She gave him a quick rundown. Mom was pretty happy; she had a nice little apartment and loved her work at the neighborhood rec center. The angioplasty had relieved the heart congestion they'd been worrying about, and her blood pressure was much better with the new medication. Cree saw a lot of Deirdre; Dee's two kids were fabulous nieces, twins but with completely different personalities, and Dee and her husband had a terrific marriage. Between Don's carpentering and Dee's teaching, they were doing all right.

Uncle Bert nodded noncommitally. "How about Cree?"

I'm great, she almost started to say. Then it occurred to her that candor might elicit the same from Bert. "Frankly? The last few months have been a little funky for me. It's coming together, though."

Another noncommital nod. "Your husband—" Bert's hand groped for the name.

"Mike."

"Mike. It's been like ten, twelve years, now. You got a boyfriend now or—"

"That issue is under review at this time." Cree tipped her hand side to side, *yes and no*. She tried to keep it light, gave him a wry grin.

Bert sucked on his cigarette. "Yeah, relationships, they can bend you out of shape, huh?"

"This is pretty well my regular shape."

If Bert noticed the tightening of her tone, he didn't acknowledge it. "So this outfit of yours, Psi Research Associates, the whole parapsychology thing . . . how'd that happen?"

"How'd a nice girl like me end up in a profession like this?"

"If that's how you see it."

"I had a very disturbing experience some years ago. At the time, I was skeptical about anything paranormal, didn't believe in ghosts. But then I got a very convincing demonstration that we don't know anything about how the mind really works, how the world works. The experience turned all my beliefs upside down. Afterward, I was . . . drawn to doing research in the field."

"That would do it," he agreed expressionlessly.

Cree would have gone on, but this was sounding too confessional, and Bert wasn't buying any of it anyway. She went on crisply, "Along the way I discovered I have certain cognitive attributes that sensitize me and make me unusually accessible to experiences like that one. I have a business partner, Edgar Mayfield, who approaches our research as a physicist and engineer, and an assistant, Joyce Wu, who covers most of the historical and forensic investigation side of it. I'm sorry she couldn't come help with this, but she had a family emergency. Our little firm is keeping surprisingly busy."

Uncle Bert said nothing, but there was something apologetic about the way he nodded, as if he regretted probing difficult territory.

"What's your opinion, Uncle Bert? You sure you don't believe in ghosts?" She was trying to make it easier for him. She couldn't shake the conviction that something must have happened during the exhumation of the bones, something that prompted him to call her.

Bert threw down his cigarette and ground it out with his toe. "My opinion is, we should get inside, look the place over while we still got some daylight. About ghosts, all I know is, I've been around one hell of a lot of dead people, and I've never seen one. At this point, I don't expect to, either."

3

THE RENOVATION CHAOS couldn't hide the fact that this was a lovely place. The front door opened to a hallway that ran back into the house, a fine staircase rising on the left side. Along the right were doorways to what in Victorian days would have been the parlor and sitting room, spacious, high-ceilinged rooms now full of table saws, tarps, stepladders, coils of electrical cord, toolboxes, all filmed with dust. The elegant proportions and woodwork were charming, Cree thought, but in the end it was the light that made the space so agreeable. The windows of all the rooms on the downhill side framed views of the bay, the hills of Sausalito, the Golden Gate Bridge, and a huge expanse of sky that would no doubt bring light inside even through San Francisco's infamous fog. Just below, the garden terrace was a rectangle of cut flagstone, with benches and raised plantings laid out around a circular garden area. An iron railing and a rim of vegetation nicely isolated it from street traffic and neighboring houses.

Bert grunted in appreciation as he joined her at the windows. "Doesn't come cheap, though. These people are doing all right to afford it."

They toured the dining room and kitchen. At the back, a side hall led to the L of the house and opened to a rear stairwell, a bathroom, a small room that had probably been a servant's bedroom, and a room with built-in bookshelves that must have been the library. Cree listened inwardly for the tiny thrill or reverberation that would reveal the presence of an entity here, but all she got was a sense of a cheerful, pleasant house, full of golden light faintly tinged with the green of her own envy—this was exactly the kind of place she'd always wanted to live in.

"You want to see upstairs? You think this is nice, they're almost done with the work up there, you can get a better idea. And the views, Jesus."

"No. I get it. This is where people go when they die if they've been good all their lives. I'm jealous as hell. Let's go see the damned basement."

She couldn't tell for sure, but she thought Bert was amused as he opened one of the doors in the rear hallway, fumbled for a light switch, and began stumping down the stairs.

It was a long way down; even the basement had ten-foot ceilings. At the bottom, they stepped into a well-lit hallway that ran the full length of the house. Bert gave her a quick tour as they moved toward the room where the bones had been found. He slapped a light switch to reveal a gardening room, with brick floor and walls lined by redwood-plank potting tables; a dark stairwell led upward to slanted metal doors that Cree figured must open to the terrace. Next, a room with appliances, counters, cabinets, and a big wine rack, apparently used as a backup for the kitchen upstairs.

"The new owners," Bert said, "I guess they like these well enough as is. It's the end room they're going to fix up."

At the end of the hall, he took down a ribbon of crime scene tape, then went ahead of her into the dark doorway. He groped in the shadows and turned on a contractor's lamp.

This was the biggest of the basement rooms. The light cast hard shadows that amplified its disarray: sawhorses, dangling wiring, clamp lamps, sledgehammers, a stack of two-by-fours. To the left, carving the room into an L shape, a subsection had been partitioned with a brick wall that was now partially broken down.

Bert turned on another lamp and tipped his chin toward the gap in the bricks. "So the plan was to fix this up as a rec room for the kids. But then they get to wondering why that part's partitioned off. The contractor figures it's maybe a feature left over from some earlier configuration, like a root cellar, and is just taking up space that could be put to better use. So they knock a little hole and see that it's an open chamber, half full of broken masonry and boards, and figure, great, more space for the rec room. They knock down part of the wall and start removing rubble. And start finding bones. They call SFPD, it's human remains, so it goes over to Homicide. I caught it because everybody figures it's just paperwork, I'll tie it off before I go."

Cree leaned into the broken-edged doorway. It was a simple, rectangular room about twelve feet square. The cement floor was clear now, recently swept. All four walls were brick, including the main foundation.

"So you come and take a look. What then?"

"You find a body, you gotta go through the motions. I called in a crime scene unit, we excavated the rubble, removed the bones. We all knew what we were looking at. Medical examiner signed off on it as accidental and historical death. The ME would have held the bones for the obligatory year and then incinerated them, but I brought them over to Skobold's shop, see if we could find out more about him."

Cree nodded. The enclosure exhaled a chalky, moist smell. She stepped into the near-darkness, looked around at the rough brick interior, and did her best to shift her sensorum, to listen to the silence and hear what might live within it. But besides the earthy, subterranean chill, the most palpable sensation was Bert's presence—his heavy, inscrutable, dour mood.

"In my work," she said casually, "we find people are often reluctant to admit they've had an unusual experience that bothers them. They're always very relieved when we tell them it doesn't mean they're crazy or superstitious."

Uncle Bert chortled. "Cree, kiddo—thanks for the thought, but don't try to finesse me here. I interview and interrogate people myself, that's half of what I do."

She turned around and shared his smile. "Then you know when somebody's holding back on you. Why bother with this, Uncle Bert? Why call me?"

He didn't answer. Instead, he came into the chamber and stood with arms crossed, blocking the light from the main room.

"Lot of questions here. One of my first was, guy's buried in four or five feet of rubble, but the foundation's intact, looks original. Ceiling is intact, floor above that is intact. So where'd the rubble come from?"

"Good question."

Bert produced a small flashlight from his pocket and shined it at the ceiling, a solid panel of dark wainscoting. "See the color of the boards nearest the foundation? They're old, but they're a little newer than the others. I figure the quake knocked down stuff from above, a masonry wall or maybe a chimney, it broke through the floor upstairs, half-filled this little room. The owners back then repaired the ceiling and the floor up there, but left the debris where it was. Either didn't know our guy was in here, or didn't want to deal with him. Or didn't want anyone to know about him."

Cree inspected the circle of light on the ceiling. On the terrace side, the varnish appeared paler, as if newer boards had been woven skillfully back into the darker, older ones.

"Good point." She smiled again and then prodded: "But you're stalling me."

He pulled back, affronted. "Whoa, little lady, maybe you better get straight about who's in charge here."

She wasn't ready for his reaction, his tone, and threw some of it back at him: "Come on, Uncle Bert. Do you want help on this or not?"

He stood mute, inhaling slowly as if he was inflating, looking furious with her. When he refused to answer, Cree felt her Irish come up, as Pop used to say. She pushed past him, and in the outer room she turned and half-sat on one of the saw-horses. Her heart was thumping, but she crossed her arms and kept a hard and expectant look on her face.

Bert took his time coming out, but when he did she was relieved to see that little smile orphaned on his cheeks.

"Ben Black's kid," he said. He shook his head, making a sucking noise through his side teeth. "I was about twice your pop's size, but he was twice as stubborn. Nobody pushed him around. I guess you got the gene."

The smile was gone by the time he got to her. He put a big hand on her shoulder to urge her along with him.

At the top of the stairs, Cree turned to watch Bert stump his way up, looking foreshortened as his thick hand clamped the bannister, slid ahead and clamped again, hoisting himself up.

He puffed into the light and shut the door behind him. "See, way I figure it, there are two ways to retire. Main one is, you're heavy around the middle and you got flat feet you like to put up on your desk. You know your case load'll never resolve anyway, so why bust your ass for the last few months? You've been busting it your whole life, nobody's going to complain you're not pulling your weight. You know you'll hand off your open cases at the end, pick up your gold watch, and then you're, whatever, you're at home fondling the TV remote 'til the bagpipes play."

Back in the kitchen, Bert opened a rear door and tipped his head to a flight of stairs that led down to the back corner of the terrace. Cree went out to a breeze that lifted her hair and tickled her cheeks, smelling of ocean and the exotic scent essence of northern California, eucalyptus. They walked together to the garden area in the middle of the terrace.

Evening was settling over the city. In the light of a sun floating on the rim of the Pacific, the sky above the Golden Gate was a swirl of peach and pink, lavender and turquoise, that threw an opaline light on the water. On the far side, the hills were mounds of luminous pastels, cut with valleys of shadow; on this side, the city fell steeply away in a sweep of dimming pink and beige punctuated already by a few window lights. Behind Cree, the house was a Victorian jewel box, its façade warmed by the colors of the sky, windows reflecting back the dying sunlight.

"And the other way?" she prompted. "The other way you retire?"

"Yeah, the other way is you hold your head up, you follow through right to the end. You don't slow down, if anything you push it harder."

"Why?"

"Because you want to be proud when you're done. That's what you gotta live with from here on out, so you want to know you did the best you could. You don't do that, you've disrespected your job, you've basically said what you did all along was useless anyway." Bert sat on one of the benches, pulled out a cigarette but didn't light it. "So I get one more John Doe. We can incinerate him and write him up as a number, no fuss, I'm clear. Or we can give him a decent burial, say a few words, maybe put a name on his tombstone." He looked back at her challengingly. "That seem old fashioned to you?"

"Old-fashioned conservative or bleeding-heart liberal."

"I also knew Horace, how much he was gonna love getting his hands on this guy. Write a paper about him, maybe."

"And you called me in because . . ."

"Don't bother. There's no goddamned ghost, okay? Nobody to psychoanalyze, either. You deal with Bert Marchetti, what you see is what you get. I got no depths for you to plumb." Suggesting otherwise, his gestures had gotten vehement again. "I called you in because you're a licensed PI, you do historical research, and I could use the help. It's half a favor to Horace, he can use supporting data about this unusual specimen, but I got other cases to attend to. I also thought, with you I got a personal connection that'll help keep it confidential. Like Horace said, we don't want attention from screwballs, and nobody will be happy we're spending our time or taxpayers' money on this—state's in a budget crisis, why do you think they elected the Terminator? This job is gonna be a lot of time-consuming work, up to your neck in newspaper morgues and historical libraries. Stuff that'll eat my clock when I got more recent dead people to deal with. And, yeah, I'm curious—how the rubble got in there, what really went down. Something fishy there."

He glanced over to see how well she was buying it and must have seen that she wasn't, quite. "And, yeah," he went on quietly, "I figured, you know, the wolfman thing, that would be kind of up your alley."

"You don't believe in ghosts . . . how about werewolves?"

The eyes slitted again. "Aw, Jesus. This isn't about *me*, what I believe, what I don't, it's about some poor freak bastard who died and at the very least deserves not to be forgotten by everyone, every time! If you don't get that, I can't explain it. I don't believe in that crap. I don't believe in *anything*, okay? Except maybe, this much, *this* much"—he shook a thick forefinger and thumb, held a millimeter apart—"in getting my god-damned job done. Jesus, why are you asking me questions when the whole idea is for you to be telling me some answers?"

Again his gestures had gotten bigger, and suddenly he stood up and strode off toward the house. "Fuck this. We don't have to do this. I made a mistake, calling you. Forget it. I'll pay for your flight, let's forget it. Give my regards to your mother. Let's go, I don't have all night here."

His intensity seemed all out of proportion, his words a slap in the face. But after a stunned moment Cree realized she knew how to handle it, how to tough out the hard spots with Bert. It felt like family, like fights with Mom or Dee, the way you let the conflict go through you and over you and then just let go of it because you didn't have a choice; you'd wake up tomorrow and they'd still be there, you were stuck with them.

She didn't turn around immediately. Instead, she let him stop on the porch stairs, let him realize he had to lock up after her and that back in the driveway her car was blocking his; he couldn't go anywhere until she did. The dramatic exit routine wasn't going to work.

She waited until she heard his lighter ratchet and caught the whiff of tobacco, then turned and joined him. He looked rumpled and spent as he leaned against the marble railing and blew smoke at the darkening sky.

She patted his lapel and tugged his tie straight. "If we're done here," she said, "what about dinner? You must know the good places. I could eat a horse."

4

CREE HAD BOOKED a room on the long flat stretch of Lombard Street, at the northern edge of the city, which had the double advantage of being only eight blocks from the Pacific Heights house and far enough from North Beach or downtown to have affordable rates. Bert followed her to the motel and waited as she registered and dropped off her luggage, then drove her over to Chinatown, where he used his police status to park in a loading zone near the restaurant. Being alone in the dark car with him felt awkward; neither said much. The same at dinner.

The restaurant had Formica tables and a greasy look to the walls and counters—somehow, Cree had expected some flourish from Bert, welcoming her to his town by taking her someplace special. But the food wasn't bad. He knew what to order and they both put away mountains of pork with mustard greens, chicken with peanuts, ginger beef. Chopsticks looked like toothpicks in Bert's big fists, but he worked them effectively, lifting his plate and levering food into his mouth just like the Chinese clientele.

She threw a few conversational initiatives at him, but he didn't do much with them and she didn't really know what to say, either. After their fight at the house, everything was a little forced, an undertone of caution and apology.

The only time things moved along was when she asked him for suggestions about historical research resources. Bert talked and ate at the same time, gesturing with his chopsticks to make a point. He began by outlining how a John Doe investigation went. You came at it from two sides, in this case Skobold getting information from the bones while Cree handled the historical side; the two halves of the investigation supported each other and could provide leads for each other.

"Obviously, on our side, we got the house, when it was built, who owned it, when. Then we got the owners. We find the 1906 owner's name and follow them down, see what happened to them—births and deaths, check on descendants alive today who might have letters, diaries, records of some kind."

"And then there's the wolfman himself," Cree suggested. "He would have stood out from the crowd—maybe there'll be reference to an extremely deformed individual in medical literature or hospital records of the period."

"Sure. And freak shows. Or circuses, big entertainment back then. Be sure to check old handbills. And newspapers, even the ads."

One of the problems, Bert warned, was that San Francisco's history before 1906 was full of holes. After the quake, the city had burned for three days in the biggest urban fire in American history. Most records had literally gone up in smoke.

"Which could explain why he was forgotten," Cree mused. "Or wasn't noticed."

"Or was so easy to dispose of." Bert flipped another piece of pork into his mouth, chewed, and went on: "And there's another reason why it can be hard to find stuff from that period. May not apply to this guy, up there in a wealthy home in that district, but given what he was, I wouldn't be surprised if there's a connection. San Francisco has what you might call a colorful history. I mean, there's an off-the-record subculture in every town, but back in the wolfman's lifetime this was like half the city. I'm talking about the Barbary Coast." His eyes scouted Cree's.

The name rang a bell, but Cree puzzled over the connection. "In Africa?"

"Yeah, they called it after the west coast of Africa, where the slavers worked out of, pirates and all that." Bert tapped a cigarette out of a pack, thumbed his lighter, and blew a plume of smoke over his shoulder at the No Smoking sign. "But here, it was, like, a . . . a red-light district, a warren, a whole underworld, catered to sailors just off the boat and gold miners and every kind of lowlifes. You gotta remember, this town was built on the Gold Rush, basically a hundred thousand horny, rough and tumble guys, hardly any women at first except the boatloads of whores they brought in. Barbary Coast was where they went to spend their money if they did find gold, or to make a living hitting people over the head if they didn't. Drinking, gambling, opium, slave-trading, crime syndicate stuff, wholesale prostitution. I mean, we're talking sex shows, kids for sale, murder for hire, gang wars. Make your hair stand on end to hear what went on. Point is, everything was under the table, so records of births, deaths, property sales, stuff like that, aren't so good. For like fifty years, a big chunk of San Francisco's life was underground. Chinatown, too, the Chinese didn't connect with the whites and vice versa. Oil and water, a whole separate world. People came and went, lived and died, no trace. If our wolfman connects back to the Barbary Coast or old Chinatown—" he made a hopeless gesture with the fat fingers that pinched his cigarette.

Bert's exposition seemed to have tired him. He looked around at the restaurant with a distant frown, and Cree wondered if he felt he'd talked too frankly around a "little lady."

"Uncle Bert," she said deliberately. "I believe you when you say you don't believe in ghosts. I can deal with that, I deal with it all the time. And for all I know, there aren't any ghosts involved here. But the question I have is, are you going to listen to me if I come up with something about the wolfman through . . . my other means?"

"As long as I get something concrete, what do I care?"

"I'll need access to the house. A key. Permission from the owners for me to enter."

"What're you going to do—go have a midnight séance?"

Again, his skepticism sounded uncomfortably like contempt, and Cree bounced a little back at him: "Like you said—what do you care? It's about results." She heard Brooklyn creep into her accent, and thought: *Already.*

Bert hunched, eyes down, thinking. After a while he fished in his pocket and came up with a handful of keys. He selected one and slid it across to her, but kept a big forefinger on it.

"One condition," he said. "Don't tell anybody what you're doing, what you do for a living. I mean *nobody*, not Horace, nobody. Anybody asks, you're a just a regular PI. Or a historical researcher from a university. I'd like to keep some professional dignity here. Go out with my reputation intact."

He didn't take his finger off the key until she agreed.

The transaction made things tense again, and conversation stalled once more. They finished dinner and drove through thickening fog back to the motel. Bert wrote out his cell-phone number on another scrap and said he'd call the house's owners. They didn't hug or even shake hands when she got out, just *You take it easy now* and Bert putting his hand to the side of his head with thumb and little finger spread, *Call me.* And then his car was sliding away, pushing a cone of headlight glow through the fog.

It was only eight-thirty, but it felt later to Cree. Long day. She checked herself in the wall mirror and rolled her eyes at what she saw. She unpacked and brought her toiletry case to the bathroom, where she ran the tap until the water was scalding, then wet a wash cloth and held the moist heat against her face. After a few minutes, she brushed and flossed her teeth. A hot facial massage and clean teeth guaranteed a 10 percent improvement in mood, minimum.

Back in the bedroom, she opened her laptop on the desk and started pecking in a few notes. Following the example of Joyce's case management methods, she started a contacts file to cache information on people and organizations that could be research resources. She created a file for the wolfman himself and another for the house, and typed in what she'd learned so far: a few details about the bones, not much on the house.

Finally, she started a new folder for the journal of her investigative day. This had always been a crucial part of her process, a place to write and organize notes on her talks with the living people she met, the progress of strands of inquiry, any thoughts or ideas at all. Most important, it was where she recorded the detailed narrative of her experiences at the site, whatever she glimpsed of the world of the ghost or ghosts, observations on her own state of mind and the psychological states of others. It all made a record that she could look back at and sift for new ideas, patterns, hidden threads of continuity.

She typed for a while, mainly noting questions about Bert, her sense of the house. It took only a few minutes.

By the time she closed the computer, she felt decidedly blue and lonesome. She went to the window and pulled aside the drape only to see that the fog now wrapped the motel, so thick that she could barely see the cars in the courtyard just below. Foghorns moaned out in the bay, some far, some near, blind ships calling to each other like lost souls.

Why so lonesome? Part of it was that coming to San Francisco, being with Bert, had awakened memories—Pop, mainly, so long dead, and the early, early days. Part of it was Uncle Bert himself, so different from the outgoing, fun, romantic guy she remembered. Now he was enclosed, unapproachable. He was tough and could no doubt handle hard situations, everything that came with his job. But he was so *alone.* Maybe if you were a career homicide cop and had seen too many awful things, you got secretly scared of human beings, disappointed with them or sad about them. So the way you survived was to never rely on anybody or anything, never get too close, and so never be disappointed. Give it thirty-some years, and Cree could easily see how you'd wall yourself off.

Yet here was Cree Black, pretty damned alone herself. A career as an empathic parapsychologist, half your life spent in a world most people didn't even believe existed, also did a good job of isolating a person.

Two months ago she would have called Paul Fitzpatrick in New Orleans and taken some comfort from the sound of his voice and the memory of being with him, intimate talk and walks along Lake Ponchartrain and the reassuring grounding of physical contact. But that was best avoided right now—pending "review," as she'd told Uncle Bert.

Paul was a genuinely nice man. Too nice. She believed him when he said he was in love with her, but she'd always known he wasn't really over his divorce. Or his ex-wife, who had recently returned to New Orleans and had been making reconciliation overtures. To a kind, sensitive guy who didn't want to hurt anybody's feelings and so needed "some space," "some time to think things over."

Oh, one of those, Joyce said when she'd told her. Joyce had a certain way of putting the behavior of men in perspective.

But Cree suspected Paul's need for space had other origins: She'd scared him away. He'd come a long way toward her, but she had no doubt her unusual outlook on life and psychology was still a bit more than he could swallow. He had been candid in expressing his reservations about her willingness—an unhealthy compulsion?—to put herself in situations of mental and physical danger.

She thought of calling Joyce, to check in on how her mother was doing and to ask advice about historical research, but then remembered it would be almost midnight in New York, too late to call. She could salve her lonelies by checking in with Dee, too, and at some point she really should call Mom and ask some questions about Bert.

Who is this guy, Mom?

It wasn't that Bert's explanations were so bad. Maybe it was just as he said: He thought the poor guy deserved at least a token effort, a name on his tombstone; he didn't have the time himself but he wanted to help his friend Horace get supporting data on this unique specimen. It could also be that Bert was feeling old and lonely and scared of retirement and had grabbed at an excuse to reconnect with the Black family.

Or there was some other element here, some other agenda. She was ready to believe him when he said he didn't believe in ghosts, but he had taken serious evasive maneuvers when she'd asked about werewolves.

She found herself at the window again, staring at nothing much through the fog. She was tired, but she didn't feel sleepy. Parapsychological researchers became by necessity somewhat nocturnal, but that wasn't the only reason. Blue as she was, she had to smile at how predictable her responses were. The wolfman had awakened that feeling she knew so well, and enjoyed: that hunger to know, to understand. Who was he?

Daytime was not good for her empathic process, and anyway the house would be full of carpenters and their noise, so her days were best devoted to conventional historical research. She'd begin that work tomorrow, but tonight a visit to the house was in order. It was generally wise to get off to a running start on these things.

5

BERT CRUISED SOUTH on Divisadero, feeling weary and heavy, unhappy with himself. He lit a cigarette, but it didn't offer much comfort. He was tired enough to go straight to bed, but when he pictured turning on the lights in his house, seeing the familiar paneling and the shag rug and the unmade bed with the deep impression of his own body in the middle, he knew he wasn't up for it. Instead of turning right on Market, he cut over toward downtown and the Tenderloin Club. He assigned himself a limit of four tonight.

He pulled up in the loading zone, got out, and beeped the doors locked. Inside, the bartender was the new gal, a skinny woman with a narrow but friendly face, who he'd seen a couple times before. She was probably about forty, but she dressed younger, tight jeans and a blousey white shirt rolled to reveal stringy, muscled forearms. She lifted her chin to him as she tapped someone's beer. The Tenderloin Club wasn't a great place, but it was unpretentious, a basic bar that saw to the comforts of its regulars. Once it had been one of the main police hangouts, but over the years the cops had drifted elsewhere. Now the customers were mostly younger guys from the DA's office and lower-level city administration who came because it wasn't that far from City Hall. There were only six or eight other drinkers tonight.

Bert told the bartender a Johnnie Walker straight up and another in a few minutes, she could bring it over. He waited for the first and took it and a glass of water over to a booth along the wall, where he sat beneath a dusty marlin and tasted the whiskey carefully. You could toss them back and then you didn't think you'd had much because it wouldn't start hitting you until you'd done more than you should, so he'd been working on drinking a little and giving it time before taking some more. That, and spacing it with water.

A regular health nut, Bert thought.

He took the cardboard coaster from his water glass to use as an ashtray and set his cigarette pack and lighter next to his drink. All lined up and ready. He lit up and savored the first draw, one of the last percs still granted cops at the Tenderloin.

Over at the bar, the bartender had put glasses down in front of a young couple, a guy of about thirty and a plump girl a little younger. The bartender leaned over and the three of them talked about a book they had open on the bar, laughing, paging through. Passing the time.

Bert took a sip of water, then drew squiggles in the wet ring the glass had left on the table.

Cree: She'd turned out better-looking than he'd expected. As a kid, she'd been homely, small and so sensitive or fragile-looking you worried you'd hurt her when you roughhoused, or if you said the wrong thing. Now she was a shade over medium height, and though she still had that sensitivity she had a gutsy quality, too, like she'd been through some hard stuff and knew she could survive it. She also had a good figure, though she didn't dress to make the most of it, nice reddish-brown hair, high cheekbones, eyes that probed but not in a judging way, just curious or maybe concerned. All in all, it amazed him that she hadn't remarried. Any guy with half a brain could see that she was a keeper. Somebody's soul mate.

She had a habit of meeting your eyes and not looking away, and you got the sense she could see through bullshit. But there was another thing in her face, a slightly stricken look. Somewhere along the line, maybe when her husband had died, or maybe when she'd had her "paranormal" experience, life had given her the big scare, the big ouch. Everybody got it sooner or later. She could play tough, but she wasn't good at it. He figured her for one of those people who desperately wanted to believe human beings were at bottom good, and who was therefore continually being disappointed.

He'd downed the rest of the whiskey when he wasn't noticing. Over at the bar, the new gal had her head together with the young couple, wasn't paying attention, so he hoisted himself up, carrying the glass with him, and bellied up to the rail.

"Sorry," the bartender said. "Johnnie Black coming up." She spun to the shelves against the mirror, found the bottle. She filled to the shot-line and kept going right to the top. Bert lifted it carefully, kissed the rim, drank it down a bit.

"What's the book?" he asked.

"Names," the guy said. By way of explanation, the plump girl flashed the cover at Bert: *Name Your Baby*. A shy smile, and Bert put it together.

"Congratulations," Bert said. He raised his glass to them, and they all clinked. The girl was wisely drinking soda water. Bert had brought his cigarette but now pinched it out, the secondhand smoke thing. "Boy or girl?"

"We don't know yet. We're looking at both. So far we've made no progress at all. But we've still got three months."

"Every name comes from somewhere and has meanings," the bartender explained. "You can't believe it. My name is Amy, so . . ." She looked expectantly at the young man, who obligingly paged through and found it.

"Um, 'Amy' . . . English, Old French. Means 'loved.'"

Bert glanced at the bartender. "So—would you say it's proved accurate?"

She made a pursed-lipped, mind-your-own-business smile. "Off and on."

Bert offered a little toast to that. The first one was coming on now and he felt more sociable.

"Mine's Alexandra," the girl confided. "Means, let's see . . . English, from Alexander, means 'defender of men' or 'warding off men.'" She laughed, patting the top of her bulging stomach. "I sure haven't done a very good job of that, have I? The warding off part."

"Lucky for me," her husband said. He nuzzled in her hair. Bert got the sense the kid was a little loaded.

"Okay," the bartender said to Bert, "so let's look you up. What's your handle, pardner?"

"Bert. With an E. Bertram." He wondered if she was flirting with him. Probably it was just good bartending skills.

She turned the book around, flipped forward and back. "Okay . . . English, Old German. 'Bright raven.' Wow. 'Bright raven.' That's intense."

"What's that supposed to imply?" the girl asked.

"Half of them don't make any sense," the guy told Bert. "We just looked me up, Lincoln, which means something about Romans at a pool or something. I mean, whatever, right?"

"But it's a wonderful name," the girl told him. "Like Honest Abe. I *love* the name Lincoln." She gave her man a look so serious and suddenly private that Bert turned away in embarrassment. They kissed again, and then a guy from one of the other tables came up to ask for another round.

Bert took his glass and dead cigarette back to his booth.

Bright raven, he thought. An oxymoron. Ravens were black. You didn't think of them as bright in any way. They were dark birds, scavengers, scrappers. Bad luck birds, birds of ill omen.

He drained his glass, signaled the bartender. After she brought beers to the other table, she swung by with another shot, but she didn't linger or give any indication she'd meant anything by asking his name. Catching sight of his own face in the bar mirror, he could see why not. He looked prehistoric: great big guy, old-fashioned haircut, suspicious face that was leathery and puffy at the same time and now had that slightly cockeyed look of someone who's starting to get a buzz on.

He wouldn't know what to do if she *had* been flirting with him. He didn't remember anymore how to talk or act to make a woman feel good. Like tonight, with Cree. He'd barely remembered the basic courtesy of asking about her family. In the house, he'd gotten prickly with her, put off by her probing, and he'd managed to insult her—the "little lady" stuff was not what you'd call cutting-edge, where the hell had that come from? Maybe all the way from thirty-six years ago, when she was knee high and ran around in princess pajamas with feet in them.

Cree was okay. She wasn't asking him anything unreasonable. He just wasn't ready with the answers yet.

He'd acted like an asshole, making it so tense that afterward they hadn't known what to talk about. She'd tried all kinds of conversational gambits and he had never once hit the ball back over the net. Part of the problem was her believing in ghosts and so on. If anybody should have seen or "experienced" a ghost, Bert Marchetti should have; he'd spent time at maybe two hundred murder scenes, and all he'd ever felt was sorrow, disgust, disillusionment, and rage. He didn't believe anything survived the wreck of the body. And if people did have anything as noble as a soul, surely it would have more sense than to hang out in the vicinity of the sad, ugly remains of its former vehicle.

The disparity in outlook made for a problem talking with Cree. What was he going to do, argue with her about her beliefs? People believed what they needed to. No matter how crazy it might be, it got them through the shit parts.

Then, what was he thinking, he'd taken her to one of his regular places to eat. He'd sat down and looked around and suddenly realized, Jesus, what a dump, Ben Black's daughter comes to town and I don't have the class to take her to a nice place. He'd choked his dinner down, trying to hide his shame.

The face staring back from the mirror was the sagging mug of an old, lonely fart who'd fucked up his whole life, exactly the kind of soon-to-be-ex cop he swore he'd never become.

Fuck this, he told himself. *This I don't need.* He decided to skip the fourth whiskey for now. He put a couple of bills on the table for a tip, slipped his cigarettes and lighter back in his pocket, and went to the register to pay up.

The bartender gave him his change. She turned back to the other end of the bar without saying anything, until just as he reached the door she called out, "Good-night, Bright Raven!" He glanced back, but she was already serving some other customer.

Bert's house on Mars Street was set on a nearly vertical slope. It was just a one-story shoebox, but from below, perched on girders at the top of five zigzagging flights of wooden stairs, it looked more impressive than it was. Fifty-eight steps and five landings up, surrounded by trees and bushes. He'd bought it twenty-two years ago, after he'd divorced Fran and they'd sold the other house and divided the money. It had been cheap back then because it was nothing much to begin with, and the stairs made it hard to get to. With the hill so steep, there'd been only three other houses on the whole block, with lots of jungle between them. He'd bought the place because he'd needed the morning light coming in. That and the comparative isolation of it: It had seemed sufficiently far from the years of his marriage and the disasters that ended it. He'd never given the fifty-eight steps a thought. Good cardio conditioning, keep a macho guy in shape forever.

Now, though the slope and the green still kept it private, they'd built upscale houses on both sides and all down the street, gentrification putting siege to his little citadel. And the stairs were a pain, especially when you were bringing in groceries or, like tonight, carrying a bunch of case files.

He left the pool of streetlight and stumped up into deepening darkness. At the top, the motion-detector light came on, blinding him. He set down the bulging briefcase and put one hand on his Beretta before unlocking the door. When it swung open, he stopped dead still and listened to the dark house inside.

Eleven years ago, a psycho he'd been looking for, wanted in a double murder, had decided to turn the tables on him. John Abel Mayhew had somehow found out where Bert lived and had come in through the bedroom skylight and waited for him. When Bert came home, he leapt out of the shadows inside, slashing with a butcher knife. Bert would never forget the shock of that sudden, unexpected explosion of activity. In the end it was more of a comedy of errors, the guy missing Bert with big swings of the blade, Bert drawing his pistol and shooting in the dark and missing, missing, missing, shooting holes in his walls, ceiling, cabinets, windows. Both of them tumbling over the furniture. He'd seen the guy only in the muzzle flashes, a strobe that froze the image of the lunging screwball in midair. Bert had finally hit him in the ankle and incapacitated him, absolutely blew the ankle to pieces, it was amazing how many bones were in your ankle. Bert called for assistance as the guy flopped around shrieking like a redlined V-8 engine with its main bearing blown. Waiting for help to arrive, Bert had gotten so sick of the noise that he'd knelt on John Abel Mayhew's chest and with the gun shoved up into his nose told him to shut up or he'd shoot him where it would really hurt. A lesson in the art of persuasion: The guy actually had quieted down a bit.

The place had been shot to hell, but aside from bruises he got from tripping over furniture Bert had ended up without a scratch. The cops and EMTs who had responded bitched about having to run up so many steps. By the end, everybody was chuckling except John Abel Mayhew, whose ankle was all over the place and who ended up getting life without parole for the murders, plus B & E, attempted, lying in wait, assaulting an officer, the whole book.

Still, it had made its mark on Bert. The firearms incident counselor at Behavioral Sciences told him all about his amygdala, how trauma permanently branded your brain with a fear reflex. Bert could still feel it. The shock of coming home to the supposed security of your castle and getting jumped by somebody. The shaky breathlessness lasted only half a minute, but it happened every time.

Tonight he flipped on the lights and dropped the briefcase on the coffee table. He quickly checked through the house, then went to the stereo, put on some music—a collection of slower numbers by Count Basie that took the edge off reentry. The sweet blue sound filled the room and made him feel both better and worse. Better because the catch in the beat never failed to give him a boost; worse because, again, he sensed he'd screwed up with Cree, and even with the tension it had been nice to eat dinner with someone. With a good-looking woman. She was a good kid, asking the right questions, doing her best to keep an old fart company. She deserved better.

Tomorrow he'd try to put his thoughts in order, show her some paper. Tell her the rest of it.

He thought about checking his e-mail and then decided against it; he had a good idea what he'd find and didn't need it tonight. Instead, he went to the kitchen to get the fourth drink he felt he was owed. He poured it into a tall glass so he could mix it with water, but then decided he'd just pour it long. He brought the glass into the living room and stood in the middle, taking the whiskey like medicine.

The house was a single floor, anchored on the slope on one side and twenty feet off the ground, on a lattice of girders, on the downhill side. This far up, its windows gave to views of the near rooftops and farther away to the glow of light from Market and Castro, so that after dark Bert had the dubious pleasure of imagining ten thousand queers going about their nightlife. A long living room with a dining alcove separated from the kitchen by a counter, then a hallway leading to the bathroom, a couple of closets, one big bedroom, and a smaller bedroom that Bert used as his office. That was it. No basements, no attics, no secrets, keep it simple. A narrow deck projected out over the slope, where in good weather he could sit and have his morning coffee. It wasn't the house in Pacific Heights by a few million bucks, but you could do worse.

The whiskey and the music came together in a good feeling in his stomach. He switched on the lamp by the couch, turned off the overhead, and then stood just feeling the music. This was a good collection. Nowadays he was into the slower, spacious numbers, the ones an older guy could move to without making a fool of himself. The Count. You couldn't count on much, but you could count on the Count. The Count said life was okay and kind of graceful, and you could almost believe him. You had less gravity when you moved to the music. Bert took a few steps, found the catch, the slide, the short step. He put his right hand around an invisible partner's waist, his glass in his outstretched left hand, and spun lazily through the room. Muted brass over a solid foundation of saxophones, rhythm section subdued, brushes on the snare, it never failed.

He closed his eyes and floated and spun for a while, then bumped his thigh on the Barcalounger and realized he was a little dizzy. When he opened his eyes, the first thing he saw was his own reflection in the sliding doors to the deck, with the darkness and lights of the valley shining through.

A big old guy in a wrinkled suit dancing with an empty whiskey glass and an armful of air.

Bert poured another splash, took his glass out to the porch, leaned against the railing. A car nosed along the street below, pulled into the curb, went dark. A couple got out and went into their house. The fog made it blurry and soft like a cameo, and the general hubbub of activity all around was going quiet. Inside, the CD had played itself out. He sat on the tube-aluminum lawn chaise, then lay against its angled back and closed his eyes. A little later he heard the clank of his glass hitting the boards, but he didn't let it rouse him. He was concentrating on the sounds of the city, a lullaby hum that floated him gently away.

6

THE CHILL AIR and the exertion of climbing eight blocks steeply up-hill, fog beading on her face, refreshed Cree and brought her mostly out of the funk she'd been slipping into. On each side the tall, narrow houses angled themselves against the slope, their warm windows revealing glimpses of the lives unfolding inside, people taking the mild domestic comforts of late evening. It felt tranquil and reassuringly mundane.

The wolfman's house was as lovely in the dark as it was in daylight. Even with the windows so blank and hollow, it didn't look forbidding; it looked like it was just wanting company—a nice house, ready to provide a happy home for somebody. She went in with only a trace of reluctance.

She left the lights off, as always. Darkness was essential to the job at hand, because it tended to induce the mental state required. She and Edgar had conducted functional microelectroencephalogram tests that verified a neurological explanation: With vision frustrated, the spectrum of other senses, physical and extraphysical, came to the fore; different parts of the brain became active. Plus it was always a good idea to avoid alarming the neighbors with signs of unexplained late-night activity at an empty house.

The obvious thing to do was to head straight to the basement to seek out perimortem resonances of the wolfman, but the charm of the place beguiled her. She was feeling no whisper, no silent trill of danger or anticipation, so she took her time and wandered for a while through the main floor rooms. She savored the Victorian era's approach to space and proportion, for which she'd always had a weakness. Finally, she got curious and went upstairs.

It was hard to see in the dim glow of ambient light through the windows, but Bert was right, these rooms were gorgeous. The floors were shiny and smelled new, the walls appeared pristine with fresh paint, the woodwork had been stripped and refinished. A few pieces of furniture stood swaddled in heavy plastic sheeting, shapeless masses in the half-light, but otherwise the rooms were empty, airy. Feeling a little like a burglar, she peered into each doorway as she made her way to the front of the house. In what must have been the master bedroom, she lounged in a broad bay windowseat and just let the house come to her. Beyond the fog-blanked glass, she could sense the steep hill more than see it—a few blurry rectangles of neighbors' windows, warm and yellow, and the sulky hoots of foghorns somewhere out in the Golden Gate.

After a few minutes, she went through her sensitization ritual: lotus position, hands laid in the *dhyana mudra*, breathing slow and deep. An inventory of her sensory and affective state didn't reveal any hidden energies or subconscious disturbances. Her pulse was steady and moderate; behind her eyelids, the phosphene field appeared as a uniform galaxy of tiny lights, and in her ears the sound current maintained a steady, silvery hiss. Her skin sensitivity registered as normal, no wandering cold spots; her emotional landscape seemed devoid of inexplicable dissonances.

Mainly what she felt was a sense of privilege, being for the moment the sole occupant and mistress of this fine place. She savored that for a while, and then it occurred to her maybe it was time to look for a new, nicer place when she got back to Seattle.

She thought she had shed her earlier droop on the brisk walk uphill, but in fact it had tagged behind like a blue balloon, wafting along in her back draft, and now it caught up: *Lovely place*, she thought, *I want this; maybe it's time to look for a new apartment; can't afford anything this nice, but could come closer if there were two incomes paying for it; what will happen with Paul, how long do I hold on to expectations there, why does it always have to be complicated; what am I doing with my life, why am I not connected with a man; why can't I be normal; what's the matter with me?*

From balloon to avalanche, starting slow but gathering speed and weight until she unlocked her legs and fled the upstairs.

She'd always been uncomfortable with close, dark, underground places. It was a natural reflex: the instinctive fear of limited mobility, of being trapped or suffocated, of being far away from other human beings, where visibility is poor and where dangerous things can easily hide. But knowing its origins didn't help contain the discomfort; being in the basement put her senses on high alert.

She used her penlight to make her way to the end room, panned the beam just once to orient herself, then cut the light and headed to the wolfman's chamber. She felt her way inside and sat on the floor in a silence that was absolute, black darkness that fizzed with phosphene sparks.

The smell of earth and stone. The faintest of movements in the chill air, invisible currents shifting. *And what else?* she asked the darkness.

She groped her way through the layered subjective impressions of the space. She felt the weight of the house above and the walls all around, fought off the fear of enclosure and suffocation, formed her mind into a empty place occupied only by a gentle question: *Hello?*

Silence and darkness and the formless passage of time.

Two hours later, she finally gave up. As far as she could tell, no revenants had made themselves apparent. Her problem was similar to Skobold's challenge with reconstruction: She lacked any precedent to draw from. Given the extent of the wolfman's deformities, she couldn't be sure what kind of mind he had. She needed to "get into the head" of the wolfman, but she wasn't sure what that head might feel like, how she would even recognize it as distinct from her own thoughts, fears, or half-dreaming imaginings. For all she knew, the deviations in his cranium had been accompanied by extreme retardation, or behavioral pathologies and affective disorders.

She stood stiffly, groped her way into the larger basement room, then paused to ask the darkness one more time, *Who are you?* But if any trace of the wolfman remained here, it gave no answer.

7

CAMERA ON RAY, bird's-eye view, Ray thinks. *A naked man, running, a tiny pale shape against the broad dark flank of the hill. Three dogs ranging in wide patrol, a shifting triangle in the knee-deep grass. Sun sunk behind the ocean fog bank, murky darkness stealing over the coastal range from the east.*

Camera on Ray: Cameron Raymond puzzles at his hawk's-eye perspective, seeing himself as a scissoring figure bounding upward. He wonders whether it's some new neuropathology or some kind of inspiration—the vertigo scares him, but the freedom is worth it. For a time he wheels above, then stoops in a steep dive and drops to himself again. Close is better. He is the hill's lover, the night's secret paramour. He runs uphill tirelessly, racing the clouds to the ridge, certain tonight will be a good night.

Take off your clothes, Ray exults. *Leave the face behind, the scarred scary stranger face, a ghost face that hangs in midair and then blows away on the breeze. Drop all the masks. Underneath is raw you.*

Everything registers. He scours his skin on branches and thorns, the night air strokes him with caresses alternately cold and warm. The mountain looms ahead, approaching clouds still far to the west. Behind, the valley lights make a galaxy of sparks caught in the bright webbed strands of highways. When the half-moon nudges above the eastern horizon, he sees his own limbs flashing pale against the grass, then mottled into shifting camo by trees overhead: long muscle bands standing out on the pumping thighs, fisted hands punching, arms corded with effort. Shock of feet hitting the ground, the inburn and outburn of every breath, the syncopated heart battering in the chest. All the parts doing their job to their utmost.

Ray thinks joyously: *What are you, really? This.*

In the scrub woods and fields, it was less a run than an obstacle course, where he dodged boulders and trees, swung under branches, leapt bushes and rocks. Sometimes where the slope steepened, he scrambled on all fours.

Ray ran near his limit, but the dogs roved and probed at an easy trot. He knew they felt what he did: that fierce electric life, expressed in the will to run and to hunt. Joyously honing the blade of self against darkness, sky, earth.

He wasn't in the condition he'd been in last year, but on a good night like this he knew he could still run as much as five miles, uphill and over the roughest terrain, and after some rest could easily do the downhill return. He'd once tried to do the same on a quarter-mile track and found himself exhausted after only four miles. The difference being the magic of the night, the scent of mystery, the allure of danger. Those things gave you power. Round and round the track, that was the treadmill of the ordinary, destination preordained. No mystery. Of course your fire dimmed, will faltered. But out here you never knew where you'd end up. Where the night would take you.

Ray knew of a dozen good places to run within an hour of San Francisco. He preferred to head north to Mount Tamalpais or Point Reyes, but when time was limited he'd stay close. Tonight he'd chosen the Fish and Game Refuge, just twenty miles south of the city. The eastern slopes of the Santa Cruz mountains rose above the densely populated valley, where the streets of San Carlos and Redwood City made a webbed orange glow in the night. But this was protected land and mostly roadless and nobody came to places like this at night. Except Ray.

People didn't come because there was danger in being alone, outside, at night. Every sense shrieked a warning. Darkness and solitude conjured images from the primal imagination, the womb from which fear and religion were born. Ray felt it and it was one of the energies that propelled him, but he also knew that he and the dogs were *part* of that danger—they *constituted* danger, too.

And that was fitting. The epiphany had come to him during another night, a few years ago: *Only when you are dangerous are you truly equal to the world*.

He had chosen the Refuge tonight because the sky had been clear at sunset yet the weather report was predicting heavy clouds later. Fog often embraced San Francisco, but this weather pattern sometimes created an opportunity for a certain kind of connoisseur. A massive cloud bank would shove in off the Pacific, a sky-borne herd of aqueous, gaseous bison. Shoulder to shoulder, blunt heads lowered, they'd roll over the lowland coast, push up the steepening slopes, and then grind to a halt against the spine of the coastal range. For an hour or two the clouds would build against the dam, piling higher and higher until the mountains could no longer contain them. First a few tendrils of fog scouted through saddles in the ridge, and soon a smothering cascade rolled over and down and blotted out the eastern slopes.

If he was lucky and arrived at the summit at just the right time, he'd find himself simultaneously at the top of the ridge of earth and at the bottom of a cliff of boiling cloud. He'd feel the pressure mount as hundreds of miles of weather pressed against the last few feet of earth. Then he'd see it break and pour, and he could join it, become it: He'd run down with the wall of mist at his heels, the clear night ahead.

If he was very lucky, he could stay on the edge. That was best. Always it was the edge of things, the brink of transformation, that was most ecstatic.

It all constituted a thrill so deep and strong it seemed to change him at a molecular level, promising all good things: power, healing, endless vigor, perpetual life. Sky, water, and earth met the fire in his head, lived on inside, remade him into an elemental being.

He knew of no one who had done this except himself. He knew of no one who hungered for it as much or had the vigor for it. Maybe no one but him knew why this was necessary, how it made you whole.

Maybe no one else in the world knew. Maybe you had to be an angel. Or maybe you had to be a werewolf.

Tonight the right conditions didn't materialize. Ray straddled the crest only to find that the clouds had stalled a few miles offshore, arrested by some dynamic of air pressure and wind. He was disappointed, but still took savor in being here, especially with his thoughts so clear, his senses refreshingly free of distortion. Anyway, there was so much to think about. Ever since the discovery of the wolfman's bones, he'd sensed some extraordinary convergence occurring, lines and forces and ideas coming together, deeply meaningful in ways he had not quite determined. These runs, the night, the moon's serene face, were also crucial parts of the ingenious riddle.

He sat at the ridge top until he got too cold. The moon had passed the zenith by the time he stood and whistled to conjure the dogs from the dark. Then they were all running downhill in long, loping bounds, gravity now an ally to flight.

The terrain was mixed here, thickets of manzanitas and junipers casting blots of shadow into clear patches of long grass made pearly by moonlight. They had barely started before the dogs began sending little signals to each other, yelps triggered by something in the scent landscape. A half mile below the ridge, running at a long diagonal, Ray saw a faint flash in the darkness a hundred yards ahead. Fritz's voice rang in a series of urgent yelps, and suddenly there was Basil, angling out of the brush on the right. An instant later Sadie burst from shadows on the left, farther back.

They'd flushed something. That was the flash he'd seen: a deer. It had been grazing at the edge of tree shadows and flicked its white tail as it fled.

Ray broke through a thicket of slashing branches to see Fritz and Sadie veer hard to the left, Basil to the right. Ray followed up the middle as they drove the deer in a long curve back toward the heights.

A hundred yards farther on, he caught sight of the semaphore tail, seesawing through the darkness ahead, then vanishing to the right. He followed the dog's voices in the dark. He hurtled through a patch of chest-high scrub, and when he emerged onto the lighter slope of grass he could see the deer ahead, just flicker and moonshadow.

The land rose hard on their left, a dark wall of bare rock and loose earth that reared on the uphill side. The deer had made a mistake coming this way. It bounded along the base of the cliff with Fritz and Sadie closing from behind, two shadows slicing low through the grass. Then Basil burst from the trees at the far end. The deer turned downhill but sensed Ray pounding up from below. Confused, it turned back toward Fritz, shied, then shied again from Sadie. At last it cut hard left and flung itself at the cliff. It clung to the slope, fell, leapt, slid down again. Basil closed in. Another terrific leap, a desperate struggle of spindle legs for purchase, a rattle of pebbles as it slid down.

Ray stopped forty feet away. He was breathless with exertion and stunned by awe. His brain was a fire, and in the fire was a blot and in the blot another kind of fire. He could see everything clearly. The slant of moonlight and the shape of land made a perfect theater, animated with a performance acted for him alone. So this would be tonight's gift: a stark truth five hundred million years old.

The deer leapt again, slid, and Fritz made the first lunge. The deer dodged and tried to leap over Basil, but the big shepherd reared and caught a haunch and they went down together. Fritz and Sadie were on it instantly, shadows converging close to the ground, humping and flailing. The kill became a single shadow animal in mortal battle with itself, a many-legged, convulsing thing. Ray watched, stunned, transfixed, for only a moment.

"Off!" he barked. "Get off!"

He ran to the wall and shouted again as he came among them. This close, the night air was spiced with blood, charged with terror and the killing urge. It seared him. When he pulled at Sadie's stub tail, the Rottweiler slashed at him with a snarl but then moved away as she saw who it was. He yelled another command as he put a foot against Basil's heaving chest and pushed the shepherd away.

Ray cuffed Fritz from the throat and growled at Basil when he started to move in again. In their frenzy, they were at the very limit of their capacity to obey, but they stood back as Ray knelt to the deer. They were ceding the kill to the pack leader.

The young buck had been badly wounded. Its chest heaved and its breath raged in its throat. Its heart thrummed a muffled drum roll in its chest. Freed of the dogs, it tried to right itself in a convulsion of flailing legs, raised its head, dropped it, tried again. Each time, a flash of moon from one wild eye. Ray felt the spray from its nostrils on his bare skin. *Calm*, he willed it. *Accept. Show me it can be done with grace.* He put a hand on the straining neck and felt the heat, the wet, the quiver and throb. Musty wet fur and the copper smell of blood.

The dogs' hunger for the kill was a dark blade of yearning. The deer's terror and its will for life was another, keen and pure.

Ray was both. And Ray was the eye of knowing.

Camera on Ray as he sits and lifts the quaking head to his lap: In the dark, he strokes the slimed fur, feels the hot spraying breath. He wills the deer to calm, but it twitches away from his touch. For a moment he can find no serious injury, and he wonders if maybe the buck has burst its very heart, its will to live that strong. The thought makes him weep. But as his hand moves along the muscle of the neck he feels a tear in the pelt and a hot pulsing flow. He tries to look into the deer's eye, to stare into its transformation, to meet the animal self in that instant. But the deer no longer sees anything. The eye is a black glistening orb, without mind, angled up at the sky. The thick pulse ebbs and soon stops. Ray waits for something to pass out of the deer. He wants to see it. He tries to feel what is in himself that is the same.

A final exhalation and then all that's left are random quivers. The tension goes out of the night and the aftermath washes in, sadness and wonder. Ray knows the dogs' hunger to kill is what makes them dogs. The deer's desire to run and to live is what makes it a deer. Ray's ability to feel both, his yearning to understand both, is what makes him human.

What are you really? This. The truth is rapturous and so hard.

"I'm sorry," Ray whispers. "My beauty," he says. "Thank you," he says.

For a while he strokes the deer's body and weeps for it and then he gives it up to the dogs.

8

D R. SKOBOLD HAD kindly agreed to meet with her during his one o'clock lunch hour, with the understanding that his time was very limited. Figuring in drive times, that meant Cree had three hours for a visit to the New Main Library; if the San Francisco History Room there didn't have what she needed, it could refer her to other libraries, private collections, or museum archives. She parked in a pay lot and walked across the plaza between the ornate Edwardian dome of City Hall and the white art deco façade of the library.

The fog was gone and San Francisco's pastels and whites were crisp against a blue sky. Despite only six hours of sleep, she felt energized by the morning sunshine, and dealing with Bert didn't seem such an imposing problem. The guy was closed off, but she'd work on him, spend some off-duty time with him. Encourage him to call Mom, too, get reconnected there; maybe help him think more positively about life after retirement. She'd figure out who his wolfman was and clear up that one little piece for him.

Today, the first step would be the house itself. Somebody had built it, owned it, lived in it; somebody had knowingly or unknowingly hosted the wolfman, knowingly or unknowingly repaired the floor above his crypt.

The History Room was on the sixth floor, a huge square space filled with rows of counters, tables, and computers, with a few microfilm cartels set up along the left side. The archivist gave Cree an overview of resources and steered her toward a likely starting point, the indexes to the Sanborn Insurance Company maps. The hand-inked neighborhood maps showed every street and structure and had been redrawn often enough that she could determine within a year or two when the house had been built. She compared her city map with the old index maps to find the right blocks, then filled out a requisition form and took several microfilm reels back to a viewer.

She scanned through the sliding frames until she found the right cross streets, and soon located the footprint of the house, just as it was today: a rectangle with its narrow end facing the street, long side stretching back into the lot, a short L wing at the rear. The most interesting feature of the 1905 map was that it showed another house immediately adjacent on the downhill side, where the terrace garden was now. She made a photocopy of the frame, then rewound and worked her way backward in time through the other spools. Both houses were represented on the earliest Sanborn map, 1886.

Next she moved to the records of the Spring Valley Water Company, which supplied water to San Francisco from 1861 to 1915. Their ledgers recorded when a tap was first turned on at a given address and who paid for it, so by going back and forth between water records and the San-born maps, she was able to piece together a rough history of the two properties. The house where the bones were found was built in 1881 by a James Marcus, then sold to a Hans Schweitzer in 1882. Schweitzer was still listed as owner on the 1905 Sanborn map and received water there until 1914, when someone named O'Brien took over the water account. The house next door had been built by somebody named Jackson around 1880, but the house had disappeared from the first map drawn after the quake, and Schweitzer's name appeared in that lot's empty rectangle.

Probable sequence of events, she figured: The Jackson house had suffered quake damage, part of it toppling into the Schweitzer house, killing and burying the wolfman; the Jacksons had not rebuilt but had sold the lot to their neighbor, Schweitzer, who had opted to leave it empty and create the garden terrace. Schweitzer had sold both properties to O'Brien in 1914, and the open space had been preserved by every owner since.

She left the library at twelve thirty, pleased with her progress. Even Joyce would be impressed—after only three hours into her first research day, she had the owner's name for the property during the period in question, plus a general history of the house and the lot next door.

The feeling didn't last. The plaza was a gathering place for homeless people, who huddled among the trees with shopping carts and bags, eating scavenged lunches. Crossing the square again, she passed close to a huge man with long hair matted into dreds and a beard full of food debris, dressed in layers of tattered clothing that made him bulky as a bear. When he saw her, he sort of *reared*, swinging toward her and baring rotten teeth. Cree quelled the startle reflex, kept a neutral face, avoided eye contact, and swept quickly past. Her chest panged in sympathy but, like anyone who had lived in big cities, she knew it was best to slip through these encounters. Joyce called it the metropolitan glide.

Afterward it occurred to her that maybe the wolfman had been in a similar situation. Maybe he'd been one of those Barbary Coast derelicts that Bert had talked about. She could easily imagine the scenario: Shunned because of his deformities, homeless, scrounging a living, he'd secretly camped out in the gangway between the Schweitzer and Jackson houses, or had found his way into Schweitzer's basement. He'd set up his nest of rags, like the homeless people here, on the night before the quake. He might have been still asleep when the world fell on him at five thirteen the next morning. The wolfman might have no connection whatever to the Schweitzers or their house, to anyone or anything. Maybe no record of his life or death existed anywhere.

She felt her mood sag, but then reminded herself it was still very early in the game. And there were always the bones.

Skobold looked up from his lunch, a submarine sandwich on a sheet of waxed paper. She was early, and from the way his eyebrows appeared over the rims of his glasses he was surprised by her sudden appearance. He was sitting behind his desk while a younger man half-sat on one corner of it, gesturing with a manila envelope. The other visitor turned part way toward her and gave her a smile.

Skobold swallowed. "Ah. Ms. Black, meet Cameron Raymond. Ray, Cree Black."

" 'Ray'?"

"Because of the last name and because I'm a radiologist. It was inevitable." Ray's grin moved further up the side of his face.

He wore jeans and a white shirt and had the rangy, trim build of a very fit man. A nice face, Cree thought, handsome yet strangely shy or self-effacing. He shook her hand with a short, firm squeeze.

"Ray works at Temple MicroImage, the lab that's doing the imaging work on our . . . um, newest guest. He's the man I turn to when I need the kind of advanced analysis we'll be doing in this case. He's just brought some new films, which I'm very much looking forward to seeing."

"And I should be getting back," Ray said. "But give me a call, Horace; we'll talk when you've had a chance to look them over."

As he turned toward the door, Cree was startled to see the scarring that distorted the left side of his face. A weal of swollen tissue like a braid stretched from the corner of his lip to just in front of his ear, pulling the skin of his face and tugging down the corner of his eye. She almost gasped from a mix of sympathy and shock, and from the way he averted his eyes as he left, he clearly noticed her reaction.

Skobold stared after him with a mournful, troubled expression, then raised a forefinger to request patience as he returned to his lunch.

Cree sat on a plastic chair and waited, feeling bad about the way she'd reacted to the radiologist's scarring. She considered asking Skobold about him, but decided it would seem rude. Through the door to the lab, she could see several people clustered around Karen Chang and her partially completed reconstruction. The pallet had been removed from the back of the room, and she thought about asking Skobold where the wolfman had gone, but then worried he'd see it as her rushing him.

To make conversation, she picked up a photo of Skobold standing next to a plump, cheery-looking woman about his own age. "Your wife?"

Skobold looked mildly alarmed. "Sister," he said through his food.

Another photo showed Skobold with his arm around the shoulders of a handsome, dark-haired young man, much younger, in a graduation robe. Cree took it from the shelf and admired it briefly. "Is this your son? He's very handsome!"

This time he looked positively stricken. "My partner, Ms. Black," he said gravely.

Cree's mouth opened and shut of its own accord. "I'm on a real roll here, aren't I."

Skobold stared at her as he nibbled a trailing tag of lettuce, then turned businesslike: "I'm happy to meet with you briefly now, but as I said, I can only spare fifteen minutes. And I haven't had time to do anything more with the wolfman."

"I'm hoping the questions I have are general enough for you to have an opinion after even your limited examination to date."

He gestured with his sandwich for her to continue.

"You mentioned that the crime scene people retrieved various artifacts with the bones. What sort of artifacts?"

"Broken china, splintered furniture . . . um, a galvanized tin bucket, that sort of thing. Bertie will have an inventory."

"Any clothing?"

"Just rags—shreds, really. The fluids of decomposition hasten cloth decay—they provide a growth medium for molds, bacteria, and insects. Really, only the hard parts survived—the buttons, some rivets. No zippers back then."

"So . . . when you find a body like this, can you tell what happened? From the position of the bones? I mean, what happened before death or at death as opposed to after death?"

"Aha. An excellent point. One of the subdisciplines of the field is called *taphonomy*. It's the science of determining what happened to remains after death—the process of decomposition, damage or distribution by natural forces or by human action. For example, you find a human skeleton distributed over several of acres of woodland. Does that mean somebody murdered the deceased, dismembered him, and scattered the parts? Or were they dragged by animals, washed by flood waters, or moved inadvertently during logging operations? Understanding taphonic factors can be crucial to determining time, cause, and manner of death."

Skobold paused until she nodded to show she understood. "I wasn't present at the retrieval, but from looking at Bertie's photos of him in situ I can safely say he died where he was found. From the position of the bones, I suspect he was standing at the time of the earthquake."

"Standing in the basement? Or standing outside and caught up in an avalanche of stuff?"

"I don't know. It's an interesting point."

She waited quietly as Skobold ripped off several more bites. At last he patted his mouth with a napkin, stood, and came around the desk. As Cree stood to follow him out, Skobold paused to tap the photo she'd commented on earlier, a grin suppressed at the corners of his mouth.

"Yes, very handsome," he said. "I'll relay your compliments to him."

He led her through the lab, explaining quietly that he had moved 3024 to the back room to keep him out of view of the graduate students who were now working with Karen Chang. He unlocked a door on the far wall, ushered her through, and shut it behind them. When the overhead fluorescents fluttered alight, Cree saw a small, windowless chamber lined with shelves full of boxes, bottles, and equipment. Skobold went to the wolfman's pallet and drew the fabric carefully down to the skeleton's knees. They both contemplated that shocking bony face as Cree unfolded the page on which she'd jotted her most pressing questions.

"Can you tell much about his condition at time of death? His health history?"

"Not too much on this individual yet, but in general—most definitely *yes.* An early physical anthropologist once said that bones provide every person with an epitaph. But now the science has improved to the point where we can more accurately describe bones as our posthumous *autobiographies.* Your bones are a diary that you've kept and added to every day of your life."

"That's a beautiful concept!"

"My favorite challenges are the osteo-archeological ones, where ancient remains are found and I am asked to decipher the social and physical environment from the bones. What did this woman do for a living? What diseases did this man have in childhood? Was this person rich or poor, a slave or a king? Was this child killed as part of a religious rite, or for the sheer nutritional value of his flesh? With current techniques and technologies, we can reliably answer many such questions."

She gazed down at the wolfman, catching a sense of the bones as Skobold saw the bones: bearers of encrypted stories, Rosetta stones of whole lives.

Skobold pulled over a floor-standing lamp consisting of a circular light tube with a magnifying lens at the center. He adjusted the reflector, then picked up one of the leg bones and laid a finger near the knob at the upper end.

"Before I can sculpt a face, I need to know everything I can about the individual I'm attempting to re-create. How old? How tall? What race? Fat or thin? Healthy, or a victim of chronic disease? Any determination I make will improve the degree of likeness I can achieve. To make those decisions, I'll look at the bones' appearance very closely, measure them, and compare their numbers to statistical baselines compiled from thousands of individuals."

"But will the baselines really be helpful? Won't his deformities throw you off?"

Skobold looked pleased with her. "An excellent point. No, we probably can't apply typical standards to, for example, his rate of growth. Or, if we see anomalies in his bone makeup, we have to ask if they're the result of environmental conditions—disease or poor diet, perhaps—or a coproduct of his deformity, perhaps caused by the way his genes triggered growth. With a subject like this, we'll have to put together data from a wide variety of indicators. And, of course, any historical information you can provide about him would be enormously helpful."

"At this point, can you tell anything about his nutritional history? Did he eat well?"

Skobold hefted the long bone as if he could gauge such things by feel. "The ridges and crests are pronounced, suggesting robust musculature and adequate nourishment. Again, I can't be certain without spending more time with him. However, I can tell you some other interesting facts."

"Oh?"

He hovered briefly, then selected a rib bone. He turned it on the table so that it arced into a little bridge, then wrestled the magnifying lamp into position above it. "Take a look."

Through the lens, the ivory-brown bone looked huge; Skobold's chopstick appeared in the brightly lit circle and traced the length of rib's curve. "Here we see healthy bone—smooth, uniform in thickness, a nice sweep through its natural geometry. But here . . . you see the thickening, the uneven surface?"

"An injury?"

"Exactly. You see, bones are ordinarily *elegant*. Each has grown to accomplish its function with maximum efficiency yet utmost economy, so they are generally smooth and graceful. But when a bone breaks, the body hurriedly sends materials of repair to the injury site, and growth then is more haphazard. An injured bone quickly adds a layer of what we call woven bone that functions like a miniature cast. It bridges and immobilizes the fracture as the bone ends knit. After a time the new bone smooths over, but there will always be a thickening, what we call a callus, at the point of fracture."

Cree pondered the slight bulge. "So . . . what sort of injury caused this?"

"Not a severe one. There's been no angulation or displacement. Just a small crack or compression . . . a bone bruise." In the viewer, the bone vanished and another rib appeared, again marked by a telltale swelling. "There are quite a few of these on this fellow's ribs. Most are on the posterior curve—his back. Also on the scapulae and the bones of the arms and hands."

Cree picked up the longer rib and put her thumb and forefinger on either side. When she stroked the curve, the swelling was more obvious to her hands than to her eyes, a girdle of thickening about half an inch long. Tactile contact with the wolfman made him all the more real: Astonishingly, she was touching what had been the inside of someone's body, the bone just above what had once been a beating heart.

"What do these callus formations imply?"

"A rough life. Of course, we often see bone injuries and self-repair. Most are caused by accidents or result from repetitive use—for example, a stonemason's fingers will show indication they were repeatedly crushed, from being hit by the mallet or having stones dropped on them. But Wolfman's injuries were inflicted by others, I'm sorry to say. He was beaten with a stick or club. The location of the injuries suggests they occurred when he was on the ground, or bent over, perhaps trying to protect himself."

"Defensive injuries."

"In the technical sense, yes. But remember, the term can mean different things. He could certainly have gotten them while fending off blows from an attacker. He could also have gotten them from someone he was attacking, who was fighting back."

Cree nodded, swarmed by questions. "How long before death? In a single beating or repeatedly over time?"

"Can't say. But given the degree of healing, I'd hazard that none of these injuries occurred within, oh, the ten to fifteen years preceding his death."

The wolfman lay in his many pieces. Knowing about the pain he must have suffered, Cree saw his bones, his unintentional autobiography, as looking sad and defeated.

"You're feeling it, aren't you?" Skobold said softly. "You want to know who he was. You feel an unaccountable loyalty to him. A determination to find out who he was, to give him his due."

"I always get that for the underdog. No pun intended." She realized he'd read her mind, and she cocked her head at him. "How'd you know?"

"I share the sentiment." His fingers stroked the arm bone comfortingly. "They look so crushed down by time and gravity. But then I remind myself they're defiant, too. They say, *We will persist. We will tell the story.*"

"I like that."

A thousand other questions occurred to Cree, but Skobold's assistant had appeared at the door. She knocked on the glass, made a throat-cutting gesture, and spun away.

"Okay," Cree said quickly, "I know we're out of time. But one thing I should know . . . not to put pressure on you, but when do you think you can get to him? I mean, I'm down from Seattle and—"

"I was planning to start tonight, after hours. I really shouldn't, but of course I can't resist. But it's going to have to be a spare time job for me, Ms. Black. Meaning it could take weeks to complete reconstruction. Unless," he finished with a prim smile, "you'd like to help me."

"Are you kidding? I'd love it! I'm flattered you'd ask!"

"It will go faster with extra hands. Just the routine processing will be time consuming, but what with the gossip factor, I can't let any of my students help. And our working together will allow us to compare notes on what we've found. But are you up for working in the evening?"

Cree had to grin. "Absolutely! I'm . . . something of a night owl, actually."

Skobold nodded thoughtfully. "Let's say eight tonight, then. I'll tell Security to expect you—you'll want to pick up a key from their office."

9

CREE GOT TO the house at three. Nobody answered the doorbell, and when she let herself in the racket of power tools explained why. In the dining room, a man was working with a floor sander that rasped and thundered and seemed to drag him after it; in the front parlor, a carpenter was using a table-mounted saw that he dropped to cut precision angles on a strip of decorative molding. A couple of men were bent over another table saw where they'd spread some papers. They looked up when she came in, and the older of them came toward her with an inquiring expression. He was dressed in a leather apron over brown work pants and shirt, and his air of authority told her he was head of this crew.

"Mr. Hernandez," she said. "I'm Cree Black and I'm assisting Inspector Marchetti with the identification effort for the skeleton you found. If you can spare a few minutes, I have some questions for you."

Hernandez shook her hand, feigning consternation. "I swear I didn't do it. I have an alibi for all of 1906."

She shared a laugh with the men and clarified that it was regarding the house—its structure and renovation history. Hernandez gave his crew some instructions and went with her to the back parlor, where a short alcove extended to a doorway opening to the porch and terrace.

"Okay," she began. "My questions have to do with the difference between what this house is now and what it was when it was first built."

"Got it."

"Originally, there was another house where the terrace is now." She showed him her photocopy of the Sanborn map. "You can see it's built very close to this house—what, five or six feet?"

"Sounds about right. The gangway would have been just wide enough to walk through. On these steep hills the lots ran long and thin, you had to build close."

"So all these windows, the protruding bays, the front porch—those would have been added after the other house came down?"

"Oh, there'd have been windows. But you're right, not the bays or the porch, sticking out so far. With the other house gone, this side would have become a more important exposure, so they articulated this facade to make it look and function more like the 'front.' They'd have broken out walls and reframed to accommodate the additions. First, they'd've built foundation extensions for the bays and the porch."

She tried to visualize the reconfiguration. "Can you see any sign of wall repair or renovation from what you've been doing?"

"Nope. We haven't had to open up any walls on this side. Sorry."

A fifth man arrived with a box of doughnuts and a cardboard tray loaded with Styrofoam coffee cups. The men shut down their tools and sat on the floor or leaned against the walls to stuff their faces. Cree declined Hernandez's offer of a doughnut.

"How about the floor boards?" she asked. "I'm particularly interested in the area directly over the room in the basement."

"I can tell you about that," one of the men said helpfully. He was young, muscular, his copper skin covered in dust except where a mask had sat over his mouth and nose: the floor sander.

"Why don't you show us, Ricky?" Hernandez suggested.

In the front parlor, Ricky tugged back a tarp and used a push broom to clear sawdust from the floor nearest the terrace-side wall. He squatted and swiped the area with his hands until he found the right place.

"The varnish is colored all the same, probably been sanded clean and revarnished a couple times since then, so it's all yellowed the same. The floor is white oak, right? No big difference in color. But you can see all these boards got a finer grain, more rays. Better wood, older trees like they had. The boards on this side, it's different. You see that? It goes back, oh, about to there." Ricky gestured in an arc that took in about a quarter of the room.

It was subtle, but Cree could see what he meant. The floorboards nearest the outside wall had been replaced with lumber from a different lot. Like the ceiling boards in the basement, they had been interlaced with the older boards so that the difference was almost imperceptible. It seemed to confirm the theory that the masonry that had buried the wolfman had fallen through both the outer wall and the floor, requiring substantial repairs.

Ricky stood up again, pleased with himself. "This like *CSI*, man! Looking for the clues? You gonna put my name in the newspaper?"

The men in the other room laughed and berated him.

They chatted as Hernandez took her on a quick tour of the house to show off the fine work his crew had done, then headed for the basement. In the back room, they turned on some lights and Hernandez brought another with them into the wolfman's burial chamber. The deep, subterranean smell was the same, but in the harsh light the room seemed far smaller than it had in darkness.

"Mr. Hernandez," Cree said, "what I'm trying to figure out is, after the stuff fell and killed that poor guy, somebody did all this work, right? And they left him in there. If I can determine what they did and how they did it, that might help me figure out *why* they did it. Did they not know about the dead guy? Or did they deliberately leave him there?"

Hernandez nodded. "I see your point."

"So, your crew opens this up, and it's knee deep in rubble, right?"

"Deeper. In the middle, more like shoulder high."

"What kind of rubble?"

"Bricks, mortar, slabs of granite that were probably windowsills or lintels. Lots of broken boards, too, broken floor joists, clapboards, pieces of crown molding. We figured a chimney or part of a brick wall fell through the walls and floor upstairs. Makes sense it was from the other house, falling this way."

"Can you tell if this room was here already, and the stuff just happened to fall into it, or did somebody build it around the rubble pile?"

Hernandez inspected the wall, pondering that. "Hm. Well, we've got a four-wythe brick wall on three sides. Four wythe means four layers of brick, which is way overbuilt for a dividing wall. If it was built after the stuff fell in, I'd expect to see poor-quality mortar work, an extruded joint, on these inner surfaces. Somebody trying to work while standing on a pile of debris, or working from the outside, it would be hard to clean up the mortar that bulges out when the brick is set. But looking at the inner face, I'm seeing skillful workmanship, a smooth V bead. I'd hire this guy in a heartbeat! I'd definitely say this room was here before the quake."

"But after the quake, somebody patched the ceiling—removed the damaged boards, carefully put new ones in. That would have to be done from this side, wouldn't it?"

"No question. Had to be done from in here."

"So . . . how does someone do all this from the inside and get themselves out?"

Hernandez frowned as he looked around, shining his light on each of the walls in turn, then looked closely at the outer wall. He shrugged, at a loss. "Only thing I can think of is there was a filled-in door right where we happened to break through. We didn't look that close, we just determined it wasn't a bearing wall and started in with the sledges. If somebody had built that section from the outer side, working the bricks in skillfully, we wouldn't have noticed. And we'd've wrecked any indication of sloppy interior mortar joint as we knocked our way through."

"When you started taking away the debris, how'd that go?"

"We had three men running wheelbarrows out through the gardening room stairs, two of us inside moving rubble. I was the one who saw the first bone."

"How far in were you?"

"We started at the doorway we made, working our way in and down. The first bone was a long bone, like an arm bone, sticking up from under maybe four feet of rubble. About in the middle here."

She pictured the situation. "Must have been something of a showstopper, huh?"

He grinned. "Well, we pulled it out and looked at it. It looked like it might be human, but we didn't know for sure. Then right away we found another long bone and some little bones I thought could be a hand or a foot. I was uncomfortable doing any more, so I pulled the guys off and called SFPD. Inspector Marchetti and the crime scene people kicked us out for couple of days and did the rest of the excavation."

The coffee break upstairs must have ended, because the racket started up again, the whine of the chop saw and some hammering. A deeper rumble told Cree that the floor sanding had resumed at the other end of the house. Hernandez was getting the look of a man with other things on his mind: three thirty, quitting time on the horizon, work to be done.

They turned off the lights and headed back upstairs.

The Schweitzer family history was becoming very important, Cree decided. Clearly, the owners of this house had not only known about the wolfman but had taken some pains to leave him in there.

10

CREE'S MAP SHOWED Mars Street as a short, curving way just above the big bend on Market Street. She followed Bert's directions and parked just as the streetlights winked faintly alight against a sunset-rouged sky. Five fifteen: She was a little early.

Bert's house stuck out from the steep hill on stilts, at the top of a wooden stairway that angled between trees and shrubs. It looked a little low-rent up there, especially compared with the modern concrete and stucco places on either side. She began climbing the steps, wondering why Bert had sounded so tense when she'd called. Maybe he'd broken down and decided to tell her whatever it was he'd been holding back from the start.

Looking up at the house, she could see through the deck doors to where lamps made circles of yellow on the inner walls and ceiling. After a moment, Bert came into view. He paused with his arms out to each side, head tipped back, then glided to the right, disappearing and then reappearing with the same smooth motion.

Puzzled, she lingered at the fourth landing. She couldn't see his legs or feet, but his big, white-shirted body turned, sidled, spun right back with surprising grace and precision. It took her another few seconds to realize that he was dancing. She couldn't hear the music, but she could see the beat in his movements.

There was something touching about a big man moving that way, an older man, his clumsiness turned unexpectedly effortless and gallant, and suddenly the memory came to her: Right, Bert danced. He used to grab Mom and make her dance to the radio, Pop looking on amused and indulgent, Mom pretending to hate it but looking pretty with her cheeks flushed. Bert was into swing and ballroom, which even back then had seemed old-fashioned. Looking at him now, Cree felt a brush of nostalgia and compassion: an older man, dancing alone—at once charmingly old school and a little sad.

"Get you anything? Beer, cocktail?" Bert tucked his rumpled shirt in over his belly and tipped his head toward the kitchen, which was separated from the main room by a high counter. He had turned off the music the moment she rang the doorbell.

"No booze yet, thanks—I'm going to meet Dr. Skobold later to help him with the bones. Maybe a Coke?"

Bert went around the bar, opened the refrigerator, and took out a can. He set her up at the counter with a glass of ice cubes, then found a bottle and poured half a glass of whiskey for himself. Cree sat on one of the stools while Bert stood uneasily on the other side.

"Place is a mess," he apologized. "Long days on the job, trying to close things out. You know."

"No, this is really nice—right in town but so private! You must have great views when the sun's up."

"Pretty good, yeah." He sipped his whiskey, bit his lips, looked away.

Actually, the house seemed worn, tired, like Bert himself. The smell of stale cigarette smoke, trails worn in the rugs, a sagging couch, not much on the walls besides taped-up posters for older popular films and jazz concerts: the house of a solitary person.

The silence had gone on for too long. "But those stairs! My God, Uncle Bert, your own Stairmaster, every day. Must keep you in great shape."

"Don't I wish." He took a swig of whiskey, Cree tasted her Coke. There was another silence that Bert chickened out of first: "Yeah, I didn't ask you about yourself much. I mean, I don't know . . . social life. Guys."

She had learned to say it concisely and without excess emotion: "I had a very hard time after Mike died. It took me a long time to stop missing him."

Bert's eyes dodged.

"I have some very good friends," she went on, feeling pressured for more. "For the last year I've been seeing a guy in New Orleans when our work schedules allow it. Now there are some complications with that. I'm a little unfamiliar with this stuff, but I gather it's pretty typical and . . . un-interesting. What about you? I remember hearing you got married—"

"Divorced. Twenty-three years ago."

"Seeing anybody?"

He looked downright unhappy again, shifting his weight uncomfortably from foot to foot. "I'm a little past my prime, Cree."

She would have disagreed just to make him feel better, but he was too tense, none of this was working out. Personal chitchat was clearly not Bert's strength, and love life was not a good topic for either of them right now.

"So what's up, Uncle Bert? Sounds like you've got something for me?"

"Yeah. There's some stuff you need to know about."

He led her through the living room and down a short hall, into a little room set up as an office. A computer monitor glowed from the clutter on a big steel desk.

"About ten days ago, I got a problematic e-mail." He clicked the mouse to open a file on the computer and after a moment an image materialized.

At first glance, Cree thought it was just a dog—the neck and head of a pointy-eared, gray dog, staring straight at her with its head slightly cocked. It took her a few seconds to notice the subtle morphing that had been done: The eyes were disturbingly human, the mouth shortened to the front of the muzzle and rimmed with a pinkish ridge that suggested human lips. The flesh-toned nose was too rounded and prominent.

A dog becoming a man. Or a man well on his way to becoming a dog.

"What in the world—?"

"That's what I've been asking."

"Who's it from?"

"Anonymous. Address is a Hotmail account, just a random string. I sent a reply, asking who I had the pleasure of addressing, but my message bounced back. 'Undeliverable, recipient's account no longer in service.'"

"A gag e-mail? Everybody's got a joker in their address book, right?"

"Except that I've gotten two more since this one. All with the disappearing address of origin."

Bert opened another photo. This one looked like a Doberman, but again the features had been perverted by adding human elements: a disturbing swelling of the forehead, human eyebrows and eyes. The head was upraised, the almost-human lips parted over snarling dog teeth. There was no mistaking the menace implicit in this one.

"So . . . what does it mean to you? Something to do with the wolf-man's bones?"

"Yeah, the part-human, part-canine thing, that was my first thought. Plus I got the first one four, five days after we retrieved the bones. But now I'm wondering if it's got some other elements. Let's go back in the other room, I'll explain."

Back in the living room, Cree sat into the sagging couch and saw that the coffee table held a dozen or more manila folders and ring binders: case files. Murder books.

Bert sat heavily next to her and lifted an ankle to his knee, jiggling his foot as he took a pull from his drink.

"I thought about whether the messages were connected to the wolf-man. Horace has been keeping a lid on it at his shop, but there's no question other people have seen the bones. There's the crime scene crew and the people in the ME's office. There's Horace's assistant, there's whoever Horace had do his lab work. But I'm thinking it's something else. Somebody with an ax to grind with me."

"Like who?"

"My first thought was, every cop has creeps he's put away who eventually get out and don't exactly wish him well. When I was in Narco, I put away hundreds of shitheads, most of them are back on the street by now. In Homicide, I've put down quite a few, and some of the ones who got murder two or manslaughter are probably out, too."

Bert stood up suddenly, swigged from his glass, and began pacing back and forth, a man working himself up to something. "But I don't think that's it, either."

"I'm listening."

He set his drink aside to lean over Cree with his knuckles on the coffee table. He was breathing hard, and his eyes were full of a dangerous worldliness. "First we need to get something straight. Back at the house, you asked me if I believed in werewolves, right? And I said I don't. Superstition, Hollywood, bunch of crap. But you're right, that's not the whole answer. Where I'm at now, I'm looking back at thirty-five years of dealing with the bad things people do to each other. I know how they prey on each other. I got a good memory, Cree. I remember it all. An endless string of bad shit—dead people, wounded people, tortured people. They do it in stupid ways and violent ways and devious ways. Nobody turns into a wolf. People who do this shit don't have to. *They're wolves already.*"

He looked so tormented and baleful that against her will she broke eye contact. She leaned away from his red face, feeling a little pulse of fear like a tiny artery throbbing at the back of her brain.

"Okay. So tell me where you went with this. How it connects."

Bert drained his glass and grimaced as he struggled to get himself under control. He came around the coffee table, tugged up his trouser legs, and sat.

"These are case files I've been taking another look at. Over the years, there are gonna be cases that stand out, right? Some are the ones that got under your skin, you can't shake the images of what you saw. Some are the ones you had a feeling about, you knew you could've solved them if you'd gotten one more break. But you never did, now they're languishing and cold and the guy who did it is still out there, laughing his ass off."

Bert half opened a file, then closed it again and looked at her with concern. "There are photos in here, not so nice to look at. You up for that, or—"

"I can probably handle it," she lied. "But thanks for asking."

11

BERT READ FROM reports and summarized each file as Cree leafed through the materials. They were older cases Bert had handled himself or ones he'd worked along with other jurisdictions. The cause and manner of death varied, but they all had one thing in common: Bert hadn't liked the outcome. There were two stabbings, a shooting, a blunt-object battery; the morphing e-mails must have gotten Bert thinking about dogs, because several files concerned unsolved dog-attack deaths. A couple were ten years old, one in San Francisco, one in Oakland, animals never identified. Four years ago, a toddler killed after wandering away from a family outing in San Bruno State Park, just south of San Francisco, death attributed to dogs or coyotes. Three years ago, an elderly woman dead in Sausalito, animal never located. Bert had even pulled up a death attributed to accident, a man who fell down the stairs in his house and then was partially eaten by his own dogs after they went unfed for several days.

After eight or ten, Cree could no longer absorb the details. When they closed the last of the folders, she leaned back, feeling stunned and sick.

"You're saying there's a murderer who didn't get caught. You had suspicions at the time, maybe you had other suspects who never panned out, who slipped through your fingers. And now the killer is sending you e-mails."

"Right now, all I'm saying is *maybe*."

"Assembling this material was a lot of work. When did you first get the idea there was something to look for?"

Bert bit his lips and turned partly away. "For the last six months, I been looking back. Wanting to clean up anything I'd let get away from me.

73

It was kind of on the side, but then I began getting the e-mails with the morphs. But it wasn't just the messages. All they did was reinforce the sense I've had all along on every one of these. Most of these files I just dug out today."

Cree thought about that. "Why would this hypothetical killer suddenly start sending you messages?"

"Guy's taunting me. I must have gotten close to him and he's reminding me. He must know I'm retiring, wants to rub my nose in shit because I didn't catch him. Trust me, these guys often do this. They like to challenge you. They half-want to get caught, and they love the attention, makes them feel important. He doesn't want me to fade away without a last fling at it, because when I fade away, so does he."

"But—"

"I figured you'd be skeptical. But take a look at this." Bert selected two files, the older dog attacks. "One of these was mine, right? The other was Oakland's, but we got together because of the similarities. Me and the lead from Oakland, we didn't like the way the animal never turned up, couple other details. We batted around the idea that these were actually homicides, somebody using dogs to kill. See?"

She looked where Bert's thick finger indicated, a memo from back then. She smelled the booze on Bert's breath and was hit by a sudden yearning for a stiff drink herself, then remembered she needed to stay alert for her session with Dr. Skobold. That gave her a jolt, and she looked quickly at her watch.

"Seven fifteen! How long does it take to get to Berkeley from here?"

"This time of night, not too bad. Half an hour."

She shook her head, trying to rattle away the dazed feeling. "I should go to the bathroom and then head over there."

Bert started stacking the case files. Cree went down the hallway to the bathroom, where she shut the door and leaned her head against it with her eyes closed, trying to overcome the sensation of hurtling. After a few minutes, she splashed water on her face and patted herself dry with one of Bert's smelly towels.

When she came out, he was up at the front of the house, putting his jacket on.

"Going out?" she asked.

"I got errands to run. I had a lot on my plate even before this stuff came up."

"Well, you're going to have to talk to me first." He hesitated, so she pointed at the kitchen bar and ordered him curtly, "I need a drink of water. Then talk. And don't give me any bullshit."

His eyes narrowed, but he went to the sink and filled a tumbler for her. She drank it greedily. Afterward, they stared at each other across the bar.

"I don't know what to think, Uncle Bert. I mean, I don't have much experience in forensics or criminology, but it just . . . I don't know. Did you talk to your lieutenant about this?"

"No. Because I know what he'd say. 'Bertie, you're hanging up your hat in three months. Why go looking for problems? At some point we all gotta hand off the baton.' Or he'd say I was reaching, the whole thing was thin. But how many times have I heard that over the years? Brass, they're thinking about budgets, case loads, processing rates. They forget about the victims, the survivors, the perpetrators. The reality!"

He came around to Cree's side of the bar and perched on one of the stools, arms folded across the barrel of his body, waiting for her response.

"So you called me here to help you chase down this supposed murderer? Because you want to go out with a bang, but you know your lieutenant won't give you any support resources, and you need someone to help with legwork? You misled me?"

"No! Jesus, what do you think I am? When I called you, all I had was the bones!"

"You said you got the first e-mail message ten days ago. You called me, what, eight days ago."

Bert's eyes slipped away, came back angry and defensive. "Like you said, at first I figured maybe it's somebody pulling my leg. I didn't put the whole thing together in my mind until like two days ago, you were already on your way. So help me. Christ, one reason I showed you this stuff is I figured you should have fair warning, it could get strange around here, maybe you want to stay out of it."

"If it doesn't tie in with the bones, how am I involved anyway? You said there was no connection."

"Maybe there *is* a connection. This guy, he's got to be someone I talked to back then, somebody I looked at or got close to without knowing it. Maybe he knows about the bones, too, maybe he's got some inside access. How the hell do I know?"

She studied him. Clearly, Bert wasn't used to being interrogated; he was used to being on the other side. She felt bad for him, perched on his chair, caught out like a schoolboy.

"Hey, Uncle Bert," she said, as gently as she could manage. "We're family, right? Almost, anyway. How about you just tell me what's on your mind. Let's sort it out from there."

He tried to keep his hackles up, but he looked relieved. He checked her face, checked his watch, checked the floor. "No way am I going to put you in harm's way. I just wanted to warn you—the bones, maybe it's not as simple as it looked at first. And as long as you're here, maybe you could keep your eye open for the connection. If there is one."

She studied him and decided he was probably telling the truth. If there was some connection between the bones and the e-mails, he was certainly right to bring it up.

"Here's the deal. I don't want you to bullshit me ever again. No beating around the bush." She paused, astonished at the Brooklynese in her voice, as if she'd absorbed it from the air in Bert's house. "Just tell me what's on your mind, let me sort it out myself, my way."

"Okay."

"And I have to be honest with you. One, I'm not a criminal investigator, I don't know anything about police work, I'm not going to be any good to you. I can't, and I won't, it's just not something I can do. Okay? Two, I'm not buying your theory one hundred percent. About your e-mails connecting to these old cases. About the cases being linked or the animal attacks being homicides. I'm sorry, but that's how I see it."

He nodded and stood up. "Good. Fine. Hey, I'd like nothing more than being proved wrong, believe me. Now we gotta go or we're both gonna be late."

He seemed more relaxed as he locked the door and escorted her to the stairs outside, as if coming clean had let some pressure out. When they got to the edge of the light cast by his motion-detector spot, Cree couldn't see a thing; beyond the top step, the stairs were just an abyss of darkness. But he took her arm in a solid grip, and she measured her steps by his.

"Takes a while to get used to it," he said. "Could break your neck. Me, by now I could do it blindfolded."

They descended into the night, into the foliage that rose thick around the stairway. In places, she was completely night-blind, but she felt Bert's bulk next to her, his firm careful hold on her arm and his steady tread. Uncle Bert, from back when.

"I saw you dancing," she confessed. "When I was coming up the stairs. I remember when I was a kid, you dancing in our kitchen."

Face invisible, Bert snorted softly. They moved on down.

"You looked . . . you looked good. Like a guy who knows what he's doing. Who's still got the stuff."

"Yeah," he said wearily, more to himself than to Cree. "A regular Fred Astaire."

12

THE CAMPUS SIDEWALKS were mostly deserted. The lights, regularly spaced along streets and walks, lit the open spaces and the façades of buildings but put impenetrable shadows under the trees. Cree presented herself at the security office to register and pick up an electronic key, then drove to the parking lot behind the Life Sciences Building and walked the leaf-shadowed paths around to the front door. The foyer and main corridor were empty except for an old man buffing the marble with an electric floor polisher. She took the elevator to the basement level, where it was much cooler, and so quiet her heels echoed. No light showed under any of the doors she passed.

She knocked at the lab door, waited, then tried the knob and found that it opened. The windows were dark, but the ceiling fluorescents were on and humming, bathing the big room in blue-white light. The counters were spotless, the computer screens dark, the various clay heads standing there looking at nothing. The smell of rot was stronger now. No sign of Skobold.

He wasn't in his office, either, though his desk light was on. Probably gone to the bathroom, she thought.

Killing time, she studied the partially completed craniofacial reconstructions. Karen Chang must have been busy today, because the head she'd been working on was no longer just plaster and spacers. Half the face was clothed in straps of brown clay of varying widths and thicknesses, and ropes of clay wrapped the post that served as a neck. It looked like a drawing from a nineteenth-century anatomy textbook: on one side, angular white bone with the long grin of teeth; on the other, the beginnings of the muscles and fat that gave a face its humanity and its individuality.

Karen had put glass eyes into both sockets, round unblinking baby blues, unsettling in such an incomplete face. Cree lightly touched the clay, found it soft and yielding, like flesh.

The buzz of fluorescents was the only sound. She wondered what was taking Skobold so long, then thought maybe he was already working on the wolfman. But the door to the back room was shut and its window was dark.

Running late, then. She went to another reconstruction, this one further along. She looked it over and opened the textbook on the counter next to it to find drawings and photos of cadaver dissections, with statistical tables next to them. One series of head shots showed a dissection in reverse order, starting with white bone, then working layer by red layer up, muscle by muscle. She found it disturbing but fascinating: the complexity of the face, the body, the way all the parts worked together. How all that engineering ended up smoothed over with skin, detailed with brows and lashes, with characteristics people could think of as beautiful or handsome, when there was all that organic machinery underneath. She wished she hadn't looked at the photos in Bert's case files, which kept spoiling what really should be unalloyed awe and appreciation.

Bert's theory bothered her. It was awful to think of a murderer on the loose, somebody who had gotten away with it but who didn't want to let go, wanting to rub Bert's nose in his failure. Somebody who, having gotten away with it before, might think to try it again. Or do something more extreme to Bert than sending e-mails.

But just as troublesome was Bert himself. True, she hadn't studied the cases and didn't have the forensic experience he did, but it looked to her like he was trying to connect dots that didn't connect. Even if he could prove there was something wrong with earlier determinations on each case, it would be quite a stretch to assume there was a common perpetrator. And he was too intense about it, too convinced, on too little evidence. As if he had too much emotional investment. As if Bert was showing some mental fatigue at the end of his thirty-five-year shift.

A sound brought her out of her thoughts. It was a low rumble followed by a dull *blump!* from the inside wall. Somebody doing something in the next room over, whatever that was. As she listened, the sound came again, that heavy rolling rumble followed by a muffled concussion that shook the counter slightly. A janitorial crew, she figured, cleaning and moving furniture.

She closed the anatomy book, starting to be bothered by the cadaver photos. She checked her watch, wondering if everything was all right with Skobold or if she should be concerned. A moment later a sharp rattle came from close by, and she jumped, hands suddenly tingling.

It was Horace, backing through the hallway door with an armload of papers and folders. "Sorry I'm late," he called. "I hope you haven't been waiting too long?"

"Not at all. I've been admiring your work." She flexed her hands, trying to shed the wired, caffeinated feeling, hoping he wouldn't notice.

"I was just finishing off some chores next door," Skobold explained after he'd deposited his papers on his desk.

"What's next door?"

"Oh. The rest of the lab. The meat suite."

" 'Meat suite'?"

He owled her with his eyes and frowned disapprovingly. "The students' unfortunate attempt to be facetious. They call this side the 'bone zone.' You don't assume all our subjects arrive as clean as the wolfman, do you? Most have to be processed next door before they come in here. I'll show you."

She followed him out of the lab and down the hall to another door she'd passed on the way in. Skobold unlocked it, groped inside, and snapped on the overhead lights. They went into what looked like a typical pathology suite: two steel tables, scales, surgical power tools, big steel sinks, rolling chrome tables for medical instruments, a bank of a dozen brushed-steel morgue drawers, a big walk-in cooler door.

The smell was strong in here, reminding her of when Mom used to boil chicken carcasses for soup—steamy, murky like that, only this meat had gone very bad.

"By the time we receive remains, the medical examiner's lab has given up on trying to determine cause of death or identity," Skolold explained. "This is often because the soft tissue remains are in such bad shape—badly decayed or burned, in states of liquefaction or mummification or what

80

have you. Mainly what we do here is get down to the bones again and work outward from there."

"Uh-huh."

He peered at her with concern. "Is it the odor?"

"I'll manage."

Skobold pointed out the industrial-size stove against one wall, where a couple of large, lidded pots were simmering. A venting hood covered the whole thing, and a fan hummed as it sucked the steam away.

"When we get remains that include a significant amount of flesh, we macerate them for several days—that's essentially just soaking. Do you see those vats near the sinks? We pour the water off, rinse the remains, and refill the vats every day. When the tissues have softened up, we simmer the remains and then scrub off any lingering bits." Skobold chuckled and shook his head. "It used to get us in awful trouble with the other departments, but with our fume hood and new ventilation system it's vastly improved. You never get rid of every last whiff, though."

"Right."

He walked her around the suite, discussing the challenges of working with various kinds of corpses. He referred to people burned beyond recognition as "crispy critters." Crispy critters required special techniques for removing the remaining burnt flesh and preparing the charred, very fragile bones. Sometimes they encountered a mudman, someone who had been buried in soil that had absorbed the fluids of decomposition and then dried to form a cement-hard capsule around the body; this demanded painstaking removal of mineral and tissue, using dental picks and toothbrushes. Then there were corpses that had been left in sealed containers of one kind or another and had largely liquefied, another set of challenges.

He offered to show her some examples. She briefly considered looking at a pre-Columbian mummy from Chile, but in the end declined.

By comparison to Bert's photos and some of the subjects Skobold described, the wolfman was beautiful. Cree understood how you could get to like bones: clean, simple, innocent, elegant.

Skobold gave her a lab smock to slip over her street clothes, and then they gloved up and got to work. He had taken scrapings earlier, in the eventuality that DNA or toxics work might prove necessary, so their job tonight was to clean the bones. They rolled the wolfman's pallet out of the back room and positioned it next to a pair of deep stainless-steel sinks with fine mesh over the drains. Skobold switched on a radio to some classical music, and then with the water running showed her how to gently brush and rinse away soil, bits of desiccated tissue, and mold stains. Cree took the adjacent sink and followed his lead.

"Even a small amount of surface discoloration can obscure important clues," he explained. "My main concern will be to look very closely at the places where bone growth has occurred, which provide the best information about his age. His development was no doubt atypical, but between the fusion of the various epiphyses, his cranial sutures, his pubic symphysis, and other indicators, we should be able to pin his age down."

Cree started with the toe bones, rolling each irregular knot under the stream, brushing gently, and offering it to Skobold for approval. When each was clean, she blotted it dry and set it back on the pallet. Two hundred and eleven bones, some of them in pieces, would take a while.

The radio played a peppy Bach concerto, Skobold sometimes humming along contentedly. But with just the two of them, alone in the depths of the big empty building late at night, the rest of the world felt very far away. The windows on the outside wall were dead black, the busts on the counters seemed frozen in silent convocation. Cree's thoughts kept coming back to her discussion with Bert.

"So," she said. "Uncle Bert. You call him Bertie—you guys must be pretty good friends?"

Skobold held up a dripping rib, found something that displeased him, and returned it to the stream of water. "I have a great affection for him. I'd like to say we're friends, but I doubt our association quite warrants the term. We have a long-standing professional relationship and . . . certain things in common."

"But you've known him for a long time."

"Twenty-six years."

She dried her toe bone and began washing the next, trying to think of a way to sneak up on the topic without making it obvious she was concerned: In Skobold's opinion, how was Bert doing? Was he handling his impending retirement okay? Anything different about him recently? Did he always drink so much? From there, maybe she could solicit his thoughts about Bert's theory.

"He sure takes his John Does seriously. Like the wolfman here. I mean, I can understand your having a clinical interest, but I wouldn't think Bert would bother. Given that he's retiring."

Skobold paused and looked at her with eyes that filled the entire lenses of his glasses, almost accusing. "Your family—you've been close to Bertram since your father's years in the Navy?"

"Well. Actually, not so close. He and Pop supposedly had some legendary times together, if you can believe a word they said. I haven't seen him since Pop's funeral, and before that we'd fallen out of touch for many years. But we all have fond memories of him, and he calls my mom sometimes."

Skobold finished his rib, blotted it, and took up the next. "I met Bertram during a difficult period for us both. I believe our mutual . . . hardships forged a bond."

"Hardships?"

"I had recently lost a son, Ms. Black. Yes, I was married once. My son was seven. He was hit by a car while riding his bicycle in front of our house."

Cree looked up, shocked. Skobold was brushing the wolfman's rib tenderly, biting his lips so hard they were white.

"Oh, I'm so sorry! God, Dr. Skobold, I didn't know! I hope I haven't sounded cynical or facetious, I mean when I'm talking about your subjects here or—" Suddenly she remembered her comment on the photo in the office, mistaking his lover for his son, and understood the real scope of that error. She felt her face flush.

"It changes you, Ms. Black. You are never the same."

"No. Never."

"My point was, given that Bertie had also lost his daughter around the same time, we forged a sense of connection. A special . . . trust, if no real intimacy."

"Wait, wait . . . I'm sorry—Bert had a *daughter?*"

"I assumed you knew."

"I had no idea! It must have been the years when we were out of touch. No one ever mentioned it! Bert never once—"

"No. He doesn't. Not anymore." Skobold looked suddenly tired, his face so gray it seemed chalky. "She disappeared on her way home from school. She was six. Abducted a block from their house. Bertie was just a patrolman then, but he turned the city upside down, trying to find her. He turned himself inside out. He ruined his marriage, he did things that almost got him kicked off the force. She was never found."

Cree was speechless. She couldn't catch her breath. She thought back to how tough she'd been with Bert. Irrationally, she was suddenly very glad she'd complimented him on his dancing.

"Only one of too many, I'm afraid," Skobold said. "Some show up here. Some never show up anywhere."

He huffed a big sigh, and continued working. The lights buzzed and the radio played some chipper Mozart, utterly inappropriate. Cree went back to work on the longer foot bones. She'd had a bunch of questions to ask and now she couldn't even remember them.

After a while Skobold was ready to talk some more. "Which explains his concern for John and Jane Does. For a long time, he would check in with me when I received remains that might possibly prove to be his daughter. He did the same with the MEs in half the state. After a few years, he'd stopped hoping to find her, it was just his . . . habit. Male, female, old, young, he wanted to give them that. Some tiny substitute for the care he couldn't give her, I suppose. I was happy to help him."

A long silence. She couldn't speak.

"Given that I understood," Skobold said quietly.

Cree was thinking about Bert's divorce and the difference between the laughing, flirting guy she remembered and the tired large rumpled man he was now, and about Skobold's handsome young lover and funeral home persona, and she couldn't say a word.

They worked for another two hours, talking only when Skobold gave suggestions or showed her aspects of the bones he considered important. He washed the cranium and mandible himself, using extreme care, frowning to look closely at interesting features, retrieving small chips and loose teeth that accrued in the drain screen. When they were done, the stains were mostly gone and the skeleton looked brighter, more cheerfully savage.

It was almost eleven o'clock when they peeled off their gloves. They removed their smocks and put them into a steel hamper, then covered the bones and wheeled the pallet into the back room.

The next step, Horace told her, was to take cores from the femurs for the osteon count, another way to assess age and health. They'd measure the bones, label them, and varnish them; Skobold would degrease the skull in preparation for taking casts of it. He'd look closely at the X-rays, compare the wolfman's metrics to standard statistical tables, then would put together his best guesses as to facial musculature and appearance with any information she might find, such as period photos or medical records. Only then could they begin reconstruction.

It would have to be done in his spare time, he reminded her, which meant they'd have to meet mainly after hours. Cree had other nighttime activities on her agenda, but figured it was manageable; she agreed readily.

"Same time tomorrow night, then. Now, I have a little paperwork to do before I close up. Please take care walking to your car. There have been some incidents on campus lately."

He opened the hall door for her, smiling wearily. But when she turned to say a last good-night, she found his face had changed again.

"I adored my son. Adored him. I had to look at his broken body with an anatomist's knowledge of what it must be like inside him. Later, I wouldn't let them close the casket, they had to pull me away. At the burial, I thought I'd die. My marriage didn't last a year. I still visit his grave on the anniversary."

Skobold's jaw was quivering slightly, and Cree felt it in him, the huge unfillable hollow, the enormity of that pain. She touched his cheek, afraid to offer more lest they both break down, and started to walk away.

"But at least I *knew*, you see," he called after her. "Where he was. What had happened. When I thought of Bert's situation, I always knew I was the lucky one."

13

BERT WAITED UNTIL Cree had driven out of sight, then walked past the city-issue Crown Vic and got into his own vehicle. It was a Chevy Suburban, biggest thing on the road short of a Hummer, pretty intimidating with its dull gray paint and deeply tinted windows. He slammed the door, started it up, then bent to unlock the metal case bolted to the floor under the driver's seat. He brought out his little Tomcat .32 and tucked the clip holster into his waistband, then put the truck in gear.

His first errand was a quick-stop place, where he gassed up the Suburban and went inside for a jumbo coffee and three egg-and-sausage sandwich things that had been in the steamer since breakfast time. Back in the driver's seat, he tore into the sandwiches and stoked himself with coffee. The coffee was good, and he felt like the truck, full tank and ready to go.

Not yet eight, he was right on time. He drove back down to Sixteenth Street and into the Mission district. He had always felt at home here, one of the few parts of San Francisco that wasn't just pastel stucco houses but also big industrial buildings more like the type he'd grown up around back east. He pulled over in the orange glow beneath the 101 overpass and let Chevy idle as he sipped coffee, smoked, and waited.

A few minutes later, Nearing's car slid past and pulled over. Rich got out and came to the Suburban, bringing a small gym bag and his own cup of coffee.

Rich Nearing was a tall, stringy black guy in his late thirties, a beanpole with sandpaper-short hair over a hatchet face and a long neck with a prominent Adam's apple. Tonight he wore black jeans, black T-shirt, and a black leather jacket that he left open so you could see the straps of his shoulder rig. He worked in the Narcotics Section, Bert's unit before moving over to Homicide.

"Hey, Machete," Rich said. He slammed the door, made himself comfortable, popped the hole in his coffee lid. First Tuesday of the month, this was the ritual. They'd drink coffee and discuss the route before they got going. In the dark cab, with the tinted windows and his black skin and clothes, Nearing was the Invisible Man, just teeth, eyes, a single gold stud earring.

"How's it going, Rich?"

"Goin' good. My boat's almost done, that feels all right." Nearing had used some of his off-the-record income to buy a third-hand cabin cruiser and was fixing it up himself. "My son's birthday is coming up this weekend, we're trying to get ready. That stuff. You?"

Bert started to shrug, *same old same old*, but then surprised himself by finding there was something to report. "My . . . niece is visiting from out of town. A good kid, haven't seen her in a while."

Nearing nodded, put his coffee to his face.

"How's it look for tonight?" Bert asked.

"Everything's routine except the new client, the dry cleaner. Mr. Zheng's son called to ask if we could wait 'til next month. I said, Sure, no problem, we're nice guys, we understand."

Bert laughed. Being understanding was not a posture that you used. He hadn't met the Zhengs. Koslowski, their partner in Vice, had gone with Nearing for the first meeting, but he knew the call meant there'd probably be some ugly stuff later tonight. Mood he was in, he almost didn't mind.

The first stop was a video store, specializing in but not exclusively devoted to sex tapes. It was run by a pair of old hippies who had opened up their shop on the periphery of the North Beach sin zone. Bert pulled up across the street and Nearing hopped out with his duffle, waited for traffic, then crossed to the brightly lit façade. Bert watched as he went inside, and through the door he could see the change in posture of the guy behind the counter. Nearing's favorite greeting for these visits was "Trick or treat!"

Bert lit a cigarette, knowing there'd be a wait. Nearing liked to chat up their clients, playing buddy and coconspirator while in fact he was just drawing it out, savoring his power. Nearing always got off on the risk, the rush of being outside society, off the record, off the charts. Playing it both ways, law and outlaw.

Working in Narcotics and Vice put you in touch with certain kinds of people and therefore certain kinds of opportunities. The guys who ran Very Very Video were typical. Storefront rentals were pricey anywhere near North Beach. You had an inventory to keep up, overhead was high, and you had competition, so of course you wanted to make extra money on the side. In the case of these guys, they had friends up in Mendocino who grew amounts of marijuana even the pot-tolerant SFPD would ordinarily be reluctant to ignore. But the tip had come first to Nearing, so word of their activities never made it into the books. All these guys did was hold the quantity shipments, stinky green bales of leaf and big zip-top bags of resinous buds until local distributors picked up their allotments. For taking the risk, they got a percentage from the suppliers.

For overlooking Very Very Video's sideline, Bert, Nearing, and Koslowski took a percentage of the percentage.

At last Nearing kicked his duffle under the counter. The guy back there disappeared from view, then stood again. The bag reappeared on the floor on Nearing's side, but still Rich had to shmooze some more. He called it "establishing congenial client relations."

Bert had been inducted into the business by the old-timers back in Narcotics, had left it behind for some years after he moved to Homicide, then got recruited again by the younger generation. When his senior at Narco had first invited him in, Bert had declined. But after a year or so he'd begun to feel that he was owed something by the scumbags who he worked so hard to police and who—one of them anyway, somebody somewhere—had destroyed his life. If you wanted to get moralistic about it, you could call it a sin tax. And if it occasionally required administering pain, you could call that punishment. There was a certain quid pro quo that Bert was uneasy about, in that their clients also expected Nearing and Koslowski to stifle cop interest or at least provide advance notice of pending action. But in the end, Bert felt these guys mostly got what they deserved.

At last Nearing wrapped up his visit, skipped across the street, jumped in.

"How'd it go?" Bert asked.

"Great. I had him throw in a couple copies of *Bad Boys 2*."

"Give mine to Koslowski."

"Hal was telling me how hard moving to DVD is on these smaller outfits. I never thought of that. You can't get rid of your tapes because for half your customers, that's still the viewing technology they've got, and now you also gotta please the people who've gone over to disc. Except where are you going to display it all when you've only got six hundred square feet? Plus you're carrying every title in both formats, twice the inventory for the same rental volume. It's tough." Nearing stared sympathetically at the storefront. "Funny, you never really realize what the other guy's up against. You know what I mean?"

Bert pulled out and gunned the engine. "My heart bleeds," he said.

The last stop was the dry cleaner's. It was after eleven, and the north end of Columbus had quieted down, storefronts dark, traffic sparse. Bert could feel pressure building as they got closer, the accumulated tension of waiting and knowing what would probably go down. Nearing was feeling it too, getting quiet, checking his gun, generally girding himself.

All-Nite Laundry was a new business and a recent addition to their list—a full-service laundry and dry cleaner that was open twenty-four hours, three-hour guaranteed turnaround. From the street, the plate glass windows showed a spotless front waiting area, a long counter with two cash registers, and an endless garment conveyor full of clothes in plastic bags, stretching back into darkness. The actual cleaning facility was a bigger room in back with a loading entry on the alley.

Between front and back operations were five windowless little rooms, occupied by five young Chinese women. Being open twenty-four hours a day, the business made the perfect front, allowing men to come in at any time without drawing attention to themselves. The tip had come through Koslowski.

They pulled up directly in front and sat there for a while, looking at the bright counter and the two increasingly nervous guys behind it. They would be wondering why this big gray Suburban was there, but with its tinted windows they wouldn't be able to see who was inside. The moment Bert and Nearing got out, one of the men inside turned and scuttled back among the garments.

"Can I he'p you?" the one guy left up front said. Big toothy grin, pretending he thought they were customers. He was about seventeen and looked ready to piss himself.

"We need to talk to the boss," Bert said.

"My uncle not here. Sorry." Still the tight scared grin.

Nearing was already going around the end of the counter. Bert ordered the boy to stay up front, absolutely not to move from where he stood. He slapped the red button that turned on the conveyor, and the whole room began to move, a rumble and swish that would provide a good noise screen. Then he followed Nearing, brushing past the sliding plastic-bagged garments toward a lighted doorway in the gloom at the back.

They went into a square room at the center of the building, where several big canvas gurneys full of clothes waited for processing and a wide doorway opened into the laundry facility. Ranged along the walls were rows of machines topped by venting ducts, the round windows in their doors showing the tumbling cloth inside. In the middle were several long tables where a half dozen men and women were sorting, folding, spot treating. They all stopped when they saw Bert and Nearing at the door. The air was full of the stink of cleaning agents and the rumble and drone of machinery.

To Bert's left, another doorway opened into a narrow hall lined by a series of doors, all but one of them closed. He leaned so he could look into the open door and saw just a bed, a lamp, and a chair.

He turned when three men appeared in the doorway to the laundry area. The oldest was the father, a gray-haired, irritable-looking man of fifty, one of those tight-faced guys who looked like a skull. Behind him was the young man who had been at the counter and a burly Chinese guy with pecs and biceps bulging out of a wife-beater T-shirt.

"You don't come in here!" the older man said. He waved his hands at them as if that would make them go away.

"Mr. Zheng," Nearing said reasonably. "We do come in here. We come in here and you give us some money. That's how it works. That's what we arranged, remember?"

"No money now." The father stood resolutely in the doorway. "You said okay you wait."

The skinny young man moved forward. He was a good-looking kid, early twenties, dressed in a blue button-down shirt, tie, trim khakis. "Please. We'll be sure to have the money for you next time." His English was unaccented.

"Oh, come on, people!" Nearing said. "This is exactly what I warned you not to do. Mr. Zheng, I told you, this is how you get in trouble."

The patriarch said something rapidly in Mandarin, his eyes moving from Bert to Nearing, full of hate, and the clean-cut young man translated: "My father wants you to know that he doesn't believe you will have us prosecuted. Because if you close us down, you will get nothing from us."

"Hey, we're gettin' nothin' already," Bert reminded him.

"Prosecuting isn't the only kind of trouble I meant," Nearing added grimly.

"We'll have it next time," the young man repeated urgently. "It's not going to be a problem. Please."

Bert heard a noise from his left and he looked over to see a young woman stepping out of one of the doors along the side hall. She was wearing a short, lacy robe, and as she turned a length of smooth thigh emerged from the blue cloth. She made an involuntary shriek when she saw Bert and Nearing confronting her red-faced boss.

At the sound, two of the other doors opened and women's faces looked out warily. They were all smooth skinned, moon faced, ebony haired, terrified. Not one of them was older than fourteen, fifteen.

"You go back inside!" the father ordered them in Mandarin.

Two of them disappeared immediately, but the first one hesitated, clenching the robe at her throat.

Bert grunted, taken aback by what he was feeling. The father was haranguing the girl, his eyes screwed up, gesturing threateningly, but still she stood uncertainly, paralyzed.

"Take it easy, Bud," Bert said to the father.

"You don't tell me! You don't tell me in here!" He went on in Mandarin, incomprehensible except for his rage, as he stepped toward the girl.

Bert grabbed his arm and flung him across the room. Guy didn't weigh anything, he flew against one of the gurneys and half fell into it. Nearing drew his gun and went into a shooting stance, freezing the two at the door. The father stood up but Bert gave him a backhanded slap that spun his head around and dropped him in a heap. Bert bent, half lifted him by his shirt, and slapped him again. The guy looked ready to spit venom, his cheeks red-bruised, choking and sputtering, and the sight of his self-righteousness filled Bert with rage. He hauled off and slugged him, put his weight into it.

"The fuck you *doing*?" Bert yelled. "They're *kids*! Don't you have any self-respect? They your daughters? Nieces? Or just kids you bought? What?"

Nearing stayed spreadlegged, gun on the guys at the door. On the floor the father moaned, his face still that weasel mask of hate, and Bert felt a tight string break inside. A terrific energy seized him. He lifted Zheng up and dragged him to the hallway where the girl had been. He held him up with one hand and threw open her door and saw her huddled on the bed, cringing and crying.

"How old is this kid? Twelve? Thirteen? You fucking piece of shit, how old is she?" But the father was in no shape to answer. Bert ground him against the door frame, shook him like a scarecrow and then tossed him on the floor like the trash he was. The girl wouldn't look, just hid her head and cried. Bert was panting and he could feel the red swelling in his neck and face. He strode out to the two who stood at the door. "You want some too?" he said. He pushed the slender young man aside and swung a foot into the balls of the muscle-bound one before either could react. The guy fell back, skated across the floor on his ass and stayed sitting there, gasping for air.

No one budged. Everything stayed frozen except the tumbling clothes in all the round windows.

Bert turned back. Nearing's face was twitching with nerves, but he managed a quick smile. Bert shook himself, shot his cuffs, straightened his shirt. Then he turned around to the son, who hovered in the doorway, wanting to go to his father but afraid to move.

"You," Bert said. "Your old man's English isn't so good, so I want you to translate for me." He gestured for the young man to go to his father, sprawled half in the hall, half in the center room. The kid scuttled over, knelt, lifted the patriarch's head to his lap.

Bert hunkered down and gripped the father's face in two hands so he couldn't break eye contact. "Tell him just as I say it. First, you have the money next time, every time. The law doesn't like what you're doing and

I don't either, so if you fight me you're guaranteed to lose every which way. You think this is bad, there's four guys out in the truck who'll come in here and put you out of business for good. Tell him."

The young man rattled it out, and Bert understood enough to know he was translating correctly. Bert held the father's head until he felt him try to nod his assent.

"Second thing, and listen closely. You're gonna be ashamed because now those girls know you're not such a big shot after all. You're gonna want to take it out on them, them seeing you humiliated like this. But I'm coming back here in a week and in a month, and I'm going to check up on them. If I see a bruise, a scratch, a frown even, I'm gonna take you in the back room there, put you in one of your machines and cook you in the chemicals. Got it?"

The son translated. The bloodied face of the father nodded with a series of jerks. Bert kept up eye contact until the flame of hate and resistance had been replaced by hopelessness in the dark eyes, then tossed the skull-like head back into his son's lap.

The clothes were still filing around on the conveyor, zombies on parade drill. Out at the front counter, the kid opened the cash registers and handed over whatever was in there, even the checks, which were no use to them.

They drove back to Nearing's car. Nearing was having a ball, recounting what happened, mimicking the expressions on their faces. Now that the adrenaline was fading, Bert felt like shit, his hands sore, a muscle pulled in his shoulder. Worse was the feeling that he'd eaten or drunk something poisonous, something that was still in his blood.

He pulled up behind Rich's car and they sat for a while as Nearing worked inside his duffle, divvying up the night's take, setting aside the bundle for Koslowski. Bert pocketed his without looking at it.

"You were in top form, Bertie," Nearing crowed. "I was ready to crap myself, but you—man! Eye of the *tiger*! You scared the living shit out of them."

"Okay, Rich. I gotta go home now."

"Come on! You love this shit! You love it and you're good at it. Admit it, man!"

"I don't love it."

"Go *on*, Bertie, you the *man*! Credit where credit's due!"

"Shut up. I mean it."

Nearing's eyes narrowed. He looked offended at what he must have mistaken for Bert's tone of moral indignation. "Hey Bertie, why do you think Koslowski and me asked you back in? We know your rep—Bert 'Machete' Marchetti. I *saw* you, man, okay? You don't think we've seen it before? You get off on it, man. Don't even try to bullshit me."

Nearing wasn't getting it. It was time for him to shut up before something bad happened, but he didn't know it. Bert held onto himself hard for a few seconds. Finally he just looked over at Nearing, nodded. "Okay, Rich. Now I'm tired, I'm an old man, gotta get my beauty sleep, yeah?"

Smiling again, Nearing punched his shoulder and got out.

14

CREE BEGAN WEDNESDAY with a terrific run through the Presidio, a labyrinth of winding streets and parkland that capped the northern tip of the city. Her AAA book said it had been the site of the first Spanish fort in the area, and then a U.S. military base that had been converted to private offices and residences and public recreation areas. Curving roads, big overhanging trees, tile-roofed buildings, broad lawns and soccer fields, ocean air spiced with eucalyptus tang: utterly lovely. One minute she was running through a neighborhood of white stucco duplexes and four-units, the next she was plunging down a steep curving lane into deep jungle where innumerable paths snaked off into the green, tempting her feet. She felt as if she could run forever.

Last night's visit to the wolfman's house had resulted in another disappointment. For a while she thought she was picking up the perimortem moments of an earthquake victim, a sense of alarm and chaos and crushing weight. But that was too easy to imagine, and was probably a projection of hers, a frustrated subconscious attempt to force her way into the wolfman's experience. In any case, it didn't tell her anything useful. Mainly, she'd spent the time thinking about Bert and his old cases and Skobold's tragic story about their lost children. She had come away from Skobold carrying a knot of his grief in her chest, and for a time, sitting cross-legged in the wolfman's crypt, she just gave up and wept. Whatever resonances of the past, the dead, might linger in the house, they couldn't compete with the overpowering emotions of the present and the living. She had returned to the motel deeply exhausted.

But the world had gone around and the sun had come up. Running helped purge the other stuff. Cool, crystal clear weather, brilliant sun slanting down in shafts of warmth between the towering eucalyptus trees and spacious pines: Even with the new complications, she regained confidence that she could untangle some of Bert's problems.

Today's agenda was mixed. According to the archivist at the History Room, the quake and fire had destroyed most pre-1906 birth and death records; in any case, she wouldn't know where to look until she had a closer estimate of the wolfman's age. But pre-1906 newspaper collections were in good shape, so at some point she could also try a direct search for reference to the wolfman. Also, the archivist had given her the names of several private sources for genealogies and other historical materials, and Cree had called to leave messages asking for research appointments.

First, though, she needed a better general orientation in her subject; it was hard to make sense of specific historical data unless she could put it in context. After her run, she drove downtown, cruised a couple of bookstores, and bought three books on San Francisco history. She carried them and a cup of coffee to one of the outdoor benches between the library and the Asian History Museum.

White collar city employees came and went, a park crew was picking up trash in the plaza, a few tourists snapped photos; the homeless people were pushing their shopping carts down side streets to do their daily foraging. Cree dove into her books, speed-reading, jotting notes when thoughts or questions struck her. Time to get an idea of what kind of world the wolfman had lived in.

General impression: San Francisco in the last half of the nineteenth century was one kick-ass wild town.

In just a few decades, it had exploded from a scruffy settlement of a few dozen people on a marshy, sandy peninsula to a major port city of half a million. The mushrooming changes made for a chaotic situation, with people arriving and needing shelter and food and water and sewage processing and entertainment and booze where none of it had existed previously. It was a place of breakneck change, danger and opportunity, fortunes made and fortunes lost.

On one hand, there was a growing population of upright, decent people coming in, establishing lives of family, commerce, church, the arts, and so on. They built houses, started businesses, worked jobs, constructed libraries and schools and theaters, paved streets, made laws and civic codes—good citizens, building civilization on the wild West Coast, land of opportunity. Within a few decades, San Francisco boasted every cultural refinement the century had to offer.

But the city had been started by the huge influx of gold-seekers in 1849, a stampede of rough guys that was refreshed by a comparable rush of frenzied silver-miners after the Comstock Lode discovery ten years later. Among them came every shade of sleazy entrepreneur, con man, and thug—as Bert had said, mostly rough and tumble guys without a lot of family responsibilities or scruples—and the city administration they created was for most of the century so corrupt that it was little more than a branch of the vice empires.

Thousands of Chinese came, too, looking for gold or to make lives in America after building the Central Pacific Railroad. They didn't speak English and were often persecuted by the whites, so they set up their own separate city in Chinatown, with legitimate enterprises as well as extensive criminal industries.

The bad guys waged continuous war on each other, sharks feeding on sharks. In Chinatown, wars between crime syndicates sometimes climaxed in pitched battles between small armies that left scores dead in the streets. Another ongoing war raged between regular citizens and low-lifes, between criminal gangs and law enforcement. One gang, the Sydney Ducks, liked to start fires just to create a distraction that would let them rob and loot without interference; the Ducks burned down as much as half the city on five occasions. In response, the furious citizenry formed vigilante armies that struck back by rounding up any men they thought might be crooks and hanging them from scaffolds in the streets. During one of these convulsions, five thousand armed men seized the armory, built their own military fort complete with cannons, and took control of the city government that had encouraged crime and corruption. They hanged a few suspected crooks and exacted some concessions from City Hall. Afterward, many of the insurrection's leaders became influential men—and just as corrupt as the politicos they replaced.

The Barbary Coast was the name given to the . . . what was it, an entertainment district? A red-light district? A no-man's land? A vice bazaar? In 1880, when the wolfman was probably alive, the area occupied about a quarter of the city on the upper east side, growing out of the docks where sailors and would-be miners came to drink, fight, gamble, and have sex. Given the shortage of women, those females who did show in the early days were in high demand and put to hard use. It wasn't long before entrepreneurs saw the profit potential and began importing women by the shipload.

Reading about sex trade made the hair on Cree's neck stand up. By 1880, tens of thousands of prostitutes were active in San Francisco, most of them in the Barbary Coast and Chinatown. The lowest caste were the older or uglier whores who worked out of stick-and-board shanties called cribs that clustered along seedy streets and alleys. One step up were the women who worked in the "cow yards," large buildings constructed by syndicates specifically to accommodate the wholesale sex trade. Some cow yards contained as many as three hundred cubicles; volume and quick turnover were the keys to financial success.

Of course, there were smaller brothels of every kind, too; only the top of that social ladder attained to the stereotypical coarse elegance of red velvet and polished brass—the stately madam playing hostess, the piano player in the front room with garters on his shirt sleeves. The brothels that maintained a pretense of gentility were called parlor houses and catered to a wealthier class of client.

Alcohol was another major industry, with melodeons and groggeries, deadfalls and "resorts," establishments that ranged from a board across two crates serving raw grain alcohol to fancy clubs selling decent stuff and providing entertainment to go with. It was the fashion to have liquor served by "pretty waiter girls," who also served sexual favors in booths around the main floor or in rooms upstairs. In 1890, the city licensed 3,117 such places, and officials estimated that another 2,000 operated on the sly. Drinking places competed for customers by offering porno peep shows, bawdy dancing, displays of the corpses of famous criminals, dog fighting, and live sex acts that included multiple partner combinations and women with animals.

Sex, booze, gambling, and drugs were the core industries, but robbery, burglary, graft, grift, extortion, murder, slave trading, real estate scamming, and picking pockets also made good livings for their practitioners. And of course shanghaiing, where sailors just off the boat got hit on the head or drugged unconscious and woke the next day as involuntary crewmen on outbound ships. Harbor masters, police, and city officials pocketed a good percentage for facilitating or ignoring criminal activity, so every form of vice, venery, scam, and ripoff flourished from the bottom-feeders right on up to the movers and shakers at City Hall.

Cree shook her head, appalled. One hell of a town, nobody's idea of a wholesome, safe, tranquil place. Yet part of her wished she'd been there, had seen it in all its unholy, wild and woolly glory. Victorian San Francisco sounded like a cross between the dense, fog-dank London of Dickens and Sherlock Holmes and a classic old West cowboy town, Dodge City or Tombstone.

So that was the wolfman's world. But where did he fit into it? Where would he have left a record of his existence?

Cree put her book aside, sipped the last of her cold coffee, and looked around. Across the street, on the sidewalk at the Asian History Museum, some event was shaping up—news vans, TV cameras, a crowd gathering. She watched it with absentminded curiosity.

Bert was right to warn her it wouldn't be easy. The mayhem, the turbulence, the mushrooming growth, the scope and pervasiveness of underworld activity, topped off by the massive disruption of the earthquake and fire: It seemed impossible that they'd ever discover who the wolfman was.

The thought made her sad, because unless her late-night visits to the house revealed something, she'd probably end up disappointing Uncle Bert. This particular John Doe meant a lot to him, as if it were symbolic of his whole career and, as Skobold said, of his lost daughter. Her abduction could also explain his current obsession with every case he'd failed to close, as if all those old cases had absorbed the colossal force of his frustration and passion. She doubted he'd ever get closure on any of that, but it would be nice to lay at least one skeleton to rest for him.

Cree looked over as a clamor of booming and clanging noises started up in front of the museum. Cameras flashed from the crowd as a dozen Chinese men in crimson costumes, waving ribbons, beating gongs and drums, began an acrobatic dance on the sidewalk.

Clearly, Bert's loss had defined his life in a way that was not healthy—it had deflected him into an outward trajectory, away from other people, into a dark view of humanity, into the anaesthetic succor of booze, into a lonely little house at the end of a very long stairway. Her immediate impulse was to reach out to him, to give him some small respite from his isolation.

But now she began to doubt she could manage it. Maybe her predicament was too similar: She had been deflected on an outbound path, too, when Mike died. She was a perpetual outsider, too, with a worldview that was incomprehensible or offensive to most people, with habits and preoccupations that were arguably morbid, with a complicated love-life defined by distance. Cree felt her shoulders slump as it caught up with her. She strove to be a complete person, an integrated person, an honest person. Yet in so many ways her outward, daily life was an act—a parody of normal that allowed her to live in the world with minimal friction. *Tell nobody*, Bert had insisted. She'd heard it before in one form or another: Tell nobody what you do for a living, what you believe, what you've seen and done, what matters most to you, who you really are. Even Paul Fitzpatrick, at gatherings with his psychiatrist friends, had asked her not to be too specific about her work lest his own professional credibility suffer.

Over the years, she'd learned the lesson: *Look ordinary. Don't advertise the fact that you creep around in the middle of the night communing with dead people. Society doesn't understand people like you.* Three hundred years ago, she'd have been burned as a witch.

"Why the sad face?"

The voice jolted her out of her thoughts. She looked over to see the man she'd met at Skobold's lab, the radiologist. He was coming from the direction of the library and stopped just short of the bench with a cautious smile.

"Cam Raymond—Ray," he reminded her.

"Ray, of course."

He stood strategically so his good side was toward her. From this angle, she thought, you'd never know: handsome profile, a tan that set off startlingly pale blue eyes, dark eyebrows with a graceful lift at the end. His khakis, blue shirt, and tweed jacket were worn casually yet were well cut to a nicely proportioned frame.

He noticed her little stack of books and picked one up to inspect it. "Reading up on our beloved city? Not from here?"

"From Seattle right now. From back east originally. How about you?"

"San Francisco born and raised."

"Lucky man—I totally and completely adore this place."

Ray glanced at the fracas across the street, then back at her, smiling. "Yet just now you had the look of a stranger in a strange land."

"I suppose that's what it was. At that moment, it was, what . . . the sense of being one thing on the outside, the person you wear for the world to see, and a very different thing on the inside." She smiled quickly, surprised at his perceptiveness and her own candor, wanting to lighten it up. "And wishing the two could be . . . you know. Formally introduced."

Ray grinned and seemed to appreciate the insight. But his hand rose unconsciously and brushed the damaged side of his face, and Cree realized she was talking to somebody who knew a great deal about that feeling. A man who walked around charming people with half his face and scaring them with the other had to have a unique sense of himself in relation to the rest of the human race.

"So you're doing the X-rays on . . . Dr. Skobold's special project?"

"Yes. I work part-time for the UCSF Medical School, part-time for Temple MicroImage. That's a private lab that does specialized radiology, ultrasound, microphoto, and magnetic resonance work. I've done jobs for Horace for, oh, the last ten years or so. I like Horace a great deal. What's your connection? I was surprised that he mentioned 3024 while you were there."

"I'm a private investigator. I'm doing historical research for the identification effort. Dr. Skobold invited me to help him work on reconstruction, too. We cleaned the bones last night, and I'll be going back there again tonight. It's a fascinating process."

Ray bobbed his head thoughtfully. " 'The wolfman.' How do you like the nickname?"

"I don't know anything about the anatomy side. I'm just looking for records of a human male with severe congenital defects, born between 1865 and 1885, died in the Great Quake."

Before Ray could reply, a professional-looking pair approached them from his bad side. The woman wore a burgundy pants suit, heels, pearls, expensive hair, and a look that suggested a career in finance or government; the man was the male equivalent, with gray temples brushed back, a deep tan, a flawless charcoal pinstripe. When they saw Ray, their faces took on a sudden, unnatural neutrality, and their path veered slightly as they slid on past. Cree knew it was just what she had done with the homeless man yesterday, but she couldn't help frowning after them.

Ray stared after them for the duration of one long, pale blue gaze and a lazy blink. It was like a slow shutter dropping on a camera, recording their image. For a second he seemed to sag, and then he was checking his watch and starting to make leave-taking movements.

"So," she asked quickly, "you going to be doing any more work on the wolfman?"

"Probably. I expect Horace will want a closer look at the palatine sutures and the cementum annulation."

The anatomy was all Greek to Cree, but she smiled anyway. "Well, maybe I'll see you over at the lab, then."

He must have seen her friendliness as social damage control after the executive couple, because for an instant he iced her with that same flat, pale gaze he'd given them, turning his face so that the scars were very visible. It was as if he was daring her to show revulsion, or trying to intimidate her, punish her for her sympathy. Or maybe once his resentment awakened, it didn't shut down immediately. It was hard to read intentions on a face so divided.

Across the street, the clamor reached a frenzied climax, followed by a rush of applause. Cree took her time inspecting his face, then met his eyes again and decided to take a chance. He was being his weird self; she'd be hers.

"So . . . would you like to sit for a while?" She moved her books and sidled to the left of the bench, making room. "If you've got any great ideas about where to look for our guy, I'd be glad to hear them."

Surprised, he lost a beat, then beamed a big smile. And then Cree's cell phone went off in her purse. She glanced at the caller ID: Uncle Bert.

"Oops! Lousy timing. I better take that," she said apologetically. "Nice seeing you, Ray. Let's get together another time, okay?"

"Another time," he echoed. "Definitely."

15

R AY DROVE EAST on Cesar Chavez toward home, looking forward
to the meeting he'd scheduled for this afternoon. Last night's marvelous, epiphanic encounter with the deer had honed his hunger in a way
that couldn't be ignored. This guy LeGrand, out at the wolf place in
Lafayette, sounded like someone who could answer some of his questions.

But first he wanted to ask Horace about Cree Black, what a private investigator from Seattle was doing researching the wolfman.

He'd enjoyed her comment about feeling like a stranger—an unexpected admission from a person outwardly so pleasant and normal and a
surprisingly frank remark to make to someone you didn't know. She was
attractive, with red-brown hair loose on her shoulders and eyes that conveyed an intriguing mix of vulnerability and unflappability. But he'd gotten suspicious when he'd learned of her involvement with the wolfman,
and added to the usual stuff he felt downtown, he'd felt the urge to test her.

And she'd been gloriously unfazed by his weirdness. Inviting him to
sit—he got the sense it was a sincerely friendly gesture and, at the same
time, a way of telling him to fuck off with the scary-face shit.

As a result, he'd liked her immediately. He sincerely hoped that
wouldn't be a problem.

Ray's house was a massive, dirty-brick warehouse, set on a channel that
fingered in from the main quay of the bayside waterfront. Truck-loading
bays lined most of the street-side façade; a mesh-fenced yard wrapped it
on the east and south, empty but for weeds and a few old cargo containers
that would have become condos for homeless people if the dogs didn't

run them off. The facility had once provided transshipping services for goods brought on the big ships, storing the box-car-size containers until they could be put aboard trains or trucks. Ray had left the Dimension Intermodal sign on the bricks, but the business had gone under twenty years earlier, and the building and grounds had gone to seed long before he'd inherited it from his mother's brother. It was strictly chance that he'd come into possession of it, but had he searched the world over he doubted he could have found a place more suited to him.

Over the years, most of the larger port-related industries had moved across the bay to deeper channels and more modern facilities, and now his neighbors were smaller warehouses, auto body shops, small-scale steel fabricators, low-end commercial printers, and a scattering of artists. Many of the buildings were empty, surrounded by rusting steel sheds and decrepit hoist equipment, creating a postindustrial wasteland atmosphere that Ray cherished. He liked the way Dimension Intermodal's abandoned, forbidding exterior masked the secret oasis of comfort and beauty inside. Sort of a metaphor for the guy who lived there.

He backed up the van, got out, unlocked the steel-clad man door, and came back to hoist a couple of sacks of dog food onto his shoulders. The dogs heard him coming and made yips and howls of anticipation.

Inside, the building was as big as an airplane hangar, one large room with brick walls cut by tall windows of milky glass, an expanse of cement floor, a flat, iron-trussed roof forty feet above. Cut into the space against the bay-facing wall were the former administration offices, which he had appropriated as his living quarters. On the ground floor he'd set up his living room, kitchen, and bedroom, and then on the flat roof above them he'd built his studio, just a big hollow box that housed his enlarging equipment, computers, and private gallery. The rest of the building he'd left as he'd acquired it: a huge, empty, littered cavern. Pigeons nested in the roof superstructure and their shit gave sections of the floor a Jackson Pollock look.

Home.

He crossed over and unlocked the interior door and the three dogs came around him. Confiding trusting gazes, noses in the crotch, leaps and licks to the chin, great olfactory interest in the dog food bags. Alpha dog was bringing home the bacon.

Family.

"Okay, you guys," he scolded. "Okay. Let me through. Down, Fritz." He dropped the bags and squatted to give the three of them some mammal time, roughing up their coats, tugging their ears, enduring their mouthings. After a few minutes, he broke away to pour kibble into their bowls. Nothing like a fresh bag; they went at it as if they'd been starved.

He called Horace's lab phone, got his voice mail, then tried his cell phone.

Horace answered immediately. "What can I do for you, Ray? I'm walking into a meeting at this very moment."

"I ran into that woman, Cree Black, downtown. Told me she's all the way from Seattle to look into the wolfman skeleton. I wondered why."

"Oh, Ray," Horace said, vastly weary. "What."

"What's the deal? Just curious. You hired her?"

"No."

"So *Marchetti* hired her? From *Seattle*?"

"She volunteered—she's the daughter of an old friend of his. She's also an extremely bright woman and a skilled researcher. Bertram's in the same position I am. He wants very much to ID the poor fellow, but he doesn't have the time or resources. I'm very glad to have her on board for the effort."

Ray felt disappointment and behind it a surge of anger and bitterness. He didn't say anything.

"It's not your concern, Ray."

"You'll need work on the sternal rib ends. There are developmental anomalies all over those bones. You'll never age him without more work on the palate and teeth."

"You're right. In fact, you're prescient. I'm planning to messenger the skull and some ribs over to you first thing tomorrow. But so what? Why—"

"I can't work with anybody connected to Marchetti."

"Nobody's asking you to," Horace said. "Just do your job, send me the bill. Why should you care? Now I really have to go."

Ray didn't say anything.

Horace didn't hang up. Ray heard him sigh, and then he said softly, sadly, "Oh, Ray. Cameron. What's different about this? You've worked on

Bertie's cases before, you've never crossed paths, we've managed just fine, haven't we? But more important, speaking as someone who admires your talents, who considers you a friend, I have to ask, Doesn't there come a time when—"

"Don't try to play the diplomat here," Ray snarled. "You're a sweet guy. Not everybody is a sweet guy like you."

The rage mounted and he would have gone on, but he heard the sound of Horace disconnecting. Ray pitched the receiver at the wall so hard it exploded into pieces, then swept the counter with his forearm so that cans and dishes scattered, shattering and rolling. The dogs scrabbled to the far end of the room and looked at him with terror in their eyes.

Instantly he regretted worrying them. He got his breathing under control and made reassuring noises as he retrieved pieces of the handset, looked them over, threw the thing away. The dogs calmed a little. He realized he'd have to hurry to pick up the mess if he was going to get to his appointment on time.

Given its small size, Ray figured the wolf was a female. Her yellow eyes flicked at his, and from the way her body stiffened he could tell the animal had gone into high alert. She no doubt smelled the dogs on him.

The wolf moved over as Judd LeGrand swung the door all the way open and appraised Ray from the hallway. He looked just the way Ray had pictured him from their phone conversation: mid- to late-fifties, maybe five-eight, with a tanned, deeply seamed face and red hair cut bristle-short and going to gray. His T-shirt and black jeans were snug on a tense, hard body. Unlike the wolf, he met Ray's eyes and didn't look away.

"Mr. Raymond, I take it. I'm Judd LeGrand. And this is Reba. Come on in—she won't bite unless you provoke her."

The house was a one-story stucco ranch surrounded by acres of mostly open land, a mix of suburban estates and older farms scattered widely among the hills above Lafayette. LeGrand led Ray back into an open-plan living and dining room, where windows gave long views to the northwest, arid downward slopes that yielded in the far distance to flatter ground, trees, a few tiny rooftops. The sliding rear door opened to a large yard occupied by a wooden barn with an attached mesh-fenced kennel at the rear. Ray didn't see any of the kennel's occupants, but as he was looking a woman came around a corner, kicked open a door in the barn, and disappeared inside.

"So," Ray began, "I take it you've been working with wolves for quite a while?"

"About twenty years. We started with just rehabbing an individual animal now and again, and then got involved with reintroduction efforts. I do some lobbying and teaching, but mainly I'm in it so I can hang out with the wolves. You want to see the setup?"

"You bet," Ray told him.

LeGrand blocked the rear doorway so Reba couldn't get through, let Ray out, then followed and shut the door. From the redwood deck, Ray could see that the whole compound was surrounded by a high chain-link fence. Toward the front, a wooden palisade fence blocked views of the road; against the gray boards stood a long row of smaller cages that Ray realized were rabbit hutches. A wolf-food farm.

LeGrand gave him an overview of the operation. They owned twelve acres, but only about a third was fenced. There were six kennels, so that was the limit of the wolves they could handle at any time. Moeris Foundation was one of a network of facilities that took in wolves that had been injured or trapped or that had been bought as pups by people who thought they wanted an unusual pet but found they couldn't manage an adult. Some were reintroduced to the wild, some brought to zoos or teaching programs. Right now there were three besides Reba.

LeGrand spoke in a gruff voice, informative but not warm, and his gestures were tight as he pointed out various features. Definitely former military and a guy who made it plain he could take you or leave you. Out here in the sunlight, his eyes slitted and seemed suspicious and appraising. Ray liked his style.

They were still on the porch when the woman emerged from the barn, carrying a couple of big plastic pans back toward the house. She was Judd's age, had the same leathery skin, and wore faded jeans and a plaid shirt tucked in to reveal a busty, narrow-hipped figure. When she got to the deck, she raised her eyes and smiled, but Ray noticed the tick of reaction as she saw his face.

"Mr. Raymond, this is my wife Emily. Sugar, this is Cameron Raymond. He's the one who called earlier."

107

Emily said hello, carried the pans past them, and went into the house.

"So," Ray began, "tell me how you got into this. Why you wanted to save wolves."

"I don't save wolves. They save me."

"How so?"

"I don't make a secret of the fact that I had a hard time in Vietnam and a hard time when I came back. Wolves turned me around. I cite my experience because I figure it shows the benefit of working on behalf of a good cause. Helping restore wolves allows me to give something back to the world. To preserve one of God's noblest creatures. It helped me get on my feet again, and it helps others, too. One of our most successful programs is geared toward putting veterans, prisoners, and juvenile offenders in contact with wolves. Alcoholics and substance abusers, too—just being around a wild animal helps them get outside the spiral of their own problems."

Ray decided that the story explained the seamed faces, the rough voices, the dulled edge just behind the sharp: Judd and Emily were ex-alkies, no doubt met each other in recovery, found wolves instead of Jesus.

"Yeah, I saw that on your Web site. Buy why wolves? Why not, oh, raccoons? Or squirrels."

LeGrand frowned. "Trying to be funny?"

"No, no. Rhetorical. I can think of a lot of ways wolves are special, but I want to hear your take on it. How contact with a big predator is different."

LeGrand turned another notch toward Ray and made no move toward the kennel. In the bright sun, his eyes were almost lost in the shadows of his brows. "You know, we didn't talk much about you. Why you're interested. What you're after here today."

They locked eyes but were interrupted when a snarling came from the barn, followed by the sound of a scuffle. A big gray wolf came into one of the runs, trotted its length, pivoted, trotted back, disappeared inside.

"What I'm after is, I want to know more about wolves. And, frankly, I'm just as interested in you. I want to know what you went through and what you found in working with wolves that helped you pull your shit together."

For the first time, LeGrand's eyes moved to the scarring on Ray's face.

He sucked his cheeks and seemed to deliberate, then tipped his head to-ward the kennel. "Let's go take a look."

LeGrand went on past the barn to the far end of the kennel runs, where he stopped and whistled. Ray could see indistinct shapes moving in the darkness of the low doorways, but no wolves came out.

"They come when you whistle?" The thought disappointed Ray.

"No. They come out when they're curious. But something's throwing them off today. That growling, that's fairly unusual. I don't know what's up with them."

"Do you ever have more wolves than there are slots in reintroduction programs?"

"Rarely."

"Rarely, but sometimes. What do you do then?"

LeGrand's eyes went to Ray's again, studying first one eye and then the other, back and forth. "They have to be put down."

"I don't believe you'd do that. If it was me, I'd pack them in my van and take them someplace and start my own private reintroduction project. Don't you ever—"

"No, Mr. Raymond. We don't. That would be illegal, wouldn't it." LeGrand's look made it clear he didn't like the question, and Ray guessed it was time to change the subject.

"So . . . Moeris Foundation. An unusual name."

LeGrand had started toward the barn, but the question put a hitch in his stride. He answered in a flat voice, "It's from a poem by Virgil. A nice classical wolf reference, sounded legit. Dignified."

"No. Moeris was a werewolf. From Virgil's poem "Alphesiboeus," written in 39 BC. Why a werewolf, as opposed to any of the famous wolves of history? If it's personal for you, the wolves-saving-your-ass theme, why not Luperca? Or Romulus and Remus?"

LaGrand spun back to face Ray. "Listen, I don't know what you got going, but I don't need it around here."

"I told you. I wanted to meet you and learn more about the founda-tion. And I'm considering making a substantial donation."

"No you're not. People who make substantial donations don't come here in three-year-old minivans. I got a radar for creeps, Jack, and you're dicking me around. So you got two choices, you can tell me what's up, or you can leave. Which is it?"

The drilling, suspicious eyes and macho tone got Ray's juices going—his arrogance, his assumption he knew enough to make a judgment of Ray. LeGrand looked fit, but Ray had no doubt who would come out ahead in a fight. For a few seconds he debated provoking him further, forcing a showdown right now. Then he decided to do things differently.

"Maybe I caught you at a bad moment. I'll go now. I'll come by again another time."

"Oh, you'll go. But you're not coming back." LeGrand pointed to the side yard of the house. "Go around the outside. I don't want you in my house."

It required a lot of self-control to walk away. LeGrand followed him to the driveway, watched as Ray got into his car, and stood there glaring as he drove back down the hill.

A headache had begun during the confrontation and as Ray drove away it threatened to blossom into a full-blown supernova, the kind that fuzzed the edges of objects with jittery rainbows of light. It was the pressure. He was never sure whether the pressure made him think a certain way and get into a certain mood, or whether certain kinds of thoughts and feelings brought on the pressure. Whichever, he decided to return later to take the edge off LeGrand's hubris and make him answer some questions. LeGrand's behavior made it all the more evident he was a good person to get to know.

He drove to a gas station in Lafayette and while his tank filled he dosed himself with a mix of dexamethasone and epinephrin, which reliably eased the head pain and gave him a charge of euphoria and energy. He also bought a county map and studied it as he had a BLT and a milkshake at the attached diner. When he was done eating, he got out his checkbook, went over his finances, and wrote out a check for five thousand dollars, which he folded and tucked into his back pocket. He read the newspaper and killed time until the sun had set, then drove back up the hill.

He parked at a turnout two miles below LeGrand's house, went up a brush-lined ravine until he was out of view of the road, then cut over the hill. With his practiced night vision, he easily found his way to the far end of the fenced area, about a hundred yards from the kennel.

He scaled the fence and dropped down on the other side. He stayed in a crouch for half a minute, listening, but heard no reaction to his arrival other than the increased agitation of the wolves. Shapeless dark forms moved in the kennel runs, up and back, spinning, swaying.

Ray appraised the layout of buildings and selected the shadowed corner of the barn on the left side. The chain-link of the first run began about six feet short of the corner around which LeGrand would likely come, leaving a place for Ray to stand, invisible even if Judd brought a flashlight or there was a yard light on the house.

First he'd say hello to the wolves. He slipped down silently, but of course they anticipated him. Two came uneasily to the ends of their runs, but the third slunk into its door, the tip of its muzzle wagging side to side in the black doorway. The two outside grew more excited, swaying, growling, lifting heads to scent the air. As he got closer, he could see that their ruffs were up.

"Hey, creatures," he whispered. "Hey, wolves. Hey, gorgeous beings." Being so near to them in the night exhilarated him and felt very intimate.

Both wolves were snarling and whining, and in the dim light their bared teeth were the brightest things about them, two savage mouths. But in fact they weren't gorgeous. From this close he could see the weakness in them. The big one was old, hair going tufted, long teeth missing on one side, hindquarters stiffening. The smaller had a pale bald patch on its shoulder, mange or a shaved area left over from some surgery. Their smell was not a good animal smell but the musty, sick scent of dirty fur and sawdust, shit and dog food.

Creatures of the cage. Ray's heart broke at the realization.

He rattled the mesh violently and the urgency of their growls increased. He kept rattling until a light snapped on above the deck of the house, throwing the shadow of the barn across the yard and the kennel runs. *So stupid*, Ray thought. *Now you can't see in the dark. Moeris, my ass.* Now the terrified wolves were flinging themselves at him, hitting the mesh and staggering back. When he heard the aluminum door open and shut, he moved into position at the corner of the barn. He hoped it wasn't the wife.

Footsteps crunched on the gravel and then stopped, someone pausing to assess the situation. In another moment, LeGrand's voice came: "That you, Mr. Raymond? If it is, you should know I'm coming out with my gun and I'll blow your ugly head off."

LeGrand couldn't be sure, Ray thought. He had to be wondering if it wasn't just a tussle between the animals, or a deer come around and setting them off.

The footsteps resumed. A second later LeGrand's shadow stretched past the corner, shadow arms at its sides, hands at the ready but carrying no gun. The instant LeGrand came abreast of him, Ray snapped out of his crouch and tackled him at the knees. LeGrand's legs went up and his body rolled off Ray's shoulder. Ray toppled him onto his face, then dropped himself onto LeGrand with one knee on the smaller man's back. LeGrand's breath coughed out of his lungs, and Ray exploited the shock to bring his arm up behind him. He levered the arm until LeGrand's back stiffened, then used it to drag him into the deep shadow at the corner of the barn. He put his knee into place again and with his free hand pushed the bristle-cut head down against the gravel.

They held the position and panted in the darkness. The wolves had retreated inside and were moaning eerily.

"Where's your wife?" Ray whispered.

"You touch my wife, better kill me first. Because I'll hunt you down and tear your guts out. Believe it."

"I don't want to hurt either of you. I just want to ask you some god-damned questions. We need a few minutes. If your wife calls out looking for you, you just tell her everything's okay and you'll be inside in a minute."

"She's taking a fucking shower."

"So much the better. Now, I'm going to explain why we're doing this. Your attitude completely pissed me off. Maybe it gets you by with used-up alkies and cons, or with kindly animal lovers who are easily impressed with a tough guy act. But it doesn't cut it with me. I don't like being insulted, and I want more than your standard song and dance. I want you to dig a lot deeper, Judd. I want all you've got."

"You're on drugs, right?" LeGrand grated. "But you don't have to be a victim here. Even right now, you have the power to choose not to do this."

"Tell me about Moeris. I've gotten information on two dozen wolf advocacy groups, but the only one named after a werewolf is yours. Why?"

"You need *help*, man. Trust me, I can help you. I've seen a hundred guys like you."

"No, you have not!" Ray jerked the arm up until LeGrand wheezed. "Treat me like an individual, Judd. Treat me like I matter. Imagine for a moment that we have something in common. Did you kill people in Vietnam? Is that what fucked you up?"

Another grunt of pain. "What do you think?"

"What else? Seeing people get killed? Seeing people killing each other?"

"All that shit. You got it right, Sherlock."

"Okay. And you came back and were a junkie and a drunk for fifteen years, in and out of jail, arrested twice for assault. Why?"

"I was fucked up. Like you are now."

Ray sighed and rolled his shoulder to relax the cramp that was starting there. He was getting tired of sitting like this. LeGrand's neck was twisted hard and the gravel had to be hurting his cheek. Ray didn't like seeing a man in that position.

"Tell me why the name Moeris. Moeris, he used herbal potions to turn himself into a wolf—is that what you did? Drugs made a monster out of you?"

"Yeah. That's right." LeGrand labored to breathe. "What's your point?"

"Can't you tell? Me coming here like this, isn't it something you might have done? To sort things out?"

When LeGrand didn't say anything, Ray thought that maybe he'd gotten through.

"So we have a lot to talk about. But I don't want to do it like this, and I don't want you to diss me again. So I've got a proposition." Ray took his left hand off LeGrand's head, reached around and found the check he'd put into his pocket earlier. He started to put it into LeGrand's back pocket, then felt something metallic and hard in there. A switchblade knife, his fingers told him, definitely an item to be kept out of the picture during an encounter like this. He zipped it into his jacket pocket before tucking the check into LeGrand's jeans.

"That's a check for five thousand dollars. My gift to Moeris Foundation. I want to let you up. If you try to run to the house and call the police or get your gun, you probably won't make it before I stop you. But even if you do, you'll never know why I'm here. I'll also put a stop on the check—what a waste of an easy five grand, right? So will you talk with me like a nice guy, or are you going to continue giving me a hard time?"

"Have to take a chance, dickhead."

Ray was getting accustomed to LeGrand's style. More than ever, he hoped they could talk. He released the arm and took his weight off the knee.

LeGrand bolted the moment he got his arm back. He beetled toward the edge of the light, and Ray had to move fast to stop him. He landed hard on LeGrand's back and bent to put his throat in a forearm choke-hold. He worked him back into the shadowed nook and lay almost entirely on his body, their faces close. Inside the barn, the wolves were moaning again. Ray heard the quick scrape of claws as they skittered.

"What is the *matter* with you?" Ray hissed. "Why can't we have a meaningful conversation?" His anger flared and he was tempted to say something hurtful: *You think those scabrous, neurotic things are real wolves? All you know is caged animals. You don't know about freedom. Your life is a lie.* But it was bad enough to humiliate LeGrand physically.

"Judd, listen, you're a strong guy. I admire you, I really do. I think you're strong because you broke once and you healed stronger than you were before you broke. Tell me about that." He adjusted his hold so LeGrand could speak.

"You don't get stuff like that this way."

"You're not giving me any other way. Give it a try."

LeGrand strained uselessly against the chokehold, but at last Ray felt a softening in the back and then a hiccup like a suppressed sob.

"I wasn't sure what people were anymore. What I was." A throttled, half-whispered rasp.

"I understand exactly! Why the werewolf motif?"

"I had seen guys turn into predators. I had been a predator. It was hard to stop. I had to think about that. When I got into taking care of wolves, it was like a metaphor. I was a damaged wolf myself. Then I started working on rehab stuff and I had to deal with all this prejudice and misinformation. It goes way back, a million years. Fear of the unknown. Fear of the wild. Fear of what's inside you. Superstitious fear. I read up on werewolves because that's where the ideas came together. About what was human and what was animal. It was like a catalyst for me. Moeris, it seemed like a good symbol for all that. That's it. So let me the *fuck* up."

Ray decided to chance it. He slid his arm out from under the throat and lifted himself away. He squatted as LeGrand pulled himself onto all fours, then sat upright and backed himself against the side of the barn. Even in the deep shadow, Ray could see him wince as he rolled his neck side to side. A wolf snout emerged from the doorway to his left, scented, withdrew. The wolves were calmer now.

"What do you feed them? The rabbits you raise?"

"Scrap meat donations from Safeway. Dog food. And rabbits, yeah."

"Alive or dead? You kill the rabbit yourself first, or—"

"Why the fuck do—?"

Ray leaned suddenly forward and LeGrand twitched back. "Or do you just toss the live rabbit in?"

"For the wolves going into release programs, alive, yes."

"Why?"

"So they remember how to kill. So that part of their instinct doesn't atrophy."

Now they were getting somewhere. Ray's excitement rose and he crabbed closer, trying to formulate the right questions. "Judd, this is very important. Do you think a person needs to kill, too? To keep the instinctive thing alive? To make contact with that primal stuff, come to grips with it? Feed it? Does breaking the taboo make you stronger?"

"You and Charlie Manson, huh?"

"What?"

LeGrand shook his head. His confidence was returning, or maybe he just didn't give a shit how this turned out. " 'Come to grips?' I killed, I saw a lot of guys kill, and nobody ever came to grips with it. Too easy to do and too hard to get over. I didn't see anybody come off wiser. And it's not all that taboo, not half enough. That's another fucking superstition. Too bad."

"More. Dig deeper on that."

"There were two kinds of guys. One kind went to pieces the first time they killed or had to lie in a shell crater with chunks of their dead buddies all around. The other kind got proud and cocky. Bragged about their kills, kept ears or scalps on their belts. Got high on it."

"Which were you?"

"But you open yourself up to it, something gets inside and starts eating you. Making you hollow. The ones who thought they were the toughest, they're the ones that had the hardest time after. They had that thing inside."

Ray thought about that. "When you killed people, when you saw people die, up close—how did that change you? I mean, the way you think your own death? More afraid? More . . . accepting?"

"More nothing. More fucking nothing except screwed up. Me, I was very fucked up. Believe it. I had to work very, very hard to get back even this far."

"Maybe you should have kept going the other way," Ray muttered darkly.

LeGrand snorted, spat, shook his head. "You're a fucking kid. Lot of abstract ideas. You don't know what any of it means."

The preaching, superior tone infuriated Ray. He leaned into the light from the porch and turned his face so that all LeGrand would see were the scars. "You," he said very quietly, very deliberately, "don't know anything about what I am. And you have no fucking *idea* what I am capable of."

LeGrand didn't react, didn't seem to care. They were quiet for a long time like that, stalemated, and Ray heard some music start up in the house, a radio changing channels. The wife must have come out of the shower. Ray crabbed closer to LeGrand, ready for a sudden move, beaming his urgency at the dark silhouette.

At last LeGrand rasped, "You're trying to figure if killing can make you free or natural or . . . what, complete? If that makes it okay? You're trying to figure out if you're a werewolf?"

"Something like that," Ray said breathlessly. He didn't know the exact questions, but they were getting close to it now.

LeGrand's dark shape didn't move. "That's something you'll have to answer for yourself. That's what it's all about, man. Trying to answer that."

Ray had to admit that was a safe assessment. He'd known it all along, but disappointment flooded him. He'd had irrationally high hopes for what LeGrand might be able to tell him.

He had just decided it was time to go when the aluminum door scraped and LeGrand's wife called from the house: "Judd! The hell're you doing out there?"

LeGrand didn't move for several more seconds. Then he lifted his head and called, "I'll be in in two shakes, baby. I'm just seeing to one of the animals."

16

CREE RETURNED TO the motel at four thirty, glad to have some time to regroup before meeting Uncle Bert for dinner. She ran the tub to its deepest and lowered herself cautiously into the scalding water until just her nostrils were above the surface: heavenly. Even on a bright day like this, San Francisco was brisk in November; after sitting for so long in the park, she felt deeply chilled. Plus, tubs were a great place to think.

Ray Raymond was insightful and even attractive in an odd way. But that icy gaze continued to trouble her. He had X-rayed the wolfman's skull and recognized its canine characteristics—was he the one sending the morphing e-mails? Then there was Uncle Bert's theory. Could Cameron Raymond be a murderer, too?

A new shiver went down her spine and legs despite the parboiling embrace of the water. Yes, it was easy to imagine that slow gaze and blink stemming from some deep hatred and resentment, possibly one requiring vehement expression.

But of course it was unwise to trust impressions like that, as she'd learned many years ago in an undergraduate class on forensic psychology. The instructor had begun the first session by showing slides, starting with a mugshot of an unsmiling, middle-aged businessman type, white shirt, tie, dark hair with receding hairline.

"This man is a convicted serial child molester," Dr. Danforth explained. "His victims were six girls, ages five through nine, each of whom he systematically befriended, entrapped, sodomized, and tortured. Let's take a close look at his face."

The students dutifully studied the screen, and they easily found the sadism in that rather ordinary face: lowered lids that failed to conceal the calculating glint of the eyes, a tidy tuck of the lips that controlled their expression, the smug bulk of those cheeks. Knowing what he'd done, Cree could see it all right there: the pathology, the secret savor of his awful acts.

After a long moment, Dr. Danforth turned to the screen and did a double-take. "Oops!" he said, "Wrong slide!" He fingered the controls and this time checked to see that he had the right picture. "Sorry about that. We'll get back to that gentleman in a moment. This is the real child molester."

The new photo showed a very different face. This was a young man, a surfer-dude type with white-blond hair, a band of freckles across his cheeks, a scruffy beard on a weak chin. He had a negligent, *I don't give a shit* look in his eyes and wore a little self-satisfied, sharklike smile. Cree could readily imagine him befriending a child, then turning into a thrill-seeking persecutor.

Then, whoops, another apology and a third slide. This one was a classic dirty old man with a lecherous face, gaps in his teeth, narrowed eyes that told of a lifetime of evil thoughts and sick deeds. By now the class had clicked to the ruse, but to drive the point home Dr. Danforth showed four more slides, letting the class read evil into every man's features.

In fact, Dr. Danforth told them, none of the men were child molesters: The businessman type was a past president of Harvard, and the surfer dude was himself, twenty years ago.

His point was that appearance could never serve as a basis for either law-enforcement action or psychological assessment. *Anyone* could appear to have sinister, criminal, or psychopathological characteristics if seen with the proper mental prejudice; scrutinized with a bias, any life story or life style could suggest a criminal history or antisocial tendency.

After class, Cree and some of the other students joked about it: "Hey, but maybe they all *really were* child molesters, even Danforth!" They went out for drinks and experimented by studying the other patrons at the bar, easily finding indications that every person present was in fact a sadistic pedophile. They laughed their heads off, but Cree remained unsettled by what she'd found in herself.

Later, with more context under her belt, she'd learned that appearance *did* sometimes play a role in the psychology of violence; people with disturbing congenital abnormalities or facial disfigurements resulting from injury did sometimes become psychopaths or sociopaths. Perhaps as outcasts they felt entitled to revenge upon the society that rejected them; or maybe the absence of rewarding human contact impaired development of the sense of empathy that normally suppressed antisocial impulses. In some cases, the original cause of the deformity, whether congenital or injury related, was accompanied by neurological impairments that precipitated violent behaviors.

Still, it would be completely inappropriate to read anything into Ray Raymond's facial appearance or expressions. Besides, aside from his scars and the defensive stuff around that, he struck her as interesting, appealing—even, in his stranger status and perceptiveness, something of a kindred spirit.

Or maybe that was just her empathic thing again. Sometimes too much sight could make you blind.

Cree felt she'd simmered long enough to macerate. She got out of the tub with muscles so relaxed she half expected to sit up right out of her softened flesh.

"The other night," Bert said, "I don't know what I was thinking. Ben Black's daughter comes to town, I should take her someplace nice."

"This is pretty seriously nice, Uncle Bert."

The restaurant he'd chosen was an Italian place in North Beach, just off Washington Square. The waiters wore short-waisted tuxedos; the tables were covered in white linen and each place was set with three wineglasses of different sizes and shapes. Cree was glad she'd dressed up a bit: dark tights, heels, a conservative black skirt, a short embroidered jacket over a silk blouse. Bert looked almost distinguished in a navy blue, double-breasted suit, a red tie actually knotted at his throat, his gray hair combed. The maître d' seated them in a corner table at the end of a gorgeous mural of Venice. Pavarotti sang quietly from hidden speakers, and the deep red-brown woodwork gave off a burnished glow as if it had been polished with hundred-dollar bills.

"Only thing is, I can't smoke," he lamented. "Most places I go, I say, screw no-smoking regs, I'm a cop, after a while they know me and don't hassle me. But here, for all I know the person I'm offending at the next table is the mayor or the police commissioner, it isn't going to wash."

Cree chuckled. A waiter appeared with the wine list; Bert looked at it, selected a bottle.

"So you saw Horace last night," Bert prompted.

"Yes. No big revelations, but we got the bones washed. What a sweet man! He sure thinks highly of you, Bert. And I learned a lot."

"Guy definitely knows his field."

"He pointed out a lot of old injury sites. Bone callus. Some are clearly defensive, but Horace said that the wolfman could have received them while attacking someone."

"Yeah. Jeffrey Dahmer probably got 'defensive' injuries."

They nodded. In the silence that followed, Cree felt their conversation stall and start to lose cruising altitude. At least this time she had some idea of why it always did so.

"Listen, Uncle Bert. At some point, we're going to have to talk about personal things. Otherwise it's hanging over us and neither of us can figure out how to talk around it."

"Around what?"

"Your daughter, for example," she said gently. "Horace told me about her."

The waiter returned with the wine, pulled the cork and offered it. Bert waved it away, then impatiently signaled his approval as the waiter tipped a half inch into one of the tulip glasses. Getting the message, the waiter withdrew and let Bert pour.

"I told your father. He must have not talked about it with your mother, or they didn't tell you, can't blame them. It was no secret, trust me. After a few years it wouldn't go away, so I tried not ever talking about it. That's all."

"Did that work?"

His mouth kind of smeared on his face. He tasted his wine.

"What was her name?"

"Megan."

Cree gave him an encouraging smile. "Pretty! Not what I'd think a Guinea from Brooklyn would name his daughter, though. Was your wife Irish?"

"Chinese. Big extended family here in town. Good people. We just liked the name."

Cree sipped from her wine, too, the glass blearing Bert's face. "So, do you stay in touch with your ex?"

"No. Fran remarried, to a Chinese guy. I guess being married to me got her over Big-Nose Devils." He was trying to be funny, but his face looked like death itself as he picked at the tablecloth and then lifted his glass and tossed off his wine. "Could we talk about something else? This was a long time ago. We're supposed to be having a good time here."

"Of course." She gave it a beat and then miscalculated by prompting, "I just thought—"

"You want to know what it was like?" His eyes seared at her. "At first it was like I could *feel* her, I knew she was out there somewhere but I couldn't *find* her. And what really hurt was, I knew I'd let her down. When she was little and she'd cry in the night, we'd say, 'Don't worry, Daddy's here, Mommy's here, we'll never let anything bad happen to you.' And she'd stop crying, she'd believe us. But we lied, because it turns out we couldn't protect her. I *knew*, I *knew*, when whoever it was grabbed her, she was thinking, *No, this can't happen, my daddy said there's no such thing as monsters. My daddy is a policeman, my daddy said he'd protect me.* But I couldn't. Couldn't find her. Couldn't do anything. I let her down. *I lied about the monsters!*"

Cree breathed slowly and shut her eyes. When she opened them again, Bert was leaning across the table, red face close to hers, cords in his neck making the loose flesh jump and shiver.

"There was a long time when I didn't think I could keep going. The department gave me personal leave, all I did was look for her. I drove my wife away. I badgered every cop in fifty miles, I *threatened* cops, my friends, said I'd kill them if they didn't help me. What kept me going was, I'd go home and I'd suck on my gun. Yeah, I'd put it in my mouth and remind myself there was that, it was a split second away if I needed it. And the only thing that kept me from doing it was that every time I got close I'd think maybe there was one detail I hadn't looked at hard enough, maybe I had a lead or a clue or a contact that would pay off, if I pulled the trigger I wouldn't be able to follow up on it."

Bert's throat was gulping air. Quietly, almost to himself, he finished,

"In my whole life there was one perfect thing, one delicate thing ever put in my hands, and I lost it. *I let it get broken.*"

He was whispering, but he was far too intense, on the verge of causing a scene. The people at the next table were glancing over. Cree covered for him by taking his big fists in her hands and nodding understandingly, as if the intensity was about their relationship, something remotely normal, acceptable.

Suddenly the waiter was there. Bert reared back in his chair, wide eyed, taken by surprise. The waiter was a short, dark-haired, middle-aged guy, a perfect Italian penguin in his tux, and though his nostrils flared wide at Bert's reaction, he managed a tight smile.

"Have you decided on your antipasto," he asked expressionlessly, "or would you like a few more minutes?"

Which is why you don't talk about it, Cree realized. *Because there's no end, no bottom, no top. No stopping it once it gets going, but no place for it to go.* A condition she was personally all too familiar with.

They ordered prosciutto with cantaloupe for the antipasto, a *primo* of *conchiglie con il sugo per gramigna* and a *secondo* of steak *alla fiorentina* and for right away another bottle of wine, a Barolo the waiter recommended. Then they sat in silence for a few minutes, letting it subside.

After the second bottle had been opened and poured, she tasted the Barolo and rolled it around the globe, sneaking a look at Bert through the red-washed glass.

"When I was talking to Horace," she said, "I asked him if the handsome guy in that graduation picture was his son."

Bert's little smile ticked one cheek.

"Point is, I put my foot in my mouth a lot, Uncle Bert. All in the interest of being Miss Honesty USA, but it still adds up to the hoof in the yap, as Pop said. You'd think with a Ph.D. in psychology I'd have some finesse. But it's a genetic disorder. Probably inherited it from Mom."

He dismissed the apology with a wave.

"No, don't let me off the hook, because I'll probably keep doing it. Especially since I have just drunk a couple glasses of wine and my judgment is even worse than usual. But I'm sorry in advance."

She'd conjured the smile again, longer, a nice reward.

"So, since I've already apologized, can I ask you something?"

"Oh Christ."

"Were you and Mom—were you ever, you know . . . sweet on her?"

"Why would you—"

"I remember you dancing with her. You'd be in the kitchen, you'd put the radio on. Mom pretended she hated it, but I could tell she didn't. Seeing you two, I thought it looked very romantic."

The memory seemed to please Bert. "We were kids. I used to goof like that, thought I was a real Romeo. Your father deserves a lot of credit for putting up with me. Far as your mother goes, sure, I was sweet on anything in a skirt and she was a great gal, a lot of fun. I didn't mind taking her for a turn on the linoleum." He checked Cree's eyes to make sure she wasn't misinterpreting. "But that's it. All three of us were old-fashioned when it came to marriage."

Their antipasto arrived, and as soon as they finished it two waiters were there with steaming plates of pasta. Bert tucked the corner of his napkin into his collar, spread it to protect his shirt. Cree noticed that the knuckles of his right hand were scraped, thought to ask about it, then decided she'd already asked too many questions; every time she ventured into Bert's personal life she hit another taboo area. She expected they'd have another long silence, but Bert surprised her.

"Your first paranormal thing," he said to his plate. "Something to do with Mike?"

Cree was taken aback. "What—Mom told you? I asked her never to—"

"No. Just put two and two together."

"I don't usually—"

" 'Otherwise it's hanging over us, we gotta talk around it.' "

Fair enough, Cree had to admit. There was a time when she wouldn't have been able to tell it, but in the last year she had managed to get some distance on it, package it as a narrative she could recite without stumbling too much or crying.

"We were living in New Hampshire. I was working for the county social services system, Mike had a hot job at a Manchester high-tech firm. One time he flew out to L.A. on a four-day business trip, so I went down to visit Mom and Dee in Philadelphia. The next day I was downtown, doing some shopping, and I saw him. I was totally astonished, he was supposed to be in L.A. He was right there, dressed in his good suit, the one I had helped him pick out. He met my eyes. But then he . . . disappeared. Vanished. It didn't make sense. It scared me terribly. Later that day I got a call from the L.A. police, saying that he'd been killed in a car accident. About three minutes before I saw him."

A rim of tears gathered on one eyelid and she swiped at it before it could spill. "Under the circumstances, I kind of came . . . unglued for a while."

Bert was rearranging the food on his plate, face expressionless, not looking her way. "And that's why you haven't remarried."

"Everyone goes through denial. In my case, it was very hard to accept that he was really, completely . . . dead. In an absolute sense. Yes. That has complicated my relationships with men, yes."

"A shame. Good-looking woman like you." He hazarded a glance at her. "What, you didn't know that? Any guy with half a brain would kill for a shot at a woman like you."

Cree smiled, surprised at how good it felt to hear that from him.

They ate in silence for a time, and then Bert sighed ponderously. "Yeah, the ambiguity. It's the ambiguity that gets you."

He walked her to her car. A short, somber stroll through North Beach. Traffic was heavy on Columbus Avenue, the sidewalk was bustling, every restaurant was packed, thousands of little bright lights, candles on the tables, flush-faced couples laughing, food smells, music from doorways. Everybody else seemed so happy and light.

Bert's insightfulness had surprised her, and as they walked she sneaked glances at him, trying to gauge what else might be hidden inside. So hard to tell. They had exhumed each other's sorrows, and there was no remedy for either. And yet it wasn't too bad. The wine made her warm and a little floppy, and she felt surprisingly close to Bert, holding his big arm against her side and liking the mass of him, the gravity he gave off. He smoked continuously, catching up after an hour and a half without nicotine.

When they got to the Honda, she beeped the doors open but didn't get in right away, reluctant to leave him.

"We didn't talk about business," Bert pointed out. "What's next on your agenda?"

"Well, I still can't do much, not without a closer age estimate. I thought I'd spend the morning in the old newspapers—mainly just to orient myself, but you never know, I could get lucky. I'm hoping to get over to the Parson Collection in the next couple of days. I'm sorry I don't have much to offer yet. But I'm enjoying working with Horace, and I had a very pleasant morning, reading some general history." She was rambling, being chatty, trying to leave things on a more upbeat note. "Funny, I was sitting in the City Hall plaza, and who should come along but the radiologist who's doing the imaging work for Horace. This guy Ray?"

Bert shrugged, pursed his lips. The name apparently didn't ring a bell.

"Talk about your foot in your mouth. Ray has very bad scarring on one side of his face—his whole left cheek was ripped open? And he obviously has a lot of issues about the way people react. Don't worry, I didn't tell him what I do for a living, but I went on about feeling like a stranger, an oddball—to a guy with a face like that! What was I thinking? Like I say, I'm sorry in advance, world."

Bert stared down the street, looking distant and preoccupied. "Okay, Cree. You say hello to Horace for me. Give me a buzz when you want to get together next, yeah?"

She had thought to give him a kiss on the cheek, but he was already gone, bulky shoulders and silver hair moving down the sidewalk and disappearing into the throng.

17

"HORACE? DR. SKOBOLD?"

The door to the bone zone was unlocked, so Cree went in and called again. The lights were all on, but she got no answer. She looked into the office and the back room, found both empty. Five after eight, Horace was running late again.

She had brought her tote bag with a pair of jeans and a sweatshirt and her jogging shoes, and decided that she could use some extra time anyway, to change out of her dinner clothes. She considered doing it in Horace's office, but then figured that Murphy's Law would require him to show up precisely when she was maximally undressed. Instead, she went back out of the lab and down the echoing corridor to the ladies' room. The basement had an abandoned feel tonight, no sound or movement, no lights under the doors, not even under the big gray door to the meat suite. She went into the bathroom, changed, and folded her good clothes carefully away.

Horace was still not in the lab when she returned. To kill time, she greeted each of the reconstructions in progress, looking over the slabs and mounds of clay that had been applied since she'd last seen them. The one Karen Chang had been working on looked nearly done, but except for the fact that it was vaguely female it had almost no personality. She wondered if it had to do with levels of skill, whether maybe Karen was not as good a sculptor as Dr. Skobold. Or maybe she just wasn't done yet.

She perched on a stool and started looking through the anatomy book again. After a few minutes she heard that rumble and clunk through the wall, a deep dull sound that slightly vibrated the workbench: *lumberlumber-lumberbunk*. That was the common wall with the meat suite. Now that she knew what was through that wall, she could better visualize where the sound was coming from. If you came into the meat suite and went past the offices near the corridor, took a right so you'd face this wall from the other side, there'd be the bank of drawers. The morgue drawers.

She went to the workbench along that wall, leaned over, and put her hands flat against the plaster. When the sound came again, feeling it also through her palms, she knew exactly what it was. The rumble was the sound of an eight-foot refrigerated steel drawer sliding out on its carriage. The blump at the end was the drawer stopping as it reached full extension. The more forceful clunk was a drawer chunking against the wall when it had been slid shut. Somebody was opening and closing the drawers that contained the customers of the meat suite, the crispy critters and the mudman and who knew what else.

She pulled her hands quickly away.

After listening to another repetition of the noise, she got impatient with it and went out into the corridor and down to the meat suite entrance. But there was no light visible under the door. She leaned the side of her head against the steel and waited until she heard the sound again. *Rumble-bumblerumblechump.* From here she couldn't feel the deep vibration of it.

She rattled the lock and knocked loudly. "Horace? Dr. Skobold? It's Cree!" Everything she did sounded frightfully loud in the cocooning silence. "Are you in there?"

No answer. She waited, her ear against the door, and heard nothing.

She thumped the door with the heel of her hand, waited, then gave it a kick of frustration and went back to the reconstruction lab feeling twitchy and hyperalert, irrationally glad she had put on her running shoes. The sound didn't come again.

A few minutes later Skobold bumbled through the door with his armload of books, so effusively apologetic that she couldn't stay irritated.

Their goal tonight was to measure every bone. As Cree had pointed out, the standards would probably not apply to the wolfman, but they still had to be systematic about the metrics. Once he had all the numbers, Skobold would attempt to pin down the wolfman's age and stature by comparing his measurements to statistical averages derived from thousands of skeletons in the Hamaan–Todd collection in Cleveland, the Terry collection at the Smithsonian, and others. When they'd finished measuring, they'd label each bone with its own control number and then varnish it. The skull would require a number of additional processes to prepare it for casting.

Horace unlocked the back room. Cree helped him carry a variety of tools out to the counters, and then they wheeled out the wolfman's pallet. Reserving the skull for himself, Horace put her to work measuring the long bones, showing her how to position them on an osteometric table. He started her with a femur, positioning the two knobs at the knee end, the medial and lateral condyles, flat against the stop board so that the bone angled out across the middle of the grid-marked table. Once it was in place, they slid a metal form over the top and placed its wire crosshairs parallel to the major lines of the bone. Cree wrote down the measurements and then used a protractor to determine the angles of the knobs and protrusions relative to the shaft.

Skobold had placed the jaw into a boxy contraption that he called a mandibulometer. With the open end of the horseshoe of the jaw positioned against a vertical board, he slid a bar across until it touched the chin area, then lowered another bar from above so that it touched the top of the jaw hinges. He didn't say anything as he jotted the measurements, but Cree could tell he was perturbed by the results.

They settled into a rhythm, Skobold leaning over to check her work, nodding when he approved, making small adjustments when necessary.

"So," Cree began, "I thought you were over in the . . . over on the other side." She tipped her head toward the meat suite wall. "Thought I heard someone working over there, but when I went over there wasn't any light under the door."

"No, not tonight. I was bringing some slides to a colleague in another building. I'm very sorry, Ms. Black, he's a talkative fellow and I couldn't break free without offending him."

"Who else might be working there?"

"This time of night, no one."

"But I heard it last night, too. It sounded like the . . . drawers being opened and closed." She tried not to show how much it had upset her.

He frowned as he made an adjustment to the mandibulometer. "Hm. The elevators, perhaps? Sound travels queerly in some of these buildings.

I can't speak to it myself because, frankly, my ears are not what they once were. I should probably get hearing aids, but I am too vain."

Cree nodded, letting it go. She finished with the left femur and marked it with the case control number Skobold's papers specified, then set it back on the pallet and started in on the right femur. Skobold bent back to the mandibulometer and explained in some detail the process of using multiple indicators to determine age.

She waited until it seemed they had a pretty good rapport going. "Horace, I have a problem I was hoping I could talk to you about."

"Oh?"

"It's about Bert. What you told me last night showed me how little I really know him. We just had dinner tonight, and I still can't say I know much. I mean, it was good, we talked about the old days, my mom and pop, his daughter . . ."

"But," Skobold prompted. He was using a caliper to measure the thickness of the mandible at various points, tipping his head to get his bifocals onto the tiny numbers.

"But he's working on a . . . project. And I'm having a hard time with it. I mean, trying to figure out whether it's a reasonable concern or suggests Bert is . . . not coping effectively with his impending retirement."

He looked at her sternly. "Ms. Black. I have no idea what you're talking about. You'll have to be more specific."

Cree had been trying to position the crosshairs over the femur and couldn't seem to get it right. She gave it up, folded her arms, and faced Skobold.

"He showed me a bunch of case files. Some are closed cases, some are open, some are unsolved homicides, some are accidental deaths, and Bert thinks there's something wrong with every one of them. A lot have to do with dog attacks. He's got a theory that there's a murderer on the loose from years ago. He sort of suggested he could use my help, because his bosses aren't buying it. The problem is, I'm not either. I keep thinking it's because he's retiring, he wants to go out with a flourish. He's created a . . . a crusade, he's invested it with all the emotional urgency associated with his failure to protect or find his daughter. He's on a quest to rid the world of bad guys and he's only got three more months to do it."

Skobold went back to work on the jawbone, shaking his head with vast sadness. "Oh, Bertie. Oh, Bertram."

"But then, what do I know? He's certainly more perceptive than I gave him credit for being. So maybe he's right. Especially given those e-mails he's been getting, I—"

"E-mails?" Skobold repeated, deeply perplexed now.

Cree stamped her foot in frustration. She was just not telling this coherently.

"I'm sorry, Horace. Bert started getting some unusual e-mails not long after they found the wolfman. He thinks the bones might have provided some kind of a trigger for the killer. About ten years ago, he and a detective from Oakland worked on a pair of unsolved dog-attack deaths. They thought maybe it was someone sending their dogs after people, basically homicides with dogs as the weapon. Now he's thinking some more recent dog attacks might tie in, too. And the e-mails could be this guy taunting him, because Bert never got him and maybe this guy knows Bert's retiring soon. They're highly skilled, altered photos of dogs, morphing into humans. Or humans who've almost turned into dogs."

Skobold fumbled as he worked to remove the jaw from the apparatus, nearly dropping it. His hands were shaking so hard it rattled when he set it down. He started to lift the cranium, then turned to look at the counter behind him and struck his forehead tragically with the palm of his hand, alarming Cree.

"I forgot the craniophor," he explained.

He started toward the back room but then caught himself. He looked devastated as he gazed down and stroked the narrow dome of the wolfman's forehead.

"Oh, my little friend," he said sadly. "What have you begun?"

18

THE OASIS WAS in the Potrero district, a big cube of a building probably built around 1935 with decorative patterns of yellow bricks worked into the stucco to give it somebody's idea of a Middle Eastern look. Over the marquee were architectural flourishes intended to represent domes and minarets, and the theme continued inside in the murals and woodwork, fake marble, doorways cut into that heart-shape at the top. The Oasis had been built long before 9/11, back before Israel-Palestine and OPEC and Osama Bin Laden and all the crap, when the Arab world was just a faraway celluloid myth of sheiks with their harems, desert palaces in palm-shaded oases, dashing dark-skinned guys, veiled women with mesmerizing eyes. Back in Brooklyn when Bert was a kid and his mother had made him take lessons, the theme varied, but all ballrooms were basically the same. A ballroom had to have an exotic look and a name to go with: Xanadu, Avalon, Stardust, Taj Mahal. You could go to any of the ballrooms in San Francisco and they were about the same as the ones back east and still mostly the same as when Bert was a kid.

Bert cranked around to retrieve his shoe bag from the backseat, turned again, and sat with it in his lap. He looked at the façade of the Oasis. Nobody was coming in yet, he was a little early. He didn't like to be the first to arrive. He lit a cigarette and thought about what he'd learned and tried to make some plans.

He'd lied to Cree again. Why? *I'm going dancing*, he could have said. *Wednesday nights, sometimes I go. Probably not your kind of scene, but you could come with if you want to have a laugh. Bunch of geriatrics like me and nerdy Pakistani kids, but, hey, at my age it's easier than confession or sex. And it's better than what'll happen tonight if I don't go.*

The world was too often without grace. It was the one failing he couldn't get over with age or forget with booze, the one loss besides Megan he couldn't forgive. But here, even if it was a fantasy of Araby that never was, there came a moment when the curling lines and dovetailed beats of sound and movement converged and at that instant you felt grace or embodied it or at least saw it across the room. On that alone, you could make it through another few days or weeks.

You could make amends to your gods after you did something, or you could apologize for your sins in advance, like Cree warning him about putting her foot in her mouth. Not that either made any difference, but thinking about what he should do, what he wanted to do, he had to wonder which this was. For last night, or for what he might do later tonight.

"Ray" with the scars. Cameron Raymond. He'd put it all together within five minutes after he'd left Cree. Horace used Temple MicroImage, Bert had seen the lab logo on materials he'd reviewed. Back at his car, he'd called Temple, knowing it was after hours, and had gotten the expected voice-mail system and one of those messages, *If you don't know the extension, enter the first three letters of your party's last name.* He tapped in R-A-Y and sure enough, *You have reached the voice mailbox of Cameron Raymond. I'm sorry I'm not available to take your call, but . . .* Bert hadn't heard that voice in many years. It brought back the whole thing in an instant.

Cameron Raymond. So that explained not only Horace's occasional mysterious uptightness over the years but the sudden spate of dog-morph e-mails. And probably the other stuff as well.

Once he'd verified that Cameron Raymond did work for Temple, he'd called in for vehicle registration information and had gotten the basics, including a plate number for his burgundy Chrysler minivan, home phone number, and current address. He'd also requested a sheet review and as he waited for it to come in he'd driven to the address DMV had provided, down near the shipyards on the Bay waterfront. On the way he got the return fax and was surprised to see that aside from a couple of speeding tickets, Raymond had a clean sheet. Which didn't mean anything one way or the other except that Ray's juvie records had been sealed.

It was dark on the industrial streets, not many lights in the buildings, a disproportionate number of streetlights burned out. The homeless encampments along the dead-end streets, tents and tarp shelters and abandoned cars, were shadowy but full of furtive movement. Raymond's address turned out to be the office and warehouse of what had once been Dimension Intermodal, according to a sign still on the side of the building.

He drove slowly as he looked the place over. It looked abandoned: a half-block-long building, probably built in the 1920s, with tall windows, truck loading bays along the right side, a steel-plate human-sized door on the left. On the east, the building faced an empty lot surrounded by a ten-foot wire fence with barbed wire at the top. A sliding mesh gate, wide enough to admit a semitrailer rig, appeared to be the only access from street to lot.

No sign of a Chrysler minivan at the moment. Bert considered whether Raymond might park inside, coming in through the roll-up doors facing the lot, but after looking at the amount of vegetation and trash along the gate decided it hadn't been used in years. So Raymond probably parked in front, using the man door. In which case, he was probably not home at the moment.

Bert bumped over some rail tracks, came to the end of the street, pulled a U, and stopped where he could observe the property from the bay side. Just to the south was the channel of Islais Creek, dominated by a huge gantry, badly rusted, intended to lift containers on and off ships. No signs of current activity anywhere. Maybe Ray didn't live here at all and it was a dummy address. Still, Bert slouched low in his seat as he drove back past.

He had driven back toward the Oasis, thinking. He'd always distrusted coincidences, and here were several that put his neck hairs up. One was that Cameron "Ray" Raymond had chosen a career as a radiologist or specialized imaging technician or whatever he was. Obviously he did path or forensic work, since he worked for Temple and did jobs for Horace. The choice of career suggested a lot about Raymond's proclivities. Plus, a job at Temple would involve networking with others in the field, putting Raymond in a position to know what was going on at other path labs in the Bay area. With his computer skills, he could probably get access to inside information on homicides. Possibly even to distort findings or records.

Coincidence? Bert didn't think so.

Then there was Cameron Raymond talking to Cree Black down at City Hall plaza. In a metropolitan area of two million people, his running into the woman who was doing investigative work on a case, the wolfman, which Raymond was doing imaging work on for Horace. Cree Black who was the niece, sort of, of Bert Marchetti. Bert Marchetti with whom Cameron Raymond had something of a significant history. It didn't wash.

Bert felt the blood come up in his face. The effrontery of it! He hadn't even rinsed the poison out of his blood from last night, and here he was, the anger welling up again. Part of him wanted to go straight back to Raymond's place to do something about it. But the guy wasn't home.

Maybe later, he promised himself.

Bert paid seven dollars to the old woman in the Oasis ticket booth, then went into the dance hall. He found a chair, opened his shoe bag, and took out the suede-soled shoes. People were just starting to arrive, groups coming in noisily, solos much quieter. Tonight was smooth dancing only. The Oasis reserved Fridays and Saturdays for Latin, disco, or rock and roll because that was what drew the bigger crowds and brought in the real money. A typical Wednesday drew only about twenty or thirty people, max. Even with the staff and the DJ, it could seem a little sparse. The smooth-dance crowd was different from the Latin and fast-swing bunch, generally older people like himself who couldn't cut athletic moves anymore or who, like Bert, used the dancing to try to calm down, not crank up.

Actually, the makeup of the dance crowd was not so different than when he was a kid. You had a lot of old ladies and very few old men, same as back then only "old" now meant Bert's own age. You had the nerds, there had always been nerds, only nowadays they were mostly Japanese or Pakistani kids over here to attend UC Berkeley or USF and trying to have a social life by taking ballroom lessons. They were usually in love with their female instructors and followed their movements with mournful puppy-dog eyes. Then you had the teachers from the dance school at the Oasis and a few from other studios around town, younger men and women, sharp dressers, many of them into competitive dancing. If you made your living teaching ballroom, you had to show up at these things to give the event some drama and excitement, keep your students convinced it had enough moxie to keep them paying you for lessons. Usually the night began with a short refresher on the steps, after which the teachers' main job was to give moral support and to matchmake the wallflowers who would otherwise be afraid to set foot on the floor.

In Bert's age bracket, the dancers were 90 percent women whose husbands had died off and who were secretly hoping for a geriatric romance to arise from a night of dancing. Except that it never worked out that way. Mostly they danced with each other, or with some punk who was wishing he was dancing with Britney Spears instead and who couldn't move for beans anyway.

Being a decent dancer and older, Bert was in high demand, to the extent that the competition for his attentions could get a little nasty. He made a point of spreading himself around, seldom dancing with the same old bat twice.

He wasn't immune to the jolt that came with dancing with one of the young female teachers. The feel of a supple waist under his hand, the way a young woman's breasts swayed as she moved, the splay of pretty hair under the lights, the flash of white teeth, it still got to him. The good ones knew to smile and wore red lipstick and eyeliner that made their faces dramatic, and their enjoyment of dancing was contagious. No, he was not immune, and there were old guys who kept up with dancing just for that.

But for him it was the grace. It was the taste of grace you got when the music started and the lights changed and created an illusory world of dash and romance. It was an antidote for the crap that was 99 percent of everything else and for the toxified feeling he felt after a night like last night. He did a little dancing most nights at home, but the house was too small. Here at the Oasis was a freedom that came only with a half acre of polished yellow boards and the slight give of a sprung dance floor. Even the old ladies gave off a spark once they got going, and Bert knew he did, too. And that was worth the awkwardness of coming here without a partner, witnessing the embarrassment of the beginners, fending off widows who wanted to make exclusive claims.

He tied his shoes carefully and for a while just sat and took in the varnished boards, the high ceilings, the decor. He tried to put Cameron Raymond out of his mind, determined not to give him that. You couldn't let him bend your head out of shape, that's exactly what he wanted.

On the far side of the room, a couple of instructors were showing some moves to a group of students. More people were coming in now. He felt the usual pang of being a single, over here on the folding chairs, and wondered if Cree would come dancing if he asked her. She was fit, graceful, she could no doubt be good if she learned the steps. He'd start her with a waltz, the basic box step, work out from there. She'd have to wear a different skirt, though, something with a flare, not the tapered kind she'd had on tonight.

She had looked lovely tonight, a sweet kid. And of course he'd screwed up again, going off on Megan, then feeling pissed at her for dragging it out of him and so turning it around on her, probing her about her dead husband when what the hell did he know about her grief, her way of handling or not handling it? Nobody can really understand another person's pain. But he had definitely found the nerve. Her face had said it all. Another fuck-up with Cree.

"Mr. Marchetti, how nice to see you! I wondered if you would be here tonight."

Bert looked over to see one of the regulars coming his way. She wore a blue-gray dress and a paste-diamond necklace, and her gray hair was wrapped against her head and held with glitter-crusted clips. Mrs. Helen Aldritch, maybe five years older than Bert, husband long dead, a pleasant age-wrinkled face, cords in her neck, liver-spotted bony hands. She had her purse in one hand and her shoe bag in the other, and she gestured at the seat next to him.

"Mind if I join you?"

"It would be my pleasure." Bert tried to smile. "You look stunning tonight, Mrs. Aldritch."

Mrs. Aldritch sat with a grateful sigh and began changing her shoes.

"Don't worry, I know I'll have to share you," she said. "I won't be greedy. But you have to save me from at least a few of these boys. They dance like robots! Zombies! It's a wonder they ever get married and have children, you wouldn't think they'd know how to accomplish the necessary. Of course, that's what people always say about the English, and they seem to have managed, haven't they?"

"Nature provides, I guess," Bert told her.

Eventually the music started. The MC worked the lights so that beams of purple and turquoise angled in the room. They began with a waltz. Mrs.

Aldritch was tall enough that they were a good fit, and though her back and hands were hard as hickory she was surprisingly spry. They whirled with the music, other couples spinning nearby.

Tonight Bert wasn't sure he could let go. He couldn't seem to shake any of it. Cameron Raymond, Cameron Raymond, there was something else he should remember about Cameron Raymond, but he fished in his memory and couldn't catch it. In the brief moments when he was able to put it out of his mind, his thoughts went to the rest of his working day. A couple of cases kept coming back at him. A court appearance coming up for the homicide of a Mexican nanny, apparently by her employer. And a teenager, son of a wealthy family, shot dead for reasons that Bert didn't understand yet, a whole sad drama. He knew he wouldn't clear that one before the end.

Then there were the older files he'd been reading and the taunting e-mails that he now knew came from Cameron Raymond. He'd dug up another case today, three years old and going nowhere, where the vic had been slashed, his face mutilated. Johnny Miller, the lead inspector on it, had treated it as a drug dealer's message hit, but to Bert's eye the drug connection had never been firmly established. And psychologically, the focus on the face was another piece that might point to Cameron Raymond.

Mrs. Aldritch misinterpreted his detachment. "I know I'm an old dried-up piece of jerky. Not like dancing with lovely Miss Escobar."

They were swinging around in the wake of Tina Escobar, an especially gorgeous instructor, and her competition partner who was gay but handsome as Valentino. Tina waltzed with all the grace imaginable, right out of a Vienna daydream, but she also trailed a sultry, sexual smoke behind her. She wore a blouse that left her shoulders and upper back bare, and the play of the gentle muscles in her back, the smooth plumped softness of her chest below her collarbones, the way the lights played in her dark hair, it all spoke straight to a man's soul.

Bert looked at the gray face in front of him, the carefully rouged cheeks, Mrs. Aldritch's old eyes intent in their wrinkles, and felt a tug inside. He could almost cry. They turned for a promenade, and when they came back face-to-face, he said, "It's nothing like that. I just got a lot on my mind tonight."

"Such as?"

"Oh, my job. That stuff."

"And what is your job, Mr. Marchetti?"

"I'm with the San Francisco Police."

"How exciting! Doing what, if I may ask. Tell all," she demanded gaily. She wasn't prying, she was doing a wifely thing, urging him to get it off his chest so he could loosen up and have a good time.

An underarm turn and she was facing him again. "Trust me," Bert said, "you don't want to know." All the awful feelings came boiling up, he didn't know if he could keep doing this tonight.

Mrs. Aldritch was leaning elegantly away, smiling, eyes blissfully half-closed like she was having the time of her life, but Bert could tell she was hurt. She was doing everything right, being witty and kind and elegant and drawing him out and she'd heard his refusal to unburden as another proof of his dissatisfaction with her. In fact, Bert realized, she was really leading without seeming to, she was covering for his inattention, making it work despite him.

The thought made him angry and ashamed. Nothing with Cameron Raymond tonight, he decided. There was a lot to think about, he should put his ducks in order first. He'd determine the next move when he knew more. Anything tonight would be precipitous.

Making the decision helped. He'd take control here. He'd think it through. And when he was ready, he'd do whatever he felt was right. *Count on that, Cameron.*

They had come in near Tina Escobar again, flashing dark eyes, red lips, blouse forever sliding off the pale shoulders. Bert caught her scent as they followed in her wake.

When they'd spun away again, Bert leaned close to Mrs. Aldritch's ear. "She's a very pretty girl," he whispered. "But you are a much better dancer. You have the spark. The grace. That's something no one can teach you."

She didn't believe him at first. But he worked on it, he caught her eye, he let the music come into his lungs and his heartbeat, grimly he let himself catch the pleasure of whirling over the big floor. His feet found it, and soon they were locked together in one gesture, perfectly synchronized, and it was all grace and lightness, space and spin.

"Perfect," Bert whispered, complimenting her turn. A moment later he said it again, "Perfect."

After a while she saw he meant it, and she took on a glow that made him feel better about himself and for a while banished everything without grace, all the blood and darkness, past and to come, from his thoughts.

19

IT WAS TEN thirty by the time Cree emerged from the lab and into the empty corridor. It had taken longer than expected to measure and mark the bones and to hear what Horace had to tell. He had explained at some length the conflicting indicators that made it so hard to determine an age for the wolfman, but mainly he'd talked about Uncle Bert. Bert and Cameron Raymond.

She pushed the elevator button and listened to the distant sounds of the machinery responding far above. She considered whether that could have been the noise she'd heard earlier but felt too numb to decide. Mostly it was fatigue, but she felt bruised, too, the feeling she'd sometimes get after working out with Joyce in the dojo, of having been hit too hard, too often in an unguarded place: no marks yet, but you know it'll show by tomorrow.

Outside, she left the lights of the entryway and turned into tree shadows cut with shafts of streetlight. The air smelled moist and good, a sweetness that she realized was probably just the natural scent of the world in the absence of the odor given off by boiling corpses.

Horace had again advised her to be cautious when walking through campus, and now as she came around a dense stand of trees and shrubs the mottled darkness inside seemed to shift. In a moment she was past it, listening hard without turning her head. But there was no brush of leaf or other sound of movement. Still jumpy when she reached the parking lot, she scanned the expanse of pavement before moving on toward her car. It was reassuringly empty, her Honda SUV an island near the middle. Three empty rows behind sat a little silver BMW, a couple of rows straight ahead a purple minivan in the tree shadows at the edge of the lot, neither of them near enough to permit a sudden attack. She crossed to the Honda, waiting until she was almost in its shadow before opening the door with her remote. Then she was inside. She checked the back, then locked the doors.

She started the engine and when the lights came on she jumped as they illuminated someone leaning against the purple minivan, watching her. She hadn't seen him in the shadows. For an instant his eyes were so pale in the headlights it was as if he had no corneas, or had reflecting eyes like an animal's.

Cameron Raymond.

He raised one hand to doff an imaginary hat to her and then just stood wincing into the headlights. Hands tingling, Cree put the car in gear and rolled in a circle that brought her abreast of him from ten feet away.

She rolled down the window. "What are you doing here, Ray?"

"Waiting for you." He smiled with what seemed truest radiance and leaned back against the side of the van. Cree got another shock as she saw that the rear window was full of dogs: three toothy faces, watching her through breath-fogged glass.

"Why? What do you want?"

"I want to talk to the woman I met in the plaza. The woman with brass to be so up-front with a scar-faced stranger." His divided face seemed utterly without guile.

After what Skobold had told her, she certainly did need to talk to him, but she was exhausted and still jittery. She watched him dubiously as she tried to decide why seeing him here awakened such a feeling of unease. Except for the e-mails to Bert and maybe that icy look at the plaza, there was no real reason to be afraid of him. Unless Bert's theory was right.

"I didn't mean to startle you," Ray called softly. "If it's any help, you scare me, too."

He followed her to an International House of Pancakes, where they took a booth at the corner, ordered decaffeinated coffee, and watched each other warily across the table.

"Ray, I'm pretty beat, so I need to cut to the chase here. What did you want to talk to me about?"

"The wolfman. You said you wouldn't mind some ideas that might help you in your research."

"Great. But I think we've got some more pressing issues to discuss. Why are you sending Bert those e-mails?"

If he was surprised she'd figured it out, he didn't show it. "Bert owes. I don't mean to me. He owes it to himself to acknowledge what he is."

"You're taunting him. Trying to make him angry. Don't do it."

"No! I'm doing him a favor!" A wry grin warped the big scar. "Returning a favor, actually. Call me a flamingly naïve optimist, but I keep thinking it's never too late to face the truth."

"Ray. Do you have any idea of how far I am from understanding one word you're saying? Horace told me what happened, what Bert did. Is that what you're talking about?"

"You're tired. This could require a long answer—you up for that?"

"Probably not. But go ahead anyway."

He was seventeen when Bert Marchetti ruined his face, twenty-three years ago. At the time he lived with his mother; his father had died in a fishing-boat accident five years earlier. Ray had finished high school a year early, but his girlfriend was still in school and he had decided not to go to college right away. So he still lived at home and still hung with some kids from school, mostly guys who'd graduated ahead of him and were doing what he was: killing time, making up their minds about their lives only very slowly.

He spent that first summer after graduation drinking, smoking dope, writing poetry, necking with his girlfriend, experimenting with photography, and doing stupid things. Once he and the guys went to the Golden Gate Bridge and climbed down into the superstructure under the roadway, where they got so drunk they were afraid to climb back out and had to spend the night clinging to girders, throwing up into the black water far below. Another time they stole the car of somebody one of the guys didn't like, drove it down the coast highway, and rolled it off a cliff a few miles south of Pacifica. They waited for it to burst into flames the way every car did in the movies, but it just bounced off rocks and landed upside down in the shallow surf, inert. Fun anyway.

By late summer, they had found a thing that got them off, which was to surprise each other, outdo each other, with the risks they took and the excesses they indulged in. It was better than any drug. The more spontaneous and unexpected, the harder the adrenaline kick and the better the high. The thrill came from going seriously beyond the norms, definitively breaking the rules; the only problem was, once you'd done something a few times the thrill began to fade. You had to keep raising the stakes.

So one time they were out walking, five of them, feeling reckless. They jumped up onto a parked car and ran over the tops of a whole block's worth, denting the roofs and hoods, a juvenile delinquent classic. Then they scooted a few blocks away and walked around until they heard the sirens. A few minutes later, on the spur of the moment, Nick and Jonah conceived the brilliant idea of robbing a corner grocery store. Half the fun was doing it under the noses of the police, who they figured would be tied up with irate car owners. Ray and the other two were leery, but they posted themselves outside to make sure the getaway was clear, or whatever they thought they were doing. Inside, Nick and Jonah grabbed the old lady at the register. They didn't have any weapons, but they shook her and knocked things off the counters, and a minute later they came tearing out with a handful of cash. The five of them ran. They were four blocks away, arguing about how to divide the spoils, when the first squad car pulled up.

They scattered. Ray cut between two apartment buildings, came out on the next street, ran to the right. He sprinted to the corner and slammed full-tilt into a police car that screeched to a stop right in front of him. Before he could even get up, this big cop jumped out, grabbed him, threw him against a parked car. Ray panicked and fought back and when he did the cop went crazy, smashing him up against the car so hard his head went through the glass of the side window. The more Ray fought, the harder the cop went on him, smashing his head against the door frame, grinding him, sawing his face on the broken edge of the window. He was afraid the glass would cut his throat, but the harder he tried to straighten, to hold his neck and face away from the slashing edge, the more the cop took it as his resisting. Even after Ray went slack, pleading, the guy kept shaking and sawing him, tearing away pieces of his temple, his cheek, the inside of his mouth, the side of his tongue. Finally some other cops came and made the big one stop. They arrested Ray and called an ambulance.

It made the newspapers. Bert Marchetti's administrative review cleared him of wrongdoing, so Ray's mother filed a civil suit. Ray testified, Bert got raked over the coals for a few weeks, but it didn't fly. The jury agreed that Ray's injuries were unfortunate, but there was no way to prove that Bert had used excessive force under the circumstances. The exact events were Bert's word against Ray's. The other cops who'd pulled Bert off Ray had gone mum.

For his part in the robbery, Ray went to juvie court, got a year of probation. His skull had been fractured, jaw splintered, skin and flesh slashed to bone. He went through several phases of surgery, after one of which he contracted one of those drug-resistant staph strains, which ate away some more of his cheek before it was stopped.

Cree tasted her coffee, but the cup had been sitting so long it was tepid and unpalatable.

"Fifty-eight bucks," Ray said.

"What?"

"That's how much Nick and Jonah took from the register. Fifty-eight dollars."

As he'd told the story, she could see him relive it, looking very much the injured, scared, disillusioned teenager. She didn't let her sympathy show.

"I hated him," he went on. "For years I blamed Bert for everything that was wrong with my life. For the first year, I was just going to kill him—seriously, I planned it all out. But between court and surgery I didn't have a chance, and then after a while I began to see things differently. I'd think about the grip of his hands on me, the weight of his body, that *energy*, I can't describe it, it's like the . . . rage of the whole world poured through him. And I knew I had to figure that out. How a man could have that feeling in himself. Whether I had it, too."

"Why do you think he did you a favor?"

"Because he made me think about all this. I wasn't 'normal' anymore. But I discovered that I hadn't been normal, would never have been normal even if Bert hadn't ruined my face. I readily admit I hate his fucking guts. But I also recognize that he's the one who showed me who I really am."

Cree nodded as the pieces started to come together. "So, sending him the e-mails, that's, what . . . returning the favor by showing him what he really is. Showing him the beast within."

He smiled, pleased with her.

"Why now? Twenty-three years later? The wolfman's bones?"

"Suddenly there was the perfect metaphor! Honestly, I'd never quite thought of it that way. With his retirement coming up, he'd have to be in a reflective frame of mind. I figured if ever there was a learning opportunity for Bert, this was it. 'Here's the real you, Bert. Like what you see?'"

She closed her eyes and rubbed her forehead, suddenly very tired. "Ray. I don't think Bert is the metaphor type. You are catching my tone of understatement here, right? The symbolic value of your perspective is not going to make a large difference to his personal development."

He grinned. "Can't teach an old dog new tricks?"

"This is not at all funny. He's in a difficult personal transition right now. If he figures out it's you, he'll . . . I don't even know how to say it. He'll make war on you."

His expression told her it had been a mistake to warn him. Cameron Raymond was clearly not planning to let Bert Marchetti get away with hurting him, ever again.

"You know about his daughter?" she asked.

"His lost daughter. Yes, Horace has pleaded that case ever since I've known him. Dear Horace. Forgive and forget. Sweetness and light. Harmony everywhere."

"Doesn't that make a difference? He was out of control, like you say, he was outraged at the world. You certainly received a very disproportionate share, but he took it out on everybody, trust me. And I believe he knows that about himself now."

Ray shook his head. "No. His daughter's abduction didn't create what's inside Bert. It just let it loose. Let him express it. Gave him an excuse."

She reached across the table and grabbed his hand with both of hers. When she first touched his skin, the hand leapt like a startled animal, but she gripped it tightly, hard enough to hurt. She was going to command him to listen. She was going to say that Bert was a harmless old man now, lonely and full of regrets, and that any pain or self-recognition he owed had probably been accomplished as well as it was ever going to be. But what happened was his hand turned in hers so that it faced hers palm to palm and lightly returned her grip. And she hesitated about what to say and then they were just looking down at their hands entwined like it was a phenomenon of some importance in its own right.

After a moment she took her hands back and wrapped them around her coffee cup.

"Ray, I'm curious about your perspective on all this, and I'd enjoy talking with you again—I think about a lot of the same things, I suspect we have a lot in common. But right now, I want you to tell me you'll quit provoking Bert. Or educating him about his true nature. Please."

He looked puzzled. "What more did you think I was going to do? I made my little point. I never had an encore planned."

Cree nodded, letting herself feel some small relief. They both sipped cold coffee; Ray stared into the darkness through the window, some thought or feeling pulling him into a different place.

"So, what were you going to tell me about the wolfman? You said you had some research ideas for me?"

Ray looked startled at the question, a man who had come back suddenly from some place far away. "Right. But I think it's my turn to say 'another time.' It can wait. I've already kept you up way too late. Give me a call if you want—I'm in the book."

His smile looked strained as he put down some money, stood, started to walk away, caught himself. "No, actually, there is one thing you might want to think about. Something that struck me in a book I was reading. This old Inuit man up in Canada, a famous hunter, was talking about living among wolves. He said, 'It's not the wolf you see that's dangerous. It's the wolf you don't see. The wolf you don't know is there.'"

He gave her a look as if this was vastly significant and then spun away and was gone.

20

S HE WASN'T EVEN going to try for the wolfman's ghost tonight, Cree decided.

She unlocked the door and stepped into the dark house, surprised at how easy and welcoming it felt, how nice to be back, even at a quarter to one in the morning. It had been a troubling day, and disappointing on the research front, but an idea had occurred to her that suggested one slender possibility, too. It was about something Hernandez had mentioned when she'd visited the house on Tuesday: Yes, the heavily wrapped furniture scattered through the upstairs had come with the place and was period stuff; for these historical houses, he said, coming with a few original furnishings greatly enhanced the value. He and his crew had wrapped up the five larger pieces and a handful of old photos—just a few old portraits and the typical scenes that people put on their walls to provide a touch of historical ambience.

Of course, there was no guarantee that any of the furniture or curios actually descended from Hans Schweitzer's time, and she certainly didn't expect to find a photo of the wolfman. So what was she looking for? She wasn't sure. A name, a date, a telling photo, a letter? The peripheral dynamics of the case—Ray and Bert's troubled history—were increasingly disturbing, and she felt an urgent need to make progress, to close the investigation out before anything went awry. But she needed one more link, one more piece of information that would open up new avenues of inquiry. Maybe some accidental conveyance from the house to her, from past to present, would make the difference.

There was only one piece in the first upstairs bedroom, a looming, shapeless mass of plastic and duct tape that she assumed was a wardrobe.

She put her flashlight in her teeth and began peeling tape. Hernandez had done a good job: It took ten minutes just to be able to lift aside the front layers. When she'd loosened enough to open the doors, she stood under a rustling canopy of plastic and played her light over every section of the interior, looking for a maker or owner's label, graffiti, anything. But aside from the scent of old wood and a whiff of mothballs, it was empty. She probed for a false bottom or hidden compartment, but found no indication of one. It took another five minutes to tape the coverings back in place.

She peeled a bureau in the next bedroom in the same way, and got a little thrill when she opened the top drawer and found several glassed frames separated by bubble wrap. The items behind the glass were clearly quite old. Predictably, the first was a photo of a cable car, with a few faces looking from the open arches of the roof and a uniformed conductor posed uncomfortably at one end. There were no notations on the photo or the back of the frame.

She carefully studied a grainy photo of what looked to be a prequake downtown commercial building, but found nothing more rewarding than a flavor of the time and place: wide-skirted women on the sidewalks, a horse-drawn streetcar, men in bowler hats. *Market Street, 1883*, according to a handwritten notation on the back.

The last was a photo portrait of some dowager dressed in Victorian finery, one hand in her lap and the other resting on a Bible placed strategically on a marble-topped side table. Her bulldog face pouted in a haughty expression, and the hand on the Bible was crusted with rings; the inscription on the back of the frame told Cree she was *Elvira Huntington Pierce, 1887*. Huntington had been a famous name in that era, Cree recalled, one of the "Big Four" richest and most influential men in the city; she wondered if Elvira was one of that clan.

There was nothing in the other drawers. Cree wrapped up the bureau again, sneezing in the dust that sifted from the plastic. She wondered if she'd be better off going to the basement after all, then figured she'd follow through and give the pieces in the master bedroom a look.

The young woman's face riveted her the moment she lifted the photo free of its bubble wrap. The portrait was one of three nestled in a magnificent rolltop desk in the big bedroom—a small photo in an oval mat not much bigger than Cree's hand; the gilt frame looked worn and nicked.

Cree puzzled at the face, trying to decide why it seemed so familiar. Not the hair, which was pulled tight around her head and probably gathered in a bun in back; not the round forehead and plain straight nose. The resemblance to someone she knew or had encountered teased her until she decided it was less the anatomical features of the face than its expression: open, genuine, somehow frightened yet determined; in the eyes, a keen, questing light not entirely suppressed by a desire to harmonize and serve.

Oh, her, Cree realized. *The person in the mirror every morning.*

She smiled at the woman, intrigued, then flipped the frame over to see if there was any inscription on the back.

Lydia Jackson Schweitzer, 1888.

So Hans had married, and, unless there was a remarkable coincidence here, he'd married the girl next door.

She studied the face more closely, searching for details that might be instructive. Lydia looked to be in her mid- or late-twenties, but her stiff pose and the straight, serious line of mouth made it hard to tell. She wore only small, discreet earrings, not the ostentatious medallions Elvira Pierce apparently preferred. Cree couldn't see enough of her clothing to make anything of it; the background was out of focus, anonymous.

Not much to learn beyond the name. And a sense of the person, which was surprisingly profound.

Jackson and Schweitzer, two houses, a marriage. She wasn't sure just how that might be of use to her research, but she felt a rising excitement as she looked at the other two items. There was nothing of interest, but the feeling stayed with her as she put the photos away and rewrapped the desk. Could Lydia be the piece she needed, the link to the past, to the wolfman?

Lydia Jackson Schweitzer, she kept thinking. *Who were you? What do you have to tell me? Did you have anything to do with the wolfman we found in your basement? Did you even know he existed?*

II

CREATURES IN PERIL

21

M Y NAME IS Lydia Jackson Schweitzer, and I am writing what is to be the secret accounting of my days. I begin this record after many years of quiet deceit because events have taken such strange turns of late, and such urgency, that I feel compelled to give voice to what I have witnessed. It must be secret, because though what I shall record should surely be generally known, it would bring shame and difficulty to those I love if they were aware of the whole round of my life. I do love my husband and believe he loves me in return; I know he is a good man who has made great accommodation for my rebelliousness and contrariety; likewise, the men and women of our church. But I can speak to none of them about these things, lest I shame them and they come to abhor me.

Conceivably I could say nothing to anyone: I could write nothing, perhaps, and bear no risk of discovery for my unusual circumstances and thoughts; yet I am also sure that if I do not tell it in some way, if I do not let some of it out of me, I will surely burst from the fullness of such a life, such events. So I speak to these pages, in solitude and secrecy, and do not burst but only overflow.

It is my belief that we are each given a unique and singular life; we are each in many ways the sole inhabitant of a unique and singular world. No one can know, from a face any more than from the exterior of a house, what transpires on the inside; yet there is, there must be, some merit in knowing, that we may each feel less alone and gain wisdom of our own life by glimpsing another's. So I record these events, writing with the outlook of a castaway seafarer who rolls a message into a bottle and flings it into the waves. There is some comfort in imagining that perhaps one day this secret accounting, having traversed a broad sea, will be discovered and read by a sympathetic eye, and be of interest or benefit to its recipient.

I have decided to write only in the lower parts of the house and only in the very early mornings, before Hans or Cook awakens. I have always been an early riser, despite my late evenings, and given the day's undertakings it is the only hour when I can safely expect solitude. I would prefer, I think, to write from the lovely bay window of our bedroom, where I could look down the hill and where the great scope of the water and mountains would inform my thoughts with some special insight; or perhaps from my old window in the other house, where the street makes an interval and opens the Golden Gate to view. But I am not discontent writing in the pantry. From its rear-facing window, our little garden is a lovely microcosm, all perfect and proportionate despite its diminutive size. A wedding garden, I consider it, for the fine stonework and plantings were Hans's gift to me upon our marrying, and the sight of it never fails to warm me.

The pantry is also convenient, because it is in the cavity beneath the lowest cabinet drawer that I have decided to secrete this journal, most convenient if Hans or Cook should awaken early. I must write in snatched moments, an ear always attentive to the sound of someone stirring. Being so old, Cook makes a good shuffling and puffing when she starts her day, and Hans is so large he creaks the floorboards above. But in case either should appear unexpectedly, I have taken the additional precaution of writing in a ledger that is identical to the one in which I keep our household accounts (also full of deception), one I can easily snap shut upon their arrival and incur no suspicion.

"Up early," I would say briskly, "and thinking of the shopping. We will be needing molasses, I think." Or such.

I am not a deceptive person by nature, and in fact I abhor the world's deceptions, which seem to me the source of much cruelty and error. And yet I came to our marriage with years of practice at it. It is as if there are two of me, one kept for the world's viewing and one kept out of sight. At times I take pleasure in imagining that Hans has glimpsed through to the secret one, and his real love, just as secret, is for her. But it is more likely that the woman Hans married was only Lydia Jackson, the proper niece and ward of his respectable neighbor, Mr. Franklin Jackson, formerly of Mobile, enterprising importer of cotton and wool cloth, active in church and civic affairs; Lydia Jackson, the only child of Franklin's brother Richard, who perished with his wife in the tragic ferry accident of 1873; Lydia, adopted by her kindly uncle.

That Lydia must have appeared to him as a young woman of good deportment and education, and, like Hans, deeply faithful and active in the church. When my uncle died, three years ago, leaving his house to me, I no doubt seemed a promising candidate for wifehood and motherhood: Though perhaps past the bloom of youth at twenty-six, I was, as he thought, financially self-sufficient, educated, Christian, holding property, in good health, and virtuous.

Within a year of my uncle's death, Hans began courting me, and did so with sincerity and persistence and what struck me as a charming old-world courtliness, derived perhaps from his German accent, his formal and slightly foreign manners. And, in truth, though I was not close to my uncle—I had deceived him as I deceive Hans and the church fathers—his death was deeply upsetting to me. He had, after all, sheltered me; he had seen that I received the best schooling a woman might in this new city; in his own way, he had cared for me. The loss of my uncle, my last mooring in society aside from the church, was difficult; when Hans made his intentions apparent, the prospect of living with another human being, after a year alone in that empty house, had great appeal.

I knew Hans first as our neighbor who dined with us from time to time, and so I knew his history. He had come here from a small German village in 1859 to seek his fortune. Only a decade earlier, as a child, he had heard that in California any man could become rich just for the effort of picking up gold nuggets from the ground; and with the famous discovery of the Comstock Lode, silver promised wealth for all who came. He was the son of a rigid patriarch and to this day maintains that aspect himself, and yet he must have been a rather daring and rebellious young man, for he was only eighteen when he left his home and sailed to America. The real circumstances of the silver mines disappointed him acutely, and he retreated, penniless, to San Francisco to pursue whatever work he might find. In this he was like many thousands of others; but, unlike most, he had apprenticed as a stone mason and therefore was highly skilled at a trade much in demand. Being also upright of character and a man of powerful determination, he did very well. After several years as a laborer, several more as a fine mason, he had gained sufficient reputation to hire helpers, whom he trained to high standards; within a dozen years, he had become a prominent contractor, operating several crews of men. Within a few more he was wealthy enough to buy the large, fine house in the fashionable district of Pacific Heights, next door to Franklin Jackson and his respectable, orphaned ward.

In intimate moments, when he lies beside me flushed with the heat of his exertion, he looks upon me with a possessive glow of pride in his eyes. He tangles his rough fingers in my hair and confesses that he considers me a fortunate match. For a foreigner of modest birth who had come with the silver rush, consorted with the roughest of men, who began in San Francisco as a menial laborer, a giant, rawboned man upon whom even tailored suits have never hung comfortably and whose massive, leathered hands will forever betray his beginnings, young Lydia Jackson seemed a prize.

Which is not to say his feelings are limited to the proprietary, as opposed to the passionate. He does love me, far more than I deserve, and I love him in return. Once, he admitted that he was drawn also to my solitude, which he feels he shares: An only child, with all my relatives dead, I share his experience as a man whose family was long ago left behind in the old country.

"Now you are my only family," he told me soberly, "and I am yours." Then, growing bold, humorous, and affectionate: "At least until we make ourselves a flock of fine children!"

At that my heart threatened to break, for again I was confronted with the awful extent of my deception.

Yet it is to protect him, as much as myself, that I deceive him. Were he to know the truth about this prize, I am afraid his love would falter; for he is a moral man and would find the truth deeply repugnant. He also loves his respected position, and takes pride in it, as well he ought, and would correctly judge that what I am and what I do daily jeopardizes it.

Yes, dearest Hans—whose heavy footsteps I now hear upon the floor above and from whom I must hide away my confessions for another day.

I will go to him and meet him on the front stairs, where I will take one of those great, rough hands in my own and lead him gratefully to his breakfast.

Despite my urgency, I was not able to write this morning, for Hans awakened early with a stomach upset and asked me to attend to him, which I was pleased to do. When at last he went to his office, I concocted errands for Cook that have left me alone in the house for some minutes before my other obligations intrude.

I am anxious to relate the events of two days past, and in fact spilled them out onto the page moments ago. Then I read my own scrawl and saw only its insufficiency. I could hardly read or understand the words, let alone grant them credibility, and ripped out the page to begin again with less impatience. For this castaway's message, I must first record my latitude and longitude, as well as I can discern them. That is, I must compose this recounting so it can be understood by one unfamiliar with any aspect of my life; unfamiliar, also, with this city and that district, because unless one has seen it first-hand, I doubt anyone could truly know what I do, with what sort of people I work, or in what sort of place I spend my days.

Our occasional visitors from Ohio or Indiana express astonishment at the excesses of the Barbary Coast, for which their wholesome towns have no equivalent. One Pennsylvania minister thought it an exact replication of Sodom and Gomorrah; another, educated in the fine arts, said it recalled to him the representations of Hieronymous Bosch. Even visitors from New York and Chicago, no strangers to squalor and depravity, express shock at what they see on their chaperoned carriage rides through the Devil's Acre—and this in daylight! Were they to witness it at night, as I do, their sentiments would be vastly amplified. (Even so, Deacon Skinner smiles as he recounts their responses, for he is pleased that a short carriage ride, with no other persuasion, begets such generous donations in support of Merciful Shepherd Mission!)

My duties at the mission occupy me every day but Wednesday and Sunday, beginning at one o'clock. By then I shall have completed the housekeeping, done the purchasing if I have not assigned it to Cook, completed my correspondence, given the gardener his tasks and the wash-erwoman hers, taken my lunch, and perhaps discussed Scripture with a group of other wives of the congregation. When these errands are complete, already dressed in the many layers a proper woman must wear, I cover myself with a mouse-gray, hooded cloak and leave the house.

There is a Pacific Avenue cable car, but I prefer the Union Avenue line, which is more direct and allows me to enjoy the steep downhill walk. If the weather is fine I swing my arms and raise my face to the sun, taste the sea-air, and delight in the broad freedom of the sky. When the wind is from the right quarter, it rises beneath my skirts and billows them wide, and I become aware of myself as a naked woman and take secret pleasure in it. I imagine the delight it would bring to wear just my skin, not only in the bath or in Hans's arms but in the sunshine, moving about freely. Then I chasten myself: What, are even my clothes a deception? Am I no different from the poor whores I care for, wanton and careless? Yet I cannot but think there are different kinds of nakedness; surely while some are corrupt and indecent, others are innocent and good: We are, after all, born that way and surely enter Heaven that way. But about these things I cannot speak to Rev. Wallace or any church member, not even to Deacon Skinner, though I know him to be a for-giving and fair-minded man.

I bear down the pavement in my broad skirt like some gray ship under full sail, and swing my arms as if I were a bird about to take flight. I skip, too, and frame in my mind mischievous arguments against the disapproval of the church matrons, were they to see me: Gravity bids me descend, Gravity is certainly the Lord's law; should I not surrender joyfully to it?

There is always something new to observe on these walks, because this is in so many ways an unfinished city. In the downtown districts, we boast fine public buildings and noble homes, orderly streets, and every system of public convenience. Yet here on the periphery, wherever one turns one sees new development, making of roads and civic places, houses being built. Industry is everywhere: digging, leveling, filling, streets furrowed as cable lines are laid, drays loaded with soil or building materials, the red-wood bones of buildings rising airily amid the clatter of hammers. Our neighborhood has only recently become a popular district, and many of the lots are still empty, or just now being dug for construction. Here is an open hillside still furred with its pelt of native grasses, brush, and wildflowers; here, abruptly, a solitary fine house in an island of perfectly tended garden, lawn, and paved walks; there, a row of several narrower houses built close upon each other, illogically, as if there were not expanses of untouched ground on all sides. It makes for a motley and ever-changing landscape.

At last I come to the relative flat of Union Street. Some days I pay my nickel for the cable car, taking great pleasure in the wind in my face, which sustains my illusion of flying. On other days, I meet Deacon Skinner, whose route brings him near and who comes with his carriage at our appointed time.

On this Tuesday past, he greeted me with, "You are looking especially lovely today, Sister Lydia," as he invariably does.

He has a twinkle in his eye as he says it, as if he knows some pleasing secret about me. At those moments I think that he, too, might guess my secret nature and accept it of me. If I am lovely and he is not just making a mischief, it is the walk down the hill, the flush it must bring to my cheeks, the wind loosening my hair from the tightest of chignons. I have just billowed down like a ship under full sail, have skipped and swung my arms and pretended to be flying, and the effects of doing so do not leave me immediately.

"And you look like Uncle Sam on his way to a funeral," I retorted. He is hook-nosed, long-limbed, and gaunt, and could be the very man from whom the caricature was derived, except for his attire which is very somber. (Tomorrow, I shall think of another witticism; perhaps I will press a nickel into his hand, tell him he has saved me the fare, he can give it to the poor.) He laughed and helped me mount the carriage, and then we trotted off to do the Lord's work.

To spare the horse the difficulty of Russian Hill, Deacon Skinner stays close to the shore, and there our conversation remains gay. But as we turn south and begin to approach our destination, we both grow serious. In a few minutes more, we enter the narrower streets and cannot help casting our eyes about for signs of carnage from the night preceding. More than once we have read in the newspaper of a murder that occurred near the mission, and then have seen the blood stains on the spot. In these circumstances, our talk turns quickly to philosophy, for that aloof moral reasoning offers a slight palliative for our grave concerns. And soon thereafter our conversation retreats to the last and only real redoubt, Faith, which, unreasoning, holds out and above a golden ideal of better things.

When he established Merciful Shepherd Mission, Rev. Wallace was determined it should be at the very center of the evil it was to combat. In this he certainly succeeded. The storefront once housed a seaman's supply store; then a brothel; last, a bunkhouse or doss-house for those indigents who could afford a few pennies for a pallet. It is a narrow, two-story wooden building among others like it, in an alley that joins at one end the larger streets and at the other weaves into a cramped labyrinth of lesser ways, where innumerable hovels are hidden between the blocks. It is one of many enclaves where the poorest women sell their services from shacks and rough men hawk grain spirits from carts or crates, where abandoned babies and corpses are regularly found in the street, and many other unspeakable things transpire. Though our building is freshly painted and our sign proudly announces soup and redemption within, during daylight it offers only a meager relief from the weary and sordid look of its surroundings. At night, when the darkness and fog fill this warren, it is more remarkable because its windows are the only ones that are lit; on either side, the occupants cannot afford gas or lamp oil, or prefer to conduct their affairs in darkness.

This is where I spend my afternoons and evenings, tending to the damaged and the faithless, the sullied and the worn, the sick and the lost. And there are so many! At times it strikes me that the world is a great, cruel grinder, into which are fed unblemished innocent children, and out of which coils and tumbles a terrible mash of broken, ruined lives.

Yet on Tuesday night late, though I had labored all day in this Hell's Kitchen, this Devil's Acre, I was not satisfied; as I do regularly, I went to conduct a secret business still deeper in this dark world. Hans and the church fathers admire my virtuous, selfless service to the poor, and it is true I care deeply for their plight; yet my devotion to the mission, like everything about me, is full of pretext and contrivance.

But now I cannot continue, for there is old Cook at the back door, banging and puffing as she trundles in with the milk and bacon, and I must go assist her.

22

IT IS JUST before dawn, and I am in the pantry with a lamp and my ledger. I am stunned with weariness, yet I have not been able to sleep for thinking about these last few days. I have fallen far behind in my narrative, for events outpace my sluggish efforts to note them.

Tuesday, by the time I set out into the night streets, I was exhausted from an especially difficult day at the mission. Sister Gertrude and I, along with Deacon Skinner and Rev. Smith, had struggled hard to feed the bellies and souls of those who came to us. Our work varies: At times, the mission seems a small, country church; at others, a dining hall; at others, a hospital. On Tuesday we had great trouble with a young whore from a nearby crib, whom I had sought out and brought to the mission. She had clumsily attempted to remove her unwanted baby, and her damaged womb unexpectedly began the contractions of labor though she was only six months along. We sent for Dr. Mahoney to attend to her in our back room, and we assisted him as well as we could while tending to our other business. Her screams were most heartbreaking, each shriek and plea eliciting a reciprocal ache in my own belly. After some hours the sound wore so on us that we began arguing over small concerns, dropping things, expressing impatience with the other unfortunates come for respite. When at last she went silent and Dr. Mahoney emerged from the back room, arms bloodied to the elbows, we all looked at him expectantly.

"The girl was lucky," he told us. "She will live. If infection does not kill her."

"And the baby?" I asked.

"Luckier still. He is dead." The doctor took himself to our front porch for the comfort of his pipe, too weary even to wash his red hands.

Immediately Rev. Smith picked up his Bible and hurried toward the back room, eager to seize the girl's remorse as an opportunity for her salvation. But I stopped him with a hand upon his arm. "Sometimes just to let be," I told him, "is the greatest kindness."

And though he looked at me strangely, he did refrain from tormenting her, and let her rest.

When it was ten o'clock, I wrapped myself in my cloak and ventured out into the dark. Rev. Smith saw me to Darby's carriage, as he always does, for after sunset no one is safe here, most particularly a woman. There was a thin fog, sliding through the streets like a vaporous serpent, and I did not mind, in that its concealing haze would suit my clandestine purposes.

Darby Jones is a simple man who is commissioned to deliver me safe to home from the mission. I pay him from my own purse, and generously, to make sure he knows where his best interests lie. Yet he is not complicit in my activities; he believes I have some legitimate errand, associated with my mission duties. We ride, speaking little, several blocks to the place where I dismount and he waits unquestioningly for my return.

And then I become submerged in the underworld. Hans would be outraged that I expose myself to such dangers, but so far I have been fortunate, and quick enough with my feet or wits to avoid injury.

Darby sees me enter the doorway of a linens warehouse where the mission does some business, where one light burns in an upper window and a solitary clerk works late. He does not know I exit immediately by a side door. I then walk alone for many more blocks, angling through secret alleys and gangways, hastening across the gas-lit streets, toward my real destination, which is on the edge of the even denser and more mysterious warren of Chinatown. Voices mutter from dim windows, or the noises of eating or fighting or sexual intercourse; I skirt dark figures sprawled in doorways, not knowing if they are drunken, drugged, or dead. The air smells of urine and bad cooking and other human smells, and sometimes of dead things or rotting vegetables.

Here my mouse-gray hooded cloak saves me, for it conceals my identity and to some degree my gender, and allows me to vanish into shadows and fog if the need arises. In those dark streets, every person is a menace to me, whether vagabond, drunk, hoodlum, madman—or, equally, policeman, businessman, minister, or city official. One kind might rob, kill, molest, or abduct me; the other might accomplish what I fear even more: discover me. Often when I see indistinct forms approaching, I am moved by an instinct of danger and do not sweep anonymously past but compress myself into a doorway or the shadow of a stoop, to avoid detection. Then I crouch, holding my breath, my heartbeat shaking me, and rue my situation in every way. Each time I pray to God and earnestly swear that if He spare me now I will go back home and never do this again; I will repent and become truly virtuous and proper and cautious.

And each time when the man or men are past, I recant every oath and vow, and so lie even to my Maker.

At last I come to a more brightly lit section, where sailors congregate and other rowdies take their entertainment. Here I cannot hide but must maintain the camouflage of a deliberate haste and aloofness, and given the drug-sodden state of the inhabitants of this place, I am quicker and can usually slide past before they react. I dodge fistfights and foul propositions, shouting matches between whores and the imprecations of half-crazed derelicts. Then I slip down one more dark gangway and at last through a battered door I know far too well. I enter a dim, smoke-hazed room where listless women lounge in their underclothes and where some rough man might linger as he makes his selection. Accustomed to my intrusion, the women look at me incuriously. If she is not among them, I step quickly up the stairs and walk down the hall with increasing trepidation to another peeling door.

Sometimes the door is open and I enter directly. Sometimes it is closed, and I wait uneasily outside. On Tuesday, I arrived just as a man emerged in a befuddled way, refastening his belt, followed by a gust smelling of poppy, whiskey, tobacco, and sweat. I went in quickly and shut the door behind me, startling the woman who was rinsing herself at the basin. The room has no windows and is lit by a smoky lantern on the bedside table, a soiled and yellow light. Its walls are thin, barely muffling the sounds of exertion on either side.

I appraised her closely to assure myself of her condition, and what I saw was this: a woman with large sagging breasts, colorless hair in disarray, some rag of a chemise pulled up at her shoulders, a wary and unwelcoming look in eyes that are far too world-weary for someone only four years older than myself.

On Tuesday, she looked me over in return, then thrust out her lower lip like a pugilist, grunted, and returned to her washing.

"Back already?" she cackled over her shoulder. "Someone might think you're starting to like the life."

I have learned to expect her surliness and distrust, and to ignore it.

"Look," I said, "I have brought you some things."

And I set out on the table the gifts I carried in the pocket of my cloak: a small waxed cheese, in the hope she will be nourished; a fine mother-of-pearl hair comb I thought she would find pretty; and a five-dollar gold piece that could relieve her of five men, if she chooses. I have concealed these expenditures in my household ledger, attributing their cost to other items and risking Hans's disapproval of my spend-thrift ways.

She looked with her customary contempt at my offerings, which she sees as tokens of condescension. But her fingers could not resist a light, quick caress of the comb; I was greatly pleased, and found that single gesture easily worth all the difficulty incurred to witness it.

For this is Margaret, my sister, the companion of my childhood, my only living relative in the world, and there is nothing I would not risk for her.

I do not visit her every night. She would not tolerate it if I did, nor could I stand to, for the harrowing walk and the time we spend together are wearing on me. But I have tried to see her at least once a week for all the years since I discovered her whereabouts.

At first when I found her and visited her, I would offer suggestions as to how she might extricate herself from her predicament: I would somehow purchase her freedom from the whoremaster, I would find respectable employment for her, get her schooled for some other trade. For each she had an argument. Perhaps I resumed contact with her too late, and the coils of her circumstance had already wrapped her too tightly. Most recently, she is enjoying the attentions of a lover named Percy; she has shown me his photograph, a dandy of a pimp who maintains various dubious enterprises, including a good business purchasing opium from the Celestials and supplying it to Whites in the Barbary Coast. He has made some arrangement with her whoremaster, so that he takes her dancing now and again; he also sells her poppy at a reduced rate, and refers custom to her—what more, after all, could a woman ask?

At times she says sadly that she would change, but it is too late, she has been branded by the life she has led, is soiled beyond redeeming; at others she argues that she has in fact made a choice to live this way, it is a gay and exciting life and a choice I would understand were I not so naïve and prudish. I cannot argue that point, but must grant her that illusion if it provides her with some strength. And she loathes my pity and compassion. We no longer discuss the remedies I dream up for her.

Yet I know she is in that terrible grinder, that she is being torn apart by its cruel mechanism, and there can be no end but a tragic one. So I visit her and bring her small things, so that there is one strand connecting her with a more wholesome and sunlit world; and, selfishly, to reassure myself that she is still alive, perhaps even has some slight advantage, even as humble as a small cheese, to help her endure. On Tuesday, when I looked at her, my ears were still full of the screams of the girl trying to give birth at the mission.

When she was done with her washing, she lounged on her bed wantonly, legs spread, as if to deliberately offend me, smoking. In the years since we've reunited, I have watched her mannerisms grow increasingly coarse, her voice becoming as rough as her complexion. It is from being so hard-used, and from so long among such rough associations; yet I also see her hardness as the vestiges of a stubborn pride, to which each person is surely entitled, and I will not complain of it.

"You'll get killed one of these times," she said. "If the hoodlums don't kill you, the dogs will. Or some Chinaman will catch you and you'll wish it had been the dogs instead."

"Dogs?" I was still standing, for I am reluctant to sit on the one wooden chair or otherwise touch anything here.

"Don't you read the newspaper? Just the other night, they got another poor bastard. Ripped him to pieces, I heard." She chuckled: "And too bad—he was a regular here."

I have often seen dogs in the district, stringy miserable curs feeding on garbage, but they are timid and scatter fearfully if approached.

"You won't scare me off that easily," I returned.

This amused her. I watched her smoke, and she watched me. Sometimes we get on well, but more often it is hard to find a starting place. If I inquire about her activities, she may see it as my deliberate attempt to expose her humiliations; if I tell her of my own life—the purchase of a pretty quilt, my work at the mission, some idea that has set my thoughts afire— she may see it as my asserting my superior virtue, or advertising the genteel pleasures of respectability. A noisier pairing commenced in the next room over, reminding me that the time was ticking away. I knew I must soon return to Darby, or he would get worried; Margaret must go downstairs, for if she did not return to duty her master would take his percentage from the money I gave her.

"Are you well?" I asked.

She shrugged. What I see is what she is, well or otherwise.

"Do you need anything?" I asked foolishly. "I was thinking—"

"Me?" She gestured with her cigarette at the four walls of her shabby room. "What more could I possibly want?" She found this hilarious, and laughed until a fit of coughing took her. She convulsed for a long moment, and afterward her expression had turned cruel.

"How about you?" she retorted. "Need anything?"

She meant to provoke me, and, being not unlike her in temperament, I provoked her in return: "Nothing but a sister who loves me as much as I love her."

My virtuousness angered her. "You've come to the wrong place, then. But go round the corner, third door on the right, there's a girl who specializes in that kind of service." She flicked her hand dismissively at the gold piece on the table. "Cheaper, too."

I was stunned by her callousness, but she was not done yet. She pretended to give me a horse-trader's appraising look, up and down.

"But no—you have the look of a woman who's getting what she needs for free. Getting it nicely from your giant Dutchie husband, are you? It's not often good, but when it's any good at all, it's better than Jesus, isn't it? I could teach you a few tricks, you know. Keep him quite happy."

I would not hear my husband insulted nor the Lord blasphemed. I opened the door to leave, speechless with outrage and sadness; even for her this was extreme and unkind. But when I turned for one last word, I was surprised to see her hard face fallen. She looked like a woman of fifty, not thirty. Suddenly she was groping in the drawer of the little stand next to her bed, and in a moment she brought out the clever wooden box, of Oriental make, that I have seen before. She fumbled off the top, spilled the contents onto the bed, and snatched at the sectioned pipe and the paper-wrapped ball.

"You are being stupid!" she blurted. She pinched off a piece of the tarry lump and began desperately rolling it between her fingers. "Your husband will find out where you go, and you'll have thrown away your one lucky chance. Or you'll get killed!" She blazed a glance at me. "You'll die in these streets and your last thought will be that it wasn't worth it. *I* wasn't worth it!"

At this a veil was pulled aside, and my heart truly broke. I understood suddenly that she shows me her cruelty and coarseness with the intent to ward me away, so that I do not come here and put myself at risk. My elder sister is protecting me in the feeblest of ways, the only way she can.

"Margaret, please," I began.

"Go away," she shouted. "You don't belong here! You're not my sister. Those are my sisters, downstairs!"

I was incautious on my return to Darby. Normally I possess excellent night vision, and by remaining watchful am usually able to see threatening persons before they see me. But on that night I stormed along heedlessly, blinded by tears, and did not see a pair of men until I was nearly upon them. They were crouched in the alley, bent over a prone figure and taking things from it, even pulling off its boots. Immediately, I stepped sideways into a gangway, where not even a window lit the ground. I should have been safe, but as I stepped back my shoe hit a bottle and sent it clattering.

"Hell's that?" a voice said. "I'll look," another said, and then I heard footsteps approach.

I fled deeper into the gangway. The buildings were three storied and I was in a long slot between them, with no visible place to hide. At the very end was an airiness indicating a small courtyard, but as I approached it I was horrified to see it cut off by a stone wall, perhaps ten feet high. The only refuge was a wooden stairway from the upper parts of the building, beneath which a last flight of steps descended from ground level to the cellar. I scuttled down into the blackness there.

I pressed myself against the wall directly beneath the slant of the stairs, wrapped my cloak around me, and brought one arm up to cover my face, all but my eyes. I was now in a cul-de-sac, a cement box perhaps eight feet on a side, with no place to run.

I stayed rigid with terror, praying most fervently and hypocritically for God's mercy. This is what I had feared on every one of my secret night-time walks, what I had avoided only by great luck all along; at last I was about to receive my due. The footsteps approached until the man's feet must have been inches from my face, for though I could not see them I heard the grit of particles beneath his soles. When he came around to the descending stairs, I could make out his dim, bulky form as he bent to peer into the deeper darkness.

For an endless moment his shape didn't move. And then he straightened and turned away. I heard him stroll along the wall and at long last make his way out of the gangway again. In my relief, I felt so faint I had to grip the rough cement to avoid falling.

I hated the darkness where I stood, the meaty, moldy stink there, yet I knew I had to give the men time to finish their business and move on. It truly seemed an eternity before I tiptoed up the steps and into the open, watchful, relieved to be out of the inky dark yet reluctant to leave its sanctuary. By then my eyes had grown accustomed to the complete absence of light, and now the tiny courtyard seemed brighter; light bled into the sky from the gas lamps several blocks away. I became afraid that the men would see me if they were to glance down the gangway again.

As I hesitated, listening anxiously, a sudden movement and noise exploded not ten feet from me. From the cellar stairwell came a scrabbling and scrambling, and then something burst out of the darkness. It came out of the shadows on all fours and I took it for a large dog: I saw the profile of its muzzle, and for an instant it swung its head toward me and I saw the dim flash of long teeth. It must have seen me, for it momentarily seemed to flinch or brace itself; then it scurried with astonishing quickness to the wall at the end of the alley. When it was reared against the stone wall, leaping and reaching to pull itself to the top edge, I saw the fully extended shape of its body and was amazed to see that it was more man than dog; and briefly, at the top of the wall, against the brighter darkness of the sky, I briefly saw its whole silhouette and knew it was neither man nor dog but something else unknown to me or to anyone.

From the instant it burst from its cover to the time it vanished over the wall was a duration of perhaps three seconds. By the time the shock fully struck me, it was already gone. The surprise, coming after the long minutes of frozen terror, left me weak and dizzy. I tottered toward the main alley, willing to risk the known dangers there in preference to the mysterious one back in the courtyard.

Only afterward did it occur to me that I had been crouched in that cellar stairwell with it, with him, for five minutes or more, unknowing, and that had he meant me harm, he could certainly have accomplished it. But he had held perfectly still and silent, just as I had. Though his profile and muscularity of movement were that of a predatory creature, it seemed to me he had checked his impulse to attack; in general, I saw that he had behaved like me—as if both of us were creatures in peril.

23

T HERE IS NO way to describe my actions but to give up and list my deceptions, lies, and contrivances. (Dearest Hans, if it is you who reads these words, I beg you to forgive me for my lies and for my hubris in defying you and all the customs of respectable society.)

First, as the castaway sending his message to a stranger on an unknown shore, I must say that, lest it seem unlikely that a virtuous Christian woman of good society have a sister like mine, it is the reverse that is really improbable. That is, what is more remarkable is that I am not like her, that anyone could have escaped those circumstances which prevailed in this forever-unfinished city.

Our father came, like thousands of others, in 1849. He was the n'er-do-well brother, fleeing the perpetual disapproval of his staid family in Mobile and determined to show his mettle by becoming richer than they through some luck in the gold fields. He came in a great wave of similar men to a hardscrabble outpost of a few thousand souls. Within two years, there were a hundred thousand such hopefuls here, all but a few disappointed, stranded far from their homes and hopes. In those early years, women were rare, perhaps one for every two hundred men; all but the tiniest proportion of those women drifted here, or were imported by shameless businessmen, for the purpose of meeting the sexual needs of the men. They came from small towns, or east coast cities, or Mexico or France, misled as to their real destiny, or desperate and having no good alternative, or forcibly abducted or coerced. Some came voluntarily to strike it rich where their services would be in much demand.

My mother was one of those women. My sister and I were two of the thousands of children that inevitably resulted from so much spilled seed.

Margaret was born in 1856, the year that the Second Committee of Vigilance made such a great upheaval and it seemed that California was in a state of insurrection; I was born in 1860. That my father lingered long enough with my mother to sire us both and to dwell even intermittently with us was perhaps the most steadfast act of his life. He was a weak man in every way. Unlucky or unwilling to exert himself, he drifted from job to job, scheme to scheme, throughout the towns and camps of the region. I am sure he and my mother loved or at least needed each other, or they would not have cast their lots together; yet when he could not earn enough to feed us, he was never reluctant to have my mother ply her former trade "to see us through." And when Margaret came into her maturity, he forced her to do the same. I am sure my turn would have come had he lived.

My father did only one other thing of any virtue, which was that he read newspapers, magazines, pulp novels, and books on mining or business or even history. He was, after all, from a respectable family, and had spent a year at university. Sometimes he read aloud, and he left his literature about so that, being bright and highly curious children, we learned to read. Thus Margaret and I at least grew up literate and with a glimmering that there was another world beyond our own tawdry circumstances.

For my first year of life, we lived in a mud-floored tent in the silver country, where my father thought he might strike it rich and where he again failed, and thereafter in whatever shack or tenement was available. What might have become of us I cannot say, but late in 1872, my father learned that his brother Franklin intended to move to San Francisco. Those were the years that a new sort of enterprising person was drawn by the prospect of fortunes to be made here, providing needed commodities to the burgeoning population. Franklin rightly saw the opportunity to make great profits in fabric and clothing sales in such a place.

When my father heard of his intent, he was both concerned and inspired: concerned that his brother would learn his true circumstances of poverty and unmarried cohabitation with a whore and her bastards; inspired by the opportunity to capitalize on his brother's respectability and industrious nature. He conceived a scheme whereby we would misrepresent ourselves to Franklin as decent people, with the goal of securing a loan (ostensibly to start a business) or a job in his firm. Motivated by this plan, my father read us the Bible, knowing Franklin was religious, and strictly schooled us in speech and deportment. He contrived a fiction of our proper lives and had us memorize its details. We sisters were thirsty for such stimulus and of course were of an age that we did not mind putting on airs, and we absorbed it all quickly. So that we could afford to dress appropriately to meet Franklin, my father put my mother and sister "to work." We were living in two rooms near the Oakland docks then. My sister was leased to a brothel in San Francisco, where the trade was brisker and, being young, she could fetch a better fee. My mother did her business at our apartment.

There is a great deal more to tell of this period, but this is a pathetic and painful recounting. It is almost impossible for me to write it down. I will hasten to the ending, which is both tragic and fortunate.

On the day we were to meet Franklin, my mother and father and I took the ferry from Oakland. The boat capsized near the San Francisco side, drowning sixteen people, among them my parents.

Ever curious, I had expressed interest about the operation of the vessel and had been invited to the pilot house by the kindly crew, and so was not at the railing with my parents. The newspapers have described in detail this famous tragedy, but I saw only my small share of it: I remember a sudden forceful thump, followed by a booming in the hull; then the floor canted abruptly and threw me against the pilot house wall. The port rail went under, and then the bulk of the ferry settled suddenly and sucked down those who had first fallen in. The crew helped me escape the listing hulk, and within moments boats sped from the docks to pick up the scores of swimmers and those who still clung to the decks.

So my parents died. And so I lived, and my uncle, instead of meeting his brother that day, simply inherited a ward: a girl of thirteen, an orphan with good speech and deportment, some knowledge of the Bible, and one brand-new but ruined frock.

My sister was not with us, as she was "at work" in the city. My uncle never knew she existed. It was ten years before I was able to find her again.

Oh, I cannot continue this. It will have to wait for another day.

Here are the ways I have betrayed and deceived everyone. This will be a terrible list, but it confronts me whenever I face these pages and I had best dispense with it.

I am the product of a sinful act between a weak and morally bereft man and a whore.

My sister is a depraved whore and an opium addict, and I love her and forgive her utterly.

I pretend to be a good woman of a fine home in Pacific Heights, yet I know the alleys of the worst sections of the Barbary Coast as well as any rat that skulks and skitters there.

I practice deception daily in my every deed, as when I dress in the petticoats and bustles and corsets that are expected of me and envy those whores lounging comfortably and shamelessly in their open wrappers and transparent chemises. Even so mundane a thing as my household ledger is full of misrepresentations that conceal surreptitious expenditures.

Hans, I cannot bear you any children because I sustained an infection of my womb that left me infertile from the age of eighteen; I am lying when I say I, too, hope and expect that we will soon start a large family.

Hans, I do not merely receive you when we engage in sexual intercourse; my ladylike passivity and seeming aloofness is a falsehood I adopt to act a woman of the class you imagine me to belong to; in fact I take great pleasure in the pressure of your powerful body upon mine and in your manhood, and I think about that pleasure inappropriately, even when I sit on the hard pews at church and feel your thigh against mine.

And that brings me to the worst of all my lies, those pertaining to my faith. I cannot, will not, deny that I am a person of faith; I believe absolutely in our Lord Jesus and in the acts of kindness we bestow in order to emulate his life and to relieve suffering. But I lie when I claim to accept the literal truth of Scripture, the strict moral admonitions of our church fathers, or the rigid habits and customs of our denomination. My demure and docile behavior is a lie; in truth, I am a willful and wanton spirit, rebellious by nature, disobedient, full of secret thoughts and longings. I have some corrupt or pagan strain of mind, for I see more of God in the sunset over the ocean or a blossom in my garden than I do in church, hear more of His truth in the creak of a cricket than in any of Rev. Wallace's thunderous sermons. I cannot abide the Thompsons and their ilk, in all their fine clothes and manners and blindered lives, their intolerance and haughty privilege. I do not condemn the criminals and sinners we minister to, only pity them. My husband and the church fathers believe my devoted work at the mission derives from a fervent desire to bring sinners to Christ; but in fact it stems from no such lofty aspiration, only a simple, heartfelt urge to relieve them of some measure of pain and misery, and to justify my regular presence in the Barbary Coast and thus provide a pretext to visit my sister. I do not believe in Satan, only in a single God who is vaster and more mysterious than we are willing to conceive, and whose intentions for us no man, no minister or saint or prophet, can claim to understand.

There, I have said it. I have written all the worst. I can hardly read my own word, my hand trembles with the expectation of some great punishment, some bolt from above. Yet though I would welcome it, none comes.

TUESDAY, MAY 21, 1889

No, no punishment came, only Cook, who startled me by appearing at the pantry door: I had been so immersed in my confessions that my attention had lapsed. I pretended my tears resulted from some irritant in my eye. I shut the ledger in an offhand way, told her I had already put water on, would she make the tea; she complained briefly of her toothache and trundled away.

I read my confessions and cringe. I realize to my horror how like my father I must be, to have become such an accomplished dissembler and schemer. And yet pouring it out has proved a relief, like opening the valve of the pressure cooker, letting the steam go; the danger of explosion is past. Afterward, I have felt a strange serenity and acceptance. Perhaps I am also like my sister and mother, far too flexible of temperament or morals. Inwardly, I make something of a shrug, as Margaret did, as if to say to God, "What you see is what I am." I suppose I am like her, willfully choosing, or claiming to choose, a shameful life.

174

But that long list has compounded my situation, in that I cannot tell anyone about the mysterious and fascinating creature. He is surely something rare and amazing, that might by his nature answer many questions we have so often considered in our religious discussion. At the very least, he lives a unique life and sees this world from a rare perspective, and I am very curious about him; yet circumstances prohibit my telling anyone, for there is no way to explain how I came to be crouched in a cellar stairwell in a gangway in that filthy warren at that hour, and so saw him.

By the week-end, I had not yet solved this dilemma, and in any case, though I half wanted to return to that gangway, Saturday and Sunday left no time for surreptitious errands. Saturday is the mission's busiest day and night, for it is when the district's enterprises are most active: men from the entire region come to find whores, sailors pour off ships and gamblers flood in to fleece them, and the saloons with their randy shows are full to overflowing. It is a time when those with any religious impulse at all are prone to sudden remorse and likely to appear on our doorstep, when already poor men gamble away their last cent and have nowhere else to turn. It is also when footpads are out in force, and their victims, along with those of the fist-fights, knife fights, accidental fires, and drunken falls, keep dispensers of mercy quite occupied.

Sunday is for church, a great relief: The somber, serene convocation in that big hall, on its placid street in the Western Addition, safely removed from the Barbary Coast, refreshes and reassures me. Afterward, Hans and I often entertain members of the congregation, and all is most proper and reverent and civilized—too much so, for me, by the end of the day. This Sunday we had the Schultzes and the Thompsons to dinner. The Schultzes are unassuming and kindly, but the Thompsons are stuffy and disapproving, and it was an interminable evening. Even Hans expresses some impatience with Mr. Thompson, but has derived lucrative contracts from their association and so feels compelled to endure his company. Among other things, Mr. Thompson harbors strong opinions about the Celestials, which he is not reluctant to express, so that I had to bite my tongue throughout our meal. And his wife is boring, which after some hours can seem a worse sin even than intolerance.

But on Monday I rode to the mission with Deacon Skinner, and conceived a bold idea that like so many of mine required deception.

"Deacon," I asked, as if it were an idle question, just banter, "what is your opinion of Charles Darwin?"

"He is a scoundrel!" he answered immediately. "No, worse—a minion of Satan. The only question is, witting or unwitting?" Then, scowling: "What prompts you to ask? You have surely heard my views a hundred times."

"Of course. But have you read his works?"

"I have indeed. I only recently finished *The Descent of Man*. Aptly named, I thought. Myself, I am distinctly in favor of *ascent*, thank you!"

He looked at me askance, knowing I was up to some mischief. Deacon Skinner is an avid naturalist, who has closely studied the flora and fauna of the Peninsula and has gathered and catalogued an impressive collection of specimens.

"So it is a flawed thesis?" I persisted.

"It is in direct contradiction of holy Scripture."

"Says the deacon and stalwart pillar of Good Savior Church. What does the naturalist say?" I maintained a small smile, as if unaware of how daring such a question was.

He was most exasperated with me, but soon became thoughtful and resigned. "Oh, Lydia," he sighed, "flawed or not, I cannot accept it. Step on that slope and I am afraid it will become an avalanche that bears all mankind down with it. Look at the wretches we tend to every day. Their aspirations are fragile enough, aren't they? Their hopes of better things? The naturalist, too, prefers to maintain a belief in divinity."

He had answered more candidly than I ever expected. In sympathy, I put my hand on his arm, and we said no more for a long time. We were nearing the mission when I spoke again, as if it had just occurred to me: "Deacon, last week a woman told me that she knew of a man in most miserable circumstances. He is elderly, she says, living in the streets, afraid to ask for help. Have you time for a short detour? She told me where he is . . . I am thinking we might find him if we go now."

In this deception there was little risk of discovery, for I am well known for seeking out unfortunates; Rev. Smith calls me his "scout," good at locating souls who have been prepared by desperation to receive Christ.

Deacon Skinner assented, and I pretended to recall the woman's directions uncertainly as I guided him toward that gangway. We found

Nottingham, turned, then came to the alley in which I had encountered the two men. This was too narrow for the deacon's rig, so he tied the horse with some uneasiness and we walked in together, Deacon Skinner looking stern and carrying his brass-headed stick prominently, though we did not encounter anybody.

"Perhaps here," I said when we arrived at the narrow passage.

I felt considerable anxiety about what we might find, but in daylight its aspect was somewhat different; the sense of menace was lessened, the air of squalor and pathos amplified. I had not noticed the buildings in the dark, but the one on the left was in fact empty, obviously fire-damaged, with its windows and doorways hoarded. We walked uneasily in the cut between, our shoulders brushing the walls on either side. At the end, the little courtyard opened, cut off by the wall, and the stairs came down just as I remembered.

Seeing it now, I realized that it would be a feat of considerable athleticism to leap and catch the top of that wall, and abruptly I became afraid that the creature might turn on us. My wish had been to have Deacon Skinner glimpse him, too, to gain both a naturalist's and a religious man's perspective, and so enlist his help in determining what this being was and what we as Christians ought to do. Thinking of the strength the creature had displayed, I became afraid I had brought dear old Deacon Skinner, knob-head cane or no, into grave danger.

But aside from refuse, the courtyard was empty. Deacon Skinner peered first into the cellar stairwell, and announced, "Well, here's his nest, that's for certain."

And when I looked in, I was shocked. I had pressed myself to the left wall, up into the shadows of the descending stair; only a few feet from where I'd stood was a pile of rags, clearly a spot where someone had slept repeatedly. There were bones of small animals, as if many meals had been taken there, and a few bottles arranged in a row. The door into the cellar was of thick oak planks, iron-bound and heavily padlocked, so he had not been somewhere inside; I had stood within inches of the creature all that time.

"Are you all right, Sister Lydia?" Deacon Skinner asked.

I had no doubt grown pale, and felt so weak I gripped his arm to steady myself. "Well, we have found the place, if not the man," I said. "It is a wretched spot to call home, isn't it?"

"We'll send a group to find him another time," Deacon Skinner said consolingly, mistaking my reaction. He turned me decisively toward the end of the gangway. "But now we had better get back to see if my horse has been stolen. Or eaten," he added darkly, glancing up at the hollow-seeming windows above us. "Or whatever they do with horses hereabouts."

WEDNESDAY, MAY 22, 1889

In the mission, speaking to those who come for spiritual nurture, we talk constantly of faith—the virtue and power of faith. I myself use the term, but realize that I mean it differently than Rev. Wallace or Rev. Smith do. We have the word to describe a form of belief that is acquired through insight, not through mere reason, and that is energized by passion. We speak of faith as an act of great courage, for with it comes the capacity to overcome immediate circumstances, to ignore the reasoning mind's observations and objections, if need be, along with pain, doubt, and temptation.

But I prefer mere hope. Hope is the real act of courage, it seems to me. To hope is to say, to admit, "I wish it could be so, I want it to be so, I can envision it so, I will auger for it to be so." It is not dependent upon any abstraction; it is not based on reason; it makes no claim to know any larger truth. It does not attempt to say, "This is how the world is; this is God's will," which must be forever subject to interpretation. Hope is to simply choose an ideal, by oneself, to want and to aspire; it is inarguable, because it is not some guess about something external, it resides immediately and palpably inside one's heart. It can be thwarted, denied, crushed; but its existence cannot be denied. Hope is thus more real, more honorable, and more courageous than faith. Hope is entirely one's own.

So I lie when I say I am faithful. It would be more accurate to say I am hopeful, deeply and irredeemably so. I hope my ministrations to others result in some relief of pain and sorrow. I hope mankind will elevate itself from its squalor and cruelty, and that my actions contribute to that elevation. I hope my sister will someday live a happier life in which she is not subject to such degradation. I do hope there is a plan for mankind and that it is a kindly plan, though I cannot claim certainty thereof. I hope I will always please and honor my husband. I hope I have not burdened old

Cook with too much work today. I hope in the long run kindness trumps cruelty, though I have no evidence it will.

Perhaps it was hope that propelled me to visit Dr. Mahoney yesterday. He makes a point of showing himself a cynical, jaded man; he drinks too much whiskey and is often surly. But he has chosen to keep his office in this district, and since there cannot be much money in caring for the residents here, I have always suspected he, too, is secretly a man moved by hope and is pursuing his own small mission in its service.

Early in my shift, I thought of an excuse to visit his office: We needed medical supplies. I walked the blocks to Broadway quickly, uncomfortable even at mid-day. The row where his office is located is comprised of saloons and shabby storefronts, and during the day a great many idle men lean against the clapboards there, spitting, smoking, and calling out crudely; though there is enough traffic that I did not fear outright attack, I was still anxious as I shouldered between them to Dr. Mahoney's doorway.

There are times when his office is thronged, but I was right in assuming that Tuesday at early afternoon would not be one of those times. Upstairs, I found his waiting room empty, and I sat for only a short time before his office door opened and his patient limped out.

I asked him for iodine, and we talked as he filled a smaller bottle from his store.

"Dr. Mahoney, I have an unusual question for you," I began.

"Now what would that be, Mrs. Schweitzer?" Dr. Mahoney comes from Dublin and retains a strong brogue; the tonsure of hair that remains around his bald dome is still red.

"Have any of your patients reported seeing a very strange person . . . a freak, perhaps?"

"What sort of freak?"

"A man who has many attributes of a dog."

I expected that he would scowl and say no, and from there I could ask questions of a medical or scientific nature, about whether such a thing was possible, or what afflictions might make it appear so. Instead, he looked greatly startled and fumbled with his bottles, dropping the smaller, which rolled on the table, splashing iodine like blood. Dr. Mahoney cursed awfully, found a rag, and began mopping up the stuff.

"What on God's green Earth would prompt you to ask that question?"

"Several people at the mission have mentioned seeing such a creature. It seems as if you have heard similar stories?"

"Yes," he snapped angrily. "There's a werewolf. It prowls from here to Chinatown and out to the docks and it kills men, ravages women, and steals babies for its dinner. If I am to believe everything I hear, I tended one of its victims myself! It is a wonder what primitive superstition will do to the mind, Mrs. Schweitzer, especially when augmented by the fumes of opium, or an excess of laudanum or absinthe. Or the late stages of syphilis."

As unlikely as it may sound, the idea of the creature being a werewolf had never entered my mind until that moment. I could not think of a reply and must have appeared dumbstruck, for Dr. Mahoney looked at me piercingly.

"Why I am so hot and bothered, you might ask? Because to a doctor superstition is a deadly enemy! It ruins more people than any disease. 'Seventh time is lucky, roll the dice once more and I will make back all I have lost.' 'This hex will keep me from all harm.' 'A woman cannot get pregnant at the new moon.'"

At that, he must have become concerned he had offended me, for he stopped his tirade abruptly and peered at me over the top of his spectacles with a guilty look. I was by then more desperate than ever to confide in someone, but I bit my tongue. He recovered himself and began filling the little bottle again.

"Yes, I can imagine," I said. "Oh, and gauze and sticking plaster as well. If you can spare it."

He stoppered the bottles and busied himself at his cabinets. "There are conditions that can make a person appear fearsome. A severe hunchback, for example. I had one as a patient in Dublin—the children would stone him. I treated a sailor whose face had been consumed by an infection that left him without a nose or upper lip, who was shunned and could no longer work because he was 'bad luck' to have on ship—whatever became of that one, only God knows. There are individuals given to growing an excess of body hair. There is even a skin condition that affects the teeth and causes them to take a sharp and conical shape, like a dog's. If there is any shred of truth to these rumors, it stems from something of that sort.

And if there is such a person here, he would seem a good candidate for the mission's mercies, Mrs. Schweitzer."

He handed me the supplies and I took them.

"Yes, in that we are in complete agreement, Dr. Mahoney. Please let me know if you hear more about him. Thank you for your trouble today; please put the expense on the mission account."

24

LAST NIGHT WHEN I came to Margaret's room she was with a man; the door being partly open, I had gone right in and surprised the three of us. I recognized him from his photo as her lover, Percy, a nervous and enterprising dandy in a cheap striped suit, high collar, and bowler hat. He was leaning against one wall while Margaret, fully dressed in decadent frills, worked at her hair with the comb I'd brought. Percy is a slight man, but has sharp features and over-bright eyes that convey utter ruthlessness, the sort of person who keeps a straight-razor or derringer in his boot-top. Margaret's eyes flared wide as she saw me, a look almost of terror.

"I'm sorry," I said, "I did not know you were with someone. I'll leave."

"No, stay," Percy said, eyes alight with curiosity. Then, to Margaret: "Who is this?"

"Just a nun from one of the missions," Margaret mumbled. She went back to preparing her hair. "Not now, Sister Lydia. We're busy."

"Some pretty special kind of nun," Percy said, shouldering himself away from the wall and coming toward me. "Who comes alone to a whorehouse in the middle of the night."

His eyes seemed to gauge everything about me in an instant. Before I could move he had reached out his hand and slipped the button loop at the neck of my cloak; taken aback by his assertiveness, I was too stunned to protest. When the cloak parted, it revealed only my ordinary clothes, yet I felt frighteningly exposed. I tugged it closed immediately, but he had seen what he wanted.

His eyes narrowed though his smile remained. "Without a habit, too . . . and a figure going to waste in a nunnery. Maybe this is the same 'nun' that brings five-dollar gold pieces to a dollar whore?"

"She's a bother. Don't worry about her," Margaret said.

Percy tossed his head, yawned and stretched, and now gave every appearance of disinterest. "Mag and I were just going out," he told me. "But I'll leave you two to your business. Meet me downstairs, Mag, when you're done with Sister Lydia. Make it quick."

He left, closing the door after himself. I wondered if he truly went away or just put his ear to the door, then decided I did not care: I was her sister and had prior claim.

The moment he was gone, Margaret rounded on me fiercely. "I don't want you ever to come here again! Didn't I make that clear last time?"

"Yes. But I can be just as stubborn as you."

"And bring grief to us both. You have no idea what you're doing. Get out."

I shook my head sadly. I took out of my pocket the little sewing kit I had brought her, a set of spools of thread of every color, good needles, and a fine, sharp scissors. I opened the box and showed her its contents, then left it on the table. She gave it barely a glance. She was gathering her things and putting them in her purse with the air of a woman in a hurry.

"What do you want this time?" she asked.

"Have you ever heard talk of a wolf-man or werewolf?"

"Sure, and every other awful thing. There are ghosts and gollums here, too. And there's far worse. Now, I have little enough time to call my own, and I'm going now. And so are you."

"What do people say?" I persisted.

"They say he killed that man two weeks ago. And the one before that. That it wasn't dogs after all."

"But what is he?"

"Some say he's the scion of some Nob Hill royalty, who changes over and comes down to feed where the hunting is easy. Billy Royal knows for sure he's a Chinaman, some perversion from the Orient, come uptown to eat White meat. People say anything. What do you care? You're safe in the arms of Jesus."

"But, truly, Margaret, I think I have seen him! He ran on all fours!"

"So what? It's what goes on two legs you should be afraid of."

She snapped the clasp of her bag and made clear she was ready to go out. Her cheeks were rouged with round spots, her lips red, eyes made dramatic with kohl, hair gathered into a clasp and falling heavily on one shoulder, figure pulled into a generous hourglass shape by her corset. I saw suddenly how a man of a certain type might find her very attractive: shapely and voluptuous, a knowing and ironic manner, her mismatched gaudy finery making her look half a fine lady and half a child waif or gypsy. Abruptly, I was moved by her, for reasons I cannot describe.

"You look so lovely!" I exclaimed. I could not help myself and put out a hand to touch the hair on her shoulder.

To my shock, she snatched my arm and clenched it so tightly her nails dug into my flesh. Through her teeth, she said into my ear, "You listen to me! When we go downstairs, do not speak to Percy. Do not answer his questions. Do nothing to attract his interest or attention or I swear to God I will scratch your eyes out!" With that she flung my arm away, pulled open the door so hard it slapped the wall, and stormed out.

Now it is late Tuesday night; I am weary from my shift at the mission and yet I am writing here in the pantry while Hans sleeps upstairs and Cook snores in her room. I have turned off all the gas and write by the one oil lamp so that I can carry it up with me when I go.

My sister's grip has left a line of little crescents in my skin, not so much painful as a burning reminder of distressing emotions. When I came down the stairs, she was on Percy's arm and they were at the door; he cast one bland glance back at me, his little smile cold beneath his moustache, and then they vanished into the darkness outside. I proceeded quickly through the gas-lit streets and into my alleys, frightened by her outburst, wondering what had prompted such intense emotion. She has told me Percy also entertains another whore whose company he enjoys and with whom she feels she competes; perhaps his crude compliment to my looks had set her jealousy afire? It is not utterly incredible, for like all sisters we battled for our parents' miserable attentions and have never quite lost that sibling instinct. And everything about her has turned base and crude; needless jealousy could be just one further expression of it.

Yet I cannot quite believe it is that simple. I realize as I think of it that in some way Margaret is right, I have always proceeded into the Barbary

Coast, and every district where the unfortunate congregate, with the assumption that mine was the actual and correct world, that my duty was to bring some light from mine into their sullied, savage, little one; that my circumstances and society, the lives of the good people of my church and those like them, are righteous and universally aspired to, while theirs are simple, base, and naïve. Given education and opportunity, I have assumed, not one of them would want anything but to emerge into the bigger, brighter, civilized world.

But hearing Margaret's urgency and authority as she gripped my arm, I suddenly feared that the opposite might be true: that my world is the smaller, the innocent, the transient one, the one built on illusion, a mere island in a vast, dark and turbulent sea. That there are ancient and inexorable workings and ways of mankind about which she knows, truths she knows absolutely, about which I have no understanding. It is a terrifying prospect; I feel the way a sailor must, when his ship is going down, feeling the ocean clutch at him and realizing for the first time its real depth and coldness.

Comes Hans's sleepy voice from the top of the stairs: "Lydia? Look at the time! Come to bed, *meine Liebling.*" And the thought of lying next to his warmth and strength in our safe place gives me some reassurance.

TUESDAY, JUNE 4, 1889

In the week since my last encounter with Margaret, I have been confused and undecided. I have gone about my business and maintained all my deceptions as I am accustomed to doing, yet have all the while been desperately pondering what to do with her. But no amount of pondering has moved me toward a decision or any understanding. I cannot solve the riddle of her behavior or her life.

Nor can I solve the mystery of the wolf-man. Whenever an opportunity has presented itself, I have asked the people at the mission about rumors of a strange freak or wolf-man, and have learned that he has been sighted here and there over some months. Each person claims some sure knowledge of what he is or where he comes from, but all their accounts are at variance. The best I can gather is that he is glimpsed in different places, always briefly, and that he is blamed for all kinds of misfortunes. It is mostly foolishness and superstition, Dr. Mahoney's bane; one old woman shook her head when I asked and told me it was bad luck to talk about him. I eagerly awaited the report of Deacon Skinner and the committee of church brothers who returned to the nest in the gangway, but they said it was empty and unchanged; having been discovered there, I suspect, the wolf-man has abandoned what was for a time his safe haven.

I have not taken the time to write here because beyond my concern there is no real news and my thoughts are endlessly repetitious and circular, not worth the ink it would require to record them.

THURSDAY, JUNE 6, 1889

I am in great upheaval and danger, and it is no one's fault but my own. In just two days, everything has changed. All my artifices are about to collapse around me, and I have nowhere to turn, no one to confide in or to help me. Only an hour ago I took Hans to me in our bed, I desperate for closeness and he full of manly passion; yet while he slumbers happily in the aftermath I have run downstairs to make this silent scream upon the ledger page.

I am an idiot. It has all come about as Margaret said it would, in ways I would not have suspected because I am a foolish woman and refuse to accept the darkness in the hearts of men and the strangeness of the world's ways. As if to further confound me, I am doubly mystified and troubled because I have seen the strange person again, the werewolf or wolf-man, under very different circumstances that cause me confusion and a different kind of anguish.

Yesterday, Hans had gone to Sacramento to explore an opportunity to expand his business there; it being Wednesday, I did not have a shift at the mission and was therefore at home in the late afternoon when the doorbell rang and the knocker pounded urgently. I hastened to the door to find Percy, Margaret's lover, standing on the step, twisting his hat in two hands, most ill-at-ease and unhappy.

"Mrs. Schweitzer, Margaret needs you," he blurted. "She asked me to come for you. If you could come at once, ma'am. I have a carriage."

"But what has happened?" I exclaimed. "Is she hurt?"

"Yes, she needs you. Just come quickly. I'll tell you as we go."

I ran to get my bag, into which I hastily threw a few things I feared I might need: gauze for bandages, iodine, paregoric. I snatched some bills and coins from the box where I keep household cash, and then ran to the door, not even taking the time to tell Cook I was going.

Percy took my arm and hastened me down the stairs and to his waiting carriage, a two-seater. We mounted and then were off in haste, down the hill.

"Should we get a doctor?" I asked. "The police?" I was so alarmed I could hardly think.

"She said just to get you. It's a bad situation, Mrs. Schweitzer. I'm sorry to bring bad news. But if we hurry it may turn out all right."

The carriage jolted and rocked so I had to cling to the board to avoid being thrown out. Percy worked the hill brake, then whipped the horse when we came to the flat. We turned east, toward the city center, narrowly missing a cable car, which rattled its bell in complaint. In the same way, we skirted other wagons and pedestrians, drawing angry looks; preoccupied by driving, Percy offered nothing more until I demanded it of him.

"Tell me what happened!"

"I'm not sure myself," he said. "I got a message and went to her. All I know is, she's afraid she's dying, and she needs to see you. She says she loves you dearly and wants you near. I'm just doing what she told me."

We drove on breathlessly, my mind full of terrible imaginings. To my surprise, we did not turn south toward her place of work but on Bay Street continued east. We rolled past drays loaded with shipped goods, and then came close to the bay shore and the old docks, where the city slopes down and falls away. To the south, closer to Market Street and the steam ferry docks, the piers are newer and very active, but at this end they are smaller and in poorer repair, and many of the boats moored are old sail ships, some out of commission and abandoned. Coming toward the waterfront, one passes poorhouses and shanties, then some warehouses, and then the broad frontage where cargo is stored as it is taken off ships. The quay appears as a maze of piled crates, bales, stacks of lumber, a few tiny shacks and roofed sheds, cut randomly with avenues just wide enough for wagons.

I had never been to this section, but Dr. Mahoney once told me it is called the Morgue by the police, a dark joke, because dead men are so often found here. Some are killed at the place, while others are brought by their murderers, to be tucked under cargo or among crates where their bodies are not found until the goods are moved or the smell alerts some stevedore.

"What could she have been doing in this place?" I exclaimed.

"God only knows, ma'am. I'm sorry. But we're only a minute away."

Percy slowed the horse and brought us onto the quay, then into the labyrinth of crates and bales. Near the inland side, we passed a rough man who sat on a tall stack of raw lumber, whittling a stick with a big knife, who lifted his chin at us as we passed. Farther in, we passed another man, walking quickly out; otherwise the avenues of the quay were deserted but for a gull or two perched atop a stack or an occasional stray cat. The sun was still above the western hills of the city, but low enough to fill the avenues with shadow. Percy chose his way carefully, pausing, then deciding, until we were deep among the stacked goods, mostly lumber in long boards and beams of irregular length.

He stopped the carriage at an intersection of lanes. It was silent but for the panting of his horse and the faint slap of rigging against masts I could not see over the stacks. I looked around for Margaret.

"Where is she?"

"Well, let's talk about that," Percy said. "This seems like a good place to talk, doesn't it? Quiet and private?"

His tone confused me, and when I turned to him I was astonished at what I saw. No longer was he flustered and anxious, but suddenly self-possessed and sharp-eyed again.

"What do you mean?"

"You," he said deliberately, "are a woman who has gone a long way out a very slender limb. And I'm guessing it'd be worth a good deal to you to climb safely back in."

"I have no idea what you are talking about! I think you had better return me to my house this instant or my husband will—"

"Will not know you're gone until he returns from Sacramento, tomorrow afternoon or evening. Don't waste your breath, Lydia. You're a whore's sister, and you're the daughter of a whore, and you don't want your husband to know about that. And do you think your church community will embrace you when they hear about your night-time activities? There's a lot of room for misinterpreting. So you have a lot to lose."

I started to bolt from the carriage, but he caught my arm so hard it seemed I felt my bones creak.

"We're in a quiet little spot here. The men you saw are with me. The dock patrol has been paid to be elsewhere and to be deaf and blind in any case. No one can help you, so you'd better do what I say. What you're going to do is, you're going to make a bargain with me on what it's worth to keep your house and husband and marriage and fine upstanding reputation. I would think that's worth a good deal."

"I have no money! My husband manages all the money!"

"But you're so clever—look how much you've hidden from him already! You can manage to pry some free, I'm sure."

"You can tell my husband anything you please! He won't believe you."

"I thought of going to him first, you know—maybe bringing Mag with me so he could see the resemblance. He would probably pay nicely to keep the world from knowing what he married."

"He would strike you down on the spot!"

Percy tipped his head side to side, doubtfully. "More likely to strike you. For making a fool of him in front of the whole world? Probably ruining him? He would be justified."

I opened my mouth to reply, but then felt a terrible doubt. I have rarely seen Hans angry, but then he glowers so that his face turns as black as his beard, and I have known him to take stern measures with his employees. As for the members of my church, too many are like the Thompsons, and they would never tolerate me again. It is their way to construe the moral impoverishment of women like Margaret as an inborn trait that runs with the blood, not a tragic accident of circumstances; were they to hear of my visits to that brothel, especially given a suggestion from Percy, they would readily believe I was in the trade myself, through some corrupt taste or proclivity. Every strange word I had uttered, every variance from doctrine ever expressed, would be remembered as proof. I do not know how long Hans would resist this same conclusion, or how long his business could endure the gossip of his community.

Still, I could not bear Percy's plotting, and would almost endure the shame and loss just to deny him his goal. Feverishly, I tried to think of a way to defy him, to escape and somehow gain the upper hand.

"I will never give you anything."

Percy shrugged and looked around us, the branching ways between stacks, with some satisfaction. "You know what they call this place?" he asked.

"Yes."

"Good. Listen, Lydia, I'm a lazy man. I like things easy. If you make this too hard, if you convince me there really is no hope of a goddamned deal, I'll just kill you. It wouldn't be the first time." He turned toward me with an expression of such reptilian coldness, such ruthlessness, that I could not doubt him. "Don't ever push your luck with a lazy man."

At that I broke into tears of despair. There seemed no way out. I loathed Percy's oily, dapper, venomous presence on the seat beside me, the trap he'd lured me into so easily. There could be no limit to the perfidy of a man who would use Margaret like this, someone for whom he should have held some affection, or to exploit a sister's love, for such ends.

Then it occurred to me that there could only be one way for Percy to have learned my name, my residence, my husband's name and work: Margaret must have told him. The thought of her complicity broke my heart into a thousand pieces. Abruptly I was that sailor again, drowning on the dark sea, not realizing until too late its merciless depth.

Percy gave me time to work this through in my thoughts. Not far above us a gull hovered against the wind, orange-lit in the lowering sun, looking down at us curiously, as if wondering what strange creatures these could be; then it let the wind gust it away.

We are such paradoxical beings. My helpless sorrow was so extreme that, with the gull's lifting and vanishing, my emotions suddenly reversed, the way laughter can suddenly give way to tears or tears to laughter. In another instant all I felt was an angry, diamond-hard resolve to die rather than let this awful man have any satisfaction from me.

I wept more piteously, and groped in my bag. "Please! Take anything! I have a few dollars here. I have a brooch of some value. Just let me go. Please! Let this whole thing pass and I promise I will say nothing to anyone. You needn't fear that I—"

"Tomorrow we meet on Market Street, and you've got a thousand dollars with you. You can go to the bank first, or you can bring your jewelry—I'm sure your uncle left you something nice. If you don't show, we can do this ride again and I can be more persuasive. Or I can visit your husband's office with this news. Or maybe just go straight to Reverend Wallace and tell him a tale that will curl his collar stays."

I pretended to be too upset to hear him and continued groping in my bag. I came out with some coins and bills and thrust them at him, then reached into the bag again as he greedily counted them. My fingers found what they sought, and when I brought my hand out, it was with the iodine bottle clenched in it. I quickly pulled the stopper and flung the stuff at his face.

He screamed like a woman as he put up his hands up to claw at his eyes. The horse half-started, but in that instant I hurled myself out of the carriage, fell, recovered, and ran into the nearest cross-avenue. I scurried along the line of stacked crates and then turned into a narrower way between two piles of raw boards three times the height of my head. Behind me I heard him cursing murderously, and knew that if his earlier willingness to kill me had been exaggerated, it was no longer.

My one thought was to head inland, to some point at which I might slip into the streets or find myself among a crowd of people with whom I could plead for help. But I heard Percy's shout behind me, apparently calling to one of his confederates, and then the noise of his boots as he jumped from the carriage. I turned into a crevasse between a line of crates, edged my way deep in, then saw a man's form cross the other end. I went at a right angle, ducked under the overhang of stacked boards, turned again, trying to find some place where no one could see me. I had no idea of the landscape beyond what I could see before me at any moment. It seemed a treacherous and random maze.

Percy, in his rage, uttered murderous curses, and his hard boots made a solid footfall. As I scurried and ducked, always trying to keep some pile between us, I heard another set of footsteps arrive and a few low words exchanged; then I knew the other man had arrived. I was sure that if they could not find me outright they would think to block my way to the west, where the city would provide me with better refuge.

So I began to work my way south. I took off my shoes so that I would not make any noise, and crept stealthily between stacks. At intervals I would hear one of them and wedge myself beneath some overhang of boards or into some crack between crates. After a few minutes of this deadly hide and seek, too afraid to continue, I found a particularly deep overhang where the longer boards had been stacked upon the shorter. I crowded myself back under them and into the furthest shadow. Once there, I ripped the lace from my sleeves so that no trace of white would betray me, and tucked my skirt around my feet. I wished desperately I had worn my cloak.

And there I crouched, terrified almost to death, certain they would soon find me. But though I sometimes heard them close by, their passing came at longer and longer intervals. Within another hour it had gotten dark, and soon it was black in the cleft where I hid.

Still I was afraid to move from my place. I was hunched into a little cave of raw boards, surrounded by their woody scent which on every other occasion I have thought among the most lovely in the world and which I now loathed. I knew that having failed to find me immediately, they would patrol the first quayside street to watch for my emergence. So I resolved to stay put. I wept and prayed continuously to God for forgiveness and mercy; not in any faith or belief it was deserved, but only in hope that, just one more time, it might be forthcoming.

At length a fog drifted in and further decreased the likelihood I would be discovered. The distant noise of the steam ferries ceased, to be replaced by foghorns out in the Golden Gate. Hours passed, and in my exhaustion, my head began to bob.

I awoke suddenly when it seemed a brilliant light was cast upon me. But when I opened my eyes, I realized it was only the early dawn, the first brightness of the eastern horizon lighting the ways between the stacks. I had spent the entire night there, and felt badly chilled and cramped; but I had lived.

I was about to straighten my aching legs and crawl out when I saw a slight movement not far away. Abruptly I saw that there was someone crouching in the shelter of another stack of beams, diagonally across from me. I almost choked on my own heart, for it seemed to jolt out of my chest. It was the creature from the gangway, the wolf-man.

Clearly he was not aware of me; I must have been asleep when he arrived, and with the wind from the west my scent was being carried away from him. He had settled into a niche like my own, and he appeared comfortable there, as if somewhat habituated to the place. The light was young and indirect, but was enough that I could see most of his anatomical form except where boards blocked my view. He did indeed appear to be half a man and half a wolf or dog: he sat with short, rounded upper legs bracing lower legs far too slender, and short feet more like paws. His arms were like a man's but his fingers clumsily short and thick. Most strange was his head, which was marked by the long muzzle of a dog but lacked the pointed ears of a wolf; I could not see whether he had human ears, however, because his hair was long and he had a dark beard that covered his chin. Yet his face was not hairy except in the normal places a man grows hair, and his arms were mostly clear of it, showing skin of a pale color. As I watched, he lifted something to his mouth with both hands and gnawed on it with his fearsome teeth. A flutter of white feathers revealed it to be a gull, no doubt fresh-caught.

I froze with fear and plummeting spirits, realizing I had escaped murder at the hands of Percy only to face some unimaginable horror far worse. I recalled the terrific energy he had displayed as he'd swarmed over the wall and knew that if he saw me now, he could cross the space between us in a single second.

Then a most curious thing happened, and despite all the terrifying and preposterous events of those hours, it is this moment that returns to me more forcefully than any other. From a gap between beams came a young cat—a kitten really, not long from its mother's teat. It came toward the wolf-man's place as if oblivious to him, and I was certain it would be snatched and eaten. But instead, it approached gaily, playfully, and he greeted it in kind, with a gesture of his misshapen hand that revealed familiarity and every attitude of pleasure and fondness. In a moment, the kitten was in his lap and he was caressing it; it rubbed its cheek against his chest. The wolf-man offered it a morsel of meat, and the kitten gladly ate one tidbit after another from those stubby fingers.

The sight had a profound effect upon me. The display of this simple kindness and fraternity came at a moment when all the world seemed bent on doing ill, when it seemed the world capable only of cruelty, violence, and deception. This act of gentleness, so surprising and unanticipated, brought tears to my eyes. The wolf-man acted as though he was the kitten's friend and fellow; or, the way any man might be affectionate with his pet.

I watched for several minutes, still in terror yet mesmerized, presented with a palette of such diverse emotions I could scarcely accommodate them. When the kitten had eaten its fill, it groomed itself as the wolf-man nuzzled it affectionately with his snout and then used his hand to stroke its fur. His fearsome and deformed countenance was composed in an expression that I can only call contentment.

And then I heard voices and footfalls. I started and turned to look toward the sound, and when I looked back, the wolf-man's eyes were straight upon me. His nostrils flared, scenting for me, and then he scuttled away in a blur. In half an instant there was no sign of either wolf-man or kitten. I crammed myself farther back into my niche, and immediately saw two Celestials striding purposefully toward the piers. From their lithe movements and the queues wrapped around their heads beneath slouch hats, I knew what they were: *boo how doy*, the feared bodyguards and assassins who work for the Tong chieftains. In a few seconds they had passed, and there was the mandarin himself, a small man in traditional tunic and cap and slippers, all richly-embroidered, walking boldly down the center of the aisle; and behind him, again, two more baleful *boo how doy*.

They passed and were gone toward the docks, and the moment I could no longer hear them I crawled out and ran. There was some risk in this, but I would far rather encounter even the most criminal Celestial and his hatchet men, for whom an attack upon a White woman would risk terrible reprisals and persecutions, than Percy and his like.

It was only dawn, and I escaped the docks without incident. Once in the streets, I put on my shoes again and did my best to straighten my clothing and hair and pretend to be ordinary; I walked south until I came to civilization and was able to catch the first cable car of the day. I slipped into my own house like a thief, and old Cook, in the kitchen, gave no indication she heard me. When I came down after changing my clothes and washing, she had a tidy breakfast waiting for me.

"Haven't you slept in, sleepy-head!" she chided me good naturedly, pleased that for once she had risen before me. And I was so grateful to see her old face and dumpy form, there in her apron at the stove, I could not help but give her a heartfelt kiss, despite the turmoil in my heart.

25

I HAVE SPENT THE last days in an agony of anxiety. At any moment all that I have, my house and the respect of my community and the love of my dear husband, might be taken from me. Either Percy will reappear and abduct me again, or he will make good on his threats and go to Hans or Rev. Wallace with tales of my misdeeds, both real and contrived by him to assure the greatest injury to me: that on those nights I visited my sister I also whored and partook of the poppy and who knows what else. I am certain that though his scheme began with mere greed as its motive, he will now be moved to avenge himself upon me for having hurt him and escaped him, and will not hesitate to do his worst. I would go to Margaret, but I am too afraid she has willingly betrayed me, or truly does not wish to ever see me again; and yet I constantly worry for her well-being. It is an intolerable situation.

At moments, despite these preoccupations, my thoughts also turn to the wolf-man: what a wonderful and strange thing he is, what we might learn from him. Seeing him with that wild kitten struck me with the force of a revelation. Perhaps it was only that I was so desperate at that moment, expecting only violence and evil, and the sight of his momentary gentleness so directly contradicted my dire expectation. But I also wonder if such a creature, so savage in appearance yet capable of such kindness and camaraderie, might not teach us a great deal about our own paradoxical nature, and how to make better of it.

And, too, I feel concern for him. He lives as an utter outcast, a stranger amongst every specie of being, and in circumstances as perilous as can be imagined; there are a thousand ways the world could abuse him. Clearly, he has survived by fleeing from temporary nest to temporary nest, always at risk of discovery and injury. With his hideous outward appearance, I could not doubt that any man might shoot him on sight, especially in that he was accused of every awful thing that happens; or that those of a certain strain of mind would see him as a spectacle worth a fortune if exploited properly. It is a miracle that he has survived this long.

FRIDAY, JUNE 14, 1889

Three more days have passed in this unendurable tension. My script is almost illegible . . . my hand trembles. I cannot eat or sleep; every knock at the door, every man who appears on the mission steps, every carriage in the street, sets my heart racing so that a sweat comes out all over me. Here it is, I think, my doom: Percy, returned to destroy me. When Rev. Wallace visits the mission, I watch his face with apprehension, afraid I will see the iron mask of disapproval there, the building wrath and accusation that will any moment be unleashed against me.

I can no longer take pleasure in my walks, for I am afraid that dapper, striped suit and weasel smile will materialize in front of me; even on the busy commercial streets, I gasp when a horse like Percy's appears, or a man of his build or bearing.

At home it is no better. When Hans comes through the door, I am all but paralyzed with fear that he will have heard from Percy, and that he will march straight to me, pick me up by my scruff and throw me into the street. And when he only appears his ordinary self, whether affectionate or tired, preoccupied or businesslike, I watch his face for signs that he has received the awful news and is concealing the fact as he contemplates how to respond.

In my mind I form all kinds of explanations, pleas, arguments, excuses; I imagine myself indignant and denying everything; or, admitting it, wretchedly repentant or steadfastly defiant. But not knowing precisely what Percy will say, or invent, or what role Margaret will have played, I cannot imagine a response that seems adequate. I am somewhat mystified as to why Percy has not already acted on his threats, and at moments indulge a wild, irrational hope that he has just decided to let it pass. That lasts only an instant, until the memory of his bright, calculating eyes comes back to me, and then I know that the delay is only because he is plotting his moves carefully for maximum effect; perhaps he is even drawing it out deliberately, knowing and savoring the misery it must be causing me.

And when I am not knotted with anxiety about this, I worry about Margaret, whether she is well, what will become of her. From my mission work, I know all too well what happens to whores as they age, as their market value diminishes, as disease and the violence that surrounds them eventually destroys them. Some few do make a break from that life, or succeed so dramatically that they become financially independent, but Margaret is not likely to do either. Does she not see the toothless, haggard, wretched women, reduced to begging and char-work, dying young, or just disappearing suddenly, all around her? I fret about whether I should visit her again, and what to say to her if I did. At one moment I resolve to visit; at another not; at one I am furious with her for what Percy has done, at the next unsure how much a hand she had in it; at times I think of closing my heart off from her forever, then a moment later am sure I would die were I to try, or ever lost my sister again for any reason.

And, such being my penchant or habit, I have conceived another urgent reason to go to my sister. For it occurs to me that she might not be so debased as to have set Percy upon me; it may be that she was in some way coerced to her complicity. Perhaps her agitation at my meeting Percy was out of concern for me, fearing that he would conceive some such scheme. This possibility fills me with hope, and the question has taken on a great significance for me. At times I think its answer might present me with a larger truth about my own kind, one that will lay to rest either my worst fears or my fondest hopes. One or another must be shed, I am beginning to think, for I truly doubt my heart can endure two such conflicting sentiments, such uncertainties, in such extreme degree.

On Wednesday, I spent the evening at home with Hans, a rare thing as our lives go now. We made ourselves comfortable in the sitting room, I with some needlepoint and he with his newspaper. At one point I looked up from the mess I was making with the thread to see him with his paper lowered, dark eyes on me in a way I took to be accusing.

I thought he would begin the terrible process, but all he asked was, "Lydia, are you well?"

"Yes, of course!"

"But your hands are shaking. And your cheeks are hollow; you haven't been eating."

"Oh, it's nothing. I'm a little under the weather, I suppose. That's all. No appetite."

He came to where I sat and put a hand on my shoulder. I flinched from the touch. He is such a large man, and with him towering over me I could feel the strength in his body, like some great engine, and wondered at how that strength might be used or not, contained in civil gesture or not, and what force or choice within him directed it to one end or another. What is it in any man, where in him is the organ, that makes that choice? I thought of Percy's words, that Hans would strike me, and wondered if he would. I could not be sure. The pressure of his hand on my shoulder was heavy even with an affectionate touch, and I knew I could never bear to feel that enormous weight or force turned against me in anger. I hid my needlepoint, lest he see what a tangle I'd made, and raised my eyes warily to his; but he was already looking across the room, his thoughts elsewhere.

"Well, you must take better care of yourself," he said. "Can't have you getting sick."

"Hans," I said, greatly surprising both of us, "do you love me?"

He looked back to me with puzzlement in his dark eyes. "Haven't I sworn to always love you, before God and in the presence of our community?"

"But what does the word mean?"

At that, he crouched down next to my chair, so that our eyes were almost level. "Have I been unkind in some way?" he asked.

"No, never once!"

His concern eased. With his thick black hair and heavy beard, his face so often appears stern, but now he only looked benevolently curious and amused.

"So you are in a philosophical mood," he said.

"I suppose I am." In fact I was suddenly on the verge of confessing everything to him, I yearned to do so and so face the consequences and have it done with, just to escape this harrowing waiting and anxiety. I suppose I wanted him to say then that he loved my secret heart with his secret heart and that nothing I could do or say, or that the world could do, would ever precede or obstruct such love. Yet I could not begin it. My heart was wrung as I realized I did not know my own husband's nature well enough to know how he would respond.

He returned to his reading, and, unsettled, I went to tend to the silver in the dining room. From there I glanced covertly at him through the doorway. There was Hans in his accustomed spot in his big chair, beneath the gas lamp, reading. His spectacles only partly concealed his frown as he read something that displeased or irritated him, and in every way he appeared a forbidding man: huge, dark-bearded, heavy-browed, massive of limb, deep of voice, stern of manner; a man of exacting standards. I thought: I have taken this man to my naked self, to body, heart, and very life; at moments he displays the greatest sweetness and tenderness; how could it be that I am not sure of him, that I cannot claim to know him or trust him? How can it be that I fear him, even, my own husband and lover?

And, uninvited, the memory of the wolf-man and his kitten came suddenly to me: the astonishing surprise and relief of encountering such benevolence in such a savage creature, and all the thoughts the vision had prompted. Oh, how I would welcome such a gesture to me, at this moment! It occurred to me that if I can extend to the wolf-man the hope of humanity, surely I can do the same for my own husband! I am without an ally in my terrible predicament, but I think I must find one, and soon; what better place to seek an ally than under my own roof?

I think: Hans wooed me, and I accepted him. Perhaps it is time, now that we are married two years, that I wooed him in return. Mine will be a very different courtship, not so cordial and gallant as his; for in courtship one generally poses and flourishes, charms and flatters, presents one's best face, wit, and manners; it is a stage-play of benevolent exaggerations and misrepresentations enacted upon the parlor floor. Whereas mine will have to begin with the truth. It will, I am afraid, be a difficult conquest to make.

III

ANATOMY OF A WEREWOLF

26

THURSDAY MORNING AT City Hall provided Cree with another series of very minor findings, long shot possibilities, and outright disappointments.

Trying to find out more about Hans Schweitzer and Lydia Jackson, she stopped at the Bureau of Records and Statistics, where the clerk told her that their birth and death records dated only from April 1906; earlier records had been destroyed in the quake and fire. Same with marriage records. Same with autopsy records. However, religious groups maintained their own records of births, deaths, and marriages, and many of those had survived; it all depended on whether the church in question had burned or not. Given that Cree didn't know whether Hans or Lydia had been religious, let alone what denomination they'd embraced, it didn't sound like a promising tack.

She moved over to property records. She knew Hans had owned the house until 1914, well postquake, so if he'd bought another place within city limits his name should show up in surviving records. She did find the deed that transmitted the house to O'Brien—as she'd suspected, Schweitzer had attached a provision binding the now-vacant downhill lot with his property in perpetuity—but no Hans or Lydia Schweitzer appeared at any other location in 1914 or the years following. She skimmed tax rolls for fifteen more years and didn't find Hans. He could have rented, relocated to Oakland or to Istanbul, or died while on vacation in Tuscany or Tahiti. There were lots of Jacksons, but no Lydia; she could have divorced and remarried, died, or moved to Zanzibar.

Cree's frustration mounted. She might never find the descendants the Schweitzers might or might not have, let alone any records they might or might not have left them, which might or might not mention the wolfman.

The morning's only real accomplishment was that she finally reached Gerald Payson and managed to wrangle an afternoon appointment to check out the Payson Collection's archives. That left a few hours for a more direct, if long-shot, search for the wolfman: the newspapers. She walked back to the New Main Library and laid claim to one of the microfilm cartels on the fifth floor, not far from the wall of gray steel file drawers that housed the newspaper film archives. She set up camp with a small thermos of coffee and a bagel with cream cheese secreted in her purse.

She pulled spools for the *San Francisco Chronicle* and *Call-Bulletin*, randomly choosing five years scattered through the period the wolfman had most probably been alive. But then another errand occurred to her.

The *Chronicle*, late summer, 1981. She found the first reference on August 12, one paragraph detailing the apprehension of five "juvenile gang members" for a grocery stickup. A few days later, three inches about TEEN OFFENDER CHARGES POLICE BRUTALITY. The article didn't offer any details she hadn't already gotten from Ray.

She didn't find another reference until mid-October, RAYMOND FILES CIVIL SUIT. This one included a photo of Ray, apparently a high school yearbook shot from before the injury. He was what she and her friends used to call a "dreamboat," the type whose name they'd write in ballpoint on their palms so they could sneak looks at it during classes and give themselves goose bumps: a handsome, thoughtful-looking boy with wonderful eyebrows, an innocent masculinity.

The last article was about Bert's acquittal, which featured a posttrial photo of Bert in a roomful of cops. He had just been exonerated; he should have been happy, and the other cops certainly looked gleeful, *score one for the good guys.* But Bert wore the face of a man who had seen hell close up and was still being chased by its monsters.

She rewound the spool and put it away, trying to decide what to do. She could be up front with Bert about Ray, tell him that's who was sending the e-mails, tell him it was a symbolic gesture; urge him to forget the murderer-who-got-away idea. Or, she could keep quiet about Ray in the hope Bert would never connect him with the messages and the whole thing would just peter out. Without any new messages arriving, maybe Bert would get distracted by other obligations, and they could move on; at some point, she and Skobold would figure out the wolfman bones, so that immediate catalyst would be removed.

She puzzled over it for a time and finally decided that right now her best option was to do the job she was here to do. She did her best to put the problem out of her mind as she threaded the film for 1866 and began scanning.

Nothing relevant jumped out at her, but then she wasn't really expecting anything. This was more like flying over the countryside in an airplane, getting a general idea of the lay of the land.

It was slow going but entertaining. There were articles about the post–Civil War Reconstruction out east, about the fortunes of various mining companies, about the Central Pacific Railroad, about corruption at City Hall, about mounting tensions between Chinese and whites and the anti-Chinese legislation pushed through at the state capitol. The Barbary Coast made the news in various ways: murders were committed, ministers and missionaries launched doomed campaigns against vice, the Board of Supervisors was badgered to act on crime, morality, health conditions, or municipal services. The journalistic style of the era was histrionic, opinionated, with a tone sometimes florid and sometimes snide; even the ads were fascinating, hawking all kinds of outrageous products whose virtues were extolled in fancy typefaces and intricate line drawings. The personal ads were astonishingly like today's, full of secret assignations, coded love notes, lonely hearts calling out.

Cree got her first possible hit in the 1876 spool in a minor article about Golden Gate Park. The planned park was being touted as a great enterprise that would make San Francisco a glorious capital of culture and finance on a par with Paris and Vienna, and work had begun in 1870. SCHWEITZER AMONG FIRMS SELECTED FOR PARK CONTRACT: The article dealt with the assignment of construction contracts by the park commission. The only useful detail was that Schweitzer Superior Masonry had been chosen to build several small stone bridges. That same issue displayed an ad for the company, elaborate curling script accompanied by an etching of a superb brick building in the Victorian style. The ad promised "Old World quality of construction" and claimed a specialty in brick, granite, stone, or marble for projects of any size.

Same Schweitzer, Hans Schweitzer? Hernandez had said the brickwork in the basement showed excellent craftsmanship; maybe Hans was the proprietor of the construction company and had done it himself. She allowed herself a moment of optimism, made a photocopy, and went on.

Another hour passed, and her eyes began to feel the strain of reading the grainy screen, following the sliding frames. She ran into other ads for Schweitzer Superior in later issues, none of them particularly informative. But as she struggled to finish the spool for 1888, a different kind of headline caught her eye.

A SECOND FERAL DOG ATTACK HAS PROMPTED INCREASED CIVIC CONCERN

The Board of Supervisors last night heard complaints from merchants and residents of the Third District who requested the Board's action to relieve the area from the depredations of feral dogs. The dogs, which roam the port area in large numbers, are said to pose an increasing danger to pedestrians.

The recent death of Ezra Painter, a laborer residing in Pacific Street, was cited as a demonstration of the urgency of the situation. Savagely bitten and mauled, Mr. Painter was found near death in Kearny Street on Tuesday morning of this week and died at the medical office of Dr. William Mahoney several hours later. Mr. Painter's is the second death attributed to the animals, with the first being Alice Drummond, a woman said to be in the employ of The Dancing Mermaid saloon, who was found dead of similar causes ten days ago.

Lanson McAvoy, the owner of a marine merchandise outlet and several entertainment resorts in the district, complained that the attacks have discouraged evening custom at his enterprises. The Rev. Wilson Filbert, who operates the Faith and Fidelity Mission of Battery Street, stated that the Board's most effective means to increase security in the district would be to restrict the sale of alcoholic beverages and to ban women from drinking establishments. Police Chief O'Donnell responded that his department lacks sufficient manpower to police any aspect of the district's activities, let alone animals. Sarah Painter, sister of the deceased Ezra, blamed the nearby concentration of Chinese residents for the increasing numbers of free-roaming dogs, citing the Celestials' poor sanitation and their custom of raising dogs with the intention of consuming their meat.

After hearing testimony from those concerned, the Board deferred further discussion in favor of other business.

The only reason she'd noticed it was Bert's including dog attacks among his old cases. Also that she was tired, getting her wires crossed. Was she looking for reference to a disturbingly deformed individual, a werewolf, or a murderer in old San Francisco? If the latter, she should also have made note of the dozens of other killings the papers had reported. There had been plenty to choose from: According to one of her history books, San Francisco had averaged over three hundred murders a year throughout those decades, a per capita rate about one hundred times the current level. Ninety percent occurred in the Barbary Coast.

She decided the article was irrelevant and scrolled on. But once the seed was planted, she couldn't help herself. She found one more story about a death attributed to dog attack, this time a bartender at a Barbary Coast concert saloon.

By then her eyes were giving out, and anyway it was time to head over to the Payson Collection.

27

FROM HIS PHONE voice, Cree had expected Gerald Payson to be stuffy, an older man with an academic's manner. But he looked to be in his midtwenties, with a long sallow face beneath a sort of pompadour of pale blond hair. The suit he wore was far too big for him: a retro-punk look.

"Thank you for letting me come, especially on such short notice," Cree said. "Really, I'm very grateful. I won't get in your way, I promise."

It had been a minor ordeal to make the appointment. When they'd talked on the phone, Payson had informed her that they were in the process of reorganizing the materials, and with the collection in disarray they would not be admitting researchers for another month. Cree's hopes plummeted, but she decided a little arm-twisting was worth trying, and when he asked what the focus of her inquiry was, she figured she'd got him.

Bert wouldn't want her to say she was helping the San Francisco Police or mention the wolfman. So she offered a harmless fiction: that her grandmother was the illegitimate child of a man who had worked as a musician in San Francisco from around 1865 until his death in the quake. They had already tried the usual genealogy routes with no success, but everyone said the famous Payson Collection would probably have posters or handbills . . . A little more pleading and flattery, and Payson had relented.

This house was better preserved in its original state than the one in Pacific Heights, but it had far less charm. Down here on the flat of Franklin Street, with other buildings close by, there was no terrace, no big view or abundant sky. In fact, Payson kept the drapes mostly drawn, so that almost no natural light came inside. The varnish on woodwork and floors had aged to a deep dull brown, the wallpaper was busy and dark, and there was far too much ornate, overstuffed furniture.

Payson led her to a desk in the front parlor, sat behind it, and appraised her briefly. The room was truly packed with furniture: chairs, love seats, lamps with ornate shades, buffets, end tables, sculpture. Awful music was playing upstairs, muffled techno-punk with brain-death bass.

"As you can see," he said, "the building itself constitutes an important part of the collection. It has been preserved just as it was built in 1874. All of the furnishings and details are period, and most are original to this actual house."

"So the fire didn't get this place?"

"Stopped at Van Ness. One block over." He had a ticcish habit of rapidly rubbing his thumb against his forefinger, and everything he said seemed to amuse him in some secret way. "The collection was started by my great-grand-uncle, based on his father's acquisitions, and has been added to by each generation since. I assumed proprietorship upon my mother's death last year. As you know, our specialty is historical ephemera, with a focus upon San Francisco's cultural and recreational life. Because my ancestor was an avid gentleman about town, we have by far the largest and best collection of Barbary Coast ephemera in the world, dating from the 1850s."

"So I understand, yes. I'm looking forward to seeing it."

"Including an outstanding selection of materials on erotic entertainments and sexual recreations of the Victorian era." Payson kept his eyes on her as if waiting to see how she'd react. As he paused, a heavy thump came from upstairs, followed by swearing and muffled laughter. He was evidently entertaining guests.

He had her sign a thick register and let her donate fifty dollars to the foundation. Then he crossed the room and slid apart the doors to the rear parlor.

Cree was appalled. Scattered electric lamps cast circles of dreary yellow light over a jumble of piled furniture, cardboard boxes full of papers and objets d'art, file cabinets, stacks of books. Stacks of canvasses and framed photos leaned against the walls along with antique signs and nautical equipment.

"The collection was originally housed on both floors. However, as I *tried* to warn you, we recently began consolidating the materials in just the eight downstairs rooms. The disorder is only temporary."

Cree put it together: Payson had moved in upstairs when he'd inherited the place, and to make room for himself and his buddies had dumped everything down here.

"Can you give me a rough idea of how it's organized? I mean, what's in which room? Where a given time period might be found?"

He handed her a slim leather-bound book. "There's the master catalogue, and the boxes all have the correct index numbers on them. But they're not sorted at the moment."

"Right."

"Of course, I would be glad to stay and help you locate what you need."

His proximity made her skin crawl. Cree turned to give him a chilly smile. "Thank you, but I wouldn't want to take your time. I don't even know exactly what I'm looking for—this could take days. You go on upstairs. It sounds like your friends are waiting for you."

"Those assholes?" His lips twisted in contempt and he made no move to leave.

"I'll call you if I need you," she stated firmly. She turned to face the chaos.

She toured the ground floor with her pad, drawing a map, one room to a page. When she had given all eight rooms a quick once over, she went through again, sketching in the general contents of the piles of boxes and file cabinets according to the index numbers she saw on them.

The catalog didn't specify individual documents, but rather provided reference numbers for subject categories listed in alphabetical order, such as Advertising, Asian, Arts and Crafts Movement, Baths (Public), Boxing, Circus, Civil War, Crime, Dogfighting. The list went on and on, through Literary, Occult, Opera, Maritime, Medical, Mechanical, Murder, Musical, Oddities, Pedophilia, Prostitution, Saloons, Spiritualism, Sports, Tong Wars, Wardrobe.

Over two hundred categories, but not one for "werewolf," "wolfman," or even "freaks."

She jotted the numbers for the most promising topics: Animals, Circus,

Medical, Miscellany, Occult, Oddities. If she didn't find anything there, she'd follow up with Crime, on the chance that the wolfman had gotten in trouble, and then Entertainment Saloons, in case he'd been used that way.

The library seemed a promising starting place, heaped with stacks of framed handbills and posters and scores of file boxes. Several boxes bore the index numbers for Oddities, but she couldn't reach them. Blocking her was a barrier of glass-topped counters with boxes stored on and under them, all bearing sex-industry reference numbers. Not a priority category, but she thought she might as well look into one to get an idea how the materials were organized. She pulled a glassine envelope from the nearest box and found a display of business cards.

Mary Monroe Washington
350 lbs. of ebony-skinned passion.
Jasmine Jones' Establishment, Pacific St.
All hours. 50C each, three for one dollar.

Livia Spencer
Secret French techniques will
guarantee your complete satisfaction!
All hours. 75¢ per each.

Nelly O'Hara
A clean Irish virgin every time.
Rate: One dollar.
Money refunded if not perfectly satisfied.

The cards, with their flowing type and flowery borders, struck Cree as both pathetic and tragic. The women who'd had them printed were long dead, the legs they'd spread for thousands of men turned to bone or burned to ash. She could easily imagine the taste or tenor of their lives: the desperate enterprise, the uncertainty, the violence and degradation. In

211

the history books, she'd read the awful facts camouflaged by those flowers and the curling script. Life for these women was a one-way, downward arc, making their best money in their youth and then commanding ever lower prices as they aged and weakened from disease. In Chinatown, there were "hospitals" for used-up prostitutes: basement rooms with rows of pallets on which women terminally sickened with STDs were sent to die, out of view. One church mission report determined that their average age at death was twenty-three.

She tucked the cards back and pulled another envelope from further back. This one held a sign printed on crumbling newsprint stock:

AN AUCTION

BY

MADAME JOHANNA

OF SIX VERY YOUNG GIRLS

AGED 11 TO 14 GUARANTEED.

COME EARLY AS BIDDING FOR FIRST SERVICES WILL BE BRISK.

8 O'CLOCK, JULY 19, SACRAMENTO ST.

Cree put it away, starting to feel distinctly dragged down. Chalk it up to the sour light, she thought, the musty dusty smell here. Was this kind of sex really related in any way with what she felt when she'd made love with Mike, or with Paul? On the same continuum? It appalled her that desire could turn so predatory, could willingly use people and use them up entirely if that's what its satisfaction required. The question was whether this form of it was something perverted, skewed, or was just another feature of the basic urge, always pulsing in secret beneath the veneer of the proper, tender traditions of love and marriage and fidelity and family. The next file she pulled contained a larger folded page, a poster with crudely typeset block letters and a hideous engraving for illustration.

SCANDALOUS FUN FOR THE ADULT MALE!

NOT FOR LADIES! NOT FOR CHILDREN!

A NEW SHOW FEATURING

BERTHA AND HER BEASTLY SWAIN.

THRICE NIGHTLY FROM NINE O'CLOCK. 25C ADMISSION

That's it, Cree thought, *I'm out of here. That's it for today.* She'd have to return another time and make a point of skipping this category.

The illustration featured a deep-chested boar mounting a naked woman. The boar had a humped back and a bristling face made all the more horrible by the artless rendering. Its stubby back legs strained against the floor while its front hooves hung down limp over the woman's shoulders. Bertha herself was fairly obese. She held herself on all fours but also appeared to have a small table or pedestal supporting her from beneath. Cree couldn't doubt that the image was drawn from life.

"Oh, yes. I have a special affection for that one myself."

Cree leapt upright and spun around to see Gerald Payson, right behind her.

"Awesome, isn't it?" he said. "There's more along those lines."

"Oh?" Cree panted. "Anything with a wolf? A monkey?"

Payson gave her an insinuating grin. "Hmm. Well, a donkey . . . Sure, dogs, but no, I can't recall any wolves or monkeys. If you had told me your interest—"

"Not just sex acts. Circuses? Freak shows? Skits? Anything with a wolf or wolfman or apeman? A wildman?"

"Wildman, that was a perennial favorite among hucksters." He shrugged. "But nothing I can point you to. There are over sixteen thousand items in the collection. It was mainly my mother's gig. I've only looked at a fraction of it."

Cree put the poster away and turned back to face Payson.

"I'm leaving now," she said, "but I'll need to come back tomorrow or the next day. I'm sure it's an imposition, but I'll pay you well for your trouble. In the meantime, I have a list of topics I'd like you to look for, and I want you to pull out the boxes so I can get at them. Arrange them at the front of each room. Understood?"

She shoved her list of index numbers and topics at him. Payson took it, grinning again as he clicked his heels and saluted crisply. His hand had made contact with hers as he took the paper, and she couldn't help wiping her fingers on her skirt as she left.

28

S HE MADE IT to the Life Sciences Building by four thirty. It was nice to arrive when it was still light outside, for once, and to see Horace puttering around the lab when she came to the door. No shadows in the bushes outside, no tense waiting in the abandoned basement, no wondering what was going on in the meat suite.

Skobold pulled a shade on the outer door and locked it behind her. Indirect daylight came from the light well and through the windows, taking the chill off the blue-white ceiling tubes. After her session at the Payson Collection, Cree took comfort in the sight of Skobold's benign face and the order and rationality of the lab.

"I am increasingly thinking that our wolfman might just provide us with a window into some very exciting discoveries. We have some interesting work ahead of us."

She took the smock Skobold offered her. "What's on the agenda?"

"We're nearing my favorite phase of reconstruction." He continued talking as he arranged tools and materials on the counter, looking unusually eager in his melancholy way. "In this case, my pleasurable anticipation is amplified by some new information I received from our friend Cameron. In fact, I was so . . . motivated . . . that I made some extra time this noon and was able to do some preparatory work on the cranium. Soon we can begin making the molds for the skull casts and begin sculpting. If you'd like, we can also create a parallel reconstruction on the computer, although I vastly prefer the old-fashioned method."

"I'm game. Just show me what to do." She had a lot to discuss with him, but thought she'd wait until they were working.

They went to the back room and Cree wheeled out the wolfman's pallet as Skobold carried several boxes of supplies to the counter. When she pulled back the shroud, Cree was startled to see the wolfman's head transformed. The upper curve of bone was intact, the hole bridged with meticulously rejoined pieces and chips, and the surface of the skull glistened.

Skobold explained. Earlier, he had degreased the skull, glued the broken pieces back into place, and varnished the intact cranium and mandible with a coat of polyvinyl acetate. It was all part of the preparation for making plaster skull casts.

He set Cree up at the counter with a can of ordinary satin varnish and had her seal the rest of the bones as he continued preparing the skull. She spread newspapers, then arranged several dozen plastic blocks to support the bones as the varnish dried. She put on rubber gloves and began brushing on varnish, following Horace's instructions to cover every bone feature without leaving drips or bare spots.

As always, working with the bones calmed her, gave her a sense of progress. One step at a time, one bone at a time, building slowly toward understanding. There was a method here, it wasn't all chaotic. Bones could be cryptic, but they couldn't lie. The brush floated over the smooth ivory surfaces, and the varnish revealed tiny pits and seams and stains.

Farther down the counter, Skobold had laid the skull on a rubber mat and was plugging the natural holes and cavities with putty. The external auditory meatus, the nasal aperture, the foramen magnum and other indented features needed to be filled and smoothed to make sure he could separate the mirror image molds after casting in plaster.

"So what was the new information?" Cree asked. "Something to do with the age indicators, I hope. Because I really need some specificity regarding his age."

Skobold's eyes lit up. "Precisely. Our fundamental conundrum. I asked Ray for additional work on the palatine sutures and the cementum annulation, and he was kind enough to do the work this morning and messenger the materials to me. The results are intriguing. No—exciting, precedent setting. Perhaps you had better take a look."

Cree put down her brush, wiped her gloved hands on a rag, then moved over next to Skobold.

"From studying his epiphyseal fusion sites, the pubic symphysis, the sternal rib ends, and the osteon count, I get an age range of thirty-six to forty-two. Ordinarily, I would consider this a safe estimate. But two other indicators create a problem for us. Let me give you some context. As I'm sure you know, the skull of the infant is composed of several pieces which gradually grow together over a period of years. In the adult, we can still see them as ragged fissures in the surface of the cranium." Skobold's gloved finger traced the lines, wandering traceries like the edges of a preposterously intricate jigsaw puzzle.

"Right."

He turned over the skull and put his finger inside the jagged U-curve of teeth. "The palate is the section of cranium on the top of your mouth, and the palatine sutures are the fissures where over the years the bone has joined together. I use a four-phase assessment to age skull sutures, the Meindl-Lovejoy scale. One assigns a score to degree of closure, then multiplies by a numerical factor determined from statistical standards. Are you following me thus far?"

"I think so."

Skobold used a clay-sculpting tool to trace the hairline groove in the wolfman's palate. "Ray's enlargements allow us to measure the fissures with great precision, confirming what I had suspected. This would appear to be the palate of a much younger person. The bones of the palate are much more recently developed."

"Which implies—?"

"Sutures exist to allow the head to compress to fit through the birth canal and to accommodate rapid brain growth in infancy. In adulthood, with growth completed, the sutures naturally close. Those in the top and back of the wolfman's skull are consistent with the other age indicators I've cited, but sutures like these in the palate and maxillary region suggest more recent growth. Consistent with an individual in his late teens."

Cree nodded, dismayed. Confusion on dates was not going to help her.

"One other point." Skobold turned the skull upright again and placed the point of his tool between the eye holes. "Do you see the striations in the bone in the area from the nasion to the end of the nasals? You see it again here, in the suborbital and inferior malar areas."

Cree bent close. "Like stretch marks. Taffy being pulled."

"Exactly. It suggests that the unusual growth in the astonishingly long bridge of the nose and inner cheek bones occurred quite rapidly."

Skobold put down the skull, then picked up an envelope and took out several eight-by-ten photos. The shapes were incomprehensible to Cree, a pattern of parallel lines resembling a tree's growth rings.

"Then there is the cementum annulation, an indicator of tooth age. I have been troubled from the start by the limited degree of attrition and resorption I see in the wolfman's canines and incisors—these appear to be full-bodied teeth, healthy and showing relatively little wear, not the teeth of a forty-year-old who lived before the age of modern dentistry. Fortunately, in humans as in all mammals, a thin layer of cementum is added around the adult tooth root every year, allowing us to measure age by counting the layers. You cut a very thin section from the root of the teeth, then look at it through a microscope and count the cementum layers. I asked Ray to take a section and provide photomicrographs for us." Skobold ticked off the striations on the photo. "The cementum annulatum substantiates the observation that the wolfman's canines and the incisors are relatively young, growing teeth. Their age is precisely consistent with the palate indicators."

"So," Cree said, "you're saying his lower face and dentition developed later. In a rapid and sudden growth phase in his adult years."

"Yes."

"Horace. How . . . can that, I mean, is it possible that—" she stopped, unwilling to embarrass herself by voicing the question.

"Bones can be stimulated to later-age, rapid deformative development in response to changes in use, to injuries, and to growing tumors. A few, extremely rare genetic syndromes can result in rapid bone growth, deformation, or degeneration. Those are the only exceptions to predictable development."

"We're pretty sure about that?"

Skobold put the mandible back on the counter and turned away to fuss with his tools before replying. "Do you believe in werewolves, Ms. Black?"

Cree thought about how to answer. "I do, yes. As a way people in the old days thought of serial killers or schizophrenics, or as a way superstitious people demonized behaviors different from their own. Last year I spent some time with a Navajo shaman, talking about Skinwalkers and Navajo Wolves, evil sorcerers who are supposed to be able to change shape.

I think of that tradition as a metaphorical transformation. I've never believed in the . . . other kind, but then you tell me this stuff and I have to wonder." She grinned weakly, trying to keep it light. "How about you?"

Skobold didn't smile. "I am a scientist. I have measured the wolfman's cranial volume, which accommodated a full-sized human brain. He was a human being. I believe we are dealing with a deformity of greater complexity than previously assumed. Clearly the genes responsible for skeletal growth were faulty and caused late-developing abnormalities. If so, it is an extremely rare syndrome, perhaps one never before clinically observed. Which is why it is so very important that we understand what happened—that we document this fellow with perfect precision and objectivity. What happened to our wolfman was not the result of some . . . supernatural event. It was encoded in his genes, which I very much hope we can study in the tissue residues I took samples of. His final shape was what you might call his genetic destiny. We must study him closely so that we may better understand the full diversity of the human condition. The rainbow of our many individual 'destinies.'"

Beautiful, Cree thought. Horace Skobold was showing himself to be a remarkably thoughtful, eloquent man, a person she would enjoy comparing philosophical notes with if she were free to reveal what she did and what insights her profession had given her. She went back to her bones and brushes. Skobold turned his attention to the cranium, pressing pinches of putty into concavities, smoothing and rounding. He had lost his eager contentedness and now looked troubled.

"Speaking of Ray," Cree said, "I, um, ran into him. We had coffee together."

Skobold's eyes widened. "And?"

"He told me the details about him and Bert, what happened back then. Understandably, he doesn't care much for Bert."

"No."

"He has some, what would you call it, unusual philosophical ideas. I was hoping to ask you about him, actually."

"Ask—?"

"You were right, he sent those dog-morph e-mails—the bones got him thinking of werewolves as a metaphor. He's saying that's what Bert is. That Bert should recognize himself."

"That does sound like Ray."

"But his intensity is a little frightening to me, Horace. And I'm worried that Bert will figure out he sent the e-mails and then decide Ray is his supposed serial killer. I guess I wanted to ask if you thought Ray could really be dangerous. Do you think he could be capable of . . . that?"

Skobold brought the skull close to his eyes to inspect some detail, then continued working the putty for another long minute before answering.

"I can't say what Ray is capable of, or what Bert is capable of. But I must tell you that I believe deeply in the fundamental goodness of mankind. The pain we inflict and endure is not an inevitability of our nature but a tragic result of unintended consequences." He looked at her as if expecting a challenge. "I have spent forty years in this field, Ms. Black. I have viewed at close hand the aftermath of every imaginable kind of carnage. I spent two years doing reconstructive identification in mass graves in Bosnia and Rwanda. So I am *well* aware of the many arguments one can make to the contrary. But I still prefer to give mankind the benefit of the doubt."

Horace stopped his work to look at her penetratingly. She returned the steady gaze, seeing it all there in his eyes, the certainty and beyond that successive layers of fear, then desperation, then determination. She suspected he saw the same in hers.

"What about you, Ms. Black?" he asked, gaze unwavering.

Cree thought about it, realizing how hungry she was for reassurance on that point and how elusive it was proving.

"In general, I'd say I share your outlook. But as regards the current situation, I'm a little worried it's going to be one of those things that . . . puts our hypothesis to the test."

"Yes," Skobold agreed sadly. "I was rather afraid it might."

29

THE HOMICIDE UNIT'S office on the fourth floor of the Hall of Justice was a cramped labyrinth of pathways between overflowing green metal desks fronting paper-stuffed half-wall cubicles. On the walls hung drymark boards listing case actions pending, interspersed with framed photos of cops arresting people or newspaper articles reporting convictions on cases apparently dear to the hearts of the inspectors. The air was close with the smell of paper and humanity.

Bert occupied the far corner, the last and most cluttered of a row of desks. Ordinarily the unit's inspectors worked in teams, he explained, but with his job mostly paperwork at this stage he was a solo for now; his former partner was already hooked up with Bert's replacement. He gestured for Cree to sit, then settled himself into a creaking chair beneath ceiling lights that cast the pouches under his eyes into sharp relief. Cree had spent another frustrating morning searching for records for Schweitzers or Jacksons, but she'd been thinking mainly about Bert and Cameron Raymond. She had decided to tell him about Ray, but the decision made her uneasy.

"How's it going?" he asked.

"Frankly, it's slow, Uncle Bert. I'm basically spinning my wheels, so far."

"We knew it would be slow. That's why I asked you. Big favor, I know it."

"I did find reference to Schweitzer. I don't know much about him other than that he was a contractor, fine masonry a specialty, and that he married someone named Jackson, probably one of the people who owned the house where the terrace is now. And I took a look at one of the private collections. It's got a lot of possibility but it's in transition and disordered, so it's going to take a while to get through it. I'll go back tomorrow."

Bert bobbed his head. "How about the bones? You and Horace make any headway?"

"We did some measuring last night. Horace says bone development is paradoxical, meaning he's getting conflicting age indicators from different bone features. The best he can do so far is that our guy was between early twenties and early forties."

"Huh. Too broad to help you. Well, when he does give you a number, you can put it in the bank. He's the best, Horace."

She lowered her voice, even though none of the nearby desks was occupied. "He told me about you and Cameron Raymond."

Bert went instantly poker faced. "Okay. Good."

"Why good?"

"Because I got to thinking about Cameron Raymond, too. After you mentioned you'd run into a guy with bad scarring named Ray."

"Shit."

"Yeah, 'shit' as in 'shit happens,' except around here we say 'people *do* shit'." Bert's voice had turned acid. "Did he tell you Cameron is an artist? Move your chair around here, you can see the latest 'art' by our friend Cameron."

Cree scooted the chair so she could see the computer monitor, which showed a page of text. She started reading, but Bert waved his hand in front of her.

"Just watch."

After about a minute, she jumped as an image popped onto the screen. A dog-faced man. This one had more human features, with the canine qualities suppressed, which somehow made it even more frightening. It vanished before she could look closely at it. The image had come and gone like a subliminal thought. Bert made a low noise in his throat.

"Listen, Uncle Bert—"

"Hang on. Keep watching."

Soon another pop-up appeared. This one was in black and white, a medieval woodcut print of a hunchbacked upright wolflike creature ripping parts off somebody on the ground. It was there and gone, leaving its reversed afterimage on her retinas.

"There's one more," Bert said. "But you get the idea. They might not show for a while and then they'll pop like this. I asked our IT guy about it, he said, Yeah, it's a problem, you're going along and a Viagra ad comes onto your screen. They're like a virus, they get into your computer and activate themselves. He's got some software that'll get rid of them but I'm gonna leave these on in case they end up having evidentiary value. In the meantime, I gotta live with them. Son of a bitch."

"When did you start getting these?"

"This morning."

So Ray hadn't backed off. She was surprised as much as disappointed. She would have sworn he'd been sincere when he'd said he was done. It disturbed her to think he could misrepresent himself so convincingly. What had he said? *The wolf you don't see. The wolf you don't know is there.*

Another inspector came into Bert's end of the room, then a second. They saw Cree, nodded, began conferring. The additional company wasn't to Bert's liking. He stood up, suggested he could use a smoke, maybe Cree wanted to go for a walk. On their way out, he introduced her to the others as his niece.

Outside, Bert lit up immediately and blew a series of smoke signals as they walked along a block made up of seedy store fronts, mostly bail bondsmen with a scattering of convenience stores and auto glass places in between. With the heavy traffic on Bryant Street and the relentless rush from the 101 overpass, Cree had to walk close by Bert's side so they could hear each other.

"So what are you going to do?" she asked.

"Take a closer look at him."

"What are you thinking? On the basis of these e-mails, Ray's your murderer?"

Bert's mouth puckered and his eyes went flat in a way Cree did not like. "Mainly, I'm thinking that if Cameron Raymond didn't get enough back in eighty-one, there's plenty more where that came from."

"You don't think maybe he already got more than he deserved?"

"These scumbags, it's never just one thing! Don't think that just because he and his buddies got caught robbing that one store it was the only thing they ever did. Don't think he's been clean since then, either."

"Horace knows Ray fairly well and thinks he's a good person."

"Yeah, and that's something Horace and I are gonna have to talk about, him working with Raymond all these years, keeping it from me." Bert spat, the idea of Horace's betrayal heating him up. "I went through an administrative investigation over what happened. They looked up every orifice in my body, they looked back at every thing I'd ever done, personal finances, friendships, everything. It put me under the thumb for a long time, even if they clear you it's a permanent stigma, you think I wouldn't have moved up a couple more grades by now? Then the civil suit, that's months of meeting with lawyers and depositions and court dates, your bosses do not like that. You sit there in court all day, listening to them tell this bullshit about you, then you get home at night and read the same crap in the newspapers. Five, six weeks, you don't know how it'll turn out, the suspense isn't good for your digestion, okay? This was only like three years after Megan. Fran and I were holding onto our marriage by our fingernails anyway, then Raymond comes along and I'm up to my neck in shit. For Fran it was the straw that broke the camel's back. So don't tell me about poor little Cameron."

Bert had cranked himself up again, enough that a couple passing the other way glanced at him with mild alarm. He threw his cigarette down and stepped on it without breaking stride.

"There's something else you should know about Raymond. He came up on my radar another time. This was eight, nine years after my first thing with him, when I was just starting out in Homicide. I remembered something, it was eating at me since you clued me to him the other night, and today I went and found it. Cameron Raymond was on a witness/suspect list for a homicide in Berkeley about fourteen years ago. I wasn't lead, but I was involved because there was a possible San Francisco link. So today I got hold of the file and looked at the contact lists and sure enough there's Cameron. He was the Berkeley side's guy, so it wasn't our job to interview him. I remember now, back when his name came up, I thought, there's that little punk who cost me my marriage and nearly my job. I thought it was one hell of a coincidence that a scumbag I knew from before was now connected to a murder."

Cree felt a shiver of wariness. She couldn't tell whether it came from the possibility that Ray was a murderer or the fact that Bert's theory was ramifying in this direction. "Tell me about it."

"It was a nasty one, a slice and dice. With those, first thing you gotta consider is a jealous lover, so the Berkeley cops looked at the vic's girlfriend and any other boyfriends she might have had. And who do you think she threw over, like two years earlier, for the guy who got killed? Your buddy Ray. They talked to him a couple of times."

"But they didn't arrest him?"

"No. I told the Berkeley people they should take a closer look at him. But they didn't. In fact, they nailed somebody else. A weak case, I thought."

"And what did the jury think, Uncle Bert?"

He waved his hand as if swatting at gnats. "Never came to trial. Guy hung himself in holding. Berkeley dicks figured that was tantamount to a confession."

"So now what are you going to do?" Cree asked.

"Whatever I think necessary."

"Did you talk to the people in Berkeley about why Ray wasn't a suspect? It seems to me you should respect their judgment."

Bert flashed her a look that was at once insulted and disdainful as he brought out another cigarette, put it to his lips, took it away and spat some tobacco. "Next order of business. Where we at with the wolfman? What's next? We need some headway on this thing."

Cree bristled at his way of cutting off discussion, his whole way of talking to her. She let the chill show in her voice: "We're meeting for a short session tonight. Horace has some other commitment later."

"I was hoping you could come over to my place, maybe tomorrow, look at some more stuff I've put together. On that other thing."

They had stopped at a streetlight as a bunch of motorcyclists went past, racketing Ninja-style Japanese bikes in every color. Cree stared at the glistening rainbow parade, fighting the temptation to return Bert's dismissive treatment.

When the din faded, Bert cleared his throat uneasily. "Maybe we could grab dinner first. Least I can do is feed you right while you're down here."

"We'll see how my schedule is."

He heard that as it was intended. He lit his cigarette and didn't say anything as they crossed the street and started along the next block.

"What I mean is," Bert continued, "fuck *me*. I'm sorry."

That pulled Cree up short. They stopped and faced each other in front of an Italian-style café with the smell of roasting coffee gusting out its front door. Bert frowned down at his cigarette, lifted his eyes with some effort to Cree's.

"You're pissed because of the way I talk. I'm working on it, Cree. I'm a little rough around the edges. Guys who spend too long in the cop shop, we get like this. You gotta know you're good for me, okay? I mean it. You show me I got a lot of catching up to do, learn how to be a human being again. Stick with it, yeah?"

She hadn't thought him capable of so much introspection or humility. Surprise: Just when you wanted to kick him, he showed a lopsided charm. He stood there with a hat-in-hand expression, waiting for some response, wary of her.

"What am I gonna do with this guy?" she said at last. The words came all the way from Brooklyn, something she must have heard her mother say. She had to grin as she took his arm and turned him toward the café entrance. "You're breaking my heart," she said. "Buy me a cup of coffee."

30

Ray's address was listed in the phone book. It took Cree a while to find the place, over on the east side in an area of warehouses and port-related businesses. Several nearby streets ended in encampments of homeless people with rows of defunct cars, stretched tarps, trashcan firepits. Ray's street dead-ended at an overgrown chain-link fence, and at first she thought she must have the address wrong. But her mental lens shifted when she pulled up at the huge dirty-brick warehouse and saw Ray's minivan parked in front. She thought of the industrial places her artist friends had moved into in New York, Philadelphia, Seattle; maybe this was a Bay Area equivalent.

It was six o'clock. The sky was still bright, but the sun was getting low and putting shadows along the buildings, and Cree briefly wondered if she was being smart or crazy in coming here.

She went up to the steel door and pushed long and hard on the door-bell button. A harsh bleat echoed inside, followed by the sound of barking from the fenced storage yard to the left. She couldn't see the dogs, but their fury disturbed her.

"Hey! Cree! Fantastic!"

Ray stood at the top of the façade wall, forty feet almost directly above her, shirtless against the bright sky.

"We have to talk, Ray," she called.

"Sure! But I'm in the middle of a tricky job. Can you wait for like an hour, or—"

"No."

"Then you'll have to come up."

He disappeared before she could answer. Out of view, he made a short, sharp whistle, and the dogs went silent.

When he opened the door, Ray was wearing beat-up fatigues, rubber boots, and work gloves. His pants and bare chest were smeared with black smudges. Now that he was closer, she could see that he was superbly muscled, the hard, squared-off build of a triathalon competitor.

"I'm in the middle of resurfacing my roof," he explained. He grinned broadly and made no attempt to avert the scarred side of his face.

Cree didn't return the smile. "I was foolish enough to hope you'd quit harassing Uncle Bert. But now he's got werewolves popping up on his computer."

Ray stepped back and turned. "We'll have to talk while I work, Cree. Sorry. I have to finish it while there's still daylight. The stuff sets up if you leave it too long, it's a big mess."

She tried not to show any reluctance as she strode past him and into the warehouse. It was huge, empty and echoing, a rubble-strewn, brick and concrete cavern without any sign of any domestic presence. But Ray led her to a subsection cut into the rectangle, and when he opened the door Cree was surprised to enter a nice kitchen with hardwood cabinets and glistening appliances. The living room was tastefully decorated with yellow oak floors, white-painted exposed brick, a good dhurrie rug, a white leather couch.

Ray continued ahead of her up a flight of stairs against the far wall of the living room. "There's a ladder up through my roof. You have a problem with heights?"

"Not that I know of."

They came out into a big open room as high as it was wide, lit by tall, narrow windows. Near the top of the stairs, a couch, coffee table, bookshelf, and some potted lemon trees made a little island of domestic comfort, but the rest of the room was all bare brick and functionality: computers and photo equipment on long work tables, huge abstract paintings on the walls, racks of empty frames, rolls of canvas. Ray's studio, she realized, where he'd created his morphs.

A metal ladder was anchored on the bay-side wall, rising thirty feet to a platform like a fire escape landing just below the ceiling. From the platform a shorter ladder angled up to a little square of open sky. Ray went right to the main ladder and began climbing.

"I sent those pop-ups along with the first three," he called back. "Like two weeks ago. They're basically just adware, with a sneaky little activation delay."

"They've really pissed him off."

"They don't do any system damage. And they're easy to get rid of, all he has to do is—"

"He's not getting rid of them. He's saving them in case they end up having evidentiary value."

Ray stopped, hanging easily halfway between roof and floor as he frowned down at her. " 'Evidentiary'? Of what?"

"That's what we better talk about."

"Huh. Yeah, sounds like we better." He continued up.

Cree watched him from below, legs and rear and the foreshortened rippling wedge of back. She couldn't help but think he'd thrown her some kind of a challenge, a test of her motivation or mettle. Or maybe not. Whichever, this was some kind of turning point, because she either said to herself, *I don't trust him, I don't want to talk to him that badly, and I don't trust myself to climb up there.* Or she said, *I trust him enough, this is important, and I can handle it.*

Ray reached the platform, clambered over to the other ladder, and disappeared through the hole into the sky. Cree considered the ladder for another moment, then put her hands on the flaking iron of the first wrung and began to climb.

When she emerged from the trapdoor, Ray was thirty feet away on a vast expanse of flat roof, shoving a push broom through a thick tarry puddle. Ten or twelve metal cans of asphalt sealer, some empty, were ranged along the edge, where a knee-wall rose above the roof surface. Ray had sketched out a square in fresh black, about forty feet on a side, and was working his way back toward the hatch. The muscles of his shoulders and arms striated as he worked, his belly divided into sharp squares now sheened with sweat. She pondered the tar buckets and the nearly superhuman effort it must have required to get them to the roof.

"Nice up here, isn't it?" he said, not looking up.

"Very nice."

Beyond Ray's building, a paved yard the size of a football field ended at a narrow canal on the south and the open water of the bay to the east. In the sunset light, the distant buildings of Oakland seemed to smolder, pink-orange and heat rippled. Far out in the bay, a cargo ship burdened with containers in faded rainbow colors pushed a rim of froth through the metallic waves; along the near shore, a ragged line of gantries dwindled away south into smog-muted distance. Cree went to the knee-wall, looked down at the littered field where the dogs roamed, then stepped quickly back, amazed that Ray had stood so casually on such a precipice.

"I just do the part over my quarters," he called. "If I had to do the whole thing I'd go bankrupt as well as crazy. Anyway, the rest, I don't care if it leaks."

"Ray, we—"

"A little preface here," Ray said. "I don't think the way other people do. I never have. I don't see the world or people or my own actions in a very conventional way."

"The fact hasn't escaped my notice."

"It's just what you said, the dissonance between self and the rest of humanity, the inner and outer? For me, the way it comes across is, the harder I try to be clear and straightforward, the more I sound like I'm trying to be scary or mysterious. If it bugs you, give me a kick in the pants or whatever, but don't hold it against me. Okay?"

"I'll remember that. So here's my preface. This isn't a social occasion, Ray. I'm just trying to prevent something stupid from happening. I came to convince you of the seriousness of the situation you've created."

He tipped another dollop of tar from a barrel, then began spreading and smoothing the glistening black spill. She couldn't help but admire the good lines of limb, the forceful grace of movement, his genuine pleasure in the day and the work. But in the angled sunlight she could see that his whole torso was etched with a skein of innumerable fine scars, paler lines just visible against the tan, and she felt a prickle of wariness on her skin.

"Bert knows it's you who sent the e-mails."

Ray glanced up, shrugged, went back to work. "So I spammed him. So sue me."

"It's more complicated than that. He still hates you for getting him in trouble back then. He blames you for his divorce. And he's considering you a suspect for some . . . for another crime from around fourteen years ago."

"What?!" He stopped, straightened, rested his broom.

Cree had watched his response carefully, looking for the microsecond of calculation or concealment in the eyes. His incredulity seemed perfectly genuine.

"Back when I was at UC Berkeley, a woman I had dated knew somebody who was murdered. They questioned me about it. Is that what he's talking about?"

"That, and some others. Including several unsolved dog-attack deaths."

For a moment Ray seemed struck speechless. "The guy's really gone nuts," he muttered at last.

"Yes, that's about what he thinks of you."

"And what do *you* think?"

"I must be hoping he's wrong."

He searched her face, a penetrating pale blue gaze. The sun glistened on the tight surface of his facial scars.

"Right," he said. "Jesus. You're a brave lady. Coming out to see a guy who's a scar-faced weirdo at best and who just might be a violent psycho. Up on the roof, too."

He continued his inspection of her eyes as if looking for something specific inside her head, then grunted softly and smiled.

"Thanks," he said.

31

THE SUN'S DISK rested briefly on the rooftops to the west, then started to slip behind them. Ray worked his way back toward the trapdoor, drawing the ring of tar closer. Between gusts of wind, the oily stink of it surrounded Cree, not unpleasant. Ray looked happy—no, joyous, she thought—as if the hard work and height and company suited him. Cree could feel it herself: the cleansing sunlight, blinding at such a low angle, the big sky overhead, the enormous but muted energy of the city all around.

"You mentioned me to Bert, right?" Ray asked. "That's what got him thinking about me?"

"I didn't know you two had . . . any previous contact. I was just chatting about my day."

"So now what? My sending him those e-mails proves I'm a killer. Got any ideas about how to defuse his interest?"

"Not at the moment."

"Terrific. Fucking terrific." Ray frowned as he worked. Cree crossed her arms and took a turn around the shrinking square of untarred roof, getting chilly. Neither said anything for a few minutes. The low beams had turned Ray into a half orange-gilded, half blue-shadowed man, and he was hurrying now, working against time.

"Can I ask you a question?" he called. "On a somewhat different topic?"

"Maybe."

"You're . . . *normal*, Cree. You look it, anyway. What you said in the plaza, one thing on the outside, one on the inside—I work on that stuff all the time. You can see why. But why should an attractive, smart, agreeable person feel that way?"

"Everybody has some dissonance there," she hedged.

Ray nodded, accepting the point, accepting that she wasn't ready to confide in him.

She found a screwdriver and levered open the last remaining bucket, then decided the best help she could offer would be to get out of the way. She climbed back through the trapdoor to the platform and down the narrow ladder to the floor.

She turned on a few lights and wandered in Ray's studio. What she'd taken for abstract paintings turned out to be hugely enlarged X-rays, all of the head and neck. In some, she could still make out the faint ghosts of fleshly features: lips, a nose, an ear. But Ray's focus was obviously the bones, cropping the images until they became abstract patterns of graduated light against the deep-space emptiness of the dark film. She'd learned enough anatomy from Horace to name some of the features: an orbit, with just enough of the nasal aperture to reveal what it was, became a portal to a vast and mysterious interior. The zygomatic arch, that delicate bridge of bone just behind the eye, enlarged so it became a cathedral's flying buttress, a lovely soaring arc. A left lateral cranial view, cropped horizontally so that the segments of cervical spine became a short, vertical band along the far right that created a rhythmic counterpoint to the horizontal palisades of the teeth. There were a few MRIs among the larger pieces, computer-generated whole-head images in overbright colors, not as successful.

Another piece of the Ray puzzle, certainly, but what did it imply? The subject matter could be seen as morbid, but back east she'd known artists who painted nothing but dead babies or women wrapped in barbed wire, and got big write-ups in the *Globe* or the *Times* for it. And the compositions were really quite wonderful, reverently turning the arcs and planes and articulations of the skull into architectural forms. Having worked with the wolfman's bones, she could understand the fascination.

What's inside, she decided. That was the central motivation she sensed in all her encounters with Ray: He was compelled to look through exteriors, celebrating the secret world of unseen forms. In fact, the X-rays seemed to probe even further than the bones, turning them into partial transparencies that revealed infinite space just beyond.

What's inside? What's *beyond* inside? She came at it from a very different angle, but her own motivations were very much the same.

The windows had gone gray by the time the hatch cap thumped into place and Ray started down the ladder. He crossed the room and she thought to ask him about his work, but when she looked over at him, she was startled to see him changed. His exuberance was gone, replaced by a strained weariness. His face was red and tar streaked, eyes bulging, the weals on his face purpling.

"Sorry you had to wait. I appreciate it."

"Are you okay?"

"Ah, just a headache. The sun in my eyes, my head's full of spots. The fumes. I'll be fine. Listen, I know we've still got stuff to talk about, but I have to go get this shit off of me and take a shower. I am also starving. Are you up for talking over dinner somewhere? I know this isn't a social occasion, but if I don't eat something I'm going to keel over."

Cree thought about it briefly. "Don't keel over," she told him.

They took her car, Ray giving directions. He still looked tired, but a shower and clean clothes revived him considerably, and by the time they made it to the restaurant he had mostly rebounded. They ordered a bottle of wine and plates of exotic noodles that combined food traditions from three continents. It was a pleasant little place on a side street in Noe Valley, only a few minutes drive from Ray's.

"I had an idea for you about the paradoxical aging indicators," Ray said. "Did Horace explain them?"

"The teeth and palate? He mentioned them yesterday."

"Fascinating, isn't it? That this guy's most 'wolfish' characteristics, the lengthening of the maxillary bones, nasals and mandible, and the growth of his big canines, occurred in a rather sudden, rather late, developmental phase."

"Suggesting to you that he was a bona fide werewolf?"

"No." Ray chuckled. "I was thinking of how to narrow your search parameters. His birth date was probably around 1866, but you're most likely to find records of him when his more extreme features developed. That's when he would really have become an oddball—would really have been noticed. Probably late eighties, early nineties."

"Good point."

"And I had another idea that might help you locate records." Ray's brightness was returning fast, and he seemed pleased with himself as he sipped some wine, gazed through it at the candle, tasted it again. "It has to do with who would have noticed him or cared about him enough to leave a record of him."

"I'm not sure what you mean."

"Well, he was a freak, a monster. Think about it—the average person on the street would have reacted to him with, what . . . avoidance, revulsion, fear, derision. But some kinds of people would have had other responses, dependent on their outlook. Hucksters, sleazy showmen, they'd have wanted to exploit him to make a buck. Doctors and scientists would have had a clinical interest, would've wanted to study him—or help him. He would've been a natural object of suspicion and accusation, so the police might have paid attention to him. He'd have elicited compassion in those inclined to be compassionate, and spiritual and moral concern from religious people."

"Pretty astute social psychology."

"But then I was thinking, you have to think about the era—how the Victorians would have reacted to him. It was a different time, beliefs were different, ideas were in flux. If he did look like a wolfman, there'd be the werewolf mythology to deal with."

Cree's cell phone went off in her purse, and seeing it was Bert, she apologized to Ray and took the call. He was just checking in, he said. He sounded distracted, fumbling for what to say, and she wondered how much he'd had to drink. Conscious of Ray's presence, she arranged to meet with him tomorrow and hung up as quickly as she could.

"Bert?"

"Bert."

"How would Uncle Bert like it if he knew you were consorting with the enemy?"

"Nobody's the enemy! I don't know. I don't know how to fix this, but I'll damned well figure it out."

Their food came, and Ray tucked into his noodles with enthusiasm. Cree found the flavors agreeable, but she had no appetite. Bert's call had brought the whole problem back. The look in his eyes as they'd walked on Bryant Street had spooked her—for all his gritty charm and offhand moments of grace, Bert had an opaque place inside him, a walled-off core that she could not see into.

"Keep going," she prompted. "You were talking about how people thought of werewolves in the 1880s."

After seeing the wolfman's bones, Ray had bought a couple of books on lycanthropy, and Cree had read up on the subject after her visit to the Southwest, trying to learn more about the tradition of Navajo Wolves. They spent the next half hour comparing notes, listing kinds of werewolf. There was the Hollywood variety, a make-believe of sudden transformation, Jack Nicholson suddenly sprouting hair and fangs and overwhelming sex appeal. But that was just a celluloid update of old folktales, widespread for thousands of years, which in turn were based on the really ancient tradition of shamans and priests seeking animal forms to gain animal powers. It was a resonant symbolic idea, but not only that. Modern anthropological research into therianthropy, animal-man combinations or transformations, showed that present-day shamans took herbs and animal glandular extracts containing powerful psychoactive chemicals that did indeed radically change their thinking and behavior.

The 1600s and 1700s saw a rash of trials of admitted, self-proclaimed werewolves, such as the Gandillon family, Gilles Garnier, and Peter Stump. Today they'd have been called serial killers, but the era lacked a scientific or psychological perspective to describe psychopaths who murdered and mutilated multiple victims. It would have been too distressing, anyway; people preferred to externalize the cause of such gruesome acts, blame them on a supernatural process and an animal shape.

With advances in science and psychology, perspectives changed. In the 1700s and 1800s came the psychiatric lycanthropes, people believing themselves to be werewolves and acting out wolfish behaviors. It was practically a fad diagnosis among medical professionals during the wolfman's lifetime, and didn't fully fade from medical literature until the 1960s. Now it was just diagnosed as schizophrenia, with a lupine delusional focus.

Cree drank the last of her wine and poured another half inch. The restaurant was tastefully New Agey, with soft lighting, candles, a string quartet playing over the speakers, impressionistic floral paintings on the walls. The dozen or so other customers were mostly couples, chatting quietly, laughing, holding hands. Ray talked with enthusiasm, as if completely unaware of how strange and dark their subject was in this context. Comparing notes on werewolves. And yet he was right, she needed to consider this. In the 1880s, scientific perspectives were just starting to take hold and were usually wildly inaccurate. The average person would probably have seen the wolfman through the lens of the old superstitions and would have felt an instinctive, visceral fear of his strangeness.

"But the biggest category," Ray finished, "is the 'werewolves' who were brought to trial, tortured and killed during the Inquisition. Garden-variety eccentrics, herbalists, hermits, holdout pagans, individualists—anybody who didn't fit cultural norms had a tough time when the witchcraft hysteria was in full bloom. Ten thousand werewolves, burned alive between 1200 and 1600."

Thinking of what that number meant in human terms awakened a familiar pang in Cree: all the senseless pain people inflicted on each other. Apparently feeling the same thing, Ray subsided suddenly, his thoughts veering elsewhere. Or maybe his headache had returned.

"So . . . which kind are you, Ray?" Cree smiled, letting him know he could take it as banter.

He glanced up, surprised, then pleased. "All of the above? None of the above? I guess I don't quite know yet. How about you, Cree?"

32

BERT PUT THE bag of tools on the front seat of the Suburban, checked his guns, and drove down toward the Bay waterfront. The area immediately around Raymond's warehouse wasn't conducive to surveillance, too exposed, but luckily the railroad and finger channels restricted the number of routes leading out. He chose a spot near the first intersection where Ray would have a choice of directions, then parked the truck and waited, hoping he was right that Ray would go out for Friday night entertainment. The position was good, with a clear view of every car that came out of that section. There weren't many.

When the red Honda SUV approached the intersection, he didn't recognize it until it stopped and the streetlight at the corner lit Cree's face. She was at the wheel, Ray was in the passenger seat. A strange sensation ignited in Bert's gut and burst upwards into his chest, somewhere between outrage, fear, betrayal, sorrow, curiosity, what else he didn't know. There was no way they could see him through his tinted glass, but he reflexively hunched lower in his seat. To his astonishment, they both looked relatively relaxed, Cree looked in control. She even chuckled at something Ray said. Like she had made some kind of social contact with the freak.

But you couldn't be sure, it could all be an act, and anyway he should know where they were going. Change of plans.

He waited until the Honda turned and was past him, then fired up the truck, figuring he'd give them a block lead before he'd pull a U-turn and follow. But then a semi loaded with crushed cars pulled up alongside and stopped at the light. Cut him off completely, no view, no way to move. Bert pounded the wheel in frustration. By the time the light changed and the big rig eased its long ass out, there was no sign of Cree's car.

He took the U anyway and scouted the streets for a time, hoping he'd pick them up again. But no luck. He tried to imagine where she would be going with Scarface, and couldn't. Waves of frustration and anxiety pummeled him until he felt shaky and breathless, and all he could think of was to call her.

He sighed out loud with relief when she answered. It was an effort to make himself sound normal when he hadn't thought through what he was going to say and was out of breath from the surge of fear.

But she sounded like her regular self. He asked if they could get together tomorrow, go over a few things, she said she could meet him early afternoon. Listening carefully to the nuances of her tone and wording, he heard nothing to suggest she was being coerced or was in danger.

"How you doin'?" he asked when he couldn't think of what else to say. Trying to sound like an uncle: "You doin' okay?"

"I'm doing fine. How about you?" A little chilly, like his question had been patronizing.

"Stellar," Bert told her.

Wherever she was, she didn't seem to be immediately at risk. So it was back to the original agenda. This might be his only chance. He turned the truck and drove back to Ray's place.

The street was dark and deserted. Bert pulled up a hundred feet west of the place and backed the Suburban into the shadow of a defunct box truck. He put on a pair of gloves, checked his guns again, and gathered up his duffle bag. His heart did jackrabbit stunts as he walked to the man door in front of Ray's minivan and bent to check the locks.

The noise of dogs barking and the rattle of chain-link came from just around to the left, several dogs really having shit fits. Bert got out his picks, but then decided the first order of business had to be shutting up the animals, they'd clue anybody nearby that something wasn't right. He dug in his duffle, found the can of Mace, walked over to the storage yard fence. Three big dogs barking and snarling and leaping, and he recognized them: his tormentors from the morphing e-mails and pop-ups. Their self-righteous territorial ire pissed him off. He took a couple of shots of them with his digital camera, portraits to match the e-mails, then came up and sprayed them as they lunged against the mesh, right in their eyes, right down their throats, and in seconds they were scraping their paws over their faces, stumbling blindly, whimpering, wheezing. There was some satisfaction in putting them in their place.

Back at Ray's door, the first lock went quickly but the second gave him trouble. It was taking too long, this had to be in and out, eventually somebody would come by and see him. Originally he had wanted this to be totally covert, leaving nothing that would clue Ray he'd been here, but he'd already done the dogs and anyway seeing Ray with Cree had ignited something inside him. It scared him to think she didn't have a better grasp of what she was dealing with, was getting chummy with this psycho. Maybe a message was in order here: Letting Ray know Bert was onto him, wasn't a stickler for procedural niceties, could very well save Cree's life.

He took out his department-issue pry-bar. It was a heavy, forked steel shaft designed for breaking open even armor-clad doors, and he worked it into the crack at the bolt and levered it with all his weight. First time nothing, then again and nothing, but the third time he heard something give in the jam. Being out here, exposed, he felt freakishly nervous, energized, strong as a bull. Another all-out crank and the door flew open.

This was where it got scary. He and Nearing and Koslowski had talked about it from time to time, about the mind-set of any cop who bent the rules. They'd agreed that with this kind of thing, once you'd made the decision you had to go at the job with a commitment to stick it out, to see it through and get it done no matter what it required. No bet-hedges or half measures. For a cop breaking the law, it was all or nothing. Stepping inside Ray's, that was the point where he crossed the line. The point of no return.

He didn't hesitate.

Inside, he could tell it was cavernous and hollow even before he panned his flashlight through the empty warehouse. For a second his wired-up high faltered: Maybe Ray really didn't live here and there was nothing to find. But then he shined his flashlight to the left and saw a brick office pod cut into the space, topped by raw plywood construction, and he put it together. He walked over to the inner door, tried it, found it locked. He put his duffle down again, got out the picks, and then thought, *screw it.* The lock popped with one good yank of the pry-bar, and then he was inside.

33

"IT IS BARBARIC," Ray admitted. "That's its allure, right? People get something they need out of it, a connection to something primal. That's my point."

"How did you even hear about this place?"

"A guy at work. He loves this stuff."

Cree sat next to him in the dark car, staring at the grimy three-story factory building, the plywood-blanked windows, and felt her doubts rise again. There were a few lights on over the entry, enough to illuminate the men who were arriving furtively in twos and threes. Two blocks south was a busy thoroughfare, but this was a quiet street that dead-ended at a gate across the entrance to a factory parking lot. It was the kind of neighborhood Cree had been trained since infancy to avoid, and her urban instincts were putting her on edge.

Ray sensed her unease. "We don't have to go in if you really don't want to. I went last week, and it is pretty . . . intense. I just thought—"

"No. We're here, might as well follow through. I want to understand your point."

Cree turned to him and was startled to see that a group of men had appeared near the passenger window, right next to Ray. They were tough-looking guys and they peered into the car with suspicious looks. Cree felt the sizzle of alarm, but Ray just turned his face so they got a better view. They moved on quickly.

Ray chuckled, then checked his watch again and tipped his head toward the factory. "We should probably go in. It's a mob in there, we won't be able to get seats if we don't get in now. But you have to be, um, kind of alert, okay? Probably you should hang onto your purse, put the strap over your shoulder or something. And don't make eye contact—some of the clientele are a little rough around the edges." Ray cracked his door, but hesitated before he opened it, looking back at her with concern. "But I did warn you, right? And you promise you won't think I'm crazy?"

"Duly warned, Ray," she assured him. "So stipulated."

They went into a cigarette-hazed foyer where four bouncers gave them the evil eye and took twenty bucks, then walked down a long cement hallway toward a muted hubbub of voices from deep inside the building. Passing a cross corridor, Cree spotted two men jockeying a big crate through a side door. She briefly heard the distant barking and snarling of dogs, cut off suddenly as the door swung shut again.

When her cell phone rang, she grabbed it and hit the talk button before she thought about whether it was wise to answer.

Uncle Bert again. What was with him tonight? She stepped out of the corridor into a doorway and put a finger in her other ear. Again Bert said he was just checking in, but he sounded worried and groped for words. Cree was sure he'd been drinking hard. This time he told her that he had some new information on his theory, and that Ray was definitely implicated. He apologized again for the way he'd talked at his office, even though they'd pretty well smoothed that out. She was cautious as she talked, too aware of Ray standing there, and was glad to cut the connection.

Neither commented on the call as they continued down the corridor.

"So my point is," Ray said, "there's a central idea or concept in play here. People have been trying to get a grip on it for thousands of years. The various kinds of werewolves, that's important to consider because it reveals a lot about human nature, and I agree, people's ideas and reactions were mostly misguided and stupid. But there *is* a truth at the center of it all. A stubborn fact. The werewolf idea was just one attempt to give it a name."

"Give precisely *what* a name?"

They had come to a pair of broad swinging doors, and Ray raised a hand and tapped the chipped gray paint. "This, I think."

★ ★ ★

They pushed into a narrow plywood tunnel, then shuffled through into a large room full of jostling bodies and the scent of tobacco and sweaty skin. Once the room must have housed manufacturing equipment, but now it was mostly full of makeshift bleachers, built so that the seats at the walls rose about eight feet higher than the middle of the room. At the center, a sawdust-floored square had been sectioned off in chain-link, about twenty feet on a side, well lit by cone-shaded hanging lamps.

The arena. The pit.

They fought to a seat high against the outer wall, just below a ceiling crossed with ducts and pipes. From here they had a good view of the bright square at the center. Down at the edges of the arena, bookies were taking bets, accepting fistfuls of cash that they passed to hulking banker-bodyguards.

The audience was mixed. Many were Hispanic, working-class men, but there were also quite a few older white guys in expensive casual clothes, plus a good sprinkling of white college kids and some sharply dressed black men. There were some tough-looking, shady types and a few real down-and-outers, but mostly they were men you wouldn't look twice at on the street. Whatever their class or race, they all had something in common: a sharp-eyed air of anticipation, a hyperanimated, sweaty look as if every one of them had some kind of fever.

A commotion broke out across the room. People pressed against the walls as a pair of men came in with a big dirty-yellow dog that strained at its leash. When they got to the pit, they opened a narrow gate and shoved the animal inside, but they kept it pulled hard against the mesh. A moment later a second dog was let into the opposite side, this one a little smaller, dark brown, some Rottweiler or pit bull in the mix. The dogs craned their necks to look at each other, quivering with fear and eagerness. At first they were forcibly restrained by their handlers, but soon both pulled away from the barrier to face each other, standing on hind legs with leashes taut, choking on their collars. The people sitting near Cree and Ray argued about their relative merits. Apparently these weren't great dogs; the better fighters would come out later.

Cree leaned close to Ray's ear. *Do they kill each other?* she was going to ask. *Do they fight to the death?*

But her question was drowned out by a roar of voices. The dogs had been loosed.

Cree had thought they'd be wary at first, circling and sparring, but the instant their collars were slipped they flung themselves at each other. They moved so fast she could hardly see them. They collided in the middle of the arena, rising up on hind legs, chest to chest, as both tried for throat holds. Their speed was appalling. After an instant of grappling, they each found a grip and came down on all fours, straining, shaking. The Rottweiler mix was more muscular, but the mustard-colored dog had a better hold, a wide-mouthed clamp on the front of the throat. Their necks twitched and tossed, legs braced and repositioned, hindquarters strained, paws scraped and slid in the sawdust. Always the two growls, gargling, muffled by fur and flesh.

The crowd went crazy as the Rottweiler gave a tremendous twist that threw the yellow dog down. For a moment the brown dog stood above, worrying frantically, but the yellow dog hadn't let go and the Rottweiler weakened and suddenly the yellow dog was up again. The Rottweiler lost its grip as one yellow ear tore in its mouth. It tried for another hold, but abruptly its hind legs splayed and the powerful body dropped into the sawdust. Its growl became a high screaming stifled in its clamped throat. The yellow dog hunched over it, tossing its head with movements of shoulders and neck so powerful the Rottweiler's whole body jerked back and forth. Its legs flailed. The yellow dog's teeth snatched a new hold right under the enemy's chin. The yellow dog's handlers vaulted the sidewall, warily noosed their animal, pulled it away. Ravening, relentless, it strained back at the twitching Rottweiler.

The loser's handlers were slower to come over the fence. The dog's jaws were snapping as the men hoisted it away, but Cree was pretty sure it was dead. The crowd subsided to a quieter gabble as the bookies paid off and private bets were settled.

"I don't know about this," Cree said weakly. It had lasted maybe sixty seconds. So much savagery condensed into one minute, an explosion. Nausea bloomed in her belly. "What're we here for, Ray? What is it you want me to understand?"

"That's what I'm trying to figure out. It has to do with the primal self, our animal self. Isn't 'werewolf' just an attempt to give it a name? To understand it?"

Cree shut her eyes. "But why the focus on . . . this?"

"The way it makes you feel."

"All I feel is sick, Ray."

"No! Look at it closely. Please. It upsets me too, believe me—I'm a dog lover! But isn't there something else in the feeling?"

The images came back at her: that furious energy, that mindless singleness of purpose. The raw murderous urge in the straining muscles. Seeing it had blasted energy into her, set every nerve firing. She couldn't deny that it echoed something distantly familiar inside, like an intense memory she couldn't quite recall. It had to do with the energy or living force of the dogs. The sheer elemental power, a tornado compressed into those bodies.

"Like fear," she told him. "But different. The power of it, I don't know, maybe . . . awe."

"Yes! Fear leads to awe which merges right into reverence. 'Fear thy God.' People need something like this to make them remember. To let them feel it again. For a while I thought it was the sheer savagery, the killing—the freedom in letting go completely, maybe we know we're not fully alive without it. But now I'm thinking it's even more basic, it's death itself. Any form of freedom has to accommodate the reality of death. It's uncomfortable for us, but a wise person has to live in the continuous knowledge of death. Has to face that big bad secret we keep from ourselves. Because death weeds weakness and irrelevance out of you! Death is a wolf in the sense that death is a winnower, the way the wolves winnow the deer herds of the sick and frail and keep the bloodlines strong. You live more urgently if you're aware you're going to die. You celebrate your existence and live each moment fully. You become strong. You know what freedom is."

"Aren't there other kinds of freedom?"

Ray didn't seem to hear her. "I mean, look at them! Every last man will walk out of here more energized, more vivid than when he walked in. He'll be a stud with his wife or girlfriend tonight. He'll look in his kids' bedroom doors and love them fiercely. Because for a little while he'll remember he's mortal! He'll feel his life as high drama, tragic, heroic. And that's what he's paid for! That's what he came here for!"

She hardly heard the last words. The noise of the crowd had risen sharply as the next dogs appeared at the outer doors. This time the animals were a little smaller, one a Doberman mix, the other some kind of terrier about the same size. Their handlers pushed them into the pit, and again there was a wait as the bookies finished taking bets for this round. With its head pulled against the mesh, the Doberman strained so hard to see its enemy that its eyes rolled white around the edges.

The prospect of watching another fight gave Cree a panicky feeling. "That's all for me," she said firmly. "I need to leave now."

They stood quickly and began pushing between knees and backs to the end of the row. When they got to the arena floor, she let Ray lead, his size and his face clearing a path for them.

The crowd roared as the dogs were loosed. Cree couldn't help herself, her eyes were drawn to the fury.

"No!" Ray whispered urgently into her ear. "Not the dogs! That's not what we're here for!" And he took her shoulders and turned her to face the other way, toward the bleachers.

All the leaning, craning, excited faces, the open roaring mouths, the scorn and concern and wild-pleasured glow in every one, row upon row. Their collective appetite seemed to swallow her, suck her in, as their eyes mirrored every awful leap and slash, heave and twist. She stood appalled, paralyzed, until Ray pulled her into the corridor and away.

34

RAYMOND KEPT A nice place. The kitchen had terra-cotta tiles on the floor, hardwood cabinets, marble countertops, a cute little wine rack. Bert inspected the kitchen and attached dining area, didn't find anything of great interest. Still, he pulled out several plastic evidence bags and scanned the floor carefully. People with dogs had dog hair in their houses. Ray's floor was clean, but Bert knelt and laid his face along the tiles and put the light under the refrigerator and sure enough, several inches back there was a good collection of hair and dust. He used the pry-bar to rake some out and then sealed it into one of his evidence bags.

Check off item number one. One nail in Ray's coffin.

He found more good samples in a space between counter sections and under the dishwasher, then moved on to the living room.

It was a hip sort of place, brick walls painted white, nice oak floors, good rugs, the pad of a swinging bachelor who made good money or had inherited or both. Decent stereo and a collection of older rock 'n' roll and classical music on compact discs. Bert shined his flashlight over the bookshelves, seeing fiction titles, some history and biography, texts on anatomy, medicine, radiology, photography, computer tech. Some dog books, too.

There was a desk beneath one of the windows on the outer wall. Bert snapped on the goosenecked lamp, bent the shade close so it wouldn't spill too much light, and fingered quickly through the stack of papers. Predictably, there were envelopes from Temple and the UC medical school, but there were also some from other path labs. He looked at a few, found a mix of technical lab reports, pay stubs and bills, nothing directly implicating. He went to work on the drawers.

The top drawer held pens, change, keys, calculator, the usual. The checkbook showed regular deposits every two weeks, probably paychecks; Ray made decent money, must add up to a hundred grand a year. The only obvious anomaly was a recent deposit that exactly covered a big check to something called the Moeris Foundation. Bert filed the unusual name in his memory for future inquiries, then put the checkbook back. He looked at his watch and was surprised to find that he'd already used up half of the one hour he'd planned to allow himself here. Had to keep it moving along.

Another drawer held more bills, receipts, extra credit cards, office supplies. More keys. Many were electronic key-cards, the plastic kind used by restricted-access places like labs. He looked closely at them, saw logos but no marking except numeric codes. Ray had keys for a *lot* of doors. Needed for getting in and out of labs and supply rooms at Temple and UC Medical? Or pilfered from his occasional visits to other labs, for other purposes? Another question filed for future consideration.

The lowest drawer held hanging files, well labeled and alphabetized, and Bert immediately saw one of his targets: dogs. A guy with three dogs would have records of shots, licenses, vet bills, maybe pedigrees. He opened the file and began scanning the pages. Fritz, Sadie, Basil: cute names for the vicious threesome he'd just hosed. Bert photographed a bill detailing rabies and distemper boosters and then another that looked like an annual checkup form, listing the dogs by name along with their ages, weights, and vaccination status. None of the dogs was older than six years, the youngest was only three.

He closed the drawer and switched off the light just as headlights crossed the window. He couldn't see out through the heavy, wired glass, but clearly somebody was driving up or driving by. Bert stepped quickly aside, froze, listened. Suddenly his heart was pumping too hard, juicing him. Could they have come back already?

But the lights went on past, blurry orbs that disappeared for only a moment before drifting back the other way. Probably somebody who had just bought some rock in Hunters Point and was looking for an out-of-the-way place to smoke it. Or maybe the other side of that ecosystem, an SFPD patrol car.

Bert finished the living room, went into the bedroom. Another example of tasteful decor, nice spread on the hardwood queen-size bed, good furnishings, some original art on the walls. The dresser top was a litter of the usual stuff, coins, tie-clips, a watch, some breath mints.

And a switchblade knife.

Oh ho, Bert thought. His first emotion was one of glee, but it was followed hard by a slug of fear for Cree, out there with Ray right now. Abruptly his hands tingled and without thinking about it he yanked out his cell phone and thumbed in Cree's number. If she didn't answer, he'd put out an APB on her car. Then he'd—

But she answered after two rings. He stuttered, unable to admit he'd seen her with Ray, but he told her to stay away from Ray at all costs, that he had a lot to tell her when they got together tomorrow. In the background, he could hear the murmur of many voices, like she was at a bar somewhere. She definitely did not sound like someone speaking under duress, just a little chilly and reserved. He couldn't blame her, the way he probably sounded.

For a moment he stood with the phone still in his hand, feeling relieved and suddenly deeply thirsty for a drink. He wondered where she was. Where Ray was, and how soon he'd return. Time to get focused again.

He snapped open the knife and studied it in the flashlight beam. From the wear on the horn and chrome of the handle, he figured it was not a new weapon but had been in use for many years, maybe something of a keepsake. The blade was long, sharp, and spotless, no trace of residues even at the hinge or in the slot, nothing he could take a scraping of. Too bad. On the other hand, there was a distinctive nick in the otherwise perfect edge, a feature that would surely leave its mark in a wound. He laid the open knife on the dresser, put a quarter next to it for a size reference, then took out his camera and snapped several close-ups.

On to the bedside table. The top drawer held nothing but a bunch of prescription bottles, which he inspected one by one. Most were drug names he didn't know, but from his years at Narcotics he recognized a couple as Class II painkillers, restricted stuff. The labels named several different prescribing doctors and pharmacies, suggesting Ray was doing the shell-game routine to conceal his habit.

So Ray was, among other things, a pharmaceuticals junkie. Bert felt he was getting somewhere now.

The lower drawer contained a half dozen photographs, eight-by-tens facedown on the bottom. Bert got another tingle in his hands. So far he hadn't found anything that looked like a "souvenir," the kind of memento serial killers often took from their crimes, maybe this was Ray's stash. But when he turned them over, he was disappointed to see Ray himself. Much younger, a teenager, bad early-eighties haircut above those pale blue eyes. In one shot he was with a fresh-faced blond girl whose smile showed braces. Ray looked clean-cut, innocent, healthy. Clear skin on an unmarked face.

Funny, Bert thought, there was a drawer like this in his own house. Photos not exactly hidden, just kept private. Megan photos that came out very, very rarely but were very, very important when they did. A ghost of recognition passed through him, a wispy gray phantom of nameless emotion that made him uncomfortable for a moment and then faded quickly.

He checked his watch and realized he had to move faster. He finished the downstairs and then went up the suspended stairway from the living room. At the top, he opened a door, turned left on a small landing, and went up four more steps into a big room that rose all the way to the warehouse roof. Some light came in here, ambient city light from four tall windows. Bert could see huge framed art works on the walls, vague in the dim light. Along one wall were tables with computer monitors and other equipment on them. A workshop or studio.

The buzz in Bert's veins was increasing. Mainly it was the tension of being here, the risk of getting caught, maybe Ray coming home early. But part of it was another feeling he knew well, an instinctive sense he was getting close to something. This was Ray's sanctum sanctorum. Coming up here, he was finally getting into Raymond's head.

He brought the flashlight onto one of the canvasses and saw what it was: an X-ray of a skull, one eye-hole and part of a nose opening, the shell of the cranium a pale curve set against empty dark. The next was the same, and the next. Every one featured part of a skull. Bert had looked at enough autopsy photos, X-rays, and MRIs to know what he was seeing. In the MRIs, he recognized a glow of something irregular inside, too soft-edged to be a bullet, had to be a tumor. In one of the X-rays, the faint outline of a broken hole, a cranial injury that had to have been fatal.

So these were corpses. Ray was bringing home pictures from work. Or had other access to bodies. The guy was a necrophiliac.

Bert felt a twitch of panic. Cree was out there somewhere with this fruitcake at this very moment. He should have followed them! His hand found his cell phone and he almost called her again, then decided he'd only antagonize her.

If he lays a hand on her, he thought. *One finger.*

Hurrying now, he looked over the computer equipment briefly, the sleepy drift of screensaver starfields, and wished he could take the time to pry inside Ray's cyber files. But it would take too long, and he was no computer expert. Suffice to know that Ray had high-end computers and clearly knew his way around them. From the pop-ups, he already knew Ray had some good hacking-type skills.

Back near the stairs again, he put the flashlight in his teeth and opened one of the file cabinets. Fingering through the row of hanging files, he found older bills and receipts, property records, car records, medical, vital papers. And dogs again.

He pulled the dog file and knew he'd hit gold. Dogs didn't live that long. Some of the cases he was looking at were as much as ten and fourteen years old, meaning they couldn't have involved Ray's current animals. But here were the previous dogs: Lizzie, a malamute from ten years ago. Sherlock, a mastiff from the same period. Rat, mixed breed, twelve years ago.

A real dog lover, Cameron.

Bert's spine tingled when he found vet records, including X-rays for dental work on a pit bull from fifteen years ago. This was pure gold, the Crime Lab could maybe match these films with bite impressions on the victims. He lined up selected pages and began snapping photos.

He had already gone well over the time he'd allotted, and the tension was starting to wear on him. He flipped through the other files, didn't find anything worth stopping for, slid shut the last drawer. Then he went to the coffee table to look over the scattering of artsy things, papers, pens. Also a book about werewolves, one on the psychology of serial killers, one on the neurology of violent behavior. For a heartbeat he felt the bitter savor of vindication: Yes, Ray was one seriously fucked-up guy. But behind it came a flood of fear. The thought of something happening to Cree made him shaky and sick. Jelly in the knees. It was a feeling that went back into the shadowed past, the hidden parts of his heart. The pain he'd kept walled off for twenty-six years. What if he'd let it happen again?

Pray to God, he thought. *Pray to God. Please, not ever again. I am not strong enough. I can't. Please.*

He found his phone, punched in her number, then closed the phone before the connection was made. One more call and she really would think he was crazy. He was too shook up, the tension undoing him. Time to go.

There was a drafting table near the stairs, and he panned his light over it, just a quick look. Nothing of interest. But there were big pieces of paper taped to the wall above it, and when he shined his light on them he saw that they were maps. Topo maps that showed every back road and house. Rural areas, state parks. There were pencilled-in lines wandering among the topo marks, apparently routes and paths. Bert lost his breath as he read the names of the places. One was San Bruno Mountain State Park.

San Bruno, where that kid had been killed by dogs or coyotes only four years ago.

He was fumbling for his camera when the windows came alight with the glow of moving headlights. Instantly his tactical reflexes took over. He scanned the room to determine the angles of view and quickly chose the area between the head of the stairs and the corner, where he'd be behind anyone coming up. The headlights shone full on the windows now as the car turned in at the front of the building.

He stepped into the shadows and drew his Beretta. He held it with both hands and aimed it at the top of the stairwell and then just waited in the charged half-dark.

35

ALONG GRAY LINE materialized in the near dark, gathered, grew, brightened suddenly, and tumbled onto the sloped shore. Before the foam subsided and slid back, another pale tube had formed against the blackness and was moving in. The cast-up spray turned to mist as it blew inland, and Cree sucked it into her lungs. Sand yielding beneath her feet, fresh sea air, the reassuring rhythm of the waves: Ray was right, this was good. An antidote.

Far behind her, Ray strolled with his hands in his pockets, head down, an indistinct shape in the faint glow from the streetlamps along the Great Highway. She toed ridges in the sand as she waited to let him catch up.

He raised his head as he approached her and they strolled on together. "Better?"

"Much. Thanks for suggesting this."

"Yeah. The first time I saw the dogfights, I actually threw up. But this helps. It's good to get outside, get some distance on human beings when they start to worry you. Do you run? If you do, this is the best place in town to do it. I run here once in a while."

"You look like you do a pretty intense workout."

"Oh, I used to. Now I mainly just run. But I usually do it out of town, up in the hills, so it's more of an obstacle course, really. Night runs, off-trail, cross-country. Another quirky habit. If I get into thornbushes, I can lose a bit more skin than I'd prefer, but it does keep me in pretty good shape. Heals body and soul."

Cree thought of the web of fine scars that covered his legs and lower torso. Ray was definitely an unusual person—a werewolf, an innocent, a kindred spirit, a stranger. Walking next to him in the dark, she sensed his deep satisfaction with the moment and knew that her presence figured importantly in it.

"So, Ray."

"Hm?"

"A man and a woman go a for a walk together on the beach at night—"

"With a priest, a rabbi, and a kangaroo?"

Cree had to laugh. "I thought they went into a bar."

"And because they're mature adults, and sexuality is always an unspoken dynamic under such circumstances, the woman wants to make it clear that she's not available. Maybe it's not good timing, she's coming out of a breakup and she's not ready yet. Or she's already got a boyfriend. She tells him straight up so there are no misunderstandings and no disappointments later. But she hopes they can remain friends. Is that how this one goes?"

Cree kicked at a Styrofoam cup and a gust carried it away. "Something like that."

Ray shrugged and hunched his shoulders a little against the wind.

"And the guy says—?" she prompted.

"I always forget the punchline, dammit." He chuckled quietly. "No. I really haven't built up some big expectation, Cree. I enjoy your company a lot, I can't pretend otherwise. But I . . . it's not the best timing for me, either."

They stood looking out at the crashing, wave-ribbed dark, the cold wind pulling at their clothes and hair. Then it was time to head back.

"But all that was going to be preface to something else," Cree told him. "I was going to ask if you'd want to help me with the wolfman research. You've had more good ideas on the subject tonight than I've had in the last four days. It's pretty tedious, but it would sure go a lot faster with two sets of eyes. Do you have any time?"

"Sure. But what about Bert?"

"I'll talk to him. I'll ask Horace to talk to him. I'm sure we can work it out."

Ray bobbed his head ambiguously.

Cree pulled up in front of Diamond Intermodal, leaving the motor running and lights on. They'd agreed to meet at the Payson Collection in the morning, but otherwise had said little during the drive from the beach. It was only ten thirty, but it felt later. In her exhaustion, Cree felt her anxiety return. The area around Ray's looked grimy, squalid, forbidding in the blue streetlights and narrow wedge of headlight glow.

They said a quick good-night that felt a little strained, and Cree began backing out. She stopped as her headlights panned across Ray's wide-open front door.

Ray leaned to peer warily into the darkness, cocked his head to listen. Cree pulled forward again and slid down her window. In the headlight wash, Ray checked the edge of the door and picked at the crimped metal jamb, then disappeared into the black doorway.

After a moment a dim light came on, and Cree shut down the car and went to the door. A couple of bulbs glowed up near the ceiling, weakly lighting the near end of the desolate interior. It was enough to see Ray, striding quickly past his apartment to the big roll-up doors. He stopped, slapped a button. One of the doors lifted noisily, Ray ducked through. Calling the dogs, she figured. Then she realized she hadn't heard any barking since they'd returned. To Ray, the silence must have seemed very wrong.

By the time she got to the freight door, Ray was emerging from the dark outside. He pulled two of the dogs by their collars and the third followed close behind with stumbling, uncertain movements. There was something the matter with them. When he brought them into the light, Cree could see their swollen, seeping eyes, the froth and vomit that streaked their faces and chests. They hung their heads and worked their mouths and tongues as if trying to expel something.

"Help me with them," he commanded her. "Dogs, this is Cree. She's our friend. Okay?" To Cree again: "Grab Sadie's collar. Lead her to the house. They can't see."

She took the Rottweiler's collar and tugged her along after Ray and the others. The dog reeked of a sharp chemical scent Cree recognized: Mace or some equivalent self-defense spray.

The door to the apartment was ajar, too. Ray snapped on the kitchen lights and they brought the animals to the sink.

"Sit," he ordered. "Stay and hold."

They sat in a row, three tortured canine faces, saliva hanging in strings from their jowls. Sadie whimpered, but the others sat stoic, trusting Ray absolutely. As soon as they were settled, Ray groped in a broom closet and came out with a baseball bat. He left them there and went into the living room. Cree saw the lights come on, heard the sound of doors quickly opening and closing. Ray searching for the intruder.

If it's Bert, she was thinking. *If he's still here. If he's gone this far.* She heard Ray's footsteps start up the stairs to the second-floor studio and suddenly she couldn't help herself, she left the dogs and ran to the living room door.

"Hey, Ray," she called.

He stopped halfway up the stairs. "What."

"Maybe I should come with you up there."

"Why?"

"What if somebody has a gun or—?"

"Just stay with the dogs. I'll deal with this." Before she could move, he bounded up the stairs, shouldered open the door at the top, and burst through it.

36

CREE LISTENED TO Ray's footsteps moving through the room above. She didn't realize she wasn't breathing until a moment later, when she let out a pent-up breath.

No shots. No sound of a scuffle.

She went back to the dogs. They were still sitting as they'd been ordered, wheezing painfully but alert and tracking Ray's movements with their ears. She opened cabinets until she found a stack of kitchen towels, then ran water from the tap. When the temperature seemed right she soaked a towel in the flow. She turned back to the dogs and saw how jittery they were and she faltered as she wondered whether they'd really accept this kind of contact from a stranger. They were all big dogs with powerfully muscled shoulders and haunches, in better shape than any of the dogs she'd seen in the pit. And very screwed up right now.

Ray appeared at the kitchen door. He put down the bat and came to the sink. His movements were crisp and taut, tightly focused. He glanced at the towels, tested the water with his hand. "Good. Okay, you do Sadie, I'll do the boys. Sadie, just hold and Cree will make you feel better."

He soaked a towel, knelt next to the shepherd, laid the sopping cloth over its eyes. The dog flinched at the contact but held still as Ray began gently massaging. Cree did the same with the Rottweiler. The eyes twitched under her fingers and Sadie's whining sharpened. Cree soaked the dog's face and neck, scrubbed the ears, the nose, feeling the bone at the brow, the knob at the base of the skull, the long jaw. Their contours reminded her of the wolfman's bones. After a few minutes she rinsed the towel, wrung it, soaked it again, did the whole thing once more. Sadie's whimpering quieted.

Ray worked on the other dogs without speaking except to murmur softly to them. When he was done, he rubbed them with dry towels and then poured fresh water into a big bowl on the floor. The dogs lapped and cast themselves randomly on the kitchen's throw rugs, wheezing and exhausted but looking much better. Ray took off his fouled shirt, gathered the towels, and threw them all into a hamper in the closet.

"He fucked around in my desk drawers," Ray said. "Went upstairs and poked around. Opened my file cabinets. I don't know if anything's missing or not."

" 'He'? You know who did this?" It sounded bogus even as she said it.

Ray turned a baleful eye on her. "You know, I don't have time for bullshit. You should go, Cree. Thanks for everything tonight, and thanks for helping with the dogs, I mean that. I have to figure out some way to lock up the outer door, so I'll see you out."

"Ray, why would Bert do this? Spray your dogs, I mean, that's just sadistic, Bert wouldn't—"

"They'd have come to the fence and barked the whole time he was in here and sooner or later somebody would have noticed. Or maybe the sound just bugged him. So he shut them up before he came in." Ray slammed a fist into a cabinet, startling the dogs.

"You don't know it was him! And even if it was Bert, you can't . . . do something back. That's what I came here for today, Ray, that's the main thing! Let me deal with this. Don't crank this up any worse. It's stupid and it's dangerous."

"What, you're going to tell Uncle Bert that Ray's a nice fellow? Ray'd never hurt a fly? You don't believe that yourself! You don't know what to believe."

"Show me, Ray! Show me what you'd do. Show me you've got a handle on your anger. If Bert did this, he's way over the line. Don't go there with him!"

Ray's rage built, his whole body stiffening with the effort to contain it. With his shirt off his torso was a study of chiseled musculature. When she didn't move, he came up to her and with one hand grabbed her shoulder and spun her toward the door. But she knocked the hand away with a hard forearm sweep and whirled back to him.

The three dogs came instantly to their feet.

Ray's face warped. "Cree, if you don't leave, I'm going to fold you up like a lawn chair and toss you out. Jesus Christ, this is *my house*! What does it take to convince you and Bert that this is *my house*?"

His face had become hard on one side and savage on the other, but what Cree felt was not fear or anger but a sudden sense of loss. The things they'd talked about all night were scary and strange, but he'd told everything with an oddly innocent excitement, an implicit trust in her. Its absence hurt her and she thought it must hurt him too and without thinking she reached for him.

His hand scythed up and snatched her arm out of the air. He held it off to the side, beamed his outrage at her.

"I wasn't going to hit you," she said.

He flung her arm away. "What then?"

She laid her hand cautiously along his cheek. Her right hand, his left cheek, it was just an accident that it was the scarred side. With her hand hiding that side he almost looked like an undamaged man, handsome, well made, symmetrical. He couldn't hide his surprise or how much he needed the touch. She held the contact until the fear of it went out of both of them.

"I'm going to help you get the place cleaned up," she told him. "Then we're going to talk until we figure out what to do."

37

FRIDAY NIGHT, THE Tenderloin Club was busier than the typical
weekday. The pool tables were loud with cracking balls and drunken
conversation, the booths and tables were packed. Bert didn't know anybody in the crowd. He took his first drink at the bar and nursed it until
around eleven the front corner booth opened up and he moved over. It
was darker here, the table lit mostly by the beer signs in the windows. He
positioned himself so he could see the entrance, then set out his second
whiskey, his cigarettes, lighter, notepad, pen. He was beginning to come
down at last.

Back at Ray's place, he'd been tense as a time bomb, and when the
headlights lit the windows he'd gotten instantly wired, stoned on the
adrenaline. He had stood with his gun in his hands, feeling a mix of fear
and power, a rush that he focused into a hard sense of righteous self-
preservation.

But nobody had come. The lights had shone onto the windows,
paused, then pulled away. Somebody making a three-point turn on the
parking apron in front. He had waited until the lights were gone, then
bolted down the stairs, outside, to the Suburban. It was only two minutes
later, roaring up Third, that he realized he'd let himself be distracted, that
he should have taken photos of the topo maps and the trails Ray had
drawn on them. He cursed himself for losing control. He needed to compare Ray's maps with the scene of at least one murder, the kid killed in
San Bruno Mountain Park. A stupid oversight, he'd panicked like a fucking rookie. But he couldn't go back tonight. Ray might return at any moment. And anyway he was too fried.

Instead he'd gone home to Mars Street. Still twitchy, he'd reviewed the images on his camera and printed up the best ones on his inkjet. When that was done, he'd hit the telephone, calling in a favor—one of the last remaining chits culled from thirty-five years on the job. Now he had a little while before his meeting, enough time to get his nerves back together and put his case in order. The booze was starting to hit and it felt like a reward, calming and smoothing him. He felt clearer and sharper than he had in a long time.

He finished his second drink, ordered a third, then opened his briefcase and took out the envelope of photos and the three plastic bags of trace evidence. On his pad he started to draw a timeline based on what he knew, filling in any corroborating bits and pieces. It was still full of holes, not enough to pry a search warrant out of a judge, not even enough to talk to his lieutenant, yet. But Hank Chambers would see it. Hank would know how to work with it.

He stared at the materials as if he might spot images hidden between the scrawled pen marks. He knew the pattern would emerge if he thought long and hard enough, and the pattern would reveal ways to prove what had happened. Every event and date and place suggested other lines of inquiry, and he made systematic notes of these as they occurred to him. He was still working on it when the front door swung open and Hank came in, pouted, and began making his way to the booth.

"Hank, I love you madly. Marry me. I'm serious. You're my fucking hero."

"I'm here, Bertie, but I'm not making promises. Right? I have to believe this is worth the effort. And you have to agree that if you come up with something admissible, you'll route it so it never comes anywhere near me. If I do this, I'm tainted. One whiff of bad procedure will sink any case you might have."

"I know the rules. How about a drink?"

"Just give me the spiel. My girlfriend expects me back."

Chambers's face told Bert he was very definitely not in the same place Bert was, that flushed feeling of hot hope and righteous bloodlust, the celebratory rush you got after a close call and a big breakthrough. Hank was in his late fifties, dressed tonight in new jeans and a checked shirt and a sport jacket. With his silver hair and yachting tan and tasseled loafers, he looked more like some CEO on vacation than a senior forensic scientist and lab administrator making an off-the-record rendezvous. He'd always struck Bert as a bit of an snide, self-obsessed prig, spoiled by the seemingly endless sequence of younger women he reeled in over the years. But professionally, Hank was old school. For the last seven years he'd been chief of the Berkeley lab of the Bureau of Forensic Services, a branch of the California attorney general's office tasked to assist local police agencies with highly technical or interjurisdictional investigations. The lab was devoted to DNA work, but Hank's position and reputation would get him access to cold case evidence of any kind, from any department in the state, no questions asked.

He and Bert went a long way back, but clearly the comrades-in-arms routine wasn't enough tonight. This was stretching it, and Bert knew another approach was needed.

"Hank—this is big. This is—"

"Hey, Bertie, you know how many retiring cops have come to me like this? Wanting a favor to help them nail down the last big one?"

Bert felt a flush creep up his neck. "But they weren't me. Not one of them was as good as me. You know that. I'd've been shown the door ten years ago if I didn't have the best clearance and conviction rates in this city. Is that worth anything to anybody right now? Tell me what's worth something, Hank."

Hank shrugged.

"Trust me, this warrants you coming down here tonight when you'd rather be doing something else. I wouldn't have called if it wasn't the only way I could go. I know I got nothing to offer in return. Except my gratitude. And maybe some satisfaction for having done the right thing."

They locked eyes, gauging each other. At last Chambers must have made a decision, because he flipped open a pair of reading glasses and slid them on, making a *give it* gesture with his other hand.

"Okay." Bert turned around the page so Chambers could read it. "General scenario is, a series of homicides, going back some years, a likely perp who never got nailed, some recent developments pointing to a particular guy. I've noted the dates, jurisdictions, and file numbers for the cases I think he might be good for. Some are old enough that they didn't have the lab tech you've got now, the evidence will need a second look. Some of these might not pan out, but I'm betting some will."

"What else?"

Bert showed him the photos. "These are from his residence. The knife is maybe the best item here. It's old, there's a possibility it was used in a couple of those. It's pretty clean, probably no organic residues to test, but I figured you'd be the guy to ask around, look for a match with the wounds."

Chambers studied the photos, scanned Bert's notes, then went back to the photos with a puzzled frown. "What's with the veterinary records?"

"Dogs. The guy has three attack breeds now, he's had dogs going back years, these will tell you the previous breeds and when he had them. Five of those cases involve canine attacks, two within the lifespan of his current dogs. For the older cases, I'm hoping you can match hair found at the scene to the breeds he had then. If we're very lucky, the dental records on that pit bull will match some bite impressions. For the newer ones, I've got the hair of his current dogs." Bert pushed over the plastic bags.

Chambers frowned at the hair and dust briefly before tucking the bags into his jacket pocket. "If they even took hair and fiber on these cases. If I can put my hands on it. If there's any DNA in the samples."

"I know there's dog hair on the one of them, the slice-and-dice. I checked. Got the list right here." Bert slid the stapled sheaf over to him.

Chambers still looked skeptical, but Bert knew he'd hooked him with the possibilities. Here was a puzzle with one piece missing, and Hank couldn't resist trying to fit his piece in. That instinct was what they had in common, what Bert was counting on.

Chambers gathered up the photos and slipped them and Bert's notes into the envelope. When he'd closed the clasp, he paused, pursed his lips, frowned like a man having second thoughts.

Bert felt a stab of panic. "Three months, Hank! I'll get my plaque and my badge in a block of Lucite, which I'm gonna toss in the trash when I get home. But you do this, you give me this, I'll have something I can keep."

Hank bobbed his head, giving up, then stood and turned to go. Over his shoulder, he said, "I know, Bertie. I know what this is."

Bert ordered another whiskey that he flourished and tossed off like champagne. He looked at his notebook and checked off items on his list.

Everything was going like clockwork. With any luck, Hank would find something that tied the physical evidence from Raymond's place with evidence from one or more of the crimes. One hair on that kid in San Bruno Park. One match of presumed dog breed with one of Ray's dogs. One stab wound that matched the blade of Ray's knife. Bert could then work up a legal pretext to go into Ray's place with the warrant that would provide him with admissible evidence.

And if that didn't pan out, there were other ways to do this. Next item on the list was to set up the contingency plan. Plan B. Fortunately, he had pretty good resources for Plan B.

38

THE HANDBILL HAD nothing to do with the wolfman but, like so many other items in the Oddities files, Cree couldn't resist looking at it more closely. The advertisement was accompanied by a collection of newspaper clippings, other handbills, even a grainy photo of something indeterminate in a glass jar. One poster featured a drawing of the head suspended in a cannister of fluid, its grimacing face surrounded by swirls of black hair, and gave more details:

Along with the poster was a clipping about Murieta, a Mexican who had come to stake a claim in gold country only to have his land taken, his wife raped, and his brother murdered by American miners. With the help of Three-Fingered Jack, Murieta went on a three-year rampage of revenge and became so famous that after he was shot to death his pickled head was used to draw custom to various saloons and dives. Among the materials was a statement by a doctor, certifying that by actual measurement the hair on the head had grown several inches since Murieta's death. The head ended up in the Museum of Horrors, where it was destroyed along with most of the city in 1906.

Cree put the file back and made a note to look further into Dr. Jordon's Museum. She straightened her stiffening back and looked across the room to where Ray was working through another box.

Asking Ray to help had been the right move, she decided again, for more reasons than one. His face had its uses: When Gerald Payson had opened the door and seen Ray with her, his mouth had dropped open and he'd stepped reflexively back from the door. She introduced Ray as her associate, then whisked past Payson and into the front parlor.

"Did you dig out the boxes I requested?"

"Frankly, no." Payson went to stand behind the desk and sullenly pushed the register across to her. "We had other pressing obligations." Before Cree could respond, Payson turned and called chidingly, "Sir! Sir! You're supposed to sign the register. And a donation to the foundation is customary."

Ray was across the room and had pulled open the doors to the rear parlor. When Payson called, Ray sauntered back to the desk. He stared hard at Payson as he snapped a crisp twenty out of his shirt pocket. Still not saying a word, he reached across and tucked it deep under the waistband of Payson's pleated trousers.

It was more than enough to keep Payson out of their hair today.

They'd gone back to the library to start where Cree had left off. You had to give Ray credit for the performance, Cree thought. Also for being a companionable research partner who didn't chatter all the time. He was as into this as she was, intent on the work.

Another saloon attraction: the display of two corpses of outlaws shot by a posse of angry citizens. Attached to the poster was a photo of the coffins, propped upright against a clapboard wall below a sign that read

THE BIG NUGGET. The bodies were roped in, wrists tied across their stomachs, rifles wedged at their sides. Four bartenders posed smiling and proud next to the coffins, invigorated by their proximity to infamous death. Ray had that right.

A few minutes later she unfolded a poster that gave her a hard tick in her chest, the charge of excitement that always came with a possible breakthrough.

THE WILD MAN

RECENTLY CAPTURED IN THE JUNGLES OF BORNEO!

HALF MAN & HALF BEAST,

HE IS ENTIRELY COVERED IN HAIR & EATS ONLY RAW MEAT!

SPECTATORS ARE REQUESTED TO STAND WELL CLEAR OF HIS CAGE

AS HE IS SAVAGE & HIGHLY DANGEROUS IF PROVOKED.

THE SEVEN WONDERS FREAK SHOW, MARKET STREET

ONLY 25¢ ADMISSION!

She fanned through the materials and snatched up another poster that featured a drawing of a furry, apelike thing hunkered over a beef joint. But reading the attached clippings, she saw it was just Oofty Goofty, a well-known eccentric of the period whom she'd encountered in her history books. The oddball entrepreneur and would-be actor had covered himself with tar stuck full of horsehair. His brief stint at the freak show had ended when he got so sick that he was taken to a hospital, where doctors went to great lengths to remove the suffocating coating. Later, he made his living in the streets and saloons as a professional masochist: For a dime, men could punch and kick him as hard as they liked, for a quarter beat him with their canes, or for fifty cents use the baseball bat Oofty Goofty carried for the purpose. He took pride in displaying no discomfort and made a living that way for years. Finally the famous boxer John L. Sullivan hit him too hard with a pool cue, after which Oofty Goofty retired with a damaged spine.

She went on to the next file, troubled by Oofty Goofty. Why would someone choose such a career, and why would so many people be willing to pay to inflict pain on such a pitiful creature? There were aspects of human nature she could not manage to empathize with.

"I don't mean to be discouraging," Ray said. "But if he was the child of Hans and Lydia Schweitzer, we won't find him in this kind of material."

Earlier, they had discussed the photo in the rolltop desk and brainstormed on ways Lydia Jackson's connection to Hans and the house could guide them.

"Why not?"

"Typical wealthy or at least up-and-coming Victorians would've hidden him away from public view. It was pretty common with deformed or psychologically troubled kids. Another of the paradoxes of the Victorian mind-set—half of society laboring to conceal things they considered 'unsavory,' half laboring to exploit and sensationalize them. It would explain why he was found in the basement."

Cree could easily envision the scenario: Hans and Lydia married and had a badly deformed baby that miraculously survived into adulthood. Maybe he was severely retarded or behaviorally impaired, prone to hurting himself or others, so Hans built a room in the basement where the child could be kept both safe and out of sight. After the quake, still wanting to hide their secret shame, Hans personally repaired the house, sealed up the brickwork chamber, and tried to forget. Later, they sold the house and moved away, and no one ever knew until Hernandez and his crew knocked down that well-built wall and started finding bones.

Ray was right: If the wolfman was their child, he wouldn't have shown up as a Barbary Coast entertainment. On the other hand, Cree decided, it increased the likelihood that he'd appear in medical records or family papers that she might eventually track down.

Ray finished the box he'd been working on, shoved it aside, stood scratching the back of his neck as he pored over the master catalog. "I want to follow up on my ideas for a different tack here. You up for finishing Oddities on your own?"

"Sure. Only two more boxes."

Ray wrestled several new cartons from the back of the room, while Cree plugged away at Oddities.

Last night, putting her hand to Ray's face had changed the energy between them. Her spontaneous touch had surprised him and spun him suddenly out of his rage and frustration. It was clearly something he needed. Of course it was. She had helped him clean up the kitchen and figure out a temporary way to lock the outer door for the night. Afterward, they had sat for a long time in the living room, Cree on the couch, Ray in the big chair, sipping fizzy water, talking. She had pleaded with him not to retaliate against Bert, if that was who had broken in, and had promised she would confront him. Later still, their talk had drifted on to other things as they'd both wearied, with the odd intimacy of relative strangers alone together in the early morning hours. She had stirred from a near-drowse on his couch at almost three in the morning. Ray had fallen asleep in his chair, and she'd had to wake him to see her out.

Today it was a lot easier to be around Ray. He was proving to be a smart researcher, quick to see possibilities and connections, and his presence made her more hopeful they'd find something useful. They shared a familiarity, some slight trust of the other's words or thoughts that came of having talked about things that matter. Even his body language had changed: He made no effort to keep the bad side of his face from view, and the immediate result of his lack of self-consciousness was that Cree stopped noticing the scarring. She wondered if they'd ever attain the level of trust where she could mention that.

The Medical files were easily as strange as the Oddities. Like everywhere else in the Victorian era, San Francisco was enthralled by an explosion of "scientific" potions and cures, quack diets and exercise regimens, bizarre technologies that promised cures for gout, consumption, alcoholism, chronic masturbation. Sanitoriums abounded where people could receive the latest treatments, often with the aid of fantastic machines. New "facts" about human anatomy and behavior were discovered daily and promised remedies for every disease, discomfort, and character failing. It was the era of laudanum, paregoric and cocaine, arsenic and leeches, water cures and electric shocks and magnetic stimulation. Cree's pulse picked up when she came across a collection of doctors' case studies of abnormalities and medical curiosities, including a meticulously illustrated tract on the dissection of a pair of stillborn Siamese twins.

By two o'clock, they had found nothing on a wolflike man, an ape-man, wildman, or werewolf, and Cree had started to think ahead to the meeting she'd arranged with Uncle Bert, a confrontation that promised to be difficult. She straightened and was about to tell Ray she'd had it for the day, but he spoke first.

"I've got something."

"Oh?"

Ray toed one of the boxes at his feet. "It's from the Religion files. Which are not much—obviously, it wasn't a priority for our fun-loving ancestral Payson. What there is mainly relates to mission work in the Barbary Coast. This is from May 1906, about a month after the quake—a program for a joint memorial service they gave for church members who died in the quake."

He was studying a black-bordered page with a flowery cross at the top. It started with some somber religious text and ended with a list of seven names. Cree followed his finger to an entry near the bottom:

Lydia Jackson Schweitzer,
beloved wife of Hans Heinrich Schweitzer,
faithful member of the congregation of Good Savior Church,
and devoted servant of Our Lord at Merciful Shepherd Mission.
B. June 6, 1860, Oakland, California.

Cree was surprised at her reaction. Her first emotion was one of loss or sorrow, the knowledge that the beguiling, familiar woman in the photo was dead. But of course she would have to be by now.

"How in the world did you spot *that*?" she asked.

"Pure luck. I was thinking of the different responses people might have had. Um, the compassion thing." His eyes met hers, momentarily shy as a deer's. "So I thought I'd try the Religion category for a while. The name just . . . jumped out at me."

They quickly searched the rest of the Religion files together, but found nothing else even remotely relevant. They straightened their aching backs and thought about it.

"Does this tell us anything useful?" Cree wondered aloud. "The name of the church, the mission—we might chase those down. Could Lydia have encountered the wolfman in her charitable work?"

Ray was nodding, frowning. "Maybe. But it tells us one thing for sure. The wolfman wasn't Lydia's child. She didn't have any children."

Disappointed, Cree had to admit he was right. Lydia wasn't listed as anybody's beloved mother, as some of the other women on the list were. More important was her birth date: Lydia had been born in 1860, and despite the paradoxical teeth and palate, Skobold insisted the wolfman had been born around 1866. Meaning she'd have been only six, give or take a couple of years, when the wolfman was born.

One possible connection gained, another lost, Cree thought. It seemed less likely that Lydia would provide the link they needed. How long would it take to find the line, the strand, that would lead them to the wolfman?

IV

THE STRANGER AMONG US

39

MOMENTS AGO, WHEN I crept into the pantry, I was startled to see a squirrel on the table, eagerly exploring among the jars and boxes of foodstuffs. It scrambled immediately for the window and vanished outside, and that brought a different kind of shock: The window was open. I shut it immediately and did not see marks of any tool on the sash or sill, and it is possible that I myself left it open, or more likely Cook, who can be absentminded. But instantly all my worst fears came rushing home again, that Percy or some hireling had come prowling and had pried the window and crept about our house last night. This possibility has left me trembling again, full of doubts and dire fears.

Perhaps it is the shock I needed, for my resolve has been fickle and fleeting. Last night, after my work at the mission was done, I asked Darby to take me to the linens warehouse, and I even dismounted and went through the door. But once I had entered the darkness, it did not seem a possible thing, to scurry fearfully through those shadows and smells to a sister who might have betrayed me, or who might again be entertaining her beau when I arrived. I hovered there only briefly before returning to Darby and the carriage. "Our business was mercifully short tonight, Darby," I told him. "Let's both go home."

But I am aware that each day I procrastinate I am in greater danger of exposure. Percy will certainly come, and unless I have pre-empted him the consequences can only be disastrous.

There is still no more word of the wolf-man, not even rumor. Perhaps he will never be seen again, and will vanish as mysteriously as he arrived among us, yet another person swallowed whole by the Barbary Coast and gone forever. If so, I fear we will have lost a great opportunity to learn from him, who must have a remarkable tale to tell.

Last night I did muster the courage to go to Margaret's. I was frustrated in this attempt, and in my journey through the streets I witnessed something terrible that has only sharpened my fears and yearnings for resolution.

The intervening time has put me out of practice for this covert race, and my trepidation at what I might discover of her had put me in a state of highest anxiety. Every small thing startled me, all out of proportion. At one point, as I paused in an alley to let a brawling group make its way past, I glanced up to see a face, only inches from my own. I recoiled as if Hell's demons had attacked me, hands up to ward them, but it was only an old woman, haggard and ghost-pale, peering from her lightless window. She pointed accusingly at me and made a round O with her toothless mouth, and I fled from her in horror. I am sure she could not see who or what I was, with my face shadowed in the hood of my cloak.

I came round the corner a block from Margaret's place but stopped when it appeared there was some commotion. There were men milling in the street, several with torches that put the others in flickering light and gave them long shadows. From their shouts and agitated movements, I understood that a confrontation of some sort was occurring. In a moment, I heard the sound of breaking glass and saw a large pane fall away from a storefront window and shatter on the pavement. Most of the men clambered quickly through the dark opening. Their torches lit the interior in a fitful and terrible way, and from inside came shouts and a woman's scream. In another moment the door burst open and the men emerged again, dragging two people, aiming kicks at them and striking them with sticks. In the wild gyre of torchlight it seemed truly a scene from Hell, and when I saw the figures on the ground feebly trying to protect themselves, heard the blows strike their flesh, I could not help but cry out. Involuntarily, I stepped into the street and found myself among a scattering of others who had gathered to observe. I stood for half a minute with these strangers, afraid to intervene, unable to leave.

Closer, I heard the foreign tones in the victims' pleas and knew that they were Celestials. The men in the street continued kicking and striking them, while inside others were running rampant, smashing furniture and ripping cloth, throwing household things through the window. From the curses and warnings of the men, I understood that these Celestials had recently rented the storefront to start some enterprise. It is only barely outside the accepted margins of Chinatown, yet they had unknowingly crossed an invisible, unwritten line and were now being shown that moving in among Whites was an intolerable transgression. The White landlord would be next, the men shouted.

It appeared to be a husband and wife who were being beaten, and I was certain they would be killed. Yet I could not decide what to do, for I know a mob in its frenzy will turn on anything that opposes it. The police, I thought, someone must go to the police! I turned to a large man standing not far from me to implore him to go find the authorities, and was stunned to see his cap and uniform and the billy at his belt! He stood at his ease, watching this outrage with a look of bland satisfaction.

"You must do something!" I told him stupidly. "They will be killed!"

The policeman looked at me as if I were a madwoman, then immediately grew angry. "You'd best go about your business, Ruby. Go back to your cow yard and do an honest night's work." With that, he turned me around and rudely pushed me so that I stumbled away. I was outraged that he would put his hand upon me, and I whirled to accost him, but his back was already to me. He idly twirled his billy as he watched the awful sport that entertained him so.

I slunk away to linger out of view for a short time, breathless, listening to the shouts and the sounds of blows and splintering glass and wood, then beat a retreat back to Darby.

So another day has passed and I have neither confronted my sister nor revealed my sordid truths to my husband, nor otherwise dealt with the enormity of the problem that faces me. Instead, it only seems to have compounded and grown, water building behind a dam.

WEDNESDAY, JUNE 26, 1889

Yesterday I could not help myself and crossed words with Rev. Wallace. It was an unwise thing to do, for he is not tolerant of dissenting views and my argumentativeness will likely be held against me should an accounting be taken of my behavior. Perhaps I made this mistake because I am so

277

worn from worry, but I did in honesty disagree with him and for once would not bite my tongue. I cannot help but think he would now be a more tolerant person if, over the years, those who found themselves at variance with his opinion had expressed their own views with more conviction.

We do not see him every day, as other church business preoccupies him, so a visit is occasion for much solemnity and piety at the mission. Deacon Skinner stopped by as well, and I was most glad to see him, for though he is also solemn, he seems somehow a counterbalance to Rev. Wallace, quick and wiry where Wallace is slow and blocky, bright of eye where Wallace only grave and dignified. Deacon Skinner's wise, narrow, dry face cannot hide his humor, and his words often seem to reveal an ironical intent, so well woven into his phrasing that it requires some wit to perceive.

Neither of them witnessed much of interest; it was a slow afternoon at the mission, and the little bell over our front door jangled only seldom. It is our custom to have a prayer circle and then discussion of Scriptural principles as the dinner hour approaches, but today we had only one petitioner, an old man whom we know only as Billy, who is innocent of a single tooth in his head and infinitely accommodating of religious instruction if it is followed by a good meal. Without any other audience, we of the mission began an informal discussion of spiritual things.

Our topic had been forgiveness. We forgive because Jesus enjoined us to turn the other cheek, even to forgive those who persecute us; it is in this way, Deacon Skinner has explained, that we hope to forgo another cycle of hurting, to stall the great wheel that otherwise turns forever round with one injury begetting another and so drives the engines of war and cruelty.

Yet we also know that there is a Hell, and that God the Father judges all but forgives only some. Since all are sinners, and born that way, how does He determine who is forgiven, who is punished for eternity? (In my impious moments, I think that when he dies, Rev. Wallace will be employed to assist God with making these judgments, for he has had such long experience at it. Indeed, he resembles God so closely, with his full, gray beard, hawk's beak nose, thundercloud brows, that were God to wish a respite from the effort of judgment, Rev. Wallace could stand in for Him and no one would be the wiser.)

I asked Rev. Wallace for clarification of this point: How does God know which sinners to admit to Heaven, and which to banish to Hell? For it has long confused me, and I have struggled with it in my own conscience: Ought I to forgive Margaret? Can I forgive Percy, for example, or the men who beat that husband and wife in the street? I am not certain I can; but if I could, could not God? If I did, but God did not, would God consider me a sinner—for forgiving? Or is all forgiveness His instrument, put into our weak hands?

For Rev. Wallace, the answer to how God knows whom to bless and whom to banish was easily come by: "Why, those who have accepted Him into their hearts! Even a murderer, if he repents of his misdeeds, reads the Word, and accepts the Lord as his master, will be judged kindly. And even a lesser sinner, if he does not, must suffer damnation. That is why we are here, Sister Lydia, is it not? To preserve the multitudes from damnation by bringing them the Word that will save them?"

Sister Gertrude and Rev. Smith and the others watched me warily, as if they sensed I would debate this point, and I could not help doing so, not out of contrariety but in honest puzzlement or curiosity.

"But what of the Celestials?" I asked, for they were much on my mind, and I thought, too, of my sister, and of the wolf-man, who must be innocent of scripture but might be capable of kindness. "And other sorts of heathen, lacking good teaching? Would a Celestial who does not know of Christ, who has never read the Bible, yet has lived a virtuous and gentle life, be harshly judged? Through no fault except the land of his birth or the language of his parents—and those being God's own determinations?"

"The Lord will make Himself known to them in His time. It is not ours to understand the ways of His will or His judgments."

"Because," I went on urgently, heedless of the signals of danger, "would that not be a cruelty, to create a child with his destiny in Hell foreordained? We do know the Lord asks kindness of us, do we not? I cannot believe Jesus intended his injunction to kindness as . . . as merely bait on a hook, to draw people with our little mercies so that they will swallow the Bible! It seems to me that we are here as instruments of His mercy, in

279

the here and now. If we are kind, isn't it simply the Lord being kind through our actions? Could not that be the sum of it—that He is using our hands to help render His intent on Earth, now, today?"

Another time, his glare would have melted me on the spot. But strangely, the trials of my last weeks must have fortified me in some way, for I endured his fierce gaze and barely flinched.

Still, I was glad that Deacon Skinner interceded for me. "Sister Lydia has raised an important point, I think. Whether in the end it is Virtue or Belief we should really strive for, and whether God might not already and continuously work His judgments and mercies through the little, daily works of our hands."

Rev. Wallace brought the hot blue bolt of his gaze to bear on Deacon Skinner then, which the deacon returned with neither defiance nor undue humility. After a moment, Rev. Wallace turned to the others and told them drily, "Sister Lydia is a gentle and inquiring spirit. But one might suggest she leave such complex questions to men of religious authority and content herself with those same little, daily works. Which would not tax her so and for which a woman is, after all, so much better suited."

I was suitably chastened, and remembered that at this juncture, of all times, I must not stand out or give anyone cause to doubt me. As if to drive the point home, the bell tinkled a moment later, and I looked up to see what I feared most, a dapper figure in a striped suit and bowler hat standing in the doorway. For an instant I did actually go into a faint, collapsing briefly against Sister Gertrude.

But it was not Percy. It was only a salesman, with a kit of kitchen wares he hoped the mission might want. We declined and sent him on his way, but afterward I was overcome with nausea and had to lie down for a time. I knew I could not wait any longer, but must go to Margaret again, whatever may happen and whatever I might learn.

THURSDAY, JUNE 27, 1889

No, it is after midnight, so it is Friday morning. Once again I am sleepless and writing by lamplight. I have been to Margaret's at last. I have learned some dreadful facts. All the world is changed, yet I cannot name the nature of the change.

After my terrible fright at the mission, I was resolved to go to her. I could not bear to passively wait for Percy's machinations to come to me, but would learn what I could and act from whatever knowledge I gained. So tonight I had Darby drive me to the warehouse, then made my way to Margaret's brothel by the winding ways I know so well. In a little, I passed the scene of Monday's violence, and found that the broken storefront windows were now boarded over. A tidy sign hung against the boards, For Lease, and below it someone had crudely painted in large, dripping letters, WITE ONLY. I wondered what had become of those unfortunate people, and passed quickly over the street there as if it were haunted ground.

I came into the dim downstairs room to find only two women waiting: a busy night, I guessed from the noises of rhythmic exertion and drunken laughter from the rooms upstairs. I started toward the stairs, but the two whores roused at the sight of me and the older stopped me with a hiss and a shake of her big head. She was the hugely fat woman I had noted often before, with massive breasts and belly, each thigh big as the belly of a sow, arms like dimpled pillows, a great broad face like a kindly toad.

"Not here," she said.

"Where, then?"

She glanced quickly toward the door at the back, where the madame or whoremaster would no doubt soon appear. "Gone and won't ever be back. And you should, too, before you bring more bad luck."

"Where did she go? What do you mean?"

The other was a slender girl with a sallow olive complexion, protruding front teeth above a weak chin, wearing nothing but drawers and a loose shawl. "Gone wherever bad girls go," she said in a high voice, "and no one the wiser."

"It was you caused it all," the fat one said. Her eyes were tiny and porcine yet oddly intelligent above the mounds of her cheeks. "With Percy. Oh, she had black around her eyes that night he saw you here, I can tell you. She wasn't kissing the Johnnies with lips cracked like that, neither."

"Are you saying he beat her?"

"Sure, he beat her! But this time it was to make her tell about you. And then a week later he come back in the middle of the night to raise holy hell. I was sitting right on this chair, and he stomps in with his face stained red, eyes all pouring, in a rage. He goes up the stairs and starts in on her for a while. Then it goes quiet. And half an hour later down she comes, all dressed and carrying her Gladstone, says nothing to no one and out she goes. And never come back."

I could hardly speak. I stammered out, "But what of Percy?"

"Still upstairs. With her fine sewing scissors in his neck and laying snow white in a bathtub's worth of blood. And my first thought seein' him was, God love you, Mag, good for you! But after the police carted him away, it was me and Tildy had to mop it up so's the room could be used again quick. And that was not such a delight."

"Do the police have her?"

"Naw!" the slender one said.

"How do you know?"

The fat one explained: "They been poppin' in every day or two ever since, askin' after her and runnin' quick through the rooms. And we tell them, Forget it, ain't this the last place she'd ever be found again?"

"And who're they lookin' for, anyway?" the thin one screeched. "A girl named Mag, hair on top, two legs on the bottom, and a dollar twat between 'em! And how many are there fit that description in our town, Mag?" For the fat one's name was also Margaret. The scrawny girl thought it a great joke and slapped her bony knee in amusement.

The fat one only gazed at me somberly as if she could see my soul plummeting. "I know what it's about," she whispered. "With the walls so thin. I know what she done for you."

The slender one had misinterpreted. "What was it? Because I can do it in her place. I don't care, men or women, it's all the same to me."

"Hssst! It's her sister, you idiot!" the fat one said, turning on her angrily, and the other's eyes grew round as if I were some astonishing thing appeared in their midst.

Then the front door opened and two sailors came in, young boys and very shy. Simultaneously, the whoremaster appeared in the back room, an evil man and always suspicious of me, and not wanting to confront him I fled into the night.

And so I am free of Percy but without a sister again. Tonight I am sure my heart will burst from the feelings that overfill it. To know my sister has not only whored but murdered. To know it was to protect me that she killed him, and with the scissors I had given her! To wonder who saved whom and how so, to wonder who is to blame and who has sinned and who needs or should receive forgiveness: What is sin and what judgements should follow seems now even more confused and uncertain.

I feel the hollow that comes from not knowing where she is, for as hard as our encounters were she was forever my sister and, in momentary flashes and glints, my friend. I wonder if I will ever see her again and what becomes of such a woman, when she tumbles deeper into the bottomless murk and shadows. Where can she possibly go?

I am astonished at the world, appalled at it. One mercy given, one taken, and I cannot understand the purpose of it. I look for God's hand and know it is there but cannot decipher its intent. I barely heard Darby's good-night as I dismounted from the carriage. I stood in front of our dear fine house, which was all dark but for the one light Hans leaves for me. I did not know what to make of any of it.

All my thoughts were confused but for this: What a clear, crystalline night, how vast the sky, how great the celestial distances, how very bright and piercing are the stars above our hill!

40

YESTERDAY I COULD not bear to go to the mission, being simply too overcome. I arranged a substitute, then stayed at home and tended to small things. I spent some time in the garden, which bestowed a bit of serenity; it is as if the green things and elegant colorful shapes emit an aura or radiance unseen by the eye (though the eye is much pleased as well) but beneficial to the spirit.

My mind will not rest from thinking of ways I might search for Margaret, but none strike me as likely to succeed. Besides, she is sought by the police, and unless she stays hidden might well be apprehended, prosecuted, and hanged. My chest contracts painfully when I imagine her out there, in a world hostile and degrading in every way, with danger from every quarter, not even a whore's security of a brothel. In this she is barely better off than the wolf-man, though she is a fully formed human woman.

With Percy's death, I have been relieved of the pressing need to reveal my sordid secrets to my husband. Yet I do not think I can continue without some revelation to him: I see now that even in the darkest depths of my fears, wrapped in the coils of uncertainty and every dire consideration, the thought of being truthful with Hans persisted as a clean, bright thing, sharp and frightening, yet welcome and needed. It would be a mercy to drop all pretense, and having imagined it so many times I now long for it, whatever difficulty it might entail.

I must be a simple person, or perhaps there is some grain of truth in what Rev. Wallace said about a woman's design and limitations. For I could not imagine how to begin this process of unsavory revelation: what the first word would be, what tone of voice to use, in which moment of the day. Instead, yesterday evening after supper, when Hans had taken his place in his chair, I could think of nothing other than to go to him, to sit on his lap and bury my face in his hair and beard.

I cannot quite say why I did this. I certainly felt an instinct to take comfort from the close company of another human being, but it was not a simple impulse. The doubts Percy had raised in my mind were still with me, about whether I might ever feel Hans's strength turned against me, and I still feared him. Thus I came to Hans also to be near the source of that fear: to study it and learn if it was a real thing, to surrender to it and so to challenge it.

Hans said nothing, and I think he was quite startled. I sat and smelled him, the sweat of his skin and the wool of his suit with its ever-present whiff of brick and stone. I felt his muscles through his shirt and the abrasion against my forehead where his beard turns so wiry just beneath his ear. I had neither thoughts nor intent; I was too weary and world worn. Hans put his great hands around my waist, still speechless.

Later, I still could not think but only let that inner wind move me where it would. Hans took his Friday bath, which delights him as much for the comforts of hot water and cleanliness as for the time spent among the bright marble and smooth enamel and gleaming fixtures; he takes pleasure in working the faucets and operating all the devices. I waited until the water stopped and I heard his great sigh as he eased into the tub, then went into the room with him. Again, it was not from decisiveness or confidence I did so, only that numb submission to my several weeks' ordeal and the need to be near him. He was somewhat alarmed at my intrusion, but I gazed at him frankly.

Without his clothes, he is more majestic, a great perfect animal in the natural fullness of his frame and musculature. In his physical aspect, I found him indeed a fearful being, capable of anything, good or ill; but with every shape and proportion so ideally squared with its needed function and every part in purposeful harmony with the other. I thought: Surely, this is Adam's shape precisely as God wanted him; surely God does love the animal of him as He does the man.

For a gentleman of forty-seven, he retains an exceptional youthfulness of physique. This is not entirely surprising, given the many years he labored; and to this day he will off his jacket and show some strapping youngster how to carry the hod, or hoist a timber, or lift and lever a cornerstone square of granite. He claims he does this only when one of his men is showing a want of application, to stimulate his resolve; but I know it satisfies Hans to apply his great strength and to exercise those familiar skills. And it certainly does not hurt his authority among his crews, who may chafe at his discipline but admire his strength and his willingness to take a laborer's role again.

His face asked a question, and of course I could not say that I was wanting to know my love and my fear, that I could not bear any further uncertainty and would rather die of a certain fact than live any longer in the absence of one.

I told him, "I have come to scrub my husband's back."

This is not an intimacy we are accustomed to. His expression remained puzzled, but he made no refusal as I took up the cloth and soap and sat on the back of the tub. I lifted the hair off his neck and tugged it around to one side, then pushed him to lean forward. His back is a great shield-shaped landscape of rounded hills and soft valleys, with a forest of small curls trailing down his neck and dwindling to nothing between his shoulder blades. I wet the cloth and rubbed the soap, then applied the lather to him. My hands followed every curve and outline, traced every knob of his spine, explored beneath his arms, stroked the great wing muscles along his sides, went up the stout tapering pillar of his neck. At every moment I expected him to show doubt or resistance, but he did not; nor did I hurry or allow myself shame in my savor of him. When I had scrubbed and stroked far more than any back could need, I tugged him back to wash his hair and beard. When I was finished, I laid his hair snug behind his ears so that he looked fiercely handsome and dashing. Then I reached over his shoulders and applied the same attention to his chest and belly, another landscape of wonderful particulars. His manhood thickened and half rose against his thigh, but he made no effort to conceal himself; for the first time I looked directly upon it in the full light, freely indulging my curiosity. It struck me as a marvelous ugly thing, and I would have bathed him there also had I dared.

Looking back at what I have just written, I can scarcely believe my daring and shamelessness. Is this a newfound strength or some strange weakness of character manifesting itself? The former, I have to think: The trials of the last weeks have confounded my former certainties and thus distilled them. When all is in doubt and in danger, one has no recourse but to the deepest reservoirs of character and belief. In my case, they are not thoughts so much as the simple impulses that have stayed steady when all else is in transition, and must therefore be the bedrock of my nature.

I had not begun with any intent, or even desire, except that unthinking wish to linger near my husband and to trace his body with my hands as if his shape alone would answer my questions. But after his bathing was done, and I had dried him and he stood pink and humid, desire had kindled in both of us. And as we went into the bedroom, I suddenly knew how it should go: Tonight I will freely admit the pleasure he gives me; tomorrow I will ask him to accompany me on my walk down the hill to the cable car, and he will see how I do that. He will accept these things of me or he will not. By degrees we will both learn whom we have married. And we will make a certainty, be it a good one or a sorry one.

41

IT IS EARLY morning and I am in the dim pantry, scribbling fast as there is so much to recount. I have seen the wolf-man again, under very different and tragic circumstances.

Yesterday early evening, Monday, Dr. Mahoney came to the mission all disheveled and whiskey-breathed, in a great state of excitement. He lifted his cap to show me his freckled pate and whispered urgently that he wanted to speak with me in confidence. We took ourselves to the front porch, where he explained in a hushed voice: He had heard from one of his patients that a werewolf is now on display at a saloon called The Red Man. My heart sank at the name, for we at the mission know The Red Man all too well as a cesspit of unspeakable depravity and excess, operated by a ruthless, Godless man named Silas Singer. Dr. Mahoney showed me a crude handbill which advertised the "werewolf" as a "blood-drunk murderer, devourer of babes" and gave times when for a fee he might be viewed in his cage or fighting dogs and men.

I was much moved by Dr. Mahoney's concern for him, for without having seen the creature his view was certain and unquestioned: this was a pitiable freak or a victim of disease, now in dire need of benevolent intervention.

"Why do you come to me, Dr. Mahoney?" I asked.

"Mrs. Schweitzer, I was certainly born Irish and quite possibly born stupid, but I was certainly not born deaf and blind. You know something of him. You have asked after him too many times, with too keen an interest." His red eyes fixed me remorselessly, and though I did not speak he had his answer.

"Know something of whom?" a voice asked pleasantly from behind me, and there was Deacon Skinner, stepping up from the street.

He took the handbill from me and read it quickly. In an instant, I saw understanding come into his face, perhaps as he recalled my questions about Darwin, or the "old man" beneath the stairs, or the fate of innocents damned by God for the innocence He had inflicted upon them. He looked at me with affection admixed with concern; he and Dr. Mahoney then gazed at each other, two men sizing each other up and for all their differences finding some common sentiment.

"I have always suspected our Lydia has aspects unseen and too little appreciated," Deacon Skinner said. A flush came to my neck, and I felt as if his bright hawk's eyes could see all my night-time walks and fears and secret, heretical thoughts. "How do you know this is not just another wild man done up hairy for the show?"

I stuttered out: "Because I have seen him."

"Well, then, is he a man or a wolf?" Dr. Mahoney asked.

Both men scrutinized me as I thought how to answer, how to sum up a month of tireless questioning and pondering. "I could not say. I have seen his physical aspect, but have no experience of his nature. And it seems that not everyone agrees upon just what qualities make us human."

Deacon Skinner looked at me shrewdly and favored me with a bitter smile. "Oh, Lydia. What a dead-eye shot you are for the precise center of the question." He glanced again at the handbill and caught Dr. Mahoney's eye. "Well, I for one am willing to risk The Red Man to get a glimpse of this rare creature. My rig is nearby, Doctor. Perhaps between your expertise and mine we can answer some of these questions."

"I want to go," I said.

"Never!" Dr. Mahoney said instantly.

"Lydia, it is out of the question," Deacon Skinner concurred. "Thursday is Independence Day, and there are ten thousand ruffians come to town for the celebrations. They will be drinking hard and every criminal sort will be out to prey. It will be dangerous enough for Dr. Mahoney and myself. But a good Christian woman—"

"Acts upon her beliefs," I finished for him. "And is not deflected from her duties. If you don't take me, I will have to walk or send for Darby to take me."

★   ★   ★

So we went in the deacon's carriage, both men quite put out with me. It was just dark when we arrived in the vicinity of The Red Man, and my companions grew silent and watchful. Dr. Mahoney took a small revolver from his jacket pocket and checked its workings with a grim expression. Deacon Skinner reluctantly left his horse and rig, hiring a young man idling nearby to watch and telling him there was two dollars for him if it was still here in an hour. Then doctor and deacon each took one of my arms and walked with me held tightly between them. I had donned my gray cloak and put up the hood, to attract as little attention as I might.

The Red Man takes its name from the Indian, and maintains the conceit in its décor and furnishings. A carved wooden Indian, dour and savage, stands in front, and inside there are souvenirs of native life: buffalo skins, tanned hides with pagan designs on them, rows of scalps hanging on a string, bows and spears and battle axes. There is even a mummified or desiccated Indian tied up against the wall, horribly shriveled so that his lips are drawn back from his teeth. It is a foul, shabby place of smoke-darkened board walls, gas flames fluttering dangerously from fixtures without globes, wired-together wooden chairs and deeply scarred tables scattered on a floor more dirt than board. The pretty waiter girls wear only an Indian's loincloth, and endure whatever fondling or insult to their persons the drinkers give them; they are constantly leading men up the stairs to assignations in the second-floor rooms. As we wedged into the crowd, we were suffocated by the stink of unwashed bodies, rotting teeth, stale alcohol, spoiled food, and worse. Moments after we arrived, a fight broke out in the far corner, although in the press we could not see it, only hear breaking glass and the shouted encouragements of watchers.

At the rear, a wide doorway leads into a second room with a raised stage along its back wall, where for the gratification of the customers women are frequently subjected to degradations I cannot bear to write of. Through this doorway, we could see what must be the wolf-man's cage, a canvas-draped rectangle that filled the width of the stage and was painted with a lurid illustration of a werewolf. It was not yet time for the "performance," and with the crowd distracted by the fist-fight, we were able to push through without too much difficulty.

A pair of large, menacing men stood at the door, one of whom moved to bar the way, telling us, "Fifty cents each to stand, dollar for the chairs up front."

Deacon Skinner opened his purse and handed over the money. When the bully stepped aside, we pushed our way in and were able to find three chairs in the second row. I kept my hood pulled well forward but sneaked glances at the cage. My apprehension grew and grew, and I was not sure I could bear to witness him again. I could not say whether it was the sheer hideousness of his appearance that caused me such distress, or the prospect of seeing ferocity from him, after I had imbued him with hopes of a gentle nature. Perhaps it was simply the prospect of seeing any creature confined and in such degraded and unhappy circumstances. At intervals the canvas shook and vibrated, as if something were moving inside, and my uneasiness mounted each time.

"Courage, Sister," Deacon Skinner whispered.

"Two dollars for her, after the show," the man in front of us said. He had turned and now gave a demanding, surly look to the deacon.

"I beg your pardon!" Deacon Skinner said indignantly.

"Oh, he begs my pardon," the awful man said to his companions. Heads turned toward the three of us, faces eager for entertainment. "A gentleman, is it? I said, pardon me, two dollars for yer whore, that's double her worth. Upstairs after the show. First or after yer done, I don't care."

Dr. Mahoney stood suddenly bolt upright, a short Irishman of middle-age, now flushing red to match his hair. "Ye airen't speakin' o' me saister now, are ye?" he inquired, cheeks trembling with outrage. I don't know if his brogue had come up so strong by itself, or whether he let it show on purpose. I hid my face, afraid of what would follow.

"What, and a fightin' mad mick, too!" By the twisting of his legs, I could see that the man was craning further around to face us. "A mick the size of my dick."

The man's companion laughed, saying, "So that'd make him a fightin' cock, hey, Bill?"

Dr. Mahoney's eyes never left his tormentor. "Step out wi' me fer two minutes an' you'll have no dick at all, Billy-boy."

But the men at the door were barking out for the customers in the other room to pay now or miss the show.

"Have to wait, Mick," the big man said. He made a derisive noise and turned front again, elbowing his chum in amusement. When Dr. Mahoney at last took his seat, I felt his panting and trembling against the side of my arm.

Soon the room was packed and the air was thick. The doors closed, and three men positioned themselves at the front of the room, each standing ready with a pistol in his belt and a determined expression. Then a man who was surely Silas Singer himself came up to announce the night's proceedings in a most theatrical way. If a man could be part mantis, I thought, he would look like Silas Singer: angular, jerky in movement, hands held up before him, mouth biting off the words. Leering continuously, he told a poorly contrived tale of how he and his men sought the famous werewolf, perpetrator of so many murders, and how they caught him at last after arduous pursuit. The means of his capture was a noose of silver wire, which also arrested his transformation back into a man. Singer explained dramatically that the desperadoes standing now to either side of the stage were there for the crowd's protection, should the monster break free. The werewolf would be revealed shortly, after which dogs would be admitted to the cage and he'd fight them. Finally, they would noose and muzzle him and men could volunteer to fight him, if any dared.

Then the canvas was pulled aside to reveal a metal-barred cage, as at a zoo or circus. For a moment it seemed nothing was inside, but then I saw a hunched form, far back where the light was not as good. It looked to be a naked man, head down between his knees, hair hiding his face, sinewy humanlike arms tightly wrapping his legs. The audience made a hiss of whispered disappointment, but only a moment later Silas Singer emerged from the wing to jab the wolf-man forcefully with a staff put through the bars. The creature sprang away to half-stand, closer to the front of the cage, in a posture of reluctance. When the better light caught him, the sound of the audience changed to awe, astonishment, and revulsion. Deacon Skinner and Dr. Mahoney uttered identical gasps.

He was as I have described before, but now appeared in a most miserable way: streaked with filth, hair knotted and crusted, skin scabbed and reddened with cuts and abrasions. But what struck me most forcibly was his solitude: a creature knowing only danger from the world, a creature with no other of his kind, unless we were they; and we had put up bars to assure his separation.

He was the most alone creature I have ever seen or could ever imagine.

Unthinkingly, I stood up so vehemently that my hood fell off and my chair tipped back. From behind came angry calls for me to sit, but I barely heard, for the wolf-man had bounded to the front of the cage and now stood fully upright, arms wide above his head, and short, clawed fingers clinging to the bars. He stared wild-eyed out at the room. In that position, every feature of his anatomy was plain to see, and in all ways he seemed half human and half canine. His male member was fully a man's, but hung between narrow, forward-bent thighs more like a dog's. It was a dog's muzzle he raised to scent the air, but his dark blue eyes were precisely those of a terrified human child. He seemed to stare straight at me just as I stared at him, and I believe without a doubt that he recognized me.

Two men appeared, dragging two tightly leashed, snarling and straining curs, at which the wolf-man let go the bars. He dropped to all fours, moved in two long lopes back to his corner, and crouched again, looking left and right as if seeking a way to flee. When the men pushed the dogs into the cage, the wolf-man crowded against the bars at the far side, showing every indication of extreme agitation and unhappiness.

I could not witness more. I stumbled out of the seating area, followed immediately by Deacon Skinner and Dr. Mahoney. They took my arms tightly again and we burrowed through the standing crowd. Behind us, I vaguely heard the sound of snarls and scuffling. As we arrived at the door, a sound pierced the noise of the crowd: high, pitiful yelps that became a throbbing, ghastly warble that was quickly throttled to silence.

42

YESTERDAY BEING INDEPENDENCE Day, all the city celebrated most extravagantly, with bunting draped from every window and cornice, every flag bright and high, throngs of people filling the commercial streets. The weather was nothing short of splendid. The air crackled as every boy in San Francisco lit caps and little bombs; all the cable cars rang their bells at every opportunity. Hans and I joined the Schultzes and the Pizagallis on Market Street to watch the parades, sun winking brilliant on the brass of the marching trumpets. On the way, riding in the carriage, Hans beamed with pride in his adopted country and leaned again and again to whisper in my ear and point out every building he had some hand in constructing. Seeing the stately façades and proud cornices and snapping banners of Market Street, it seemed inconceivable to me that only forty years ago there was nothing here but swamp and empty dunes. Nor did it seem possible that only a few blocks to the north lies the exotic labyrinth of Chinatown, and, just beyond, the Barbary Coast with all its treacheries and perversions. To think of our city's queer disparity or doubleness disturbed me greatly, as if emblematic of the very nature of humankind.

Throughout the day, I could not help myself but scanned the faces of the crowds, searching and searching but never finding the face of my sister, and at times it required some effort to conceal my sorrow from my companions.

It was a noisy and colorful day, but wearying, and in my unrelenting concern I could not take as much pleasure in it as I ought until after dark, when the fireworks began. These made such lavish, luminous flower gardens in the night sky that I shed some of my preoccupation with my troubles and cheered along with the others.

When at last we came home and took to bed, Hans became amorous and his attentions soon aroused the same response in me. We are both bolder in this now, to the point that our intimacy has grown to include words as well as caresses. Neither of us shows any trace of these moments in our daily life, nor makes any reference; it is a secret between us.

That thought became a sweet revelation: Here in the safe enclosure of our dark bedroom, we are building a shared secret life.

Afterward, in the dark, he played idly with my hair as he does, and talked candidly.

"My father," he said, "did not want me to go to America. He was afraid for me, and also he needed me to help with the work. So many good reasons to stay, only one to go, which was my wanting. He was angry at what he thought a selfish and willful desire."

"What was it you were so wanting?"

"I said it was only to make money to send home. But I was not so truthful. I wanted to escape from our little village. And from my father, yes. I wanted to have an adventure. I had read adventure books, though my father forbade it. Pirates and bandits and brave seafarers and treasure seekers were in my mind. I was just a boy. I thought to try it out."

"How did you ever manage to leave?"

Hans sighed heavily, sadly. "We argued often. I was . . . not obedient. One night he told me he would beat me if I persisted in talking about it. I said, yes, go ahead and try, I am not so little anymore. He did not make good on his threat. It was a sad victory for me. I left the next day. I had a ride on a turnip cart and I cried for many miles. I knew my mother would be heartbroken. I was not a good son."

I had never heard these details before, and I was quite touched. "Even a good son must choose his own path at some point," I reassured him.

"Later I wrote letters to my parents, but they never replied. Then I wrote to our minister, but got no answer. I do not know if they are dead, or simply refuse to acknowledge me. I still write a letter sometimes. I tell them I am wealthy now and will send them money if I am sure where to send it. But still no reply."

He rearranged himself uncomfortably on the bed and his breathing was irregular and deep, as if he were struggling with himself. I was silent, letting him approach his trouble and choose his words.

"Lydia," he said after many minutes, as if it were a matter of grave importance.

"Yes, my love?" I expected a deeper intimacy, and welcomed it wholly.

"I have been thinking." He paused a long time. "I have been thinking to get the electricity put in. McGuire has it now and is very pleased with it. It is an expense we can afford. And the trunk wires are not so far now as they were. I am thinking we should have the electricity."

I was unprepared for this tangent. His taking it and my expectation of something so different seemed to sum us up so well, the two of us caught in a photographer's flash, that I could not help myself and I laughed out loud. In a moment he began laughing, too, and we both lay side by side, laughing hugely, for many minutes. And I am sure neither of us could have said precisely what we were laughing at.

SATURDAY, JULY 6, 1889

I have spoken of the wolf-man to Hans. My intent was to do so in a way that would be familiar to him and would not overly tempt his curiosity. I told him that Deacon Skinner and I had learned of an unfortunate who was being ill-treated by The Red Man, and that I planned to plead with Rev. Wallace and the Mission Council to adopt his cause and to try to free him from this immoral exploitation. It will not be the first time I have made such a plea on behalf of some suffering person.

But Hans persisted in inquiring about the wolf-man, asking me to describe him, and I answered as honestly as I was able, presenting his appearance as a deformity only. We were upstairs as Hans prepared for his day, trousers on but shirtless and suspenders down as he trimmed his beard. When I described the wolf-man's characteristics, Hans's face in the mirror darkened.

"And how is he being mistreated?" he inquired.

"He is in a cage and is tormented by his captors. He is made to fight dogs. They are calling him a werewolf. It is a ridiculous hoax and very cruel."

The face in the mirror grew darker still, and then he turned to me. "A werewolf is not a thing to take lightly. Perhaps he is best left in the cage."

"Surely you do not believe there is such a thing!"

His eyes wandered. He turned back to the mirror but did not resume his grooming. "Our village knew of werewolves. From the time I was little, my father would tell me of a famous werewolf from near Köln, Peter Stumpf was his name, in the old days. Three hundred years later and still people did not forget, how terrible the things he did. And when I was six years old, the full moon turned the color of blood, I saw it myself and was very frightened. After, there was much whispering, that such a moon begot werewolves. The next day, the miller's daughter was murdered only two miles from our house. The whole village was frightened of what walked among us. My mother did not let me out of the house until the new moon had come."

"This is no werewolf. This is a man."

"Who can be so sure?" he muttered ominously.

All my fears rose again, that I would expose my secret world and bring disaster on myself by helping the wolf-man. And at Hans's words, a feeling of dread horror crept suddenly over me: that there might be truth in the old legends, that we should not forget them so readily. But I would not show my doubt.

"I can," I said briskly.

I snatched his towel from the hook, took it to the hamper, and replaced it with a fresh one. Hans's eyes watched me from the glass, curious and doubtful.

I have been inwardly preparing myself for my meeting with Rev. Wallace and the Mission Council. This pending appearance causes me much uneasiness. I know them to be good men, and Deacon Skinner will support my petition, but I cannot be certain how the Council will respond. There are currents and countercurrents of belief and moral sentiment even among those six men, let alone the larger congregation; and by his very nature, Deacon Skinner fears, the wolf-man offers uncomfortable questions and may awaken divergent opinions. There is also the matter of how I came to know of him, for both Deacon Skinner and Dr. Mahoney observed that he seemed to recognize me, scenting me and fixing me with his eyes. I did not offer an explanation, and though their curiosity was plain, they did not press the point. But I worry that Rev. Wallace or the others might open that question.

This creates a quandary for me, in that I cannot explain the center of the issue or why the wolf-man's captivity distresses me so greatly. Having witnessed him with the kitten, I cannot help but think he must be, in part at least, a gentle creature. And if gentleness can reside in so fierce and strange a being, I think, cannot we make a similar claim for the worst of us? In appearance, at least, the wolf-man seems the very embodiment of our paradoxical natures; were we to know his mind, his ways, we might also draw some conclusions about those who claim full humanity.

And, too, there is simple curiosity: Does he speak? Does he reason, can he read and write? Does he have spiritual impulses and moral sentiments? Where did he come from? Who are his parents? How did such a creature come into being? How was he raised?

How does one live, being such an outcast, such a stranger, without the solace of any companionship except, fleetingly, a wild kitten from the docks? Surely, there could be no creature as alone as he is, cut off from every living thing. This last I will tell them, for I can admit to having seen his stark solitude in his cage at The Red Man.

For reasons I cannot explain, this seems the crux of the issue.

Perhaps it seems so because I myself have so long lived two lives, one concealed, one apparent, and therefore feel an outcast or stranger in my secret thoughts and beliefs, a state I would not wish on any being. Perhaps I think, too, of Margaret, who now lives as a fugitive and an outcast, alone and ever at risk. I mull many thoughts on this subject and wish I could discuss them frankly with Rev. Wallace and others, for I am convinced they bear upon the heart and soul of our faith. This is surely the center of it.

I do truly rue my foolishness and my daring and all my unconventional acts and thoughts. But my adventures and trials have changed me; birthing by degrees in me is a resolve I could never have anticipated. "I can," I answered Hans: though only partly true, such bold words! Increasingly, I rebel against the suppression of my hopes and observations, the silence imposed upon me by both my own cowardice and society. I am increasingly determined to act upon what I believe, no matter what convention it contravenes. No, belief is not the issue; it is only hope, again. But there it is, undeniable, a seed in my heart, and action is the nurture that will allow it to grow.

In our church we are always told that no mortal should stand between one's conscience and one's Maker, that each one's connection to God is personal and direct; yet in this we are hypocrites. We have no pope, but we allow the forceful personalities of our patriarchs, a fixed and uncritical interpretation of Scripture, and the rigid conventions of our brothers and sisters, to intrude between our questing, seeking consciences and the steady, sure guidance of Divinity. I have pressed my conscience hard, and it has offered an unequivocal and unvarying answer. I must honor it, and I will.

At times I consider if this is not an irrational resolve. Why concern myself? After all, I know nothing about the wolf-man; I hardly knew my own sister, can barely claim to know my husband. I experiment with the answers I will give to Rev. Wallace and the others, whose views I cannot fully anticipate but whose hearts I must win to gain their aid, and none seems quite right.

There is no perfect way to express it, for wisdom that can be spoken comes only from the mind, while the heart's wisdom is wordless; and the soul, wisest of all, only sings a song, a beguiling but distant melody we follow in the darkness. But I think it comes down to this: The stranger amongst us is no stranger but only ourselves reflected in the mirror of another; and what we fear and dislike most is either an imperfection in the glass or, more likely, a too-perfect reflection of those aspects of ourselves we would prefer not to see.

V

THE OPEN DOOR

43

BERT CAME IN through the front entrance, a white-pillared portico with manicured succulents in boxes on either side. The place looked good in the morning sun, irrigated lawns so green and closely trimmed they looked like Astroturf, the buildings a crisp modern Spanish colonial nicely set off by trees and shrubs in bull's-eyes of redwood bark.

A fluttery, sick feeling in his stomach had tormented him for the whole drive to San Mateo. Like this was very important in some way he couldn't put his finger on. Maybe it had to do with the fact that this was his first visit to the Oaks in over two months, the longest break he had ever taken from his formerly ironclad ritual. It was not easy to see her, you never knew how it would go, and now on top of the usual anxiety he felt a little rusty.

He went into the spotless lobby to the reception desk, pressed the call button, and waited. The place looked perfect as always, floors glistening, vases of cut flowers on the waiting area tables. He wondered if she would like the birds he'd bought in Chinatown—three papier-mâché things each about the size of his thumb, cleverly decked in real feathers with bead eyes and wire feet.

He hoped she would. The trick was to make her smile. He hoped today would be one of the days she'd smile.

In another moment he heard the chuff of a door seal and turned to see a white-uniformed staffer come into the lobby. She smiled tentatively as she came around the desk to check him in, remembering his face if not his name.

"Marchetti," he said. "Bert Marchetti—"

"Oh, of course." She made a compassionate half smile as she tapped in an exchange number and lifted a phone to her ear. She waited for a moment and then said gently, "Hi, Carol? Mr. Marchetti's here to see Megan."

A nurse led him through the door on the left side of the lobby. The core of the Oaks was a central block flanked by two long residential wings that gave it a U shape. The arms stretched back into more lawns and plantings cut with sidewalks that eventually meandered into the cluster of big California oaks that had given the place its name. Bert had never been into the right side, which was for the geriatrics.

Ten o'clock, breakfast and morning meds over, lunch not on the horizon yet, many of the residents loitered in the day rooms, some in wheelchairs, some ambulatory. Most wore the all-purpose uniform of blue-gray sweat pants and shirts.

Bert turned with Nurse Sanchez into the main corridor and marched past the line of residential rooms. He avoided looking at the shapes of people inside, the humps in the beds or silhouettes at the windows. Hovering near his door, a young man with a dented forehead looked up with one goggle eye as if the sight of Bert appalled him.

"How is she today?" Bert asked.

Nurse Sanchez shook her head. "It's not a great day, Mr. Marchetti. She's been a little depressed."

"Why's she depressed, you think?"

"We don't think it's degenerative. We think there's a cyclical element. It may be hormonal."

Degenerative, that was the big worry—that the injuries weren't done damaging the brain, that small strokes were still occurring or that existing impairments were causing atrophy. Dr. Maris had warned him that brain function could continue to deteriorate over time. They'd seen some of it in the first two years, but she'd been relatively steady for the last three.

They didn't say any more as they entered the far hallway and continued to room forty-two. No one was inside. Bert poked his head in and saw the pretty things he'd brought other times, lined up on the shelf above her bed.

"She's in the alcove then, that's a good sign," Nurse Sanchez said. Trying to cheer him up. He must not have looked cheered up, because she continued quietly, "You know, the staff, the doctors—we all admire you."

"Oh yeah?" He honestly couldn't imagine what she meant.

"For doing this all these years. For caring. For sticking with her."

He almost tried to explain, to set her straight. But why disappoint her?

"Thanks," he said. "That means a lot to me."

The wheelchair was turned to the big glass doors and the view out into the lawns, her head just visible above the chairback. There were a couple of other patients floating in the bright room, too. Several orderlies stood apart, chatting together but watchful.

Bert's stomach tightened as he came around the chair and saw her slumped there in her blue sweats, hands twisted against her chest. Her eyes panned past his and settled somewhere else. Nurse Sanchez squeezed Bert's arm and headed back down the corridor.

"Hey, Megan. Hey, it's Bert. Look, I brought you a present." He fumbled the little birds out of their bag and offered them to her. They looked ludicrous, there on his palm, still with their price tags on. Megan's eyes scouted them but then went away and remained indifferent.

"You want to go for a walk outside, Baby Kid?" Bert asked.

She turned her head toward the bright glass, and he took that as indication that she would. This indirect responsiveness to verbal communication, along with her ability to laugh, cry, and sometimes vocalize in response to stimuli, had convinced Dr. Maris that she retained some level of cognitive function.

Bert put the birds onto her lap blanket, then got behind her and rolled the chair to the doors. One of the orderlies keyed it open so Bert could push the chair through. Megan winced at the sunlight and put an arm over her face and moaned. But she didn't get cranked up. Relieved, Bert rolled her along the winding pavement and out into the grounds.

Everybody agreed that she had been a pretty girl. Hard to tell with her hunched back and slack face, but her skin was smooth and the people at the Oaks kept her hair clean and well brushed, a straight sheath of glossy ebony that hid the scars where her skull had been broken.

Whoever had beaten this girl had meant to kill her, but some fierce spark had kept her alive. The doctors had told him that, the first day—that she was a fighter. It was one of the things that had earned his devotion right away.

Bert had gotten the call five years ago from an old contact in the San Jose PD. Twenty-some years after Megan's abduction, and the guy still remembered Bert's quest. A critically injured woman found behind a Dumpster, about the right age, half-Asian and half-Caucasian. Naked, no ID, unconscious, couldn't speak, didn't match any missing persons description on the databases. Bert was at the office when he took the call and the room had shuddered like there was an earth tremor.

He went to see her at the hospital in San Jose before calling Fran. The young woman was swaddled in bandages and puffy from surgery, he couldn't tell if there was any resemblance and anyway she had been only six, who knew how she'd grown up. He'd stood over the drug-drowsing woman and beamed his thoughts into her bandaged skull like he was a human X-ray. So many questions: Is that you, Baby Kid? Where have you been? What happened to you back then? Who did this to you? Standing there, he'd picked up her slack hand and just as he did her fingers suddenly clasped his. It was just some reflexive movement, but it was magical to him, signaling she felt the same deep, instinctive recognition he did. At that instant he felt something slip or purge out of him, so intense it was like some kind of orgasm, one he'd been building toward for two decades. Or maybe it was like a knife being pulled from its sheath. He'd stood there for another half an hour before he had let go the hand and gone to a phone.

"Fran," he'd choked out, "Frannie, there's a girl here at the hospital. You better get over here."

Bert rolled the chair slowly out the winding path, smoking a cigarette and talking to her. You had to have faith that on some level they were in there and were hearing you.

"Sorry I haven't been coming down so much," he said. "I just been so busy. I told you last time, right, I'm punching my ticket pretty soon, there's a lot of work to get finished up. That's all."

Megan's head turned as she looked around at the lawns and plantings and the green-brown hills in the distance.

"Nurse Sanchez says you been a little off. What's up with that? Tell you the truth, I been a little off myself, I know what that's like. What're we gonna do about it, you and me, huh?"

By the time he finished his cigarette and flicked the butt under a shrub, they were nearing the back of the grounds, where the sidewalks converged in a big circle around one of the oaks. Along the curve were benches where sometimes there'd be other residents and their visitors or orderlies, but today they were alone. He was relieved. He rolled her around to the far side and took a seat on the bench next to her. She wasn't smiling. In fact she looked uneasy. The birds had fallen to the side of the chair, but when he put one into her hand, her fingers moved on the feathers and then the other hand joined the first. All the doctors said that sometimes tactile or kinetic was the only way to get through to them—movements and sensations talking to the deeper, older parts of the brain.

They stared out at the remainder of the groomed lawns, past a few more oaks, into the manzanita scrub. A quarter mile uphill a subdivision began, rooftops peeking from foliage.

As soon as her condition stabilized, he'd had her moved to a private hospital with a good reputation for neurosurgery, and then, eventually, on to the Oaks. If she'd been just an unidentified adult ward of the state, the accommodations would have been very different, and he wanted to be sure she had the best. Ordinarily the added cost would have been impossible, but at first Fran and her husband had chipped in, and anyway he had started up with Nearing and Koslowski a few months before, still hadn't made up his mind about how to spend the extra money. "Younger women": a private joke he'd thought up to deflect Nearing when he asked what Bert did with his share.

Bert had tried to convince himself it was Art Wei, Fran's husband, who insisted on testing, but he knew better. Finding the girl had put Fran and Bert in frequent contact again and she wasn't comfortable with it. Plus she'd had doubts about her from that first day, and the expense didn't help, Fran had always had a stingy streak. Without telling Bert until it was a done deal, she had gone ahead with DNA profiles of her blood and

Megan's. She didn't even call Bert herself with the results, just let the administrator here at the Oaks do it.

No match. This young woman was not the daughter of Fran Marchetti Wei.

At first Bert refused to believe it. He followed up with another DNA test based on hair follicles from a hairbrush of Megan's he'd saved, asking Hank Chambers to personally oversee it at the Berkeley DNA lab. Definitive results: The girl who was registered at the Oaks as Megan Marchetti wasn't Megan Marchetti. But the staff had been calling her that the whole time, and anyway, what was the alternative? The name had stayed with her. By then Bert had been coming to see her twice a week for five months, and had found something steadying about the ritual. Plus he'd managed to make her smile a few times, she'd vocalized in a happy way, giving Bert one of the best feelings he could remember. By the time they did the testing, it had become habit—visiting her, bringing her things, paying the bills at the Oaks. And maybe they were feeding him a Pollyanna line, but the staff invariably said how good his attention was for her. They said that you never knew what normalizing contact could do, that the embrace of familial love had incredible healing powers. Dr. Maris cited actual cases of recovery that had happened even when the strictly clinical prognosis was grim. Like there was a ray from your heart that could fix anything.

Fran dropped the girl cold once she found out. Bert had argued with her, asking why it really mattered, when they'd thought she was Megan it was easy to make room for her in their hearts, what did it matter whose DNA she had? What, you decided stuff like this on the basis of some fucking *molecules* it took a whole laboratory and computers even to figure out?

But he could see her point. With so many damaged, lost people in the world, there was no reason anybody should invest so deeply in some random Girl X. Who was probably a prostitute anyway: When the tests confirmed she wasn't Megan, the San Jose cops concluded she was an illegal alien brought over by some bride service or sex importer, somebody living so far under the radar that her disappearance didn't beget a call from anybody.

One of the things that made him resist the finding initially was how he made her smile the first time. When the actual Megan had been a little kid, Bert had found she liked dancing with him. He'd put on one of his records and pick her up, holding her on his hip with his right arm, other arm out and hands clasped in a wildly lopsided frame. He'd rock her to the music and they'd swing through the house and if she was in a bad mood, tantrums, sulking, anything, he could always pull her out of it.

The first time this girl had started to go into one of her anxiety things, the side-to-side struggling against her seat belt, hands scrabbling at the arm rests, the high moaning, he'd been scared to death. They'd been out here by the big oak, alone, he didn't know what you were supposed to do. But the doctors had said *tactile and kinetic, tactile and kinetic.* And it occurred to him maybe she'd remember. So he'd started swinging her chair, weaving it side to side and back and forth, trying to find that same swing rhythm, humming the music. It was like magic. After a while she'd cranked her head around to see what he was doing, and she was smiling, sort of a Mona Lisa smile, like she was listening to something in the far distance. To him, it proved absolutely who she was. Some part of her remembered the times they'd danced, and the movement brought back that good feeling.

Now, he didn't know why he came here anymore. Maybe that explained the sick feeling in his stomach on the way down. He had sort of decided to stop coming. Once he retired and wasn't making the side income with Nearing and Koslowski, he wouldn't be able to afford this place, she'd have to move, he wasn't sure how that would go. It wasn't really about caring, the nurse had it so wrong, he was all ashes inside now and besides this Megan probably didn't know who he was or care whether he came or not.

So it was almost but not quite pure habit. Okay, so what was that little remainder left over? The best he could do was, it had to do with seeing her smile, like there was some remedy in it. It had to do with that thing about the healing embrace of love, the power of that heart ray. Right now he needed to see that smile, at least one more time. Like in life you could accomplish at least that.

"You going to smile for me today?"

Megan looked at the bird in her fingers, then crushed it awkwardly right up against her eye. She held it there and rocked minutely side to side.

"You want to dance? We could do that. You know it makes Bert feel good, when you smile, right?"

He stood up from the bench and the movement drew her eye. She looked up at him as if she hadn't known anyone else was there.

"Here we go, Megan Kid. Here we go."

He swung the chair away from the bench, then looked up at the sky and took a deep breath and found the rhythm with his own feet before he moved it to the chair. It had to be slow and sweeping. Megan's head lolled with the movements.

Beyond the trunk of the oak and through a thin screen of laurel, Bert could see two orderlies, pushing a pair of geriatrics in wheelchairs. They were still fifty yards away, but they'd be here in another minute. A sweat broke on his temples.

He moved the chair to the inner music, picking up the tempo, wishing Girl X would turn her head so he could see the shape of her lips. If you could just find the center of it, he was thinking, if you could find the soul or core of what was graceful, surely you could convey it to her, to anyone. But it was so rare—so hard to find, to feel all the way. It was eluding him now as it always had.

"Megan, baby, let me see you smile," he pleaded.

Now the orderlies had rolled their charges onto the far end of the circular walk, and the desperation turned into outright fear. He'd have to stop moving this crazy way in another ten seconds.

"Megan, you got to give me something here," Bert begged. "This is important, Baby Kid, right? You got to give me something here."

44

CREE CLIMBED THE fifty-eight steps to Bert's house. The name of Lydia's church was a datum full of possibilities, and she should be feeling some renewed excitement, but all she really felt was a rising anxiety about this meeting. She'd have to confront Bert with the break-in at Ray's. If he had done it, she'd have to fight with him about it. Even if he hadn't, her knowing about it would reveal that she'd been with Ray, and he'd be angry with her. It wasn't going to be easy.

Again she paused at the fourth landing to look around. Three o'clock Saturday afternoon, and the street below was quiet but the thoroughfare of Market Street, invisible beyond the near rooftops, hummed with traffic. Looking up, she saw Bert swing into view briefly in the big front window. Dancing again. She waited, but he didn't reappear.

She walked up the rest of the way and rang the bell. This time the music was still playing when Bert opened the door, some big band playing lush, smooth melodies with a gently charged rhythm underneath. From the smell inside it was obvious Bert had been drinking. In the daylight, the place looked more stark and worn than it had by lamplight.

"Get you anything? Drink? I'm having a drink."

She hesitated, then decided a companionable gesture might help defuse what was coming. "Sure. Whatever you're having."

That pleased him. He went behind his counter and put together a couple of whiskeys on the rocks. His shirt was wrinkled, and his puffy face had the look of somebody who hadn't slept. He pushed her drink across the counter and raised his in a quick salute before drinking off half of it. Cree tasted hers. The music brought her back to hot nights with the kitchen windows open to the back stoop, Daddy and Bert in their undershirts, radio playing.

"Music too loud? I can—"

"No, it's fine. I like it."

He nodded, flicked his eyes at her, put his hands on the counter, stared out the front window. "So . . . do anything interesting last night? Friday night in San Francisco, got a great nightlife here."

"Working, actually. How about you, Uncle Bert?"

"Ah, the usual. A little work, a little R & R."

"Oh? Was breaking into Ray's place the work or the R & R?"

His red eyes came back to hers, angry and afraid. "What're you talking about?"

"You tell *me* what I'm talking about."

He didn't answer. Instead he came around the counter and past her into the middle of the living room. He stood on the rug, shifting his weight in time to the music, a new cut with a faster tempo. She followed him, threw her purse on the couch and sat into the cigarette smell. The pile of case files on the coffee table looked bigger than last time.

"Know who this is? Basie. The Count. Him and Ellington, the succor and salvation of my later years, so help me God. Guy came along and reinvigorated the whole swing movement, put the blues roots back into it. At least at first. Later he moved up to New York and got co-opted. But still."

Cree held her drink and waited.

"You ever dance to this stuff? This old-time stuff?"

"About once every other blue moon."

"C'mon. I'll show you the steps. It's easy. Takes the edge off. Makes everything more . . . manageable, you know what I mean?" He illustrated the movements. Even drunk, he moved with elegance and precision, handling his weight with economical flourish.

"No thanks. I'd look like an idiot."

"C'mon, Cree. Do me a favor. We got stuff to talk about, I know. But sometimes you gotta . . . you have to . . ." He looked perplexed, trying to name it. "You gotta find a good place first. Before you get to the other stuff."

"What other stuff?"

He gestured for her to stand, held his arms out to her expectantly, still moving to the music.

This was painful. She was tempted to do it for him, but there was too much tension to allow it to be real. "I think you're drunk, Bert."

"Yeah, just a little. Fifty-eight steps up here, do it every day, but on the other thing I never got through the first twelve." He didn't smile at his joke. "Saturday afternoon, why not. C'mon."

She made her decision. She knew it would hurt him, but she had to make him earn it, she had to have something to hold over him.

"Bert, no. Not until we've talked about what's going on. This is all getting too crazy for me."

He stopped moving. He looked vastly sad for a few seconds and then his face reddened and at first she thought it was rage. But it was shame, shame that he'd asked her. He had spilled a little of his drink and now scuffed at the wet spot on the carpet.

"Okay," he said. "Okay. Another time, maybe." He looked like a broken-hearted man.

Bert sat at the other end of the couch and for a few seconds leaned his head back against the cushions with his face to the ceiling. Cree waited. When he brought his head forward again, he was more composed.

"There's good reasons, Cree. Just hear me out first, then tell me to get fucked, get my head examined, whatever. But listen to me first."

"I'm listening."

Deep breath. "Okay. You remember I told you about that murder, the one where Ray was on the list in Berkeley?"

"The boyfriend of Ray's ex, you called it a slice-and-dice."

"Yeah. There never was a trial because the presumed perp hung himself in jail. Cops over there think that's good enough, but technically there was never a finding. So I went and located the evidence inventory. Take a look." He passed her some stapled-together pages. "Second page. About halfway down."

She flipped the page and looked where he told her. Items fifty-nine through sixty-four were collections of hairs identified as dog hairs.

"The victim didn't have pets," Bert said.

"So he had friends who came over with their dogs."

"Maybe so. But the same or very similar dogs were at the girlfriend's house, Ray's ex's house. Evidence techs vacuumed her place, too. She didn't have dogs, either."

Cree looked at the new pages he handed her. "So they had mutual friends with dogs. Bert—on the basis of *this* you break into somebody's house? You hurt Ray's pets? You—"

"You said you were going to listen first!" He was getting the baleful look in his eyes. "Look. I start getting e-mails with canine images in them, I gotta figure the taunt has to center on dogs. A reminder of something from the past, maybe evidence overlooked at the time, the grudge element. So I go back and pull up stuff that had dogs figuring in it, I showed you those. Then I go into Ray's place and find all kinds of corroboration. You been in there, you saw the art on the walls, you—" He pulled up short, realizing what he'd admitted.

"So you were watching his place? You saw us together. That's why the calls on my cell. Checking up on me."

"I, I was in there, and I got scared to death about what I was seeing. Yeah, I saw you, that's another whole can of worms we gotta get to. What the *fuck* are you doing, driving around with a psycho at night?"

"He doesn't seem so 'psycho' when you see him up close."

"Oh yeah? How close did you get, Cree? After I've been warning you?"

Cree stood up. She bent to snatch her purse and then stalked to the front hall. It was all she could do to speak to him again.

"I was going to try to talk sense to you, Uncle Bert. I was going to try to talk you out of taking this any further with Ray. But you're not hearing me, you're acting irrational and obsessive. Listen to yourself! Now you're making assumptions about what *I* do, too, you're judging what I do or don't do. If you want to convince me of anything, you're not going to do it with some drunken, paternalistic jealousy thing or another paranoid fantasy, you have to show me some *facts* that have any bearing on this! I'm trying to give you fair warning. Ray could report you. So far I've persuaded him not to, but if this goes further, so help me, I'll support him on it. *Malfeasance*, Uncle Bert—that could cost you your pension."

Bert's red face had gone to a mottled white. He wasn't healthy, she realized. Suddenly she was afraid for him, and she held herself in the hallway, looking back, her heartbeat shaking her.

"You're right," he said quietly. "You're right. Except on one thing. Listen to me and hear me out. Then you can tell me whatever."

She didn't say yes, but she didn't move. She stood near the door to make it clear he had better say something that made sense.

He got up to pace around the room as he explained. As before, when he laid out his forensic case he came across as focused and organized.

He had taken the extraordinary step of breaking into Ray's because he deeply felt he was onto something. He ticked the reasons off on his thick fingers: the dog-morph e-mails. The old witness/suspect list. Ray's criminal history as a juvenile. Working where he did, Ray had access to inside information on dozens of homicides over the last twelve years. Ray knew computers and the e-mails showed he had hacking-type skills. Ray hated Bert for what had happened to his face. Bert looks into unresolved older cases, and too many involving dogs kept coming up.

On the basis of that, he goes into Ray's house. What does he find? Suspect has three big dogs, all of them attack or security breeds. Mail is full of correspondence with path labs around the state. Files show he's owned big dogs for many years. He's got an unusual hobby: doing huge photo enlargements of X-rays and MRIs of dead people with tumors, skull injuries. That in itself constitutes a crime, the theft of confidential medical records, but more important demonstrates a morbid obsession, necrophilia or some other psychopathology. His facial disfigurement, whatever its origin, mea culpa, Cree, fine, that fits that profile, too, one of the old cases involves facial mutilation of victims. The books on Ray's table, what's he reading about? Werewolves, the psychology of serial killers, violent behavioral disorders.

"What does it take, Cree? What? To convince you something is not right with this guy?"

Cree felt her certainty falter. Intuitively, empathically, she now felt she knew Ray fairly well—she'd glimpsed something true about him on the rooftop, on the beach. Clearly, he was an innocent, asocial, individualistic person with an unusual philosophical or mystical bent, on a very private, very determined, quest to understand. But how far would he go on that quest? She couldn't be quite sure. Who *was* he, what was he? There was also that odd dissonance she'd felt from the start, the hidden part, a piece of the puzzle of Ray that she couldn't fit to the rest.

Still, Bert's case was so circumstantial, she had to throw some of it back at him. "You know what I do? I fly all over the country to investigate and study the minds of dead people. Take a look at my library, my private files. I must be a murderer, too, right?"

A big hand batted the suggestion aside. "He's got these maps on the wall upstairs. They're topo maps of rural areas, with paths or routes pencilled in, okay? One is San Bruno State Park, that's just south of here, Ray's drawn paths all over it. I didn't take a photo, I could kick myself now, but then a car came, I got ready for a fight." Bert looked more confident now, his lips working better, words not so slurred. "Cree, that case where the toddler was killed by dogs or coyotes, that was in San Bruno Park. Coyotes, gimme a break! I went into the files today and got the spot where it happened on the map right here. You can imagine how much I'd like to compare my map with Ray's." He looked at her thoughtfully. "You bring a camera with you from Seattle?"

"Of course. I'm on a job here."

"Then that's something you could help me with. The map. Next time you're 'seeing Ray up close,' go upstairs and—"

"Bert. Stop."

But she felt like she was standing on something that moved, a sandy slope, sliding gravel, no footing. She took a couple of steps back toward Bert, found a chair, sat.

"There were hairs taken as evidence in the San Bruno case and those two older attacks, too. Back then, they didn't do much DNA, but now it's easy. I took some samples from Ray's place and I also got history on his other dogs, maybe the genetics guys can identify dog breed from the follicles. It's already in the works, Cree. It's already being processed."

She thought about it as the music went into a number that would have sounded slinky in other circumstances but right now just sounded sneaky and deceptive. Bert gave her time. He stood at the window, fingering his lighter and looking out.

"So what's next? That's what I'm concerned about. You've got Ray angry as hell. As it is, it's all I can do to persuade him not to do something back, and now—"

"Oh? So Ray's gonna do precisely *what*?"

Cree realized her mistake as the anger surfaced in Bert's red eyes. He'd heard it as a challenge. "Nothing," she said firmly. "Not if I have anything to say about it. Nothing."

"So my visit got Ray provoked? Good. Maybe it'll provoke him into a mistake."

"No! Nobody's doing any more provoking! You've—"

"I'll make that decision." A clipped voice.

Cree stood up. She started toward him, then changed her mind and went to the CD player. She slapped the stop button and the music cut off instantly. In its aftermath, the silence was merciless. She went over to where Bert stood and took him by his shoulders.

"I'm going to make something very clear to you. You will not do any more illegal or violent things to Ray. If you've got a case, you make it by rules of procedure and law. You—"

"Or what? You'll walk away from the wolfman research? Go ahead. We're into something else now."

"I won't be party to anything illegal. I won't sit back and let it happen, either. You're going to figure out legitimate ways to implicate Ray, or you're going to get off his ass. Or so help me, I'll testify against you if something goes bad. You back off this whole thing, starting today. This minute."

"Comes a time when things take on a life of their own, Cree. A momentum."

"You heard me, right?" She glared at him and stalked to the door, then caught the overtone and had to turn back one more time. "Like what, momentum?"

Bert's mood had veered again. He had gone distant and secret and sad. When he answered, his voice was resigned. "Cree. Voice of experience talking here. This kind of thing, it can go from complex to simple real fast. At that point, and I think we're there right now, you don't have the luxury of indecision or weighing two sides or trying to reconcile them. You just have to choose which side you're on."

45

THE ESSENTIAL PRINCIPLE, Ray had decided, was that you had to look straight at things—most especially, the things you feared most or found most awful, distressing, or ugly. Then you had to find the courage and strength to celebrate them. That was what reverence meant. You observed and you said, *there is no part of the world I do not revere and honor; I will not turn my eye from one thing in it.* It was the impulse of all real spirituality and real art: to frame anything at all within a larger scheme of truth and beauty.

Sometimes it was easy. Sometimes it seemed impossible.

He was pleased with the X-ray compositions that sought to look inside and look at the scary things, the human mechanism people generally didn't want to acknowledge carted them around every day. The MRIs were proving to be something of an artistic challenge, still beyond him, and he didn't plan to work on them again. But he thought the visual light photos, though very difficult, were worth another try.

Saturday night was always busy in the emergency room, but down in the basement the morgue and path sections were usually quiet. The UCSF Medical Center was familiar turf for Ray, and he had the keys for the pathology suite. Plenty of patients died on Saturday nights, but they were mostly iced upstairs until daytime, when the path staff were on the job to process them, or just waited on stretchers until the overworked staff could wheel them down.

The Medical Center was a massive hospital complex on Parnassus Street, just below the eastern end of Golden Gate Park. From the street it looked like three blocks of uninterrupted walls and windows, but in fact it included innumerable wings and connectors and tunnels to other buildings. After all these years, Ray could find his way inside blindfolded.

He let himself in through a twenty-four-hour staff door. You couldn't be truly inconspicuous with a face like his, but he had already changed into scrubs and once he was inside he put his ID around his neck. Walk with a brisk, purposeful stride, and no one would bother you.

Down in the basement, he followed the corridor to the T, took the left hallway, then a right. He stopped at the morgue doors, set down his backpack, sorted through his collection of keys, found the right card. The electronic lock snicked and he pushed his way inside.

The room was dark. He found the bank of switches with his left hand, but before he turned on any lights, he stood motionless for a long time.

Always study the dark, Ray reminded himself. *What do you feel? What do you sense? What's inside you and what's in this place?* Darkness answered better than bright places. What he felt on his skin was air turned very cool and dry by a heavy-duty climate-control system. What he saw was spacious darkness punctured by a scattered constellation of red and green lights: equipment switches, surge protectors, telephones, intercoms. Silence but for the hum of refrigeration and ventilation equipment, almost below hearing. It felt clinical and sterile and at the ready, an ambience he liked.

Inside, it was different. A sullen throb of pain had started deep in his head, and his thoughts were strange things that seemed to spring out unexpectedly from different places, startling him. The lights of the room were ringed with oily rainbows. His affect seemed irrationally out of synch: He should be tense, worried about what was happening in his head, about being discovered here, about whether he could find the strength to find beauty in the dead, about Bert Marchetti. But instead a paradoxical ebullience bloomed in him, joyously defiant and inappropriate. *Pathology or inspiration?* Ray wondered. *Wisdom?* Only time would tell.

He flipped several light switches. The fluorescent tubes blinked, then glazed the tile floors and steel tables with a chilly light. He experimented with the switches, killing all the overheads he didn't need and leaving on only those at the far wall. When he'd gotten it right, he crossed over, turned on the lights inside the cold room, and opened the heavily insulated door. He looked over the rows of tables, about half of which held the plastic pods of zippered body bags. He picked a bag at random, set his backpack on the pallet next to it, and slid down the zipper.

He looked at the old man there and his skin contracted. Not a good death, not one he could look at. He pulled the zipper quickly shut. When the bag was sealed again, he felt a little dizzy and for a moment the ceiling lights went eerily chromatic.

The next bag held a middle-aged black woman. She was plump and serene and had not yet received the Y-incision. Her skin was relatively taut and her native pigmentation hid some of the lividity and blanching. He felt bad for her and wondered what had happened to end her. She had short, stylish hair, long earlobes pierced by holes for multiple earrings. Her eyelids were parted enough for a sliver of sclera to appear, like a person catnapping. Even with cheeks sunken in death, she had a pleasant face, lines that suggested she had smiled a lot, had lived a good life. The tag said her name had been Millicent. A lovely name. She scared him.

He wondered what she would say to him if they could have met, and abruptly the words came into his head as if she really had spoken: *Ray, you fool*, she'd say, *what you doin' looking at my old meat self? You go out and get movin' while you still got the spark, like I'd damn sure be doin' if I could.*

He almost laughed out loud. *Lovely, wise Millicent*, he thought. *Magnificent Millicent. I'm going nuts, but you're absolutely right.* He gently patted her springy hair, zipped her up again, and picked up his camera bag.

Half an hour later, he turned the van into the picnic area access road, cut the lights, and pulled up just past the closed gates. To avoid police suspicion or a ticket, he rolled his orange disabled vehicle tag into the top of the window, then got out, locked up, and sprinted across the parkway. Deep darkness, no cars in either direction, a clean break from civilization. Tonight the wind was relentless, blowing a hard, cold fog that shook the eucalyptus leaves and tossed the heads of smaller trees. Ordinarily, he'd strip to run, but tonight he didn't feel up for a battle against the cold and left his clothes on. San Bruno wasn't his favorite run, but it was nearby and there were some wonderful places in the little island of wild. When the wind was right the air could be the sweetest in the world, intoxicating, something about the particular mix of vegetation on the slopes.

At first he ran on the Radio Road, but after a couple hundred yards he cut southeast, straight up the steep hill and into the dense, clutching chaparral scrub. He vaulted over waist-high buckbrush and tore through manzanita thickets, sucking in the wet sweet air like a ramjet. One thornbush ripped a gash just above his wrist and it hurt like hell and bled copiously and he was glad for it. In the past he had run this gauntlet all the way to Oyster Cove and back and he was tempted to try it tonight. Run fast enough to leave his face behind, flung away like litter in the wind. Burn it all out, empty out all fear and sadness, hope that wisdom would rush in to fill the vacuum. Maybe tonight the air would relieve the pressure in his head.

But after ten minutes of hard uphill work, he knew he didn't have the juice for it tonight. The admission came with a stab of panic, which he fought down by reminding himself it wasn't unexpected, it was bound to happen, it was hardly the first time. He would not take it as a bad sign or let it dismay him on this beautiful night of insight. You needed resolve and certainty. If you veered and vacillated, you could easily get lost. He had been lost and knew what it felt like: an unending deranged screaming inside. He wasn't going to go there, ever again.

With a last surge he burst out of a thick patch of scrub and came to a stop in a more open area where the long grass had won out against the chaparral vegetation. Softer, here. The lights of the radio tower were blurs of sullen red, a dying dragon's eyes hovering over the invisible crest of the hill. Below, the streets of Brisbane smeared in a barely differentiated dull glow. A few miles straight past that, he knew, somewhere in the dimensionless murk, was his own house, his little earthly haven and shelter. He stopped and caught his breath and stood looking out that way as if he might see himself there, see Ray coming and going and living the life he lived, as if from this safe distance he could put it into perspective.

After another minute he sat down in the rough grass, staring out at the distant glow as he held himself against the cold. He put his mouth over the cut on his wrist and tasted the blood. After a while, one hand strayed to the scars on his face. The familiar, hated topography felt different. Like it had changed in some minuscule way in his thoughts.

Cree, he decided. Touching him there.

That explained tonight's strange emotional tenor. All his anger at Bert had vanished instantly, vaporized by that slight warmth of palm against his cheek. What an amazing person. Really, she was an astonishing gift, serendipitous, just as the wolfman was, as the deer had been, Judd LeGrand, the rest of it. It proved that wisdom was magically provided when you most needed it—if you could recognize it when it came. In another era of his life, he would have wanted to court her and make love with her and live with her forever. But of course now everything was so different.

He tasted the blood on his arm again. He knew that he should stay away from her, that she'd throw him wildly off balance, confuse him. But to run away would be cowardice, would be turning his eye from the world.

Ray laughed out loud at himself, feeling the reckless joy of surrender. *Whatever, Pilgrim*, he told himself. *As if you could resist!* He could not stop himself from loving her, seizing every moment and atom of Cree Black, even though the loss of her would be a terrible thing to endure.

46

SHE ARRIVED AT the Life Sciences parking lot after sunset to find that, sure enough, the shadows were again full of shifting, waiting things. On her way to the elevator, the building yawned empty all around: a weekend evening, everybody was gone. The long basement corridor and its many doorways seemed to flicker with stealthy movements.

She was glad Skobold was in the lab when she came in. He had already wheeled the wolfman's pallet out into the big room and was working on the cranium.

"We're approaching my absolute favorite phase of reconstruction," he told her.

Yet he looked anything but enthusiastic as he set himself up with a metal mixing bowl and an electric eggbeater. He explained that earlier he had painted a layer of separating compound onto the skull and was now about to coat it with alginate, a seaweed-derived compound that would dry quickly to a flexible mold. He opened a box of powder and measured it into the bowl, then filled a pitcher with water and poured some onto the mound. He turned on the mixer and stirred thoroughly, adding water occasionally, turning the alginate into a pale, creamy mass. When the consistency was right, he began painting and puddling it onto the skull. For all the obvious skill in his hands, his movements seemed tentative, indecisive.

"Horace?" Cree asked finally. "You okay?"

His hands jerked as if she'd jarred his elbow. "Odd that you should ask. I was about to ask you the same question."

"Well, there have been some developments that—"

"Yes, I know. I know because I received very troubling phone calls from both Bertram and Ray. Ray called at three thirty in the morning, very upset, to tell me what he found when you and he returned to his house last night. Then this afternoon Bertram called me. He feels I have betrayed him by associating on friendly terms with Ray all these years, not telling him. He was in a towering rage. Truly apoplectic."

"If he called this afternoon, he must have been pretty drunk, too."

"Yes, that, too. And I have learned to be wary of his heavier drinking phases."

"So what are we going to do about this?"

Skolbold's eyes drifted, either admitting he had no idea, or, it occurred to her, as if he had more to tell her but was reluctant to do so. Cree let him think it through as he finished applying the alginate and then moved quickly to the sink. She helped him rinse the mixers and brushes.

"Next we must support the alginate," he told her. "It is too flexible to stand on its own as a mold, so we must reinforce it with plaster. When that has hardened, we can separate the skull from the alginate with confidence the alginate will retain the correct shape. We'll pour a solid support mold for the shell, and when that dries we'll be ready to cast the skull."

"So many steps."

"Yes. It is painstaking, and some say it's outmoded." He went to the skull and lightly touched its uneven rubbery coating, which apparently had not yet cured to his satisfaction. He frowned and turned to Cree with a disconcerting gaze. She got the sense he was working his way around to something. "So, while we're waiting, perhaps I should tell you a bit about the virtual modeling process. Personally, I prefer the old-fashioned methods, but digital reconstruction can be useful, and it will help me explain some important issues."

He led her to a computer on one of the central tables and turned it on.

"We can now scan photos and X-rays into one of several facial modeling programs. From those, the computer builds a 3-D image of the naked skull. We then input the likely tissue depths that the computer uses to create a 3-D surface image of a head and face. We can sculpt by hand from that image, or we can employ a CAD-based carving process and create a bust out of plastic foam."

When the computer booted up, he clicked through several screens to an example, a hollow skull seemingly made out of a mesh of glowing blue wire, with a scattering of red dots burning on its virtual surface. At Skobold's command, it rotated or tipped forward and back.

"That was the first stage of our 3001, a female in her midtwenties whom we call Remedios. Next we added our tissue depths, using the thirty-four index points of the Helmer method."

The new screen showed the skull clothed in light brown virtual flesh with lifelike eyes and dark hair. Skobold rotated the image to the profile and back.

"Does it look like anyone you know? We're still searching for 3001."

"I'm sorry, Horace, it seems sort of . . . generic. It could be almost anyone."

"Precisely! Because tissue metrics are based on averaged measurements from thousands of individuals. But no real person is ever average! If you create a likeness using only those averages and avoiding any intuitive guesses, you end up with this. The appearance may be *consistent* with a specific person, but one can't claim it *is* that person."

"Right."

"On the other hand, if you imagine or intuit too many particulars, you end up with a very lifelike model, very much someone specific. But you might have guessed wrong, and have a very real-looking face that resembles no actual person who ever lived."

"So how do you get around that?"

"For forensic cases, where too much personality in the model might cause a living person to misidentify, we often stay a little on the generic side. For archeological ones, where the goal is to give vitality and personality to historic or prehistoric persons, we use more license. We tend to the artistic side."

Cree studied at the bland face of Remedios 3001. "Average tissue depths won't help you with the wolfman at all, will they?"

"No." Skobold opened a ring binder and paged through until he found some tables in which he had pencilled in the wolfman's numbers. He drew a finger across the many erasures and question marks that suggested ambivalence about his calculations. "I will have to apply more of a 'Russian school' approach—I'll rely less on tissue metrics and more on basic skeletal and muscular engineering. One starts with the major muscles of the neck, then builds the face out from the bone by adding each muscle and tendon. Only when they're in place does one finish with the fatty tissues and skin. I generally use a combination of both approaches, but for the wolfman, I will have to rely almost entirely on the fundamental engineering." He brought his vast eyes to meet hers. "And I will rely upon *you*."

"Me."

"Yes. It has become all the more important that we corroborate our informed guesswork with historical photos or drawings of him, or written descriptions. Period likenesses or written history often play a pivotal role in creating historical reconstructions—Wilhelm His's reconstruction of Johann Sebastian Bach is a famous example, as is Prag and Neave's work on the skull of King Philip II of Macedon. Or the recent reconstruction of King Tut. Portraits, legends, poems, the subject's clothing, likenesses on coins or pottery—all can provide important clues."

Horace started a computer file for 3024, opened the blank index grid, and showed her where to enter the values he'd listed, then busied himself with other chores. Cree pecked in some numbers as he drifted back to the wolfman's coated skull. For a few moments he just caressed its lumpy surface with his fingertips, like a blind man reading Braille.

"I have another point to make, but it requires I tell you a personal story. May I?"

"Of course!"

He worked his lips, hands fretting among his tools. "Twenty-six years ago. After my son's death. As I told you, I went through a difficult period. I didn't react the way Bert did, but I became . . . unhinged in my own ways. For several years. I divorced and never spoke to my wife again. I became something of a lost soul, Ms. Black. I was drowning in sorrow and loss and confusion of every sort. And the terrible thing was, beneath all that was anger. I was a volcano inside. Not just at the person who ran over my son. At the world at large. At mankind. At fate. At God. At whatever, whoever. At the peak of the angry phase, I did some awful things. Yes, Horace Skobold, idealist, humanist, optimist—yes, I did."

"Like what, Horace?" she asked gently.

"Oh, all sorts of nasty things. I gutted the career of a colleague at another university. It was sheer malice. I did it by poisoning people's minds about his qualifications and integrity and private life, and I rather enjoyed the process. It was only one of several pointlessly cruel things I did." He stopped, gulped air, eyes alarmed. "This is very difficult to relate, Ms. Black."

"Please go on. That was a long time ago. I'm grateful that you're telling me."

"One evening, here at the lab—on the other side—I was alone, working on a new subject. And my hand slipped and I made an unnecessary incision. And then I began . . . making more wounds. I began punishing the corpse of an unidentified middle-aged man for the death of my son and for my own suffering and for this being a rotten world. You cannot imagine the things I did." He stopped, appalled at himself.

"But you got yourself out of that state of mind. How?"

"I did *nothing*! I had no solution, Ms. Black. Who knows, perhaps I would have begun . . . inflicting such punishment upon the living. But a few days later, I met Patrick. He was a new employee at the print shop, not much more than half my age. I was picking up some materials and he said something, accidental no doubt, that affected me. I was so moved that I touched his arm. He took my hand briefly, a . . . a compassionate gesture. A few days later, we met for lunch. Then for dinner. I had never slept with a man, never once felt that inclination. When he suggested it, I was shocked and told him so. And yet two days later I was knocking at his apartment door in the middle of the night. I was crying and shouting, I was desperate and out of control and didn't know why I was there. I must have sounded like a madman, yet *Patrick opened his door*, Ms. Black. You see? I did *nothing* to heal myself. The world turned its kinder face to me once again. All I did was . . . accept its kindness."

He had calmed a bit, soothed by the memory. "Patrick healed me by letting me out of my loneliness. His affection showed me that life goes on and there is, after all, some reason for living it. Witnessing his humanity brought me back to my own."

Cree had long since stopped entering numbers into the computer. She sat on her stool as Horace's colossal agony and his subsequent rescue from it resonated in her. She could almost *see* his emotion, a shimmer of painfully contrasting colors.

"I never again felt a desire to injure anyone," he said, more composed. "And I came to believe that *loneliness* is the ultimate root of the pain we inflict upon each other. And that to remedy the pain, all we must do is address its root."

Cree nodded slowly, giving that its due. "I tend to think along similar lines," she said carefully. "And I'd like to believe it. The problem is . . . it might work for you and me, but I'm not sure it's something we can apply to the rest of mankind. What about greed, lust for power, racism, all the other awful motivations? It would be hard to argue that the Holocaust happened because Hitler and his collaborators were *lonely!*"

His certainty did not waver. "Oh, yes. Absolutely. Imagine how alone such a person is—one who feels so very, very removed from his own kind that it is possible, even enjoyable, to torment or kill them? To be so removed, to know so little of the humanity of those you hurt, to have so little faith they might know you or care about you? To have so completely abandoned hope of knowing or caring about another? Oh yes. What more exact definition of loneliness could one conceive? That is the absolute distillation of the state."

An elegant summary, Cree had to admit. It was very close to her own basic principle, the truth or theory or hope at the basis of her methodology and her survival. Hearing this old man say it made it a little less tentative.

When Horace spoke again, he had gained back every bit of his professorial assurance. "To the point of my long soliloquy, Ms. Black. Your relationship with Bert and new friendship with Ray means that—aside from myself, with whom both are incensed right now—you are the only person with a connection to both men. With any investment in both or any leverage with them. With any chance of helping them avoid—"

"'Unintended consequences?'" It came out with more irony than she'd intended.

"Yes, those." Skobold remained unruffled. "It appears to be up to you to open the door."

"Um, Horace, I don't—"

"I have utmost confidence in you, Ms. Black," he said sternly.

47

BERT WAS THINKING: Saturday night, after a day like today, you needed something, you deserved something. But it was all Latin at the Oasis and rock 'n' roll at the Metronome, no outlet there. At least the Tenderloin Club could reliably deliver its anesthetic, and besides there was business to attend to. He ordered his whiskey and managed to grab the same corner seat where he'd met Hank Chambers. He liked a good view of the door.

This afternoon, after Cree left, he'd felt like he had fire ants under his skin, all this pent-up energy and no place to put it. In his eagerness and frustration he'd stupidly called Hank. The conversation was short and not sweet.

"Don't badger me, Bertie. You know it'll take a few days. Jesus, it's Saturday! Don't you have a life? Because I *do*, okay?"

"Yeah, I know that. I was just checking in."

"I'm on it. I told you I'd do it. I even looked into your dog attack in Sausalito, on a *Saturday*, Bert, and that hair evidence isn't worth shit. No follicles for DNA, the microphotos won't prove anything, you can scratch that one off your list. The others I start on Monday. But don't badger me on it."

Disappointed at the Sausalito case falling out of the mix, pissed at Hank's attitude, booze at the headache stage, he'd called Horace and blown his top for ten minutes. He'd ended it by slamming the phone down on the old man's excuses, then stalked around his house just feeling desperate, pissed at Cree, scared for her, hating Cameron Raymond. He wished Cree could see the light and do one thing for him, get a photo of that map on Ray's wall. That could break it open. Again he berated himself for failing to take the picture when he'd had the chance. Another five seconds then and he'd be in much better shape now. That had nagged at him unbearably and he'd felt his urgency spike. It was a day or two ahead of schedule, but he'd broken down and made the calls to set up tonight's appointment.

Bert downed the rest of his second drink, checked his watch, and only a few moments later looked up to see two men come through the entrance of the Tenderloin Club.

Right on time, bless their bent and dirty hearts.

Nearing waved and slouched toward him, long legs in black jeans, snug gray turtleneck. Behind him came Koslowski, dressed in sweat pants and a baggy nylon workout jacket that didn't hide the bulk of his shoulders and upper arms. Koslowski had white-blond hair cut so short he looked bald from a distance, a thick neck, a wise-ass smile in a face unlined by conscience.

Nearing slid into the other side of the booth, scanned the crowd, rubbed his hands together. "Drinkie, drinkie," he said expectantly.

Koslowski came over to Bert's side and chucked him on the shoulder. "Rich tells me you boys had a good old time at the Laundromat the other night. Says you really rocked, Machete." He waited for Bert's half-hearted high five, then sat next to Nearing.

They made a good pair, Bert thought: sharp skinny dark-skinned Nearing, bulky blunt-headed pale-faced Koslowski. Both of them lethal, both cocky. The fuck-you attitudes with a paranoid edge. As they'd sat down, Bert had seen the lump where Koslowski's hip holster pushed out his windbreaker. It gave him a dark pleasure that they'd read his wishes so well from his earlier phone call and that they were willing on such short notice.

"So what's the deal, Bertie?" Nearing asked. "You're Mr. Mystery here. You got a tip for us, or what? Something with profit potential?"

Bert had planned to keep it all in character, the wise-ass tough guy attitude, but now he felt his purpose seeping out of him, their attentive faces reminding him of the many times like the Laundromat and the soiled feelings and confusions that came after.

"No. This one's more from my side of the job. Something you do to redeem your poor lost souls, for the good of mankind. Or to make old Bert happy in his sunset years. Whatever. It's about going to a guy's place and getting photos of some evidence. If it requires busting the guy's head, so much the better."

They looked at him with heightened interest. Bert felt the moment stretch, but any force he'd owned had leaked out of him and he couldn't think of how to get off the dime. First it occurred to him just how pissed off Cree would be. That, he rationalized away by reminding himself that Cree being mad was a better end result than Cree being hurt or dead. But then he realized that she might even be there, she could get hurt that way, too. Meaning he'd have to tell Nearing and Koslowski about her, tell them not to go if her car was there or if they had reason to believe she was inside.

It was getting too complex. For several seconds, he didn't think he could bring himself to go further, and anyway they didn't look like they were buying it.

But then Koslowski made a little grin, a *why not* shrug, and it changed again, turned back into a kind of game, that satisfying mix of machismo and dark-hearted righteousness, us against them where us was Bert Marchetti and the two guys in front of him right now. He felt a wave of gratitude and with it a renewed determination.

Koslowski checked Nearing's face and must have found assent. "Are we talking tonight?" he asked.

48

R AY ARRIVED HOME well after midnight. He had barely run at all, but the cold wind and darkness had proven to be the gift he'd needed. Now even the grimy dark of his own street looked pregnant, expectant. It was as if the pure black of infinite space shone down through the fog-diffused glow of the city, bathing the silent industrial streets in the absence of light. Darkness was the raw material of all creation and being immersed in it gave him energy and power.

He locked the van, went to his front door, and gave it an experimental shove. Its solidity pleased him. He had spent the afternoon replacing the jamb and then reinforcing it with a heavy steel plate, six feet long, that he'd bolted deep into the bricks of the wall so that it overlapped the jamb. Then he'd fixed the inner door with a new, heavy-duty lock set. When he'd left the house earlier, he'd locked the dogs into the residential section. Bert wasn't going to get in again.

He had just opened the locks when he heard something on the parking apron behind him. His heart leapt with the irrational, joyful trepidation that it might be Cree. But an instant later he knew it wasn't. Wrong noise. This was the quick quiet sound of someone coming at a run from the deep shadows of the first loading bay.

He stepped into the black of the doorway without showing any haste, just a guy coming home late, not worried, no. The instant he was inside, he started the door swinging shut and leapt to the right. Leaning against the wall was a three-foot length of old plumbing pipe left over from when he'd installed his kitchen sink. He couldn't see it, but his hands found it immediately.

The door bounced open hard and slapped against the wall and in the faint light near the opening he saw a burly form land in a fighting stance. Its blunt head ticked left and right.

Ray swung the pipe. It slashed out of the dark and connected with the guy's forehead. The big figure went over backward with a shriek, sprawling into the doorway, but immediately a second shape eclipsed the light, coming over the fallen body. Ray reacted too late, and something hit him on the side of his neck just under his ear. He toppled back into the building, shocked, disoriented. Distantly, he heard the clank of his pipe hitting the floor and the dogs starting to bay and the fallen guy swearing.

The new attacker was almost invisible, a quick black shape in the darkness. Ray fell hard on his right shoulder but recovered his senses enough to roll the instant he hit. The club or stick smacked the pavement just behind his head as he rolled again. When he came up, he scuttled sideways toward the depths of the building, the shelter of deeper darkness. The area near the door was empty except for the guy he'd hit with the pipe, who had come up to sitting position. Just as Ray spun to scan for the second intruder, the club hit him again, right above his temple. He backpedaled, off balance, tripped over a loose brick, fell again, rolled instinctively. A crazy swimming fog and spangles of lights filled the inside of his head.

He fought to stay conscious by telling himself there was a way to do this. It was to use the spectrum of senses he used in his night runs. Eyes were no good. In darkness, you felt space on your skin, you made a picture of a place with your ears, you intuited presences. Quick tiny gritting noises told him the invisible guy was over to his left, coming in a fast arc toward him. He threw himself toward the sound, lashed out with one foot and felt it hit. Not enough to hurt anyone.

Ray ducked down onto all fours and scrabbled deeper into the building, the movements close behind him. He cut hard right and spun and from here he could see a flitting silhouette against the doorway glow, closing fast. He drove his shoulder into the dark man's belly and followed him over and put his weight on top as they hit the cement. He couldn't see a face, but he felt a leather jacket and a strong, whipcord-lean body. The guy had to be stunned, but Ray felt snapping punches land near his throat, the strikes of somebody with martial arts training. He sprang off and by kinetic memory knew where the head would be as the man sat up. Ray pivoted and flung his foot out and felt it make solid contact.

A brilliant light came from near the doorway and somebody shouted, "Freeze, motherfucker!"

It all came together in Ray's mind, *the first guy must have gotten up, freeze means a gun, a cop,* and he knew these were Bert's friends and maybe Bert himself was out there and soon to come in. Outrage flooded him. It was like the second stage of a rocket igniting, a powerful pulse of force. He sprinted toward the light, eyes averted.

A flash lit the room, but he wasn't looking and all it did was give him a better idea of the space. He barely heard the explosion of the gun, even though by now he was close enough to feel the pressure wave of the blast. At the last instant, as the flashlight spun to track him, he dropped and went hard to the left on all fours. His hands ran into a cinder block and grabbed it, and he stood up with it just as the wedge of light caught up with him. The cinder block came around and eclipsed the light and the next muzzle flash before it crunched into the gun hand. The light beam panned wildly and then was rolling along the floor. Ray saw enough of the big form outlined against the fan of light to swing the block again. It made a solid sound when it connected with the guy's head.

When the second light came out of the darkness twenty feet away, he pitched the block at it. The block ghosted out of the beam and the light flicked to track it, a momentary distraction that was all Ray needed. He could *feel* the dark man in his space, he could *smell* him, knew where the light had been and where the man would move. He went toward that space and collided with the sinewy leather-clad body. Now the guy had a flashlight in one hand and a gun in the other, but he was off balance and Ray caught the gun in both hands. He spun so the gun was at his shoulder, then bent hard at the waist and twisted it free. An elbow to the face to put the guy down, then a hard heel to the temple to keep him there.

The hulk of the other man lay half in and half out of the fallen flashlight's beam, unmoving. Ray grabbed the nearer man's jacket and dragged him across and laid him alongside, tested the bulky man's pulse at the carotid and found it steady and firm. He retrieved the flashlight and then the guns in case Bert Marchetti was out there and planned to make some grand entrance. He shined the light on the thinner man, then knelt and rummaged through his pockets: extra ammunition clip, digital camera, several pairs of plastic handcuffs, and at last a wallet. A police ID. Richard Nearing.

Ray held the guns in his lap as he sat on the black man's chest and caught his breath and thought about what he should do. After a moment, he realized the dogs were still barking and going crazy in there, ripping the kitchen door to shreds.

"Dogs!" he called sharply. "It's okay. Basta! Quiet!"

They obeyed instantly, as always.

He thought about the darkness outside and wondered why with all his clarity he hadn't felt these men waiting. He hoped Bert wasn't out there, because if Bert came in it would be fatal for one of them. He was very angry at Bert. And it would only get worse when the endorphins percolated out of his blood and the pain in his neck and head and hands came roaring in. Just under the veneer of momentary satisfaction, rage was building. It seemed to bulge outward from the fire blot in his head and emanate through his whole body. He hoped he wouldn't let the anger unravel the gains he'd made tonight, and that he had the strength to channel it wisely.

The rage was there, but still he felt surprisingly good. It was what the books called a paradoxical affect, pretty typical: clear, clean, focused, very much alive. And full of energy. Which was good because it was now looking to be a very long night.

He felt the skinny guy's chest beneath him take one labored breath and then another. He toed the big bulky guy and got a slight groan in response. At last he got up and limped to the kitchen door to let the dogs loose, intensely grateful for their patience, their obedience, their unquestioning love and loyalty.

49

THE HISTORY ROOM didn't open until noon on Sundays, so Cree killed the morning in the basic reference section and the newspaper archives. First she wasted an hour trying to track down Lydia Jackson Schweizter's church through historical records, only to end up finding it in the current phone book, still in operation.

She called, got lucky, and reached a Reverend Michaelson who told her that Sunday was a prohibitively busy day in his trade, but he'd be happy to show her their archives tomorrow. They made a morning appointment and Cree moved on to the newspapers, claiming a microfilm cartel within arm's length of the wall of file drawers. Looking through even the narrowed range of four years was a huge job, and she knew it would go faster with two sets of eyes. She wished Ray had answered when she'd called earlier.

Still, it was easier this time. Her sense of urgency propelled her, and she was better with the viewing apparatus. She started on the 1888 newspapers, the likely year that the wolfman had begun to experience the rapid, unprecedented growth of his palate and front teeth. It was also the year the feral dog attacks in the Barbary Coast had first been mentioned. Coincidence? Probably. Or not.

This time she had equipped herself with two fine-point markers and an 1890 San Francisco map that she'd photocopied from a history text on the main floor. She scanned the *Chronicle* for all of 1888, and when she encountered reports of murders she marked the crime scenes on the map with a blue dot. Soon the Barbary Coast area was thick with blue, and the blocks near the intersection of Broadway with Kearney and Montgomery streets, called the Devil's Acre back then, accumulated so many dots they began to layer on each other.

When she found the three reports of feral dog attacks, she marked them in red, nestling the dots right there in the heart of the blue cluster.

She finished the 1888 spool, rewound, and took a moment to look at her map. As forensic sociology, tracking crime patterns, it was rudimentary, but she found satisfaction in seeing it laid out like this. She felt a little pumped up as she threaded the spool for 1889.

More murders, more blue dots. In March, another mention of a dog attack, red dot. More murders, assaults, petty crimes. Lots of the usual urban scandals, celebrity gossip, cable car issues, other civic projects. Articles on city council meetings reported charges of corruption, complaints about sanitation, harangues from religious leaders outraged by the city's tolerance of liquor and sex, tirades about the continuing influx and pagan habits of the Chinese. Talk about paradoxical Victorian values: The police log showed arrests for spitting in public or use of profanity, while the same cops did nothing about the hair-raising vice industries of the Barbary Coast.

Another couple of hours, another spool and another, and her enthusiasm began to wane. By the time she was done, it was gone entirely. In not one article, ad, or editorial did the newspapers of 1889 to 1891 contain any reference to another dog attack, let alone to wildmen, wolfmen, or werewolves.

But it was one o'clock, and the History Room was now open. She called Ray again, on the off chance he'd join her, but no one answered. Then she thought to check in with Bert. She tried his home, cell, and work phones and got no answer at any of them. A distant alarm bell began shrilling in her head, but she decided it was baseless. She suppressed it and concentrated on the work at hand.

The marriage of Lydia Jackson and Hans Schweitzer had triggered some questions, and now she had a good idea of how to answer them. Going back and forth between Sanborn maps, the Block Books, and the City Directories, she was able to piece together the entwined history of the two houses.

The City Directory from 1882 showed who lived at the Jackson house: Franklin and Lydia Jackson—Lydia living with some relative, either her first husband, father, brother, or uncle. By 1886, though, the directory showed only Lydia. The Schweitzer house was occupied by Hans alone until 1887, when the occupants were listed as Hans and Lydia Schweitzer.

Likely scenario: Lydia lived with family until they died or went elsewhere. She lived alone for a while, then married the newly wealthy contractor and moved one house up the hill.

The Block books had Schweitzer as the owner of the former Jackson house in 1887 and again in the 1890 and 1894 editions, proving that the couple didn't sell the property. So who lived there after Lydia married and moved out?

On to the Spring Valley Water Company tap records, which showed that until 1887 the tap was billed to Lydia Jackson. Later in that year, her account was closed and somebody named George Samson opened the tap at that address. Likely scenario: Hans and Lydia rented out the place when she moved next door.

Samson payed for the tap until 1890, when his account was closed. She checked out more microfilm spools but couldn't find any record of a new tap turned on at the Jackson house from 1890 to 1906. The year the Great Earthquake brought it down.

Prime real estate left empty for almost sixteen years? Puzzled, she turned her attention back to the Schweitzer house, and found that Hans was still paying the water bills until 1914, when his account closed and the new owner, O'Brien, paid to have the tap turned on.

On to the Great Register. Since women couldn't vote yet, it wouldn't include anything about Lydia, but it was rich with information about Hans. First registered to vote in 1868; born in 1842 in a German town called Gottingen, emigrated to San Francisco in 1860, naturalized as an American citizen, registered to vote in 1866. He had listed his occupation as "mason," and his address when he first registered was over in what was then a poor neighborhood, North Beach. A long way from the hilltop nouveau-riche neighborhood of Pacific Heights.

She got the sense of a man of humble beginnings, coming to the new world to seek his fortune, maybe trying his hand at the Comstock silver but instead plying his trade in the growing city. Became a successful contractor, married around 1887, when he would have been forty-five,

Lydia twenty-seven. True love, Cree wondered, or nineteenth-century pragmatism—the Jackson family marrying off a "spinster" daughter, joining two moderate family fortunes?

An image of Lydia's portrait photo came back to her, the determined sincerity with a faint, wild and lovely hint of astonishment in that face.

Love, Cree decided.

At four o'clock she left the library with her phone at her ear. She called Ray again, got no answer, left a fourth message on his machine. Then all three of Bert's numbers and again nothing, nothing, nothing. Where were they? After her last attempt she snapped the phone shut and distinctly felt a cold slithering in her spine. The fact that neither man was answering his phone was starting to scare her.

50

BERT'S PLACE LOOKED like a treehouse, perched up in the fog-thickened shadows of foliage. There were no lights in the windows, but Cree trotted up the steps anyway. Starved, she had taken the time to grab dinner and drop her research notes at the motel, and night had come while she'd showered.

Talking with Horace last night had filled her with a contradictory sense of anxiety—no, more like dread—and hopefulness. She swore that if Bert was home she'd drink with him, she'd dance a waltz or a goddamned tango if that's what it took to make contact. His vocabulary for intimacy was so different from hers, but she swore she'd decipher it.

Open the door, she thought. Let him out of the confines of his loneliness, his obsession with past injuries and horrors. Let a little light in.

She rang the bell and knocked on the door, but there was no answer, no sound of movement inside. Almost seven o'clock: She wondered where he might be at this hour on a Sunday night, and that begot a fresh wave of concern. She hurried down the steps, into the car and through the night streets to Ray's house.

The east-side streets were anything but picturesque, not San Francisco postcard material. Some blocks were lit with acid orange, some cold blue, both turning the gritty industrial streets a harsh chemical color. In the darker side streets, a few lanterns glowed under the tarps of the homeless encampments, but aside from a few ragged shadows lurching on the side-walks there were no pedestrians and almost no car traffic.

An idea had occurred to her as she was leaving Bert's. A plan, actually. It was a little risky, certainly, but probably the best option under the circumstances. A way of killing several birds with one stone. It was not really conniving, not duplicitous, she kept telling herself, not if she did it with genuine concern for Ray's well-being and sincere interest in him as a person, as a friend. And she was curious. There was an important element missing from her understanding of him. She could almost *see* it in him, a knot of idea and feeling she couldn't untangle with either her psychological training or her intuitive, empathic skills. She was increasingly certain it was central to Ray and to the whole problem.

The lights in Diamond Intermodal's windows showed he was home. She rang the bell, heard the dogs bark and go silent, and a moment later Ray opened the door. She sensed more than saw the dogs, moving in the darkness behind him.

"Where have you been, Ray? I've been calling all day!"

"Just being incommunicado for a bit. I do that now and again. But it's great to see you. Come in."

"It's not too late for a visit?"

"Are you kidding? For you it's never too late!"

The dogs had mostly recovered. They greeted her with cautious interest, flattered her with wagging tails, and followed behind her into Ray's living room. Ray gestured her to the couch and sprawled onto a big leather chair, one leg over its arm, face angled so she saw only his good side. He looked tired, pleased to see her, and worried.

"I've always been the bad-news-first type," he told her guardedly.

"Nothing particularly new to report. I was coming back from downtown, thought I'd . . . just check in, see what's going on."

He looked at her skeptically. "As in making sure I haven't done anything stupid?"

"Not exactly. But you're welcome to reassure me."

"If you're talking about Bert, no, I haven't seen him or killed him or whatever you're worried about. And he hasn't succeeded in killing me, apparently. But I did do something stupid."

Something about the way he talked, she had to wonder if there was dodge hidden in his words. But that was probably just paranoia. "What was that?"

"Went for a run after what was already a long night. I wanted to go yesterday, but it took me all day to fix my doors, and then I got called in for a late shift at the MC, a couple of the radiology people were out sick. So I went for my run afterward, down on the coastal range. Predawn's a beautiful time to do it, but stupid when you're that tired—I fell and knocked my head, scratched my hands up. Actually, I haven't been to bed at all, it's been this and that since the minute I got home." He winced a grin as he showed her the bruises near his ear and the abrasions on his hands.

"Ouch," she sympathized. "Looks like my timing is bad. I was hoping maybe you'd want to go for a drink or a walk or something. But you should get some sleep."

"Sleep? Hey, it's still the weekend for another few hours. The body is tired but the soul is ever willing." Her proposal clearly pleased him. He swung his legs off the arm of the chair, groped on the floor for his shoes, and began putting them on.

"I'll bring you up to date on my wolfman research," Cree said. "I found a few more details. Maybe you'll get another one of your brainstorms."

She couldn't see his face, but his hands hesitated at his shoelaces. "Brainstorms," he echoed quietly, "I can pretty well guarantee."

Ray knew the esoteric pleasures of his home city. Cree drove as he navigated them north to Lombard Street, then west past Cree's motel and on into the Presidio. The great bridge appeared and disappeared as the streets wandered, great orange glowing towers and twin arcs of amber orbs muted in a thickening haze. They parked in a pullover and got out into a chill, moist wind. Cree put on a sweater and the windbreaker she kept in the car, but Ray didn't seem bothered by the cold.

They hiked along the road, through the visitor center lot, out onto the bridge. Traffic roared past only a few feet away, but its manic energy and noise couldn't compete with the majesty of the structure and its setting. The towers were impossibly tall, fading into dull glows toward the tops. Below, the plane of dark water was rimmed in lights of different colors, streetlights along the shore promenade, crisper city lights along the southern shore and the blurry ones on the far side. Lost in the expanse, the scattered running lights of smaller boats and huge freighters moved slowly. The great cables soared upward in a steepening curve, while below the bridge deck an abyss of empty space gaped. The Pacific was invisible, but she could hear its vastness in the music of half a dozen foghorns, near and far.

"This is perfect, Ray," she said.

"Strong medicine," he agreed. In the regularly spaced sidewalk lights he looked weary but unmistakably proud, as if the mighty bridge and heroic landscape were something he'd made himself.

She caught him up on what she'd learned about the house. It took fifteen minutes just to reach the first tower, geologically massive and dizzyingly foreshortened seen from so close. Cree admired the great iron plating and rivets, then bellied up to the railing on the far side of the pillar to stare out at the Bay and the distant, hazed glow of the cities on the eastern shore. The tower offered a welcome bulwark against the traffic rush and unrelenting ocean wind.

"So," she said, "tomorrow. At the church. Any ideas about what we might find?"

"I don't know. Something about Hans and Lydia. They were fairly prominent, well-off, probably big givers at the plate, right? And she volunteered at the mission. There's got to be something on them."

"Think there's any chance of finding reference to the wolfman himself?"

"No." He looked a little dejected at the admission.

They both hunched on the railing and stared out for a while as the moist cold worked its way into Cree's clothes. A tanker slid out from under the bridge in the center of the channel, and they watched the line of running lights stretch like train windows, froth silvering the hull. Two or three blocks long, Cree thought, yet tiny as a silverfish beneath the monumental, impossible bridge.

After a time Ray asked quietly, "Doesn't it kind of drive you crazy? Wondering who he was? What was going on?"

"Completely. My mind won't leave it alone. Horace is the same way—he can't stand a mystery that eludes him. Sounds like you're one of the same species, huh?"

"Yes." Ray grunted. "But what kind of critter is that? The kind so strongly compelled by a mystery?"

"*Homo sapiens*, I think they're called." Cree grinned.

"I mean, what? Was he . . . deranged, retarded, they kept him down here like an animal, a prisoner? Was he actually dangerous, violent? Or was it just a matter of keeping him *hidden*, of Victorian shame—could he have been Hans's kid from a prior marriage?"

She could feel Ray's urgency mounting, tilting toward desperation, and she needed to damp it before it swept her along with it. "We're working on it, Ray. We'll figure it out."

"Or maybe he *preferred* being down here, out of the light, away from people, I could easily see that. Or—"

"Or maybe he didn't live down here at all. If we'd found the bones in a bathroom, would you assume he lived on the crapper?"

Ray looked at her, astonished. " 'Crapper.' "

"Born in Brooklyn. Pop was a plumber." She laughed at his expression. "And now I think we better head back before I freeze solid."

Back at Diamond Intermodal, Ray opened a bottle of Shiraz and they sat in the living room to sip it and talk.

Another late-night session, easier this time. Ray put on some cello music and turned on a little gas fireplace, blue flames lapping to orange. If she hadn't felt so uneasy about her plan for later, it would have felt very nice in his living room. Outside, the chill fog smothered the building, but this was a sanctuary of warmth, color. Ray sprawled sideways, hammocked in his big chair, Cree stretched out her legs on the couch. The dogs drowsed noisily on their various rugs.

Their second late night together, the trust had grown, and at one in the morning it didn't seem strange to ask if she could spend the night on his couch. Ray had begun to look strained, eyes bloodshot, face puffy, and was clearly staying up only to be polite. He made a bad joke about priests, rabbis, and kangaroos to reassure her, then set her up with a quilt and pillow and bumbled off to his bedroom. The dogs shambled after him.

Cree turned out the living room lamp and lay on the couch, but she didn't undress. At the end of the hall, Ray's light went out, and she faintly heard the creak of his bed as it received his weight. She waited until she heard Ray's snores, deep and slow, then sat up and pushed the quilt aside.

Not duplicitous, she kept telling herself. *Not sneaky, Ray, truly. Just necessary.*

51

THE GLOWING DIGITS of the clock on Ray's desk ticked ahead to one fourteen. Cree groped in her purse and dug out the digital camera and her little high-tech LED light. Barefoot, she crept out of the living room and into the hall. The bathroom seemed a good place to start: If Ray did wake, she'd have a reasonable excuse to be there, and with the door closed she could risk putting on a light. The dogs appeared in the bedroom doorway with a little rainfall noise of claws on hardwood. The advancing wall-to-wall big animal shadows gave her a little jolt, but they were calm, just checking on who was up and around. They put noses to her and wandered peacefully away toward the kitchen. She let out a breath she didn't know she'd held.

She shut the bathroom door soundlessly, turned on the overhead, and stood wincing in the glare. Cree Black stared at her from the mirror, looking guilty as hell.

Not betrayal or hypocrisy, she kept telling herself. *Not cold and calculating. Not deceitful and invasive, not in this situation.*

So why was she so wired up? She was 99 percent sure she'd find only exculpatory evidence, or none. Mainly, it was the question of what would happen if he caught her at what she was about to do and took it the wrong way.

Ray, you have to understand. This is the only way I'm going to prove to Bert that you're okay. If he keeps on like he is, something bad is going to happen. I'm going to give him the information he wants so that I can prove him wrong, so that he'll get off your case.

There was also the missing element, the secret side of Ray that even in his most candid moments wasn't quite clear to her.

She swung the cabinet door open and found only shaving cream, shampoo, the usual. No suspicious collection of pharmaceuticals. Ray must keep them all in his bedside table, as Bert had said—if Bert was even telling the truth about that. After the medicine cabinet, she went through the chest of drawers and the linen closet. Just bathroom stuff. *No mummified fingers or ears, Bert.*

She turned off the light and slipped back into the pitch-black hall. For a few seconds she held still, letting her eyes readjust, listening carefully. Ray's snoring came faintly from the bedroom, its cadence unchanged.

She glided into the living room, thought about the desk and the drifts of correspondence on it, decided to go there last. A single big dog shadow drifted in from the kitchen, paused, turned around, vanished. Cree crept up the exposed stairs to the studio, forgetting the top door's noisy hinges until the screech startled her. She froze and waited until she'd gotten her heartbeat under control before she eased the door slowly open and just as slowly shut.

Colder up here. The ambient light was a little better, vague city-night glow coming through the tall windows, enough to make out the contours of the room. The maps Bert had mentioned were at the top of her list. She spotted the drafting table straight ahead, not far from the head of the stairs, started to go over, then thought she'd wait until her eyes had recovered better from the bright bathroom.

Instead she padded over to the workbench with the computers and other equipment. She scanned the equipment, saw nothing of particular interest: cameras, printers, cables, pads with notations or sketches on them. A professional-size vinyl sign printer explained Ray's enlargement process.

Back at the end wall, she used her light to look at the huge photos Ray had hung. As before, her primary response was ambivalence. As pure compositions, they were gorgeous, celebrations of beautiful curving forms, pale arcs set against a deep darkness like the night sky, like the vaulted ceiling of a planetarium before the show began. They captured something mystical and revelatory. But cranial injuries, broken bone edges or foreign bodies, were always just visible, too, clearly part of Ray's intent. And the thought of someone taking these shots, manipulating and lingering over their cold dead subjects—that was unsettling. Which was the real key to Ray? Beauty or death?

A few MRIs were hung with the others, much smaller and not as successful. The computerized process made uneven blots and irregular rings of rainbow hues in the sectional view of someone's skull. One clearly included a peanut-shaped thing with branching roots, probably a tumor. They were too digital for her taste, the colors too harsh, the compositions not at all elegant like the others. She shined her light behind the MRIs and a few of the big ones, but didn't find any titles or other information.

Back at the coffee table, she swept her little light over books, a thick manila envelope, a scattering of pens. As Bert had said, the books were medical and psychological titles concerned with violent behavior. Suspect? Ray made no effort to conceal his desire to understand the more troubling aspects of human behavior, and Cree had a whole library on similar topics. There was also a lycanthropy book Ray had mentioned, *The Werewolf: Myth, Madness, and Metaphor*, spread open, facedown. When she turned it over, she found that it was open to a horrible woodcut of the Beast of LeGevaudan, ripping and rending one of its many victims. Abruptly it occurred to her that the Beast didn't fit any of the neat werewolf categories she and Ray had talked about. One of history's best-documented werewolves, yet no one had ever figured out what the creature really was. It made her wonder if she'd oversimplified things, overlooked something important. Her heart fluttered as she turned the book over again. Sneaking around in someone else's house, without his knowledge, was not good for the nerves.

The manila envelope contained photos. Cree slid out the thick sheaf and fanned them on the table and got another shock as her light revealed faces—the faces of corpses. No mistaking it. She controlled her breathing with difficulty as she looked through the collection. There were at least two dozen black-and-white studies of heads and faces, some badly damaged and gruesome, some serene and perfect. On many, Ray had drawn crop lines and other notations, as if he'd played with compositional ideas. From the steel surfaces or zippered edges of body bags visible around the edges, it appeared that every photo had been taken in a lab or morgue. *Not at crime scenes!* she reassured herself. The memory of the noise she'd heard from Skobold's meat suite came back to her, the long drawers opening and closing, and suddenly she knew where Ray had gotten at least some of these.

Okay, she told herself breathlessly, *photos of corpses. Not souvenirs, a project. Art works, an artistic experiment.*

Or was it? Ray was a student of death. Why the obsessive interest? And how far had it taken him? For an instant she remembered the savagery of the dogfight and, worse, the darkly joyful reflection of it in the faces of the audience. Would Ray be tempted to delve into that as well?

Her hands shook as she put the photos away and positioned the envelope as it had been. The cold was beginning to ache in her feet and creep up her legs. Time to look at the maps and go downstairs. Then she'd leave this place. Get a little distance on Ray.

She could see the maps better now, four paler rectangles against the wall above the drafting table. She stifled her jitters, crossed over to the wall and put her light onto the maps. The legends at the top told her Bert was right, they were topo maps of state parks. Where Ray took his night runs, his wild pilgrimages. The one on the far right was where that toddler had been killed, San Bruno State Park, traced with pencilled-in paths and X's that marked points of particular interest. She wished she had looked at Bert's crime scene map and could see right now whether it corresponded with Ray's markings.

Maybe she should have taken Bert more seriously.

She got her camera ready, fighting her swelling anxiety: Ray really might get a little uncool if he caught her at this. She set the camera for low-light mode, checked the LCD to make sure the map was tightly framed, and snapped the shot. She zoomed in and took a series of detail shots, then reviewed the photos in the monitor to make sure Ray's pencil lines were visible.

Everything seemed a lot less certain than it had an hour ago. Maybe her empathic identification with Ray had confused the rational part of her brain, which just like Bert had been telling her there was something amiss. It wouldn't be the first time. One of the gravest dangers of her penchant. She was panting in shallow breaths and had to shut her eyes for a moment: *Easy now. Easy. Slow deep breaths. Settle. Go slow. Don't get spooked. Go slow.*

Back downstairs. This time she remembered the creaking door, but the agonizing slowness it required made her very tense. All she felt was the desire to hurry, hurry to leave here. At the same time, she knew she should try to keep perspective. Okay, Ray took pictures of corpses, but it didn't mean he was a killer. Yes, he had an urgent fascination with some morbid issues, death and violence, but he'd been out front about it. *Urgent*, definitely the word for Ray. Maybe just too urgent? The way Cree was urgent about similar topics, or some other way? Similar, she decided, but not the same. Coming at it from a different angle, a different motive. For a moment she felt a pattern taking shape in her thoughts, but she was too jittery and it darted away from her.

She descended into the living room with utmost stealth, then stood and studied the dark hallway to the bedroom until she verified that nothing was moving. She couldn't hear Ray snoring anymore, but the dogs weren't up and there was no sign of activity.

Over to the desk. Holding the flashlight between her teeth, she leafed through the many envelopes to find that Bert was right again—path labs, hospitals, some police labs. But which ones? Were any of the labs connected to Bert's collection of dog attack deaths and murders?

She slipped papers out of one envelope, tried to make sense of the medical jargon, couldn't quite. Looked at more pages from different labs, read carefully, thought maybe she understood some of it. By the third she'd begun to see the pattern. She grabbed at the other envelopes, pulling out one sheet after the other. A sensation like vertigo hit her as she realized what she was looking at.

A little noise whispered behind her.

She spun, heart hammering. Something moved at the end of the hallway, then materialized as a canine shadow. The other two dogs followed, and all three took up a position in the middle of the room, oriented toward her. A half-second later she noticed the shape that was higher up at the edge of the hall doorway, the dark motionless blob of shadow.

Ray's face, leaning out of the dark hall to watch her.

"Hi, Cree," he said quietly, sadly. "Finding anything good?"

52

BERT JAMMED THE brakes as soon as the furthest wash of his head-lights picked out Cree's red Honda, cozied up against Ray's van. His face went numb. Seeing her car here, well after midnight, everything that implied, it was something of a last straw.

He idled for half a minute, torn between conflicting impulses. Conflicting, but all of the *fuck it* category: *Fuck Cree if she's that stupid. Fuck yourself, too, Bright Raven, give it up, lost cause, you're old and burnt to shit and don't have what it takes, go home.* The other side of that was, *Fuck it, it's lose-lose anyway, might as well have it out, high noon in the middle of the night, who cares about the consequences.*

He settled for a provisional decision. He cut the lights, put the car in reverse, and slid over to the curb. The position gave him a long angle view of Ray's front door. Tired as he was, he knew he'd never sleep tonight. Might as well keep watch as he sifted through the mental dregs and cinders of one of the worst days on record and tried to decide what to do.

This time last night he was at home, still waiting for the call from Nearing and Koslowski. Planning the operation, they'd agreed that since Bert was already on Ray's radar he shouldn't be anywhere near the action, no possibility he'd be connected. And anyway somebody had to make absolutely sure Cree wasn't there. Bert had driven to her motel, verified that her car was in the lot and that the lights were on in her room, then called Nearing with the go-ahead. He'd gone home feeling giddily pleased, sick, scared.

By three A.M. the call still hadn't come and the tension was getting bad, and he'd almost called Nearing's cell. But then he worried that his call might come at a critical moment, might distract Rich. So he'd held on, dosed himself with whiskey. At last he'd fallen asleep on the couch with his house phone and cell on his chest.

He'd awakened with a jerk to realize that it was Monday morning and there'd been no call. His head was pounding and his teeth were fuzzy, the light from the sliding doors was a death ray hitting his eyes.

First he called Nearing's cell phone. No answer. Koslowski, same result. So he gave it up and called Nearing's home number. His wife was practically hysterical: Rich had said he was going out for a drink but he hadn't come home, did Bert know where he was? He tried to reassure her: Probably he'd gotten called in on some late-night situation and just hadn't had time to check in.

He called Koslowski's place, got basically the same message from his girlfriend. When he hung up, he called a guy he knew at the Night Investigations Unit, who he figured would know about anything serious involving cops. He asked if there'd been any unusual action last night.

Jackpot. Burning up and down the cop grapevine was the news that early this morning, two guys from Narcotics/Vice Division had been brought to the hospital in very bad shape. Some people were saying there was something messy about it, because the brass were not broadcasting the news or calling up the troops. Like maybe Nearing and Koslowski had gotten hurt while engaged in something dirty that needed to be kept quiet pending internal investigations and some spin control.

Bert turned suddenly cold and shaky. It could all unravel from here. If he got caught in it, he was screwed. All the other stuff they'd been doing for the last six years would come out. Hearings, trials, maybe jail. No pension. And if the lid blew off soon, he'd get so tied up he wouldn't be able to follow through on Ray, legally or otherwise.

Damage control time. He needed to find out exactly what had happened so he could consider his options.

It took a while to find out where they were, people didn't know or wouldn't tell. It was almost noon when he drove to the hospital, hoping desperately that it hadn't gotten administrative yet, he wouldn't be prohibited from talking to them. Assuming they were able to talk.

He got a jolt when he found a pair of inspectors already in the room, but then it turned out they were both General Works inspectors. Not Management Control Division. That fact brought Bert's shoulders down a full inch. General Works meant it was still routine, they were just waiting for the victims to be in shape to talk so they could start their assault investigation.

They met him in the hall, so he couldn't get close to Rich and Pete, but through the door he could see two motionless figures in the beds, with bandaged heads and a tangle of IV tubes and monitor wires. They said Nearing had been conscious when the medics brought him in, if pretty out of it from a concussion. But he'd required surgery for a lacerated jaw and was still under the anesthetic. Koslowski was in worse shape, a serious skull fracture, but supposedly the prognosis was okay.

"What the hell happened?" Bert asked.

Minken, the taller GW guy, who seemed to be the lead, answered: "Hospital gets an anonymous tip about two guys in a car over near the arena. They send an ambulance and call the PD. A black and white goes out, gets there and sees two badly hurt guys but an undamaged car, so it's not a car crash, it's assault. No ID on the victims, they had to run the plates to figure out the car owner is Richard Nearing. Naturally the captain at Narcotics heard and got very interested, they put us on it right away."

"Your buddies, huh?" the second inspector asked.

"Rich Nearing is a great guy," Bert said carefully. "His wife's a terrific gal, got a couple of great kids. I hate to see this happen to that family."

The second inspector grunted. "Could have been a lot worse—both their guns were in the car, one had been fired, but whoever the bad guys were, they didn't reciprocate. Used a brick or a rock or something on them. Couple other funny details."

Bert almost slipped up. He almost asked, *Dog bites?* He couldn't imagine any other way Ray had gotten the upper hand with two guys like Nearing and Koslowski. But that would suggest he knew something he shouldn't. He just frowned and asked, "Oh, yeah? Like what?"

But Minken had shot the other guy a look. He shrugged and gave a casual, dismissive toss of his head. "Just little stuff. Who knows if it's worth anything. You know how it is."

Bert knew not to push it. Minken's eyes had gone suddenly flat, and the signal between them had been a reminder: *Don't talk about it.*

He stopped at a restaurant and stuffed some food into his face even though he was anything but hungry, then went to a bar chosen at random for a couple of shots. His cell phone went off, but the caller ID told him it was Cree and there was no way he could talk to her now. The next time it went off, he was afraid to even look, maybe it was the first little hello from MCD, the first beat of his career's death knell.

What had gone wrong? The plan had been to go into Ray's, inflict enough damage on Ray to cause him major hurt and keep him laid up until Bert could put him away. They were to take pictures, toss the place and make off with some valuables to make it look like a robbery—a common enough scenario in that neighborhood, easy to fake. What had gone wrong?

More to the point, what would happen next? He forced himself to think systematically about the likely progression of events. By the time he drove home, he felt certain that unless Nearing and Koslowski had a lot more imagination and strength of character than he figured them for, they'd blow it while trying to make up a story about what had gone down. The Narcotics/Vice people already had their antennae up, Minken and the other guy had been warned, so they would separate Pete and Rich for the interviews. The fairy tales wouldn't match, so they'd bring in MCD. A little pressure and soon Ray's name would come up, and Bert's name, and it would all blow.

How soon? How long did he have?

And for what—a fast exit to Mexico? A serious visit to Ray and then the gun in the mouth? Because there was no way he could see being put through that wringer again. Not at this age, this stage. No way.

Bert realized he'd been sitting in the dark car outside Ray's for over an hour. His legs were stiff and cold. He checked his watch and saw that it was almost three o'clock. Time to fish or cut bait. Do something here or go home.

He thought of Cree, in there, getting it on with a guy like that. So deceived. So unaware of how dangerous he was. The rage, the frustration, everything came roaring in. Again he considered storming the place right now. But it wasn't really an option. Ray would have fixed his door, probably armored it this time, and after Nearing and Koslowski he had no doubt taken other precautions. What could he do, stand on the street and shoot at the windows? Even if he somehow got inside, Cree could easily get hurt in the ensuing drama. Or even come in on Ray's side, what would happen then?

He started the car. There was nothing he could do tonight. It would all have to wait until tomorrow. If the internal investigation wasn't casting its baleful gaze his way yet, maybe he could still do something. Maybe Cree could pry herself away from Scarface long enough for Bert to catch him alone. Or Hank Chambers would come up with something on the evidence side.

Actually, that could solve the whole mess: Pin a murder on Ray, even demonstrate a reasonable presumption of guilt, and any internal investigation had a good chance of quietly fading away.

The thought rose quick and bright, a spark of hope. He shook his head at himself as he pulled the car around and started toward home. *Yeah, Bert Marchetti in a nutshell*, he thought, *the incurable optimist.*

53

I CAN'T TELL YOU how disappointed I am." Ray sounded vastly weary and sad.

"Don't scare me here, Ray."

"Scare you? Why should you be scared?" He came fully into the room to stand among the dogs. They were all just shadow shapes.

"Ray, turn on the light so I can see your face. I didn't tell you earlier, but Bert, he's seriously after you, he's—"

"Yeah, I'm starting to get that impression."

"I was sure he was wrong! I wanted to *prove* it to him, so that he'd—"

"Still so sure?"

"You turn on the light and look at me and see me and we'll both tell each other what's true. Goddamn it, Ray!"

Ray's shadow held for a long minute, but then he did it, he went to a lamp and turned it on. The glow lit the room. He wore only his boxer shorts, and he looked impossibly strong, every muscle chipped and carved. In the better light, she could see his left eye ticking, shivering, from side to side, independent of the right. Cree tried not to shake as they stared at each other from ten feet away.

At last she tipped her head toward the desk. The envelopes. The reports from oncological path labs and the letters from doctors that spelled it out. "Why not just tell me? Why the big secret? Does Horace know? Does anybody?"

"It's nobody's business. It's just my situation. My little challenge. I have my way of dealing with it."

She wanted to go to him, hold him, but the fear sweat was freezing her, she was shaking and couldn't think straight. "I don't know how to do this,

Ray. Help me. I don't know what hurts or helps, or what part I might have in anything. I don't know how to talk to a dying man."

Ray passed a weary hand over his brow. She couldn't make out what was in his eyes. "Everybody's dying," he said. "I'm just aware of the fact."

Much later there was a vertical band of warm rainbow colors, bright against the cool blue of shadow. It was lustrous and mesmerizing. Cree stared at it for a long time before she realized she was conscious. She was sitting hunched at the end of the couch, and the band was a narrow shaft of sunlight slicing in a long diagonal onto the bookshelf and making the book spines glow. Little motes of dust hung in the invisible beam.

Morning.

She stirred and the ache in her shoulders brought her awake. Sprawled against the other end, Ray shifted and slowly raised his head. Their eyes met across the length of the couch and held. More curious than wary, not a shadow of pretense, no deflection available to either of them.

Ray groaned and sat up. The dogs lifted their heads and the Rottweiler came to demand some affection. He roughed her coat and nuzzled her with his face when she insisted on more.

"Okay," he croaked. "Okay, Sadie. The dog food machine is awake and on duty." He stood, wrapped his blanket around himself, then shuffled off to the kitchen with the dogs.

Cree stared after him, astonished that he could be this way. *Dead man walking.* A guy with a tumor deep in his head that sometime soon would bring him down and kill him. She had demanded the details from him, and he had spent a few minutes telling her the particulars, the type of tumor, the positioning and infiltration that precluded surgery, the first tumor board's unanimous opinion, the second and third boards' concurrence. His ability to keep running at this stage was highly atypical, his doctor said. The glioblastoma mainly created intracranial pressure and pain, but it also changed brain function, made for weird sensory disturbances, unpredictable mood changes, strange thoughts. Sometimes the effects were troubling, but they could be fascinating, too. He'd been terrified when he'd first learned, but he'd more or less mastered that. He'd studied death and tried to make it beautiful. Took him to some strange places, but it felt like it was sorted out now. She had pressed him for more, but Ray said he wearied easily of the topic and was done for tonight. So then they'd talked about other things. Cree watched him closely throughout, aware that for all the times and ways she'd dealt with death, she had very little real experience of it from this side of the divide.

Now the clunk of the cabinet doors came from the kitchen and the sound amazed her. *That's how you do it,* she thought. *Hey, gotta feed the dogs. Another day comes with its demands and problems and pleasures and you muster through it because for now you're alive, and what would you do different anyway?* She wanted to tell him his courage was marvelous, but she doubted he wanted to hear it. He'd say something like, *It's not courage. It's just the absence of a choice.*

After a minute, she got up. She picked up the empty wine bottle and the glasses and brought them into the kitchen, where Ray was opening dog food cans. He put down the bowls and watched with obvious satisfaction as the animals choffed away.

"So," he said, "today we do the church records?" Drowsily normal. Instructing her on how to do it.

"If you have the time."

"Wouldn't miss it. I've got some sick leave coming at work."

Ray turned to the sink and began filling a teapot with water; Cree opened the refrigerator and scanned the shelves for breakfast foods. Like they were an old married couple. Just your ordinary heart-wrenched empathic parapsychologist trying to uncover the hundred-year-old secret of a wolfman; just your regular dying mystic doing his balancing act, resigned, doing his best to succumb completely to both life and death.

Cree took out eggs, butter, and orange juice and put them on the counter. It didn't really feel artificial. Mainly it felt like a ritual—a tea ceremony, maybe, something to be done with greatest delicacy and precision. She wanted to touch him, even just briefly on the arm, but was afraid to break the spell.

54

R EV. MICHAELSON WAS a cheerful, athletic-looking man in his
midforties, dressed in khakis and a blue shirt. He welcomed them at
the rectory door and led them past a pair of offices and a sitting room,
then down a stairway into the basement. The two records rooms were
each the size of a racquetball court, their walls lined by file cabinets and
other storage containers. A long library table stood beneath the bright
ceiling lights at the center of each room, flanked by an eclectic array of
chairs.

"I only came on here two years ago," he told them. "The downside for
you is that I haven't handled many requests like yours and so I'm not that
familiar with our early records—hey, it's been all I can do just to get to
know our living congregation! The card catalogue will help you locate
materials by type and by date, but it's not very content specific. This room
is basically our vital statistics—births, baptisms, marriages, deaths. Community projects, mission work, charities, administrative, financial, legal,
that's in the other room. It's all chronological. As you can see, it's a ton of
stuff. For a while we thought we'd have to find more space, but the Lord
intervened and brought us the era of digital media. All our new archives
are on disk."

He grinned, invited them to use the photocopy machine, and left them.

They quickly found Hans and Lydia's marriage, recorded in the ledger
for 1887. Lydia's death was recorded, but unlike other entries hers did not
include burial information—no funeral service on record, no cemetery
specified. Conclusion: she was one of the hundreds lost in the cataclysm,
buried deep or burned to ashes.

Cree was disappointed. She had successfully damped hopes for direct reference to the wolfman, but she had held out for some trail of crumbs that would lead to relatives who might retain personal effects that would mention him. The wolfman had somehow entered the Schweitzers' lives, or at least their basement, and surely their diaries or letters or other papers would have mentioned such an extraordinary creature. But there'd been no kids, there was no indication of where Hans had gone when he moved, and nowhere did they find the names of any relatives who might have inherited family records.

That left them to look for mention of Jacksons or Schweitzers in the other room, the mountainous paper trail of the church's activities for a hundred and thirty years. Lydia's Barbary Coast mission work was clearly the most promising starting point, and again they opted to begin with 1886. That left only twenty years' worth of papers to go through. Ray took '86, Cree took '87, planning to leapfrog each other through the years.

The papers gave Cree a good sense of Good Shepherd Mission. It was apparently something of a personal crusade for the church's charismatic founding minister, Rev. Wallace, who dominated church affairs for thirty years. There were texts of his fiery exhortations about sin and mercy, ledgers detailing the number fed and clothed and the smaller number claiming conversion, petitions for money, broadsides against the vice-tolerant City Hall, and occasional statements issued by Wallace or other members of the mission's steering committee on their plans, problems, and doctrinal concerns. The lists of the mission's lay volunteers and financial supporters always included Lydia Jackson Schweitzer.

The mission operated out of a storefront near the old shipyards, providing shelter, food, medicine, and moral instruction to the most miserable of the human wreckage churned out by the Barbary Coast. Its comforts attracted seamen too aged to sail, alcoholics, syphilitics, old and diseased whores, cripples, orphans, the dissolute and disaffected and marginalized of every kind.

Could it also have drawn the wolfman?

Quite possibly, Cree decided. The mission could easily have been the means by which the wolfman had come to the attention of Hans and Lydia. Maybe this wasn't such a wild-goose chase after all.

The occasional photos were compelling: sepia-tinted, fading faces from a different century, sober-faced men with beards and bowler hats, pale women with hair drawn back hard and lace at their throats. One showed a dozen men and women posing on the porch of a wooden building that she assumed was the mission. The women wore broad skirts and aprons and bonnets, the men black suits with high collars. Cree picked out Lydia immediately: a dark-haired woman of medium height, with eyes rounded, brows slightly elevated, lips just parted. The open, earnest, slightly astonished expression of a person always somewhat undone by life.

Cree felt herself pushing against the cloaking barrier of the years. The past survived only in snippets and snapshots, leaving huge gaps, tantalizing and frustrating. Seeing the photos of Lydia made it more urgent because it made her more real. Cree opened folders and envelopes and spread out ledgers, looking for their names, their faces, something to do with their affairs. *Just one little lead, one little clue,* she thought. *One thread to the wolfman or the present day.*

She was halfway through the 1889 section when she opened a folded sheaf of papers and got a shock. She straightened up, unbelieving.

"Ray," she croaked. "Ray. We got him. We got him!"

She spread the pages flat on the table, five sheets of parchment, typeset and easily legible, probably printed on the same church press that had churned out their tracts and handbills. Ray came to stand behind her so they could read them together.

Report on deliberations by the Mission Council regarding the
"Wolf Man" displayed at The Red Man resort.
Authored for the Council by Rev. Geoffrey D. Wallace
July 19, 1889

Of late our congregation has endured much troubling discussion regarding the plight of the claimed "wolf man" featured as entertainment at a certain infamous saloon. This has led our community to difficult considerations about the very nature of man and animal, and whether the soul might reside in the beast, and how we ought to conceive the Mission's undertakings in light of such concerns. In service to Christ's work and in the interest of preserving the unity of our congregation, the Council offers this report to record our observations and deliberations, and to render our decisions in the matter.

As our brothers and sisters will recall, it was first brought to our attention by Sister Lydia that The Red Man claims to have in captivity a "wolf man," who is to be seen at their establishment on Rowland Street. The Red Man has previously come to our attention as a pit of unspeakable depravity which presented for entertainment despicable acts occurring between women and animals. Lydia reported that a creature resembling both man and wolf (or dog) is encaged and is nightly put on display, and that for a fee patrons may watch him in combat with dogs or with men who fight in exchange for a share of the wagers made upon the outcome of the contest. Lydia attested that he is forced to live naked and in his own filth, is fed only upon leavings and rotten meat, and suffers from innumerable festering wounds received during his combat with man and dog.

Acting on our esteemed sister's heartfelt plea, a Mission Council committee consisting of myself, Mr. Osbourne, Mr. O'Shaugnessy, Mr. Grossbach, and Rev. Smith was formed and dispatched to The Red Man to observe the "wolf man." We were accompanied also by Mr. Franklin Wilson, a Pinkerton guard we thought it advisable to hire because The Red Man is widely known for the drunken and violent nature of its patrons and employees, which are of the lowest and most depraved class.

We did observe the supposed "wolf man" and concur that he cannot be described as either a human being or a beast, but in appearance seems to be some admixture. We confirmed that he exists in a most pitiful and disagreeable condition, and that he is nightly forced to enjoin physical combat with dogs and men. When fighting dogs he uses his limbs and his wolf-like teeth; when fighting men (we are informed; we did not see him fight a man as there were no volunteers that evening), he is made to wear a leather harness or muzzle over his mouth so that he cannot inflict fatal harm. This combat appears to cause him much fear and distress, and during our observation of him he seemed to join in it most

362

unwillingly; however, once aroused, he acts with extreme savagery and was able to kill all three dogs which were set upon him.

We remained at The Red Man long enough to verify to our satisfaction that such a creature did exist, and that his nature and appearance are not products of an actor's hoax or illusion intended to deceive the gullible out of their pennies. We inquired of Mr. Silas Singer, proprietor of the resort, as to where he procured the "wolf man," but he could not or would not tell us and responded in a surly and bellicose manner when informed we were acting on behalf of the Mission. When we threatened to call for a Police inquiry, Mr. Singer showed great amusement and quite gaily urged us to do so, naming several prominent police officials whom he claimed were among his most loyal patrons. An argument ensued with Mr. Singer and half a dozen ruffians in his employ over the disposition and treatment of the "wolf man," at which point Mr. Wilson advised us that he could no longer assure our safety and insisted that we depart immediately. We thought it prudent to abide by his recommendation.

We of this Council are keenly aware that it is the objective of Good Shepherd Mission to extend care and kindness to even the most depraved and sinful of men. It is to this very end that we have established our Mission in the most abject district in our city, thus to bring the Light of Christ Our Lord to those most direly in need of His Mercy. During the last fortnight, however, our congregation has been riven by dissent about said "wolf man," not out of argument concerning his unfortunate condition and many physical discomforts, but out of disagreement as to whether he is human, possessing a soul to be redeemed; or animal, and thus naturally subject to the whims, cruelties, and rightful usages the world imposes upon beasts; or a perversion, possibly of Satanic origin, and thus to be despised as unworthy of the Lord's ministrations.

This Council has therefore taken upon itself the task of determining a final position regarding the "wolf man" and to decide what, if any, actions on his behalf are justified. To this end we have invited the opinions of our congregation and have engaged in impassioned discussion, Scriptural consultation, and thoughtful deliberation, summarized below. In the interest of preserving our unity in the face of our greater common objectives, we have determined not to specify the names of those who argued one point or another, but merely to present their views. It is our belief that all who spoke did so with highest moral purpose and faith in God, and, in recognition of the fallibility of any human opinion, with deepest humility.

As regards the "wolf man," the varied opinions of our congregation can be represented as follows:

1.   Several of our brothers and sisters have persuasively argued that if he possess any human attribute whatsoever, one drop of human blood or one atom of human soul, he is entitled to receive our compassion and to be considered worthy of redemption.

2.   Two of us who attended The Red Man, however, having witnessed the "wolf man" in his unspeakable savagery, were inclined to believe he is a form of animal like the apes or monkeys, perhaps an African Baboon partially shaved and in some other wise doctored to enhance its similarity to a human being.

3.   Two of our committee, who also witnessed the "wolf man" first-hand, argued that such a creature could not be a Godly creation, but rather an unholy and wicked wretch, perhaps a werewolf or a form of witch or demon, that has been brought into existence through malefic powers. If this be the case, they believe, the creature has only found its just worldly fate in the hands of a brutish man like Silas Singer and must face its judgment by the Almighty without our intercession.

4.   Several of our number believe him to be the offspring of the sinful intercourse of woman and dog, a spectacle for which The Red Man is regrettably well known. Those voicing this view were in turn divided in their opinion; one side suggesting that he is thus a creature of such depraved origin as to be unworthy of the ministrations of Christ, the other contending that, as his evil origins are not of his own choice or doing, he himself cannot be called evil and is therefore deserving of compassion.

5.   Others offered the question, if the mere existence of a creature, half-man and half-beast, might suggest the veracity of the views lately

espoused by Mr. Charles Darwin and his apologists, that Mankind has emerged from a progression of beastly states. In this view, the "wolf man" is a member of some less advanced tribe or people extant somewhere on our planet, or a freakish throwback or link to a more primitive stage of mankind's development. It is the unanimous opinion of this Council that the latter conjecture is at odds with Scripture and has no bearing upon our thoughts or actions.

We are aware that all who have offered their opinions on the matter of the "wolf man" have done so in the best interests of our common goals, and it is in the interests of these same goals that we render our decision.

Our Mission was founded to serve the many, with the greatest good in mind: to wit, to bring all Mankind to the Light of Christ. Our divergence over the question of the "wolf man's" humanity threatens to divide us and thus weaken us in our service to the many. If our opinions about him are in conflict, we must recall ourselves to those purposes for which we are certainly united. If in overlooking his plight we err by failing to win or provide comfort to one soul, we must remind ourselves that there are untold thousands of souls requiring our ministrations here, that our Mission must turn its purpose to administering the greatest good to the greatest number. This is especially true in the current instance, when we cannot claim a firm conviction that the "wolf man" is in fact a man, has a soul worthy of being saved, or indeed possesses any soul.

It is therefore the determination of the Council that Good Shepherd Mission will take no action regarding the "wolf man"; that we will in humility relinquish any further preoccupation with him and surrender him to God's mercies or punishments; and that this Society will return with one mind to its original duties among those we know for certain to be human, and in need, and capable of the higher moral sentiments that make them accessible to the persuasions of Christian kindness.

VI

THE GREAT RAID

55

I AM GREATLY DISTRESSED, but I am not angry at them. To his credit, Rev. Wallace submitted the question to our whole congregation, and there was a great deal of discussion. It has been an uneasy two weeks for me, in that I had hoped for an immediate decision, and I fear that the wolf-man will not survive his captivity. Even so, I must credit Rev. Wallace for wisdom and fairness in seeking broader discussion and consensus.

Nor can I be angry at our fellow church members, for in their thoughts they were only expressing their natures, just as the wolf-man expresses or embodies his, and they are so entitled. Their comments seem to me a fair expression of the diverse sentiments I see daily, all around, in other arenas of life.

Being one of the Council, it was Deacon Skinner who broke the news to me at the mission last night. I have rarely seen him angry, and it is not a pleasant thing to witness. His lips turn white in his narrow face and his eyes become chips of flint rimed with frost. He would not say a word against Rev. Wallace or others who opposed our viewpoint, but his unhappiness with them was clear.

He left the mission and returned a short while later with Dr. Mahoney, and the three of us parleyed in the back room. We resolved to act independently, not as representatives of the church but as citizens only. Deacon Skinner proposed that we offer to buy the wolf-man from Silas Singer, but Dr. Mahoney said he had already returned to The Red Man with that intent, in the interim. He offered two hundred dollars, at which Silas Singer laughed outright, saying he had paid that much to buy him in the first place and was earning more than that from him every night. Dr. Mahoney also said he saw the wolf-man briefly as they threw slops into his cage (his dinner), and that he appears very ill; the doctor believes he is close to dying from injuries, infections, malnourishment, and, no doubt, heart-sickness.

We considered going to the police, but in the end believed Silas Singer's claim that he had patrons among them, or could easily purchase their cooperation with his interests.

It came down to our independent action or nothing. Here was a test of our claimed compassion and resolve. I told the deacon and the doctor I would speak to Hans and solicit his help.

He was still awake when I returned home at ten thirty, writing out some business at the sitting room desk, knees barely fitting beneath it. He greeted me as I entered, but distantly, for the discussion of the last two weeks has not pleased him. Old Cook had long been to bed.

"They have decided about the wolf-man," I told him.

"And how have they decided?"

"That the church will not intercede on his behalf."

He adjusted his spectacles on his nose and returned to his papers with a scowl. "As I expected. And just as well, I say."

I drew up a chair to sit near him, saying nothing. From our frequent discussions, I knew that when consulted by the Council, he had supported my view only with the greatest reservation. In the last two weeks, he has watched me present my case to the Council, and to other individuals of the congregation; the issue, and my prominence in it, clearly makes him uncomfortable. It seems to have brought a distance and formality between us.

"You are short with me tonight and have been for many days. Is it that you are ashamed to have a wife who is so outspoken? Who wears her emotions so plainly?"

He put down his pen to look at me gravely. "Would you like to know what I thought as you addressed the Council?"

"Very much," I said, though I was afraid to hear it.

"I looked at you standing there and I feared for myself. I feared that I am so besotted that I cannot think straight. I am preoccupied with thoughts of you. You looked like an angel to me, good and virtuous, and brave to talk before those imposing men. And I remembered our bed the night before and was ashamed of myself. I think I must be a weak man."

A smile sprang to my face and I felt so blissfully pleased that I couldn't speak. I would have kissed him had he not stayed so very somber and concerned.

"I know," he continued in a funereal tone, "what you are going to ask of me. I don't think it is safe or prudent. But I have known from the beginning, when I saw your resolve."

I was stunned that he saw me so clearly. "Then what is your answer?"

He mustered a great stern look and did not answer immediately but for a time made a rumbling in his throat. "Only two times in my life have I shown much of an adventuresome spirit. The first was in leaving my home and coming to this far-away place."

Here he paused for a long time so that I prompted him: "What was the other?"

"Courting you," he said quietly. "Yes. Walking from this door to your door, it seemed as long as being on the ship. Don't look so surprised. I was a bachelor for a long time. I had no experience in . . . with . . . with a good woman."

"How did these adventures go for you?" I asked.

"In both I believe I have profited greatly." He roused himself, and looking greatly discomfitted went on, "So the answer to your question is that I am a weak man and can refuse my wife nothing. Even if it means my downfall."

I took his hands in mine, like holding two big slate shingles together, and we looked at each other, eye to eye, for a long time, most candidly, most seriously and concerned for each other. He would have been relieved, I knew, if I had backed away from the request.

But I told him, "Then we shall have an adventure. You shall be a bandit and a pirate after all."

TUESDAY, JULY 23, 1889

We have plotted through the week-end, Deacon Skinner, Dr. Mahoney, Hans, and I. I was glad to put the three men together, for the doctor and deacon have strengthened Hans's resolve and he their optimism. They are worthy men, but he has the advantage, in that he is of imposing appearance and accustomed to command men, with over fifty laborers in his employ.

Our plan is to attempt to purchase the wolf-man, raising the offer considerably, though we fully expect another refusal from Silas Singer. Having consulted among his workers, Hans has learned more about Singer's gang of infamous hoodlums, who not only keep order at The Red Man but run other several criminal enterprises for him as well. How many men, we could not ascertain, but Hans estimated Singer could muster twenty or more if he desired. One of them, his apparent lieutenant, is none other than Jack Bell, once the most ruthless crimp in the shanghai trade. He was famous for being able to knock a mule to its knees with one bare-handed punch, and known to hit sailors so hard that, as Dr. Mahoney says, "they woke up dead, often as not," on the outbound ship.

Thinking of the guards at the door and the evil-looking men at the front of the stage-room, with their weapons, I am afraid that I have asked too much, that in my inexplicable obsession I have put my husband and the dearest and best people I know at grave risk.

Fortunately, Hans also has access to hardy men, even if they are not so familiar with the ways of fighting or so ready to use a knife or pistol as Silas Singer's are. A number of them are from Germany, one from the area where Hans was born, whom he recruited for the quality of their craftsmanship; they are particularly loyal to him out of a countryman's bond and gratitude for the good wages and the respect he pays them. Several I have met at building sites or here at the house, when Hans has invited his foremen to supper.

When we met at our house this morning, Hans introduced us to the crew he has enlisted after confidential conversations and sworn pledges of secrecy. There is Labinski, a Pole nearly as large as Hans himself, ruggedly muscled, gentle as a draft ox but quietly firm of character. Krauss is not so big, but again is strong; he is yellow haired, ever cheerful, a very efficient worker, Hans says; his affection for Hans and me runs deep because we assisted his wife when she was very ill last winter. Dietch is one I have never liked, for he strikes me as sullen and gloomy, secretive; yet Hans insists that is merely the introspective mien typical of the Ost-Freislander, that he is very trustworthy and capable, and was an infantry sergeant in the Civil

War. Finally, Hans brought a young man named Winston, barely in his twenties, born in the state of Maine, who is rope thin, cocky, and handsome. He enjoys a reputation among the crews as a fierce boxer and a man ever willing for trouble in whatever form it might offer itself.

And with the doctor and the deacon, that is the sum of our little army, the seven of them.

They have made plans to go tomorrow at mid-morning, not so early that The Red Man will still be closed, not so late that there would be much custom. They will take one of Hans's covered vans pulled by a company team, empty of stone but with four men inside, and Deacon Skinner and Dr Mahoney will come in the deacon's rig and meet them near The Red Man.

It was a startling thing, to see the men growing more sober and keen as they laid the details out. All wore grim faces and their eyes grew hard, warriors preparing for battle. They talked of contingencies and how to respond, and of the risk of weapons coming into play. Dr. Mahoney talked of how to handle the wolf-man himself, who will likely be agitated at the commotion and may himself be dangerous. He has prepared a room at his office to receive the wolf-man, where he will stay to receive medical attention, with boarded window and good locks.

Dietch began calling their mission a "raid," and soon they all did: the raid upon The Red Man. There is no question of my participating, for Hans has stated most firmly that he will not hear of it, and I dared not argue the point, most especially not in front of the other men. I would be afraid to go, in any case.

And yet I am afraid not to go, for fear that something terrible will happen to Hans or one of our men. It will be my fault, and tonight I cannot sleep and am full of self-recrimination for having instigated this dangerous enterprise. There is no doubt that Hans and his crew are strong, and little Deacon Skinner and Dr. Mahoney determined, but the men in Silas Singer's employ are a different matter altogether: men practiced at violence, intimidation, and no doubt murder, and careless of danger. They will be on their home ground and will no doubt outnumber our side; and Singer himself, though not physically imposing, is a man without any moral constraint or scruple whatever, and fond of his evil fame.

★   ★   ★

373

Now it is still later and the house is all dark but for the candle I write by. Tonight after Hans went to sleep, I dropped to my knees at the bedside and prayed feverishly to God that no one will be hurt or killed. With Hans snoring above me, I prayed for forgiveness if I have misinterpreted His intent, or put my dear husband at risk for a foolish and useless enterprise.

I had left the kerosene lantern alight on the bedroom table, and as I cried and muttered and pleaded, a moth circled it and suddenly plunged unerringly down the chimney and into the flame. It crackled and flared, and in a moment the stink filled the air. I cannot help but take it as a bad omen. Now I understand Hans's doubts, and cannot comprehend my earlier determination, which seems like madness. But it is all in motion. I am afraid it will be a long night.

56

THE RAID WAS done yesterday, for better or for worse. There is no way I can report it without telling it as it happened, even if I did not witness all of it. Each event led so rapidly to the next, and it was so chaotic and strange; to relate events out of sequence would confuse and misrepresent them.

I awoke from a fitful, short sleep when Hans did. He was distant and resigned, not happy to be doing this yet quite deliberate and firm, as if stimulated by the prospect of what was to come; I think there must be something in a man which relishes danger or battle, the chance to test one's mettle and confront one's enemy. He dressed as if for a regular business day, in his fine suit, and washed and groomed himself with as much care as if he were going to meet an important client. I attended to him closely.

At nine, the other men came for him in a great, heavy dray, Schweitzer Superior proudly emblazoned on its panels, with two big horses driven by Labinski; Winston, the boy, came on his own mount alongside. They waited outside as Hans put on his good pigskin gloves. He embraced me only formally, though I would have held him harder and more tenderly. I thought frantically of a blessing or a wish to bestow, some way to state my love and gratitude.

"Please return to me," I told him. And I meant it in many ways.

"I have every intention," he said curtly.

And then the door was open and he was down the steps and the dray moved away, Hans and Labinski towering on the driver's bench, Winston making a dashing outrider. Then I was alone with Cook, but could not bear her kindly prattle and went upstairs to our bedroom. I could not sit for a moment, but paced and fretted with my hands so that I snapped a button from my dress. I picked up Hans's pillow from the bed and buried my face in it, just for the scent of him, and, still pacing, stupidly cried until it was quite soaked.

What I know of the events that occurred in my absence, I learned from Winston not long later, and from the others since.

It was a clear day, promising to be hot. Inside the box of the dray, Krauss and Dietch sat, dressed in their masons' leather among a collection of tools of the trade they thought might prove useful. Winston rode ahead. They met Deacon Skinner and Dr. Mahoney at the assigned spot on Stockton Street and proceeded to The Red Man, pulling to a halt directly in front of the carved Indian.

Even the worst parts of the Barbary Coast go quiet at some point, as vice exhausts its enthusiasts, weariness sets in, and drink's effects accumulate. At nine thirty, the downtown streets are bustling, windows being washed and sidewalks swept, wares being arranged in displays, business men hurrying all brisk in clean suits, carriages and cable cars coming and going; but morning is the low ebb for the Barbary Coast streets. There were still drunkards asleep in the doorways when the raiders arrived, and the litter of trash and broken bottles of the night's activities had not yet been disturbed by traffic.

They could see from the street that a few men moved inside The Red Man, for even such a place must replenish itself, bringing casks from the cellar, raking out the worst filth, mopping up the spilled whiskey and blood to prepare for another day's inundation.

In the hope of a civilized transaction, Hans went in with only the deacon and Dr. Mahoney; the others waited outside, with Winston at the door to watch for any signal they were needed. Silas Skinner stood behind the bar, counting his take from the night before, assisted by Jack Bell. An older man now, Jack Bell looks every bit like a pirate, even to the ring in his ear. His face is scarred, no doubt from knife fights, his teeth yellow streaked with black. He looked up with a challenging expression as these three well-dressed men came through the door.

"Wrong place, wrong time," he rumbled.

At the sound of his voice, the other two men, working at the far end of the room, looked up.

"Mr. Singer," Hans said, "we have come to buy the wolf-man from you."

Singer, stringy white hair hanging on either side of his mantis face, did not look up from his counting. "Isn't that same little mick I told to shove off last week? I have no patience with stubborn men, and today I've got a headache. Pester me at your peril."

Hans pulled a wad of bills from his pocket and laid them on the counter. "We're both gentlemen here. Let's start at four hundred."

"He's dying anyway," Dr. Mahoney put in. "You'll only get a couple more days out of him. Why not sell him while he's still worth something?"

Jack Bell laughed uproariously, and in the most obscene language said that they already had plans for his future: When he got too weak to fight, they would put him in sex shows with human women and female dogs. "We'll make a real killing then. And won't he be a happy dog! When he dies, we'll stuff him and still get a quarter to see the dummy."

"Five hundred, then," Hans said, putting more bills down.

Singer shot an irritated glance at Jack Bell, then went back to stacking bills and coins. Jack Bell scowled and snapped his fingers in the air. "Boys! Didn't I tell you to clean up the place? Throw this garbage out."

The two men approached Hans and the others from behind as Jack Bell went to come around the end of the counter, and another man appeared in the back room doorway. They were all tough men, ready fighters and confident of themselves. But Hans turned and looked down at them. Hans's eyes, when they grow serious, have an effect. The men paused two paces away and went no closer.

"Six hundred, Mr. Singer," Hans said. "Or nothing. Choose now."

By then Jack Bell had reached Hans, full of bluster and glowering with rage. He swung at Hans with his famous fist. Hans made no move but to catch his arm in one hand, then turned it so that the elbow locked and pushed it down and down until Jack Bell had to kneel or have it break. Hans did not even lift his other hand.

Singer looked up with poisonous ire in his face, and in another second he had reached below the counter and come up with a shotgun. He lifted it to shoot but hesitated when he saw that the scatter-gun would hit Jack Bell and his other men as well as Hans. In an instant, Hans lifted Jack Bell and bodily threw him over the bar and against Singer, and they went crashing over into the shelves of bottles.

"Mr. Winston," Deacon Skinner called, "if you please."

Within seconds of the sound of so much breakage, both doors erupted: Singer's other hands coming through the back, our little army through the front. The two men nearest Hans flung themselves at him, but he brought his fist down on the first and crushed him to the floor, and though the second managed to grapple with him he too only lasted an instant. Hans tossed him and made a great wreckage of the tables and chairs.

Labinski and Krauss had come in with mason's hammers, the short-handled ones with ten-pound heads, with which they drive their stone chisels; Dietsch had chosen a pickaxe handle. In all, Singer had nine men besides himself and Jack Bell. There was a melée between the men from each side. Old Deacon Skinner was the first to fall, pushed easily aside. Hans laid down another of Singer's men, but then as he grappled with the next, another swung a chair that broke over Hans's head. It hit with such force that blood gushed out immediately, soaking into his hair and over his face. But stunned as he was, he managed to command himself and do the wisest thing, which was to go around the counter to where Singer and Jack Bell were sorting themselves out. He "put Jack Bell to sleep with a tap to his head" as Dr. Mahoney said, and lifted up the sputtering Silas Singer by his hair.

A pistol fired from the back doorway, and Labinski fell down, but immediately Krauss flung his hammer and hit the shooter's chest so hard he fell back and down. Another drew his gun, but Winston boxed him on the chin and then broke his nose and that man dropped, too, losing both his gun and his nerve.

Hans ignored his dizziness and blindness. He lifted Silas Singer by his hair, right off the floor, so his men could see. "Tell them to stop," he ordered. "Or I will get angry with you."

Silas Singer spat and hissed like a cat, but hanging there like a marionette, he did as Hans told him. It took another few moments for him to be obeyed.

Labinski was the worst hurt, a bullet through his thigh. Dr. Mahoney began to tend to him immediately. Our crew made the others stand together and, having retrieved their guns, ordered them to keep still. It was a very tense situation, with all the men so angry, their blood up to fight. Humiliation fed the ire of Singer's gang. They were contained for the moment, but the trouble had just begun.

In the abrupt silence, a strange noise came from the back room, a violent thumping and rattling and a half-human voice that moaned and keened. The wolf-man was agitated. From the door, our men could see the whole cage shake and quiver beneath its canvas.

Deacon Skinner recovered himself and with Krauss went to the cage. They pulled away the canvas and saw the wolf-man in his terror, bounding at the bars, baring his teeth, and making every fearsome display. Though he was clearly ill and damaged, fear had filled him with a raw frenzy. The sound he made chilled their blood, so like a man or a woman, so much an animal's senseless cry.

Deacon Skinner spoke in reassuring murmurs, and sidled closer to the cage. The wolf-man bristled and retreated, putting himself in the farthest corner and posturing himself in the way that an animal or man will when he is signaling he will fight to the death.

Our men had planned poorly for his response; they had thought he would be too weak to resist by now, or would respond to words of reassurance; or might welcome them when they made it clear they were his rescuers. But there had been too much commotion, the air was full of the scent of anger, gunpowder, and blood; his instincts told him it was a moment of fatal danger. Though they might have violently subdued him, as Singer and his men had, that was anything but our intent and would have begotten his mistrust forever. And it was not possible in any case: As it turned out, not one of Hans's men would dare try to compel him by force. They were afraid of the effects of a werewolf's bite.

They were discussing the problem when a group of Singer's men made a sudden break. Dietch and Winston brought them up short, but not before one had made it to the front door and out it. In an instant, he sped down the street and disappeared.

Our men feared he would go rouse reinforcements and there would be a bloodbath. Yet there seemed no way to bring the wolf-man out. It was a very uneasy situation for them as the wolf-man shook his cage and Singer's men grew more restless. Hans had started to feel weak, and had sat himself in a chair, still gripping the hair of Silas Singer and forcing him to sit on the floor in front of him. Blood was pouring into his eyes so that he could hardly see. Without his leadership, the other raiders became indecisive and dispirited.

Deacon Skinner and Dr. Mahoney took it upon themselves to make a decision. They pulled Winston aside and sent him to get me.

I cannot forget the moment when Winston dashed up on his lathered horse. My heart quailed, for I feared he brought unbearable news. In that moment I drained empty of myself, no faith or hope or anything at all. But Winston seemed quite gay, as if the battle had pleased him greatly, and said only that they needed me in a hurry, to calm the wolf-man. I ran to put on my gray cloak, and then he helped me mount behind him and we were off through the streets. It was another ride that turned heads and caused consternation among pedestrians. As we went, Winston described what had happened, so I had some sense of what to expect.

The front room of The Red Man was a motionless tableau, just as Winston had described it. Already a wretched, seedy place, the resort was now a wreck of tipped tables, broken chairs, shattered glass, wounded men. The tension among our men was palpable; Labinski's leg was already bandaged and he had positioned himself at the window, ready to give the warning if more enemies should appear. Dr. Mahoney had tended to Hans in the interim, and washed his face enough that he could see, but though he had recovered considerably the sight of him nearly stopped my heart. I went straight to him, and he was clearly very angry at me for coming there and at the others for conspiring to bring me. He accepted my kisses but did not return them. Silas Singer looked like a snake, ready to strike, on the floor at Hans's feet.

Hans lurched upright and gave Singer's hair to Winston, who took it gladly. "Now we go see what you can do," Hans said. "If he won't come willingly, and fast, we will have to leave him."

Hans and Dr. Mahoney and I went together to the back room. The wolf-man had calmed somewhat, but when we approached he hunched himself and crouched at the ready. His limbs were trembling with weakness, the exertion almost more than he could muster.

His appearance was awful to see. When I had seen him at the docks, though he was fearsome and deformed, he was also healthy and comfortable, his hair tangled but glossy and full, skin unmarked and of a good color, eyes brilliantly clear: whether man or wolf, a fit and free creature. Now he was corpse-pale, and not one inch of skin was without a scratch or festering wound. His impressive muscularity was gone, replaced by a sallow slackness, and his hair was crusted stiff. Worst of all were his eyes, from which the light seemed to have fled. They were the eyes of a creature which knows absolutely that the world, God's creation, is a cruel and hopeless thing, and that only. And I thought: It is up to me to show him otherwise.

"Do you know me?" I said softly. "Do you know me?"

His look changed and he focused on my face, scenting thoroughly.

"Lydia, for the love of God, not so close," Dr. Mahoney whispered urgently.

But I felt no fear, and in any case would display no fear. I had resolved to act with the trust that begets trust. I would not only stay the wheel but turn it the other way. I went to the stage and sat on it, turning to put my face directly to the bars, though I could hardly bear to see him.

"I know you are not a werewolf," I said gently. "I know you are a person. I know you will not hurt me. And I will never hurt you. We are here to free you and care for you."

His posture eased, ever so slightly. Encouraged, I put my arm between the bars and extended my hand to him, as one does with an unfamiliar dog, to let him scent it. Behind me, Hans made a warning sound in his throat. The wolf-man moved slightly from his corner, tentatively, then made one wobbly, four-legged lope toward me.

"You may come to me," I said. "You may come closer. Please come closer."

The men held themselves tensely, ready to spring to my aid, as the wolf-man made another lope and came near my outstretched hand. I thought he would scent it, but he did not. His legs weakened and he sat awkwardly, off balance, a confused look in his eyes, then toppled to his side on the floor. Still, he made a last gesture. He raised his hand and with his short, crude fingers, so rough and filthy, nails thickened like claws, he gave my hand a gentle swat or caress. Then his arm fell slack and he was unconscious.

Overcome, Dr. Mahoney whispered hoarsely, "Ough, God, what this poor man has been through!"

57

IT IS NIGHT again and my house is quiet. I am weary but would record these events and thoughts now, lest I forget them.

It was I who went into the cage. The wolf-man was only partly awake as I wrapped him in my cloak and put the hood up over his head. Then Hans carried him out of that room forever.

But leaving The Red Man was not easy. Winston had still worn his rascal's smile when we'd left him with Singer, but when we returned it had been replaced by a dangerous line of mouth and narrowed eyes. While we had been with the wolf-man, Silas Singer had heaped the most horrible insults and threats upon young Winston. From his accent, Singer rightly placed Winston as a Mainer, and told the boy that when he'd worn the gray uniform during the War Between the States, he had killed many Mainers and found it pleasurable, "like potting rabbits as they run." It was a poor choice of jibe, for in fact Winston's father had returned from his service with one leg gone and other miseries. Singer had also bitten the young man's arm, and in pulling him away Winston had tugged out a big hank of hair. When we came out with the wolf-man, Winston had him on his back on the floor, a boot on his throat, and their eyes were locked in mutual hatred. Singer choked out a continuous string of curses, which he turned upon Hans the moment we emerged.

"You are a dead man, Dutchie! Silas Singer doesn't forget! You think you'll ever sleep a night in peace again? Think your wife is safe on the streets?" He would have gone on, but Winston increased the pressure of his boot.

Hans gently laid the wolf-man on the bar and walked to Singer. Towering over him, Hans looked like a creature from Hell, with his suit front black-red with blood, blue eyes peering from a red-dyed face. I feared he would do something terrible, but he simply tossed the money, six hundred dollars, onto Singer's face, saying "You have been paid in full."

Then Hans went to Singer's men and looked them one by one full in his face, taking all the time in the world as if he were memorizing their every feature. Some looked away, some stared back defiantly, but none made a move against him. When Hans had inspected each one, he stepped back two paces and asked Krauss to unlock the front door and open it wide.

"I will never see any of your faces ever again," he said. "Not anywhere near me, or my house, my business, or my men. Not even by chance on the street. Never. If you understand this, you are free to go. If you do not understand, I will explain more clearly, right now."

The man he had thrown earlier bolted on the instant. The others hesitated until Hans took a step toward them. Seven men, and they shied at his approach. Another sidled and ran and then they were all at the door, out it and gone.

We left in a tight group that would keep the wolf-man from the view of passers-by. From the floor, Singer spat oaths of vengeance, swore he'd have me himself while Hans watched and then he would cut out Hans's heart and eat it raw.

We were able to get our charge into the van without being seen by passers-by and, along with Dr. Mahoney and Hans, who would not leave my side, I rode in the stifling box to Dr. Mahoney's office. We installed the wolf-man in the room the doctor had prepared, stripped of furnishings and with boarded windows, and I stood near as Dr. Mahoney applied antiseptic to his worst wounds. His patient was exhausted and half-drowsing. Not knowing what he preferred, we provided him with different foods and water, and left him to sleep.

Then I acted as nurse while Dr. Mahoney stitched Hans's scalp and closed the wounds in Labinski's leg. The other raiders waited in the outer room, looking in, trading their tales in great detail. There had been abundant heroism to go around.

The raid was on Tuesday morning. This afternoon, though a Thursday, I did not go to the mission but helped Dr. Mahoney tend the wolf-man at his office. He was drowsy with paregoric the doctor had administered, and we were able to wash him thoroughly and tend to every wound. The doctor and I discussed his future disposition, where he should live and under what circumstances, but could make no conclusion as we did not yet know how his health would rebound or what nature or character he might demonstrate when recovered.

I was at home when Hans returned from his office; he was early, he said, because his head was hurting again.

He let out a big sigh and said, "Too bad. I lost a good man today."

"Oh? Who? How?" I was frightened that Singer's vengeance had begun.

"Winston. He called in for his wages a day early and was gone. Too bad. He was a good worker. Though he could make trouble sometimes."

Without another word, Hans tossed his newspaper onto the table and went upstairs to change his clothes. The paper had been folded to the second page, where the headline read, A FIRE AT THE RED MAN RESORT. A fire had started in the dark of morning and had destroyed the whole building and part of a stable behind it. The article stated that The Red Man was widely reputed to be the headquarters of a crime syndicate run by Silas Singer; the report further opined that the city would not miss this nest of vipers.

I do not think Hans was behind it. I believe it was Winston, all on his own, an impulsive boy and too ready for adventure. Singer had erred in making an enemy of him in such a way.

I do not know whether this will make Singer less or more dangerous as our sworn enemy. I planned to ask Hans about it tonight as we lay in bed, in the close sweet shelter of our shared secret place. But he had questions of me.

"How did the wolf-man know you?"

"I saw him once, weeks ago, by chance. He did not attack me. I felt pity for him. I thought he would know my scent."

"But you did not think to tell me? Such an unusual creature, and you did not tell your husband? There must be more to the story."

I was quiet for a long time. Again I felt the yearning to tell him of Margaret, and everything, but could not bring myself straight to it.

"I had gone to care for a woman who was in dire trouble. I could not tell you about the wolf-man without revealing that I had gone alone to a dangerous part of the district. I knew you would be angry with me."

"As I am!"

"I promise I will not do it again. Put your hand on my heart, feel it beating there. It beats entirely for you. And I swear on it I will not go there again."

He did put his hand beneath my breast, and after a time seemed grudgingly mollified. We were quiet for long enough that I assumed he'd fallen asleep, but he startled me: "What became of the woman? Were you able to help her?"

"No. I could do nothing for her. I no longer even know where she is."

I was already just barely holding my feelings in check, coming so close to the subject. But, on hearing it so plainly admitted, out loud for the first time, my heart split like a lightning-cleaved tree. I began to cry, most wrackingly. My husband put a consoling hand on my shoulder, thinking my sorrow was for a stranger. When at last I stilled, he said commiseratingly, "Sometimes even the best we can do is not enough. Then we can only accept."

I am not wise enough to know when to accept or yield, or when to struggle on. I have certainly not at all accepted the loss of Margaret, have not abandoned hope for her, and refuse to.

But I consider myself fortunate beyond measure. By degrees, Hans is coming to know how strange I am, how foreign, and though at each juncture I fear his love will fail, it has shown no sign of doing so. On the contrary, our love seems to grow greater, as each strand of our bond is tested and found taut and strong.

After my storm of crying, Hans reassured me at length, like a parent calming a frightened child. Singer may hate us, but he has lost the main source of revenue that kept his crew in his service; and Singer, too, has competitors in his world, who have seized his problems as an opportunity to strike at him. Already, Hans has heard that a rival gang has taken over an illicit distillery Singer ran, killing one of his men. Hans is confident he will be too preoccupied with other enemies, closer to hand, to bother with us.

His sore head is just fine, he said, itching more than hurting. Labinski is strong as an ox and is already at work, limping about and smiling mysteriously when asked how he acquired his injury. I should not worry about

Winston, who is a resourceful boy and easily makes fast friends wherever he goes; he had been talking with enthusiasm of opportunities in Seattle. There is a great contract coming up for a new municipal building, and Schweitzer Superior is sure to win some part of it. The electricity will be a great pleasure and convenience for us and for old Cook.

I laughed a little at his long catalogue of boons and blessings that should cheer me. But I had to ask him, "Was it foolish to rescue the wolf-man? To do something so dangerous?"

"It was perhaps foolish, yes. We can't know the worth of the effort until we know what he is."

In that I knew he was right. "You are angry with me for going there."

"Yes, I am very angry. I would have preferred Silas Singer had never put his eyes on my wife. I am angry. I will not pretend otherwise. In the future, you must be more candid with me." His voice confirmed that he was, indeed, very angry. "I will be stern with you, Lydia. You must know I will be very stern with you."

"I understand," I told him. "I promise." We lay in the darkness for some time, thinking our separate thoughts. I felt very much chastened and deserving of it, yet I had just promised candor and could not withhold my true thoughts from him.

"But, oh, you were a good pirate!" I burst out, for I had been yearning to tell him how gorgeously formidable he had been. "Such a lovely, terrible bandit! I was never so proud in my life, Hans! Your men are in such awe of you. It was a splendid adventure!"

He was indignant that I had brought any levity to a chiding. "It was not a game, Lydia! You are incorrigible!"

I said nothing. He was right. Men's lives had been put at risk. He stirred uncomfortably for a long time and I held myself to my side of the bed, afraid he would chasten me further. But then he surprised me utterly by exclaiming, "But, heaven help me, yes, it was. Yes, a good adventure. If my father had seen me, what he would think! Worth a crack in the head, forgive me God. Worth every bit, God help us all!"

And we laughed together, for there we were, caught in the photographer's flash again, just as we are and nothing more nor less.

★   ★   ★

387

But I have been preoccupied with a thought that I must put down and will be considering carefully, one that seems important to me.

Dr. Mahoney and I have talked at length about the wolf-man, comparing our limited observations of him. He confounds the doctor more than me, I think, for Dr. Mahoney is a student of the body and is astonished at the profound strangeness of his anatomy. I cannot help myself but am more concerned with what is in his mind than the shape of his muzzle.

We know he is not "tame" or civilized. We know he is capable of violence and capable of gentleness. We know that when he is healthy and free he is physically vigorous, and we know he has the intelligence to fend for himself, to recognize a familiar person, and to distinguish a friend from an enemy. But that is the sum of our certainties.

Dr. Mahoney spends a great deal of time wondering at his origins: his parentage, his place of birth, how he lived, whether he was born just as he is or has changed as he has aged. And of course I am also very curious about these things.

But it troubles me less that we cannot know, and may never know, where he came from. Most important to me, and most reassuring to me, is that we can know, because it is in our hands to decide, where he goes henceforth, what becomes of him hereafter. He shall know a kinder part of the world, and whatever his nature, its best aspects shall have every chance to flourish.

Yes, what becomes of him hereafter: This is all that matters or should matter.

And what will become of him? Perhaps it will be difficult with the wolf-man. But as I think through these events, the tangling thicket of doubts, confusions, and fears through which I have struggled, I remember a Latin phrase I heard from a Kansas minister, who visited our mission from those once-wild plains. It was meant to refer to the difficulties of the first settlers in that wild place, and to their endurance despite them; but as I reflect it seems to sum up all our wanderings in life and our strivings of spirit, hope obstructed and hope triumphant.

Ad astra per aspera, he told me: To the stars through the wilderness.

VII

BRIGHT RAVEN

58

B ERT SPENT MONDAY morning trapped in a second-floor court-
room at the Hall of Justice, waiting for his call to the stand. The pros-
ecutor had expected to put him up around ten, but a series of defense
motions had slowed things down. Bert was to testify against a forty-
year-old investment counselor who had murdered the live-in nanny who
took care of his two kids. The way Del Peterson, the Homicide lead, had
put it together, he did it to prevent the nanny from telling his wife about
the affair they'd been carrying on for two years. The nanny had been a
pretty Mexican girl, with a big family who now sat silently in the gallery.
Another sad and unnecessary mess. Bert's role in the investigation was
small, but he'd done his bit and his testimony was part of the prosecution's case.

He didn't go up until eleven fifteen. Half an hour on the stand and
then he was excused. He nodded to the impassive faces as he passed the
prosecution table, trying to look self-assured, but his shoulders flinched
when the gavel announced lunch recess. He joined the throng at the door,
dying for a cigarette and determined to get out of the building before he
had to make eye contact with anyone else from Homicide.

He got home at one. Six hours of sleep in three days, it was starting to
tell on him. He wasn't thinking straight. Up the long stairs, into the familiar rooms. Too tired to even go through his little posttraumatic stress
thing. The liquor bottles gleamed at the back of the kitchen, but he ignored them and went into the living room. He thought about playing a
CD but didn't know which one could possibly do the job. Instead, he
took off his jacket, tossed his gear onto one end of the couch and flung
himself down at the other. He lay hugging one of the pillows to his chest,

not able to get comfortable, then folded the jacket across his eyes and fore-head. The tiny cocoon of darkness helped.

The sliding doors were dark when a strange sound awakened him. He opened his eyes and the shadowy angles of his living room seemed foreign to him for a moment, as if he'd been in a faraway dream. His watch said it was seven thirty. The sound happened again and he realized it was his cell phone, muffled because it had fallen between the couch cushions. He dug it out.

"Bert. It's Hank Chambers."

He was instantly wide awake. "Hank!"

"How are you doing?"

"Been better, been worse," Bert lied. He wondered if the question meant Hank had already heard something from the rumor mill or it was just a standard formulaic greeting. He tried not to sound breathless as he went on, "But you could easily improve my day."

Hank chuckled sourly. "Funny, your name came up today. I mentioned you to one of my DNA techs, we were talking about one of your old cases, the double from over near Seal Rock? You know what he told me?"

Bert felt a chill of fear, but ordered himself to stay in character. "No, but ten bucks says you're about to tell me."

"About Bertram—your name. Means 'raven,' and it's the name of Noah's raven, from the Bible. Did you know that? That's your namesake?"

Relief: It was just Hank pissing around. "First I heard about it. So what?"

"Noah had been on the ark for a long time and he wanted to find out if any dry land had emerged yet. So he sent out Bertram, the raven. Raven flies forever back and forth over the waves, never finds a place to alight, it was only later Noah sent out the dove that found the mountain. I was thinking, is that Bert Marchetti or what? Looking and looking, never find-ing the place to come down. What is it with you? Never satisfied. Never give yourself a break. Lot of guys, they do their bit and accept they can't fix everything, but not you. Never in, what—thirty-some years."

"Thanks for the words of wisdom. So now you gonna tell me some-thing, or are you gonna yank my chain for another half hour?"

Hank laughed again, and Bert heard the rustle of papers. "You owe me a yank or two. I busted my hump for you today."

"And?"

"On the dogs, you're not gonna like it. No matches on the hairs or bite impressions. No obvious match on the breeds your guy has had over the years. The dog evidence on those cases is lousy anyway, it was all a long shot."

"How about the slice-and-dice?"

"Dog hairs at the scene don't tell me anything without hairs from your guy's dogs of that time. But the knife used on the vic was definitely not the knife in the photo you gave me. Same story with that facial slashing— definitely not the same weapon. Which means you came up dry, Bertie. None of the stuff you gave me connects to any of those cases. Nothin'."

Bert didn't say anything. He couldn't tell if he was relieved or crushed. Maybe he'd been all fucked up and crazy about Ray, maybe he could let it rest. But a big part of him yearned for a reason to hate Ray, an excuse to do something to him.

"But," Hank said. A grin in his voice.

"Hank, you piece of—!"

"But with all our new evidence analysis tech and digitalization, we've been opening our cold cases, right, getting great convictions? So with the old stuff on active status, the records are in good shape. I had a guy run your knife against older blade profiles. And it came up, Bert. Homicide in Palo Alto, nineteen years ago. Deep stab wounds, clear blade profile, even the tearing from the nick in the edge. Got another match from a nonfatal knife assault from like eighteen years ago, vic never named the assailant. So there you go. Looks like you're onto something after all. I'll send you back your pics and the records on those two. And whatever you do then, guess what? It isn't going to involve me. I never heard anything about this."

Bert's heart was struggling to catch up with the flush of raw adrenaline that pulsed through him. After he closed the connection he had to sit, sucking air and gathering his thoughts.

The first thing was to call Cree, get her the hell away from Ray. If it wasn't too late.

Going on eight o'clock Monday night. He called her cell, got no answer, called the motel, no answer there. Maybe working with Horace? He called the lab phone and got Horace's voice mail. Then he called Horace's home phone, got Patrick: No, Horace wasn't at the lab tonight, he had a speaking engagement in Sacramento.

She could be anywhere. She could be dead. She could've gone to a movie or something and had turned off her phone. Maybe she was doing research somewhere, she seemed like the worker type, a real bulldog on a case. But where, at this time of night? Most likely she was at Ray's and wasn't choosing to answer her phone. Or wasn't able to.

Bert retrieved his gun, put it on, found his keys and wallet. A few hours of sleep and Hank's call, one solid thing on Ray at last, it had charged him up completely. When he left the house, he trotted down the stairs, never touching the rail, like he was thirty again. He jumped into the truck and fired up the big engine. First stop, Ray's place. Play it by ear. Take it as it fell out. For the first time in weeks, he felt wonderfully free and unfettered.

59

I T'S GOT TO be right, Cree. What other scenario works?" Ray gestured around him at the dark, fog-cloaked terrace as if it provided
corroboration.

Cree turned away, going through it again, hugging herself against the
chill. Nothing had changed. The house loomed dark above them, all the
empty windows. Down here, the flagstones glistened with condensation
and the garden leaves were trimmed with droplets. Another night of
foghorns.

Ray's excitement was a little frightening, but she couldn't blame him.
Finding the Mission Council's report had thrilled them both. They were
getting so close. And yet it had posed as many questions as it had answered. They figured that Lydia must have disobeyed the church patri-
archy, had rescued the wolfman, had made a home for him here. But then
what? Could he talk? Could he tell his story? Did Lydia make an effort to
find out where he came from, who his parents were, how he had lived?
Did she write down his story, or keep a diary about their life with him?
Did they take him to a doctor—might there be medical records?

And was he confined to the basement chamber? It didn't seem likely
that Lydia had rescued him only to imprison him forever in an underground crypt. Unless it was his preference—maybe Ray was right and he
was cripplingly light-aversive, or agoraphobic, or terrified of human contact. Or maybe he proved so behaviorally defective, violent, and unpredictable, that they had no choice. Or maybe he roamed the house freely;
maybe it was just chance that he got caught in the collapse of the Jackson
house, and Hans had built the brick chamber after the quake, sealing away
forever the secret resident of their household.

It all came down to what kind of creature or person he was. How he lived, what he felt. How human he was. That was the question at the bottom of everything, the one that had eluded everyone, Skobold and Ray and Cree, the patrons of The Red Man, the mission council. Maybe it was that question as much as compassion that had compelled Lydia and Hans to rescue him. And it couldn't be answered by bones or by the most realistic reconstruction even Skobold could accomplish.

She was moved by the mystery, but Ray really was far gone. The wolf-man had captured his imagination from the start, as if he saw a crucial parallel to his own life, as if all the secrets of the world were contained within that strange skull.

The tease of the council report had fueled an afternoon of frenzied work as they tore through the records. Rev. Michaelson brought them tea, but they didn't even break for lunch. They continued to find occasional reference to Lydia, always a devoted worker on behalf of the good cause. They found more Mission Council decrees and reports on one project or another, one battle against sin or another. They found an accounting of donations that included substantial contributions from Hans and Lydia. They even found a later portrait of both Schweitzers, posed with another couple. Their first glimpse of Hans showed him to be a truly imposing figure, with huge, rugged hands that rested possessively on the back of his wife's chair, a stern face gentled by wire-rimmed spectacles.

But by five o'clock, when they finished the last of the 1906 files, they had found no clues to Hans Schweitzer's fate, no name of a family doctor or lawyer, no hint of relatives or disposition of family effects. And not one more word about the wolfman.

Starved and disappointed, they'd gone out for dinner, talked it over, fitted the pieces together this way and that. After a while it began to seem like a few did fit, which had brought them back here to the house. Just to think it through one more time. She had toured Ray through the first floor and the basement room, where Ray had inspected the walls and ceiling closely. Then he'd wanted to come out here to look at the place from the perspective of the old Jackson house.

Ray paced with her around the central planting island, enumerating the suggestive facts.

"They rented out the Jackson house for three years after they were married. But then in 1890 it's vacated and left that way for sixteen years. Water records show no water service, so no one lived in it—officially. Why would they do that unless they put the wolfman up in it, Cree? Lydia was hell bent on helping him, but my bet is she was also a dutiful servant of her church, didn't want to openly disobey the Council. So she kept him secret. Kept the whole thing secret from them—we *know* she did, because the church records don't mention him again. Maybe Hans went along with the rescue but didn't totally approve, was afraid of scandal or shame, didn't want to be associated with anything unsavory that could jeopardize his business or his social standing. Neither of them would have wanted attention from oddballs and opportunists, for the wolfman's sake as much as their own. So they made a secret home for him."

"Why build the chamber in the basement? Lydia wouldn't have rescued him just to put him in a dungeon."

"She didn't! I think that's how they got into the Jackson house. Didn't want to be seen going over there several times a day with food, water, and so on. I think Hans built it down there as an entry chamber. I think there was a door in it originally, that Hans bricked up after the quake. Either he was so good there was no sign of variation in the bricks, or Hernandez is right, he and his guys broke through right there and wrecked any indications of a door. Maybe that's where they kept his larder and his chamber pot, made it more convenient to bring him things and dispose of things. It was only one end of the tunnel between the houses. Maybe the opening weakened the Jackson foundation, that would explain why the worst collapse happened right there. Hans no doubt built it well, he just didn't anticipate the worst earthquake in American history."

"Ray, that's a lot of supposition. I think you want a solution, you want answers. But you're guessing."

"No! Listen. They set him up in the Jackson house basement. Maybe he wanted it that way, or maybe he made noise. Or people would see him at the windows, or he wasn't really . . . safe. So Hans builds a basement suite for him. Out of view, masonry walls, safe containment if needed. Maybe Hans had some other reason to keep it secret, but it must have been important to him. Why else would he put those deed restrictions on the property when he sold the place? He wanted to make sure the lot was never developed. Make sure nobody ever dug in there and found the wolfman's suite. And the wolfman himself. And Lydia."

Cree stopped pacing. "Oh, now wait a minute—"

"Think about it! Her body was never found—"

"Lydia and hundreds of others!"

"Right. But where would she have been at five thirteen in the morning? She sure wasn't out shopping. I don't see her as the type to be out with some clandestine lover. She was *in there*, Cree—she was up and seeing to their . . . guest. Their . . . pet. Their surrogate son. Whatever he was to them."

Cree looked down at the expanse of paving stones and decorative walkways, the patterns just visible in the blue dark. Yes, such good craftsmanship—such *old-world* craftsmanship. Lydia's bones could be beneath her feet at this moment.

"It's not possible. What, Hans single-handedly took down the ruins, disposed of tons of rubble, covered over the basement, and built all this? One man?"

"No. He had crews available. He used his most trusted men. Maybe he swore them to secrecy. Maybe he did the most sensitive parts himself. Think of that photo—the guy was a giant, physically powerful, and a superbly skilled mason. He rebuilt the hole he'd made in the foundation wall so you couldn't tell. He filled in the door in the chamber. He built the terrace."

"Why didn't he retrieve Lydia's body? Give her a religious funeral?"

"I don't know. Some kind of personal monument?" Ray bit his lips, shook his head, stumped. "The mysteries of the heart, Cree. The mysteries of human nature." She could just make out his quick grin in the dark.

Cree blew out a breath, a plume of steam within the fog. "Anyway, what can we do about it? Not much. And I am freezing. I'm going inside."

Ray's grin widened. "I was just going to suggest that," he said.

★ ★ ★

398

He went straight through the kitchen to the back hallway and the basement door, pounding down the stairs so quickly that she didn't catch up with him until he'd made it to the back room. He turned on some lights and went to the collection of tools leaning in the corner, then selected a sledgehammer and hefted it experimentally.

Cree's jaw dropped. "Whoa—wait, Ray—"

He was already in the wolfman's chamber, legs spread wide, hammer behind him.

"Ray!"

The first blow made a dull *chunk* and sent up a puff of brick dust.

"Ray, stop! You'll only make trouble! There's nothing in there!"

"Only one way to find out." He grunted as he put his whole weight behind into another swing. Another ground-shaking *thunk*, dust, a falling chip of brick.

"Even if you're right, if there had been a suite, it's got to be filled with rubble, right? You'd need a backhoe or—"

"Maybe. But bricks in a brick house are on the outside walls, the middle would have been just wood frame like this one. And the outer wall fell this way. So maybe not." *Chunk.*

"Ray, we'll find out some other way. This is *not* our house! We—"

"You go. Stay out of it. If I get caught, I'll say I broke in."

She couldn't move. Three more swings and Ray stopped to take off his jacket, roll his sleeves, inspect the fist-size crater he'd made. Cree started toward him, but he gave her a warding look and quick shake of his head. He picked up the hammer again and blasted another spray of chips into the little room.

Cree was swearing to herself. She could fling herself at him, but she doubted she'd be able to dissuade him. She could threaten to call the police, but she knew it wouldn't stop him: Ray was a person with absolutely nothing to lose and a yearning to *know* fierce as the flame of an acetylene torch.

And maybe it *was* just one of those situations where even a good citizen could justify breaking the rules a little. Maybe there *was* something important to find through there.

Ray fell into a rhythm, pounding like a machine, the muscles of his forearms standing out like cables. Several bricks fell away, revealing another course behind them. The clatter scared her again and nothing felt right about this.

"You're not the wolfman," she rasped. "You won't solve Ray by solving him."

That made him pause. He panted as he looked at her with an expression suddenly sad and doubtful. "No. You're right. There is no solution."

For just an instant she thought she'd succeeded. But then his face broke into a wide smile that even with the scars looked gleeful and irresistible. "But, oh man, I'll be goddamned if I'll get this close and not go for it!"

He attacked the wall joyously, ferociously. Cree stood, half scared to death and half struck by him, the power of his body in its utmost effort, the desire embodied in his force. Chunks of bricks began to fall as cracks radiated from the hole.

She watched for a few more minutes, sneezing in the dust. Then she rigged one of the extension cords and plugged in another lamp. She positioned it in the doorway to the wolfman's chamber so that Ray's growing crater was bathed in light.

Complicit, she thought. *Accessory. Whatever.*

60

CREE'S CAR WAS not at Ray's and there were no lights visible in the windows. Bert drove up to the entrance door, not caring if Ray saw him. He opened the truck door and stood out of it to look over the place. The muffled sound of barking came from inside. He waited to see if Ray would show, but after three minutes of muted dog hysteria no one opened the door and no light showed. Bert climbed back into the truck and drove away.

He tried her cell phone again, knowing it was pointless, then decided to swing by the motel on the off chance she was there, maybe taking an early night after carousing with Scarface. But when he pulled into the courtyard parking lot, her car wasn't there. He got out anyway, went up the stairs, knocked at her door. No sound, no light. Curtains across the window, air circulation not running.

He checked nearby streets in case she'd parked outside the motel lot, but didn't see her car. After that he just drove aimlessly for a time, not sure what to do.

The streets of San Francisco: foggy tonight, charming as ever yet also urban and hard, so familiar after all these years. He knew the hills and the roads that wound around and up them through the pastel neighborhoods, he knew the alleys. His world for over thirty years now. He felt oddly nostalgic and wondered if that meant it was all ending, or if he could salvage something after all; if with a murder to pin on Ray he could escape. For the moment he was empty of direction, the mood was darkness tinted by the acid light of streetlamps. He lit a cigarette, took some solace in it, then fumbled a music CD into the dash player without looking to see what it was. Louis Armstrong. Not quite right, but there were some great numbers on this one. "Wonderful World" had always broken his heart and it did now. This was his town. At least once upon a time.

Then it occurred to him that maybe Cree was at his place, that'd be ironic, looking for him while he was out searching for her. Or maybe she'd lost his cell number and had left a message on his machine. Driving with one hand, he dialed his own number and punched in his remote code to listen to the messages.

There was only one, from his lieutenant: "Bert. Check in with me when you hear this message. If you get this after midnight, plan on coming directly to my office at eight tomorrow morning."

So there it was. That was the beginning. Jack would inform him of the questions surrounding Nearing and Koslowski and that MCD was interested. He'd ask Bert some pointed questions, advise him to procure counsel, then place him on suspension. Jack would be cautious and scrupulously neutral and do it by the administrative book. Then he'd turn him over to MCD.

Fortunately there was the knife. Bert would show him the pictures, prove there was some justification. *Good* justification. They'd make allowances for bad procedure. Ray would be in no position to complain, especially since he apparently hadn't been badly hurt and he'd bunged up a pair of cops. Even the most tight-assed brass took a visceral exception to that, even if the cops in question had overstepped. There were always ways to finesse things, procedural means to sweep details under the rug.

Louis had gone into a snappy number and Bert's confidence inched up. But then it got smacked flat by another thought: Ray might have gotten rid of the knife by now. Of course he had! He'd know Bert would have seen it when he broke in, would have looked into it. The knife was long gone by now, probably thrown out Ray's van window off the Golden Gate Bridge.

Bert didn't have any justification or evidence. What he had was a couple of photographs of some knife on some bureau at some location. Without the knife, picked up during a warranted search, there was nothing on Ray at all.

So that kind of decides it, Bert thought. *That decides what's left. What's next.*

The realization actually soothed him. Simplified everything. He felt reconciled and empowered in a way he couldn't name. It was like a high of some kind. The streets above Market flowed by and he observed them with huge affection. He punched the backtrack button on the CD player, all the way to "Wonderful World" and it was glorious. Louis's honey and gravel voice. The gravel made it believable, like the singer had had to go through something hard to get to the sweetness, and it was worth it.

He got back to his own street, took a turn at the cul-de-sac, scanning the curb and looking up at his stairs in the hazy gloom. No sign of Cree. Where would she be? Why wouldn't she answer her phone? Cell service could be locally spotty due to the hills, but generally it was okay.

A bad thought came to him. Ray would want to hit back at Bert for the first thing and now Nearing and Koslowski. No way would Ray let that pass. But exactly what would he do? It would be devious, like the e-mails, clever. What would be the worst?

Cree. Ray would figure that out. He'd do something to Cree.

Bert's gut clenched and squirmed like some cold snake was uncoiling in there. His arms and hands felt a spray of ice on their skin, adrenaline goosed by near-panic as he admitted he had no way to find her.

But then an idea appeared in the dark of the cab, and he grabbed at it and suddenly he knew exactly where she was. He knew it for a certainty, even though he had no basis for it. Or it was just gut instinct. Or the guidance of fate, you knew it when it came to you. He turned the truck around and began the ten-minute drive to the house in Pacific Heights.

61

A BIG SECTION OF bricks fell away from up near the ceiling. Ray jumped back as it hit the floor and shattered and the chamber filled with a new gout of masonry dust. He stumbled out of the little room, coughing, put his face into his shirt.

Even through the dust, Cree could see there was a hole. A hollow darkness on the other side.

They both stared at it. A slight pressure of air wafted out of it, gently moving the dust cloud out into the larger room. Neither of them said anything for a few seconds. Their eyes met. Then Cree turned away and headed to the hall doorway.

"I guess I'll round up some more extension cords," she called back.

She ended up making two trips upstairs, bringing back a pair of fifty-foot cords, another lamp, two pairs of rawhide gloves, and two pairs of contractor's kneepads. They put on the protective gear, and then Ray gave the wall a few more shots to widen the gap. At last another section fell, leaving a ragged oval hole three feet wide from ceiling to about waist height.

Cree brought in the lamps, laying out the cords behind her, and they shone them into the hole. The brick-walled tunnel was about six feet wide. A mound of loose brick and masonry and boards filled it from wall to wall to within a few feet of the ceiling. Above the rubble a deep gash stretched back into pitch black, exhaling a gentle breath of cool, humid air scented with mold and earth.

"Are we sure we want to know what's in there?" Cree whispered.

"I've never been more sure of anything in my entire life."

Ray was covered in orange dust that had stuck to his sweat and had smeared in streaks when he'd wiped his face. With his eyes on fire below the streaked orange forehead, he looked like some tribal person, a shaman engaged in some unfathomable rite. His chest pumped from exertion and excitement and Cree could feel his heartbeat from two feet away.

"I mean, maybe it's not a happy story here, Ray. The wolfman, Lydia— maybe it's not going to turn out to be . . . you know. Whatever you're hoping for. You prepared for that?"

Ray coughed hard, hacked up orange spit. "Only one way to find out."

He clambered into the opening, raking bricks and chunks of concrete back and to the sides to provide more clearance. Cree crawled behind him, advancing and positioning the lights, managing the cords, waiting, following as Ray dug and shoved forward. Sharp edges of masonry and boards poked at her arms and legs, clinking and shifting as she crawled.

After about ten feet, the mound tapered toward the floor and they could sit upright on the uneven slope. They tugged the cords up and beamed the lights into a wider corridor that was completely free of debris. The hallway ended about thirty feet back at another brick foundation wall, where a solitary wooden chair and tiny side table stood. Doorways led to rooms on either side, nicely framed and trimmed.

The ceiling was ribbed with heavy beams capped with stone slabs. In places, plant roots hung down between gaps, tattered curtains of dark mesh. Here and there, waterfalls of gray-green moss coated parts of the side walls, indication that after a hundred years the terrace had sprung a few leaks. But otherwise it was perfect. Hans had done a masterful job.

Ray's exultant mood had softened. Even in the glare of the lights and the hard cut of shadows, he now looked subdued. He started clattering down the rubble slope, then stopped to look back at her. He reached out to touch her lightly, one gloved finger on her arm.

"What?"

"Mainly, thanks."

"For . . . ?"

"I don't always handle my . . . situation so well, sometimes I spin off into bad places. But you've done good things for me. It's like all this, the wolfman's skeleton, you, the church report, this place . . . it's all perfect. Is there a word for the opposite of paranoia? Where you think the world is conspiring to do you good? This all, you—it's what I needed. You most of all."

Cree rocked with that for second, trying to see it as he did. *Talking to a dead man.* "Thank you, Ray."

He looked troubled. "But I wanted to explain one thing. This whole problem with Bert—I know it's my fault, the e-mails. I was out of control. I . . . vacillated from decisions I'd made for myself. I wanted to explain that to you."

"You know I'm glad to hear about it."

"There's only one established environmental risk factor for brain tumors. You know what it is?"

Puzzled, she thought back to her graduate school neurology courses. "Radiation exposure, isn't it? So . . . your job? Fifteen years of—"

"No. I'm very, very careful. And the doses we use nowadays are a fraction of what they used to be. But there was a time when I got dozens of head X-rays, over a period of months. Back when I was seventeen, Cree. That's the most likely etiology on this one. See what I'm saying?"

She saw it. Whatever violence Bert intended against Ray was unnecessary in more ways than one. There was a strong probability that Bert had already fatally wounded him, twenty-three years ago.

Ray's forbearance was astonishing and tragic and beautiful. *And goddamn everything*, she thought hopelessly. Tears sprang to her eyes and two rolled down her cheeks. Not just for Ray, for Bert, too, and everyone.

Ray was watching her closely, his dust-rouged face now more like some kid's poor attempt at a Halloween tiger. Without thinking about it, she untucked her shirt and used the clean hem to wipe the dust off his face.

"You should see yourself," she chided him hoarsely. Two more tears hurried down her cheeks and she smeared them away. "Both of us. Shit. There. Better." She finished with him, then pushed him away. She gathered up her light and clanked and rattled down the slope.

The first of the four doorways led to a small square room that was set up as a bedroom. The walls had been plastered and papered, and even with the paper discolored and hanging loose in places Cree could easily visualize the room as it had been. There were framed paintings on the walls, a bureau with a mirror, a bed frame with nicely carved headboard and four lathed posts around a rectangular heap of decayed cloth that had once been a mattress and bedding. A china basin stood on the bureau, an oil lamp on the bedside table. It smelled old in here, earthy and mildewed, and with the room lit unevenly by their lamps, it all had an archeological feel. Archeology in some time-warped, parallel universe, Cree thought: They'd opened an Egyptian tomb and found a Victorian bedroom.

"Not a dungeon," Ray whispered. "They put effort into making this room pleasant. Normal. What does that say about who he was?"

"It might say more about who Hans and Lydia were."

Ray nodded. They moved across the hall to find an amazingly intact Victorian sitting room. Again, the walls were mildew-darkened but wallpapered. A painting in a carved frame showed a landscape: Through the shotgun spray of mildew, they could still make out rugged coastal bluffs rimmed by trees, waves foaming against outlying rocks. At some point a piece of Hans's ceiling had fallen, leaving a pile of broken stone in the middle of the floor. Cree got a jolt when her light picked out a glistening white curve among the rubble, but when she toed it free she found it wasn't a section of skull after all, just the belly of a broken bone china water pitcher. The divan frame held another mound of decay, but the wooden furniture was fine. On a small table, photo portraits of Hans and Lydia stood propped in little wooden brackets, and a small, leather-bound Bible lay with a ribbon bookmark protruding.

"I think he was human," Ray said. "I think they helped him be human. I think they tried to give him as good a life as he could have."

"Could be." She stayed noncommittal because she couldn't bear to encourage or discourage him. He wanted the wolfman to have been human and treated like one. The same way Skobold wanted every cruelty to be the result merely of unintended consequences. *The way Cree believes you just have to untie the knots, that's all that keeps us from becoming the good and free beings we're intended to be. The way we're all always hoping.*

The cords made it to the farthest doorways with only a few feet to spare. The left room was badly water damaged, and heavy mats of roots hung down like funeral curtains from cracks in the stone ceiling. There were humps of rotting wood mixed with black spongy material, what might once have been upholstered chairs, and a sprawled collection of boards and moisture-swollen black blocks that had been a bookshelf and books. Cree felt Ray's frustration rising. He ripped away the hanging roots, kicked and grappled through the rubble, picking up objects and then tossing them down impatiently. In another minute he hurried out and across the hall to the last of the rooms.

She followed him reluctantly, unwilling to find Lydia, afraid again of what might be there. What was she thinking? Shackles on the walls? Human bones with canine tooth marks on them? Why was she so on edge and morbid about this? Maybe it was just too dark down here, too damaged, too old and too long secret.

Ray adjusted his electrical cord and went in, but Cree hesitated in the corridor as she heard a sound from the direction of the Schweitzer house. That clinking sound of bricks sliding against each other. It made her heart race in a way that revealed how much tension she'd been holding back all this time.

She turned off her light and stood in the darkness, staring back at the distant cleft of light made by the lamps they'd left in the bones' chamber. She didn't see any movement, didn't know what she was expecting to see.

"Cree," Ray called. "What are you doing? Get in here! Jesus, you've got to see this!"

But the shifting clink and clatter came again and for some reason it really put her teeth on edge. She turned on her light again and headed back down the hallway. Maybe just bricks moving, disturbed by Ray and her. Or rats—there had to be rats down here. She walked back toward the opening to the Schweitzer house, then stopped abruptly as her trailing cord snagged on something and yanked the lamp out of her hand. It fell and the bulb popped and then she was lost in blackness. The walls rushed in, smothering. Desperately she turned to check the rectangle of light at the far end, Ray's lamp, then spun again as she heard clattering again, much closer.

The light in the narrow gap above the rubble mound was eclipsed by a big moving shadow. It was the shape of a man clambering on all fours over the uneven debris barrier, moving awkwardly but purposefully. After another second a circle of light blinked from the shadow form, a flashlight beam that briefly lit the side of Bert's determined face before it struck Cree and blinded her.

62

BERT SAW HER face in his flashlight beam and felt both relieved and betrayed. He scrambled the last few feet, ignoring the pain in his shins and knees, then half-fell down a slope of shifting rubble into a more open space. Some kind of underground warren, a catacomb beneath the terrace. Cree must have figured out something with the wolfman and then she and her freak boyfriend had gotten rash and opened up the wall.

He got to his feet and drew his Beretta and held it alongside the flashlight with his wrists crossed. He put the light full on Cree, then angled it down a bit as she winced and put a hand up to cover her eyes.

"Where is he?"

She didn't answer but the involuntary tick of her head made him look past her, to the rectangle of light at the end of the hallway, forty feet away.

"Cree, he's a killer. Go back into the house, get in your car. Get out of here and let me handle this."

"You've got it wrong. He's not what you think he is."

"You don't know crap about what he is! Guy's a *freak*. A murderer. Get back here and let me handle him. Do as I *say*! I don't want you hurt."

"Nobody's going to be hurt!"

Bert saw the light change at the end of the hall and he brought his flashlight and gun up again. Cameron Raymond came out of the doorway with a contractor's lamp in his hands. From here it looked like his eyes reflected.

"Cree?" Ray called. He put up one hand to block Bert's light.

"Ray, it's Bert. He's got his gun. He—"

"Don't fucking move, Ray. Move and I shoot a hole in your ugly face."

Ray's light clattered to the ground and went out and then he was just gone. Bert started down the hall, but Cree got in front of him. When he swept his arm at her to get her out of the way, she dodged and grabbed his forearm and was back in his face.

"Bert, you stop. You *stop.* He's not a killer."

He shook off her grip, but he hesitated. She was still in front of him, and he couldn't catch his breath he was so mad: pissed at Cree for letting it come down like this, for complicating it, for taking *Ray's* part. He took a step back and brought both arms up in front of him again, flashlight in Cree's face, gun aligned with the beam. She fell back a couple of steps, still blocking the middle of the tunnel.

"Hey, Ray! Cree says you're not a killer. Why don't you tell her about your switchblade? Maybe you saw it yourself, Cree, in his bedroom? The knife on his bureau?"

"I didn't see it. You mentioned it to me."

"Yeah, that's right, probably Ray dumped it before you got there. But I took photos. And lo and behold, it matches exactly two separate knife attacks, one a homicide. Right down to the nick on the blade. Hey, Ray, tell her about it."

Cree had her forearm across her eyes, but her mouth bent in a way that suggested she was having second thoughts.

Still no sound from the end of the hall, and Bert goaded him: "Cat got your tongue, Ray? Sure there isn't something you want to 'fess up to Cree?"

And then Ray was there. He came out of the room on the left and stood in the center of the hallway. Cree was between them but she was so much shorter that Bert still had a pretty good view of him. Ray winced against the flashlight glare, and his chest and face were as clear in Bert's sight as the profile targets at the department shooting range.

Cree half-turned her head. "Ray, don't come out. Don't even answer him. Let me talk."

But Ray just stood there. "That knife wasn't mine. I took it off a guy who was acting like he might use it on me. I was asking him about wolves and werewolves and killing and he didn't like my questions. Maybe because he killed whoever Bert's talking about, maybe that's why he was so touchy, I don't know. I don't have it because I mailed it back to the guy. I had never meant to keep it."

"Yeah, the other guy did it," Bert jeered. "Heard it before, Ray. Smart guy like you should be able to come up with something more original."

"Cree," Ray called. "I'm telling you the truth. And Bert is a werewolf. I was right about that. You're the worst kind, Bert. The kind that doesn't even know it's a wolf. The kind no one sees until it's too late."

"Whereas Ray is Mahatma Gandhi. He's Mother Teresa and Jesus all rolled into one."

"I know what I am," Ray said quietly. "How about you, Bert? Do you even remember you were human once?"

Bert's anger made flashpoint and he pivoted his locked arms slightly, shifting the line to the right of Cree's head. When the gun fired, the flash lit her whole body and the glare seemed to tumble her aside. The explosion was deafening. Down on the floor, Cree rocked in pain, gripping her head with both hands, but Bert decided the cordite spray couldn't have burnt her too badly, she'd had her arm up to block the light. And he didn't mind getting her out of the middle of the corridor and putting her out of commission for a while. She was a loose cannon here, hard to tell how she'd come down.

Bert could see the divot the bullet had made in the wall behind Ray, well to the right. He'd expected Ray to dart away again, but instead the freak raised one hand to block the light and started forward. He seemed more concerned with Cree than with Bert.

Bert fired again, and the hand that Ray had been holding up snapped back and spun him half around. He bent at the waist, folding himself over his forearm, gripping it with his other hand. A wet pink splash had appeared on the far wall. An exultant sense of triumph rose through Bert, sweeping from his heels up his legs and groin and then bulging through his belly and chest, ending in a shimmer of sensation at the top of his head. He drew a huge gulp of breath and put the light and the gunsight square on Ray's scarred face.

Which wasn't right. The face wasn't crumpled in pain and fear and Bert very much wanted to see both expressions there. Ray was holding his forearm with his other hand and walking slowly forward with a freakish calm. Bert's fury crested in a feeling of absolute determination and exquisite clarity. He felt the weight of the gun and the crisp return pressure of the trigger and the hate that welled up and commanded his hand.

He would have fired but there was something wrong with the face and the hate and he needed just a second to consider it. The hate was aimed at Ray but when he pictured what it was he hated, he realized its face didn't really look like Ray's. What, then? Bert recoiled from the question, took a step back, turned his ankle on a brick, stumbled backward and sat hard against the rubble mound. He kept the gun raised, but he didn't jump right up. Off to the side, Cree rolled and sat up and blinked at him.

Actually there was a lot to think about. And the gun was heavy. He set the flashlight aside and put his hands in his lap to rest his arms and then he lay back against the hard angles of the bricks. Just to take a load off, catch his breath. Just to have a moment to think.

There was a shape hovering above him in the indirect light. A face. It was Fran, her smooth skin and nice hair, that look of concern in her eyes that always made him feel at the center of the universe. Frannie was a woman to be proud of. Chinese women, most beautiful in the world, bar none. But then he thought no, Fran was sixty-one, this woman was too young, and anyway her features were not so Asian. His chest clenched as he realized it was Megan, she was alive and full grown and beautiful and she'd found him somehow and that meant he could let go of it all. Let go that sinewy ropey relentless thing held so tight in his guts all these years. He could forgive the world, at least for that. That would be good.

"Uncle Bert! Try to answer me! Is it your heart?"

Her voice startled him. *Right. Cree. Cree Black, Ben's kid. God, Ben was a long time ago.*

"Yeah," Bert croaked. "Yeah, it must be my heart." Bad joke. What heart? He almost laughed out loud.

Cree was doing something and he noticed his head wasn't hurting from the corners of the bricks, she'd folded something soft behind him. Then her face was gone and he heard clinking noises and there was another face. Ray. Ray's face, watching him closely. Fucking ugly son of a bitch he turned out to be.

Okay, yeah, I did that, Bert thought *I am the wolfman. I am the werewolf.* Now it seemed right. Feeling bad about Ray was part of the ropey thing. *I was crazy when that happened, been crazy half my life. Got a thing in me, comes up and hurts people.* He looked up at the dark subterranean ceiling and it felt familiar. *Those bones that were in there, the wolfman, that freak, that's me,*

Ray. Whatever was left over of me, walled up and sealed in and forgotten and no-body ever knew. He wasn't sure if he was thinking it or talking out loud.

"She's gone upstairs to call for help," Ray's face said. "Her phone doesn't work under here, she had to go upstairs. She'll be right back."

Bert was thinking about being a wolfman and a werewolf and for a while it definitely seemed right. Everybody was a werewolf. Ray was, whoever took Megan, Rich Nearing, probably even Cree or Horace, it was always down in there, waiting, dangerous. Too fucking sad.

But then he lost the logic of it and it didn't seem quite right. Wrong animal. Because it wasn't that, or not only that. All his life he'd been looking for a certain feeling. Even just wanting it, that had to be worth something. He'd found it fleetingly when he danced. The sweep and glide and upbeat bounce. The weightlessness, that was it. You wanted weightlessness. To be unbound. Airborne. He could almost feel it right now, like he was swooping or skating airborne above an endless smooth surface.

He looked at Ray's face and was surprised by what he saw. *Jesus, he's another one, he's going back and forth forever and can't find the place to come down. Another poor restless fuck.*

He felt his arc rise steeply with a jab of scary vertigo and something sweeter, breaking or releasing. Suddenly he understood it clearly. It was very important, an astonishing truth. He could hardly make his mouth work, but he wanted badly to tell Ray.

No, he said or thought, *not wolves. We're birds, see. We're dark, shiny birds. We can fly.*

63

Y OU REMEMBER THE discussions we had," Horace was saying, "about
pure tissue metrics versus the Russian school?"

"Yes." Cree was glad to see him again. He had met them in the lobby
of the Life Sciences Building to walk them down to the lab. Ray had
greeted Horace warmly, but now wasn't saying anything. He'd admitted
that the prospect of seeing the wolfman's face, at last, disturbed him.

"My assistant and I each did a reconstruction, intentionally independent of each other—a differential experiment, you might say, similar to
the Tutankhamen project of last year."

"How have you found time, Horace? With all you've been doing? Ray
and I have kept you pretty busy!"

Horace tapped the elevator button and smiled sadly at her, his eyes
swimming huge in his glasses. "Yes. Well, your discovery lit something of
a fire under my behind," he said.

It was only eight days since that night. By the time she'd gotten back from
calling for help, Bert was dead. Ray was sitting at his side, staring intently
at him, as if keeping a vigil.

Of course the police had taken them in, Ray to the hospital for his arm,
Cree to a police station for a long night of questioning and a short sleep in
a holding cell. In the morning, she had called Horace, who came down and
corroborated what he could. Fortunately, Bert's autopsy got expedited and
left no question as to the cause of his death. He was overweight and chain-
smoked and had been an alcoholic for forty years; probably it was only his
fifty-eight steps, twice daily, that had kept his heart functioning this long.

Cree also sensed that Bert was in some kind of trouble anyway, because the investigators seemed only too willing to believe he'd gone over the edge. After they'd both been released, Ray told her about the two cops Bert had sent to his place. He didn't tell her earlier because he didn't want it to get in the way of anything. Revenge or legal action would be complications he didn't need, distractions. He didn't have time for distractions.

It had been hard to explain what they were doing, knocking holes in somebody else's basement wall. Horace helped with that, telling about the wolfman's bones, how Cree had been retained to investigate and had the owner's permission to enter the house. The police had called the owners to verify that and to report the incident, and later Ray and Cree called to promise they'd pay for replacing the bricks. The owners were actually very glad to know about the secret suite attached to their house. It made them reconsider whether to even move in—the whole thing upset them, and they had their kids to think about. They declined to file a vandalism complaint.

When he'd heard about the underground apartment and Ray's discoveries in the last room, Horace had swung into action. Within days, he'd secured permissions from the house owners and university administration, then put together a research team of professors and grad students from the Anthropology and History departments, headed by himself, to systematically explore and document the suite.

The lab looked the same as it always did, orderly and bright. Karen Chang looked up when they came in, welcomed them, then led them to the workbench where the two reconstructions stood side by side. Skobold had done his sculpting in the back room, she explained; she had concealed hers whenever Horace was nearby or when she was not working on it. They had both used plaster casts from Horace's skull molds, but Karen had copied the features supplied by the computerized modeling program and strictly applied tissue metrics, while Skobold had used the "Russian school" approach and more of his own intuition.

They looked at the two faces in silence. Ray looked stunned at first, cradling his bandaged arm as he looked from one to the other. After a moment, he smiled.

"Gosh," he said. "Let me see if I can guess which one is yours, Horace."

The bust on the left was a ghastly creature, lipless, very little protrusion of nose, mouth stretching all the way back the sides of the muzzle to reveal the rows of teeth. Karen had opted for slightly pointed, projecting ears. The final effect was of a brutal, alien being, inhuman and expressionless, devoid of any emotion or intelligence.

Though its basic proportions were the same, Skobold's was much more detailed and much more human. With rounded human ears tucked close against the head, fuller lips and nose, a shorter mouth, more padding on the cheekbones, brows that looked mobile, eyes full of alertness, he'd built an expressive face, wary but curious, lined with the creases of a life's experience and feelings.

"I should add that as part of the experiment," Horace explained, "I made full use of the clues available in Lydia Schweitzer's journal, whereas Karen wasn't allowed to read it prior to her sculpting. Lydia reported that his ears were normal, for example. She refers to his 'expression of contentment' or 'despair,' or 'relief,' suggesting mobile facial musculature and a human vocabulary of emotional expression."

"I can't wait to read it," Cree said.

Horace turned somber and gazed at her thoughtfully. "Yes. I imagine you will find it . . . compelling. I suspect you will find you have much in common with Lydia."

Hernandez and his men were almost finished, and the upstairs glowed. Much of the carpentry equipment had been removed, and the spacious rooms begged to be lived in. They didn't stray into them, though, but headed straight for the basement stairs.

The back basement room had been transformed into a research station, with folding tables and chairs, laptop computers, stacks of folded storage boxes, sifting screens, camera tripods. A researcher looked up from her computer to greet them, then went back to typing. In the wolfman's crypt, the team had opened up a full doorway and had removed the rubble from the tunnel. But in the subterranean suite, they had so far done little beyond labeling artifacts, mapping, and photo documentation. Everything was just as it had been seared into Cree's memory, except that the team had rigged good lights that made the details more visible and the ambience less threatening. A pair of researchers worked in the sitting room, but the rest of the suite was empty.

The end room was the largest and by far the best preserved of the four. At its center, a coffin lay on a fine funereal stand. It struck Cree as a beautiful coffin, simple but built with exquisite craftsmanship, pale hardwood boards joined with dovetail joints. At its head stood a little table that had clearly been set up as something of a shrine. It held a photo of Lydia in a gilt frame and a crystal vase draped with the black remains of roses. There had also been the two ledger books that contained Lydia's journal, but Horace had removed them to a humidity-controlled vault. He'd had them photocopied by technical preservation experts, and would give Cree a copy later.

They spent fifteen minutes in the room. Cree couldn't seem to pay attention to Horace's narrative. Lydia's face stared out from the oval frame with eyes that seemed to ask a question of Cree. What was the question? Cree automatically began her inner process, spiraling in toward subconsciously registered perceptions. When Ray called to her, saying they were heading out, she asked if she could stay a few minutes longer, alone. He and Horace left, chatting as they headed down the corridor.

Alone was better. Cree shut her eyes and let herself feel the space in its three dimensions, then in the fourth, time. Time stretched back, invisible, and fanned into other dimensions of consciousness. Cree felt as fully aware as she had ever felt, as open and clear as she could imagine being.

Lydia?

Against the empty canvas of perception, there was only Cree breathing steadily, alone in the silent room.

Lydia?

She gave it a few more minutes, but there was no one here. She roused from the state with some difficulty to realize that almost twenty minutes had passed. Poor Horace and Ray would have been waiting patiently all this time. Still, she stroked the coffin's polished boards for another moment, reluctant to leave the room.

Why no ghost, no affective trace, of such a person? she wondered. She hadn't yet read Lydia's journal, but that face told a great deal about who she had been. And a woman with the compassion, the passion, to rescue an unknown freak or werewolf: Surely such a heart would leave an echo.

417

Unless at death Lydia's heart's arrow had been sprung and had been received where it belonged. Unless no unrequited feelings had been held. Unless no unresolved emotions had remained to perseverate. A life so fully and roundly lived—was such a thing possible?

Definitely something to think about, Cree decided. She caught the photo's eye one more time and left the room.

64

THEY PARKED THE van at a place Ray knew, let the dogs out, and
locked up. Ray had showed her the area on a map, but once the
headlights went out Cree had no sense of the landscape at all, no sense of
direction. Down here at the bottom, the coastal ridge was skirted with tall
eucalyptus trees and some pines that cut lacy black silhouettes against the
lighter dark of the sky. She couldn't see far enough even to tell where the
mountain was.

They walked down the road to its end at a wooden fence, climbed
through, continued along a path so narrow the leaves on each side brushed
her shoulders. The dogs vanished into the darkness ahead. The air was
clear as a piece of deep blue sapphire. Ray had said the fog would come
later, and if they were lucky they could watch it roll in when they got to
the top of the ridge.

After a few minutes, they came out from under the tree canopy into a
mixed landscape of grass and brush, where she could see the rising slope as
a lighter gray-blue mottled with patches of dark. It rose to an indistinct
peak that she could barely tell from the sky. They stopped and looked up
at it and it struck Cree as imposing.

"I can't run up there. It's too steep. And too rough—Ray, I'm a sissy,
I'm used to urban jogging paths!"

"You're going to do great. And you're going to love it."

Ray was wired with excitement. She could see how important these
night runs were to him, and that her joining him for this secret joy was a
huge thing for him. She doubted she'd ever seen anyone being so pleased
by her company. It was a humbling experience.

"But I'm not going to take off my clothes," she told him. "And I'd like you to keep yours on. I know there's probably nobody out here, but don't want to be worrying the whole time about somebody seeing us."

Ray laughed quietly. "This once."

They walked farther and soon the trees became just an undifferentiated mass of black behind them. Ray's bandaged forearm was the brightest thing in view. The dogs checked in and ranged away again. She could just make out their shapes going to and fro, stopping, disappearing, emerging again. They were as wired up as Ray and she were.

She knew the feeling from her own nighttime adventures. Just being outside in the dark put her on edge, made everything feel secret, mysterious. It was shot through with a sense of expectancy, of possible danger that gave her mind a sharp clarity. When you cast loose from the habitual and the familiar, you never knew what might happen.

They were fifty yards farther up when the whole slope brightened inexplicably and the bushes sprouted shadows. Startled, Cree spun around to see a mound of light nudging above the distant line of eastern mountains.

The moon.

Ray turned too, and they just stood looking at it. It rose amazingly fast, as if a giant just beyond the edge of the world had let go of a huge pale-mustard-colored balloon. It had to be near full, she thought, the kind of moon that turned people into werewolves. And sure enough, here she and Ray were. As it rose it lost the orange tint and took on more of a jonquil hue and finally a lustrous pearl. It gilded the land with a serene chill glaze.

She was taking her cues from Ray, and right now he seemed content to watch the moon rise. So she sat in the dewy grass and brought her knees up and just watched, too. Breathtaking.

She had spent the afternoon reading Lydia's astonishing journal. It told so much, yet left so much unexplained. Either there were more volumes yet to be discovered, or volumes that had been lost, or Lydia had stopped writing after their rescue of the wolfman. Or Hans had done something with them. As for the questions Ray so desperately wanted answers for— exactly what or who the wolfman was, how the Schweitzers treated him, whether they loved him or he loved them—Cree doubted they'd ever know.

And then there was Hans. Cree was sure he'd been deeply in love with and devoted to his wife. But his feelings toward the wolfman were not clear at all. What did it mean that he'd left the wolfman where he'd died, concealed him so well? Why did he inter Lydia there, rather than giving her a church burial? Why did he finally leave the house where his beloved was buried, and where did he go?

The mysteries of the heart, Ray would say.

Bert's death made her sad: a charming guy, so lost in the world. When she'd called her mother with the news, they'd cried at both ends of the line. And yet they couldn't say they knew him, or that he'd been important. Part of the sorrow was the unspoken sense that they'd lost one of the last few links to Pop, to the early years.

The harder thing was Ray. He had deteriorated markedly in just these last two weeks, the sideways shimmy occurring more and more often in his left eye, the occasional oddly dissociated monologue. She'd decided to stay on a little longer. She was determined it wasn't going to be sad and scared. It was going to be strong and good and brave.

So far, sometimes it was. Sometimes it was just easy and fun, Ray was amazing that way—his resilience. Other times it was more like a tea ceremony again, beautiful but fragile, requiring utmost delicacy and restraint. She wasn't sure how long she'd stay, or just how she would leave. That was the hardest part.

Cree's thoughts bothered her and she stood up next to Ray again, brushing off her jeans. She had to say something but couldn't find the words right away.

"Ray. I don't know if I can . . . you know. Make it all the way." She tipped her head vaguely toward the slope as if that's what she was talking about.

"You'll do fine." He kept staring at the moon a little longer before turning back to the hill. "See that double bump to the left of the saddle? That's where we're headed. When you get closer, you'll see some boulders. Just keep them in view, you can't miss the spot. Now we better boogie, Cree. Timing is everything."

The dogs came at the sound of his voice, checked in, wagged, looking eager, *Come on, come on, come on*. Ray roughed their coats and laughed quietly.

They began to jog, slowly at first, side by side. Cree felt her breathing pick up and the night shifted again as her blood moved faster and she felt the changing contours of the ground through her feet. Ray ran effortlessly and seemed happy. This was good. This *was*. Running uphill in the wild dark. *Ad astra per aspera*. Ray's way of working through it was teaching her a lot. A man just this side of becoming a ghost. It would be hard later, but staying had been the right thing to do. The sense of joyfulness stabilized in her, and she got more confident she could linger in it.

She was in shape, good for five miles on the flat, but she wasn't used to the uneven ground and the relentless slope. Soon Ray began pulling ahead, his eagerness tugging him uphill. She put on some steam and managed to catch him for a while, but then the terrain slowed her and soon he was moving away again, an increasingly indistinct shape dwindling in the luminous dark.

And that's how it was going to be, she thought. That's how it would be.

"Hey, Ray," she called. "If I fall behind, you just keep on. You go on ahead. I'll get there, okay? I'll meet you at the top."

ACKNOWLEDGMENTS

My sincerest thanks and appreciation go to Walter Birkby, Ph.D., D-ABFA, forensic anthropologist at the Human Identification Laboratory in Tucson, Arizona, for clarifying aspects of his discipline and for applying his expertise to the conundrum posed by the wolfman's bones.

Thanks are also due to Dewayne Tully, SFPD Public Affairs officer, and Homicide Unit Inspector Michael Mahoney, for providing information about the San Francisco Police Department. Thanks, too, to Richard Vetterli, medical investigator, and Allen Pringle, chief investigator at the San Francisco Medical Examiner's office.

Also making great contributions to this book were the well-informed, helpful staff at the New Main Library's San Francisco History Room and at the Haas Lilienthal House.

Finally, I thank my wife, Stella Hovis, for her tireless support and great patience.

A NOTE ON THE AUTHOR

Daniel Hecht was a professional guitarist for twenty years. In 1989, he retired from musical performance to take up writing, and he received his M.F.A. from the Iowa Writers' Workshop in 1992. He is the author of five previous novels: *Skull Session* and its prequel *Puppets*, *The Babel Effect*, and the two previous Cree Black novels, *City of Masks* and *Land of Echoes*.